Niccolo pushed her ~~back into the~~
vehicle and slanted his mouth over hers.

His hands cradled the back of her head as he deepened the kiss. No one had ever kissed her so passionately, with such desperation.

Before she knew it, she was stroking his tongue with hers, and within moments, he had her aching. She knew that only the feel of his skin, of their bodies merging, could possibly extinguish that little blaze—okay, forest fire—scorching her insides.

Niccolo broke the kiss, leaving her breathless. "If I don't stop now, I will not be able to. And you must go before they catch up to me," he'd said.

Helena nodded, her mind a jumbled mess of hormonal overload and adrenaline.

"Helena, remember what I said. Do not think of hiding from me. I need you, and I've never needed anyone."

"I-I don't understand," she'd replied.

He placed a soft kiss on the corner of her mouth. "You were born for me—to save me from this hell. I will not rest until we are together again and you are safe with me . . . forever."

ACCIDENTALLY MARRIED TO... A VAMPIRE?

ACCIDENTALLY MARRIED TO…
A VAMPIRE?

MIMI JEAN PAMFILOFF

FOREVER

NEW YORK   BOSTON

Forever
Hachette Book Group
237 Park Avenue
New York, NY 10017

www.HachetteBookGroup.com

Printed in the United States of America

Originally published as an ebook

First mass-market edition: November 2013
10 9 8 7 6 5 4 3 2 1

OPM

Forever is an imprint of Grand Central Publishing.
The Forever name and logo are trademarks of Hachette Book Group, Inc.

The Hachette Speakers Bureau provides a wide range of authors for speaking events. To find out more, go to www.hachettespeakersbureau.com or call (866) 376-6591.

The publisher is not responsible for websites (or their content) that are not owned by the publisher.

This book is dedicated to Javi, whom I accidentally met and who accidentally became the loveliest souvenir from Mexico a girl ever could hope for.

Dear Mortal Female,

Are you one of those unlucky women whose life has been bamboozled by a deceivingly hunky vampire? Are you looking for a way to fix that train wreck you now call your life?

If so, then I will savor your agony because everyone knows that playing smoochie fang with a vampire isn't wise.

Yes, yes. I hear you ... *But I thought he'd eat caribou and sparkle.* Or my personal favorite ... *Oh, but he was sooo hot, all brooding and bulging with muscles.*

Well, you know what they say about excuses, don't you? They're like backsides. Everyone has one, and they all stink.

But fret nyet my little people pets! Auntie Cimil, Goddess Delight of the Underworld, is here to help you out of your sour pickle. This little tale holds the secret to separating yourself from an unwanted vampire mate. But be forewarned, "Until death do us part" has a whole other meaning when you're talking vampires.

Mine Truly,
The Fabulous Miss Cimil

PS: If you've read Book #1 and hope to discover what happens to our hunky, beloved Tommaso or to Emma's grandmother, then I will also enjoy watching you suffer. The author, whom I have every intention of smiting for revealing the gods' secrets, has no plans to disclose their fates for several more novels (although you'll get a hint in Book #3). Oh, but it's going to be *sooo* good! In the meantime, here's the next piece of the puzzle ...

ACCIDENTALLY MARRIED TO... A VAMPIRE?

Prologue

July 12, 1712. Bacalar, Southern Mexico

Delirious with hunger, the weary vampire sat hip deep in mud, his broad back against a hollow tree as he glared at the crisp blue sky. The monthlong summer rains had abruptly retreated. Now how much longer could he wait for her? Hours? Days? Sunshine was not Niccolo DiConti's most cherished friend.

"*Magnifico*," he grumbled.

His gaze shifted to the nearby pool. "Where the devil are you, woman?" he growled. Endless days had passed without as much as a ripple on the water's surface. This ancient Mayan ceremonial pool was the goddess's favorite portal to the human world when she came scouting for souls—he'd paid a king's ransom for that information—but she'd yet to materialize.

His shoulders slumped, and he sank deeper into the

sticky jungle floor. Shards of painful sunlight pierced the tree canopy and danced across his face, a face gloriously referred to by many as that of a hardened warrior—dark features, a few character-building scars, and capable of producing a soul-chilling scowl when necessary. Today, however, he could not muster the strength to frighten a small child.

You are a pitiable mess, he thought for the hundredth time.

Struck hard by the irony of his situation, he let out a bitter chuckle. He was legendary for his raw power, intrepid leadership, and ruthless will to survive—no, not just survive, thrive. In any situation. Any century. But as soon as he saw her, he might actually beg like some lowly mortal serf.

Bene, anything it takes, he reminded himself. *And count your blessings that your men are not present to witness your mental shipwreck on the Island of Self-Pity.*

He closed his eyes, attempting to push away his bitter frustration, but his thoughts only swiveled toward his gnawing hunger. *Hmmm, a rabbit or monkey...I must catch a little something to quell the hunger pangs—*

"Well, well. What do we have here?" said a sultry feminine voice.

Niccolo's eyes snapped open to find a dainty woman with long, wet ropes of red hair snaking down her naked body. "*Cristo sacro!* It is about bloody time," he barked.

The woman arched one coppery brow. "Oh my, aren't we a cranky little thing? And dirty, too. Had a little mud bath, did we, vampire?"

With her lean, almost boyish frame, the Goddess of the Underworld reminded him of a delicate fairy. But he knew better than to underestimate Cimil. Not only was she infamous for instigating mischief and being twelve cookies shy of a baker's dozen, she also possessed powerful sight—thousands of years ahead, millions of possible outcomes. She was his last hope. Sad really.

"My sincerest apologies, goddess," he said. "It is my lack of nourishment speaking." He pushed himself slowly from the muck and stretched. "I have been waiting weeks, and as you are aware, the sun weakens my kind." He wiped his dirty hands on his black trousers and then ran them through the length of his damp hair, shaking out the leaves.

She ogled him like a giant confection. "Well, well. If I'd known *you* were waiting, little dumplin', I might have dropped in sooner. But I was deep in a trance, connecting to a future version of myself. Had to catch up on *Dexter*. What a hottie! That guy puts the *errr*," she purred, "in killer. Ya know what I mean?"

Niccolo shook his head slowly, unsure of how to respond to her bewildering jargon. Having lived in a hundred countries and speaking dozens of languages fluently, Niccolo considered himself an educated man of the world. He'd even learned English from an Oxford scholar. Yet, he had never heard such colloquialisms.

"Not into *Dexter*?" She looked confused. "Oooh, I see. You're a *Walking Dead* kind of guy!" She winked. "I gotcha." She suddenly jumped to one side, away from a butterfly fluttering past, and then froze for several moments.

Unsure of what else to do, Niccolo cleared his throat.

She instantly snapped to life. "Hi. Who are you? And are you aware that good hygiene has made a comeback?"

Masking his confusion and ignoring the slight on

his shabby appearance, he bowed his head and replied, "Niccolo DiConti, general of—" He caught himself and stopped. Perhaps he should not call attention to his identity. The gods might not be on his list of admirers. Although they should be. What was not to like?

Cimil's eyes lit. "*The* Niccolo DiConti? What an honor!"

Niccolo stood a little taller then. "Yes, I seek your assistance."

Cimil rolled her eyes. "Well, no duh. You didn't abandon your queen's side, risking her wrath, to see me in my fabulous birthday suit. Although..." she began slowly, pacing like a slinky cat. "You and I could have some fun together. I don't mind a little dirt, especially on a tasty treat like you." She licked her lips.

Despite her odd speech, Niccolo understood the gist. He ran both hands through his hair once again, this time with worry. Sex was the last thing on his mind at the moment, and the last few centuries, for that matter. Too much killing to do, he supposed. But a coldhearted female like her would never warm his blood, even if he had the urge.

Regardless, she was right. He had taken a substantial risk abandoning his post. By now, the queen was likely hunting him via their blood bond, and it wouldn't be long before she caught up. Indeed, he needed Cimil's help. Urgently. Only it had never occurred to him that she might ask for sex as payment. On the other hand, what woman wouldn't want him?

He squared his shoulders and stared down at her. He could do this. Any price for his freedom, right?

"*Bene*. If that is what you wish, I will bed you in exchange for your assistance."

Laughter exploded from Cimil. "Oh, would you relax, vampire? First off"—she held out her scrawny index finger—"I don't need to blackmail men into sleeping with me." She snorted loudly. "Because I'm loaded!"

Loaded?

"I do not see you carrying anything. In fact, you are nude," he pointed out.

Cimil looked down at her body. "Oh, look! I *am* naked." She frowned. "Heeey, it's not polite to interrupt. I was telling you a story. Let me see..." She scratched her head. "Oh yeah. I was explaining how I'm so moneyed— that means 'wealthy' to you, Bo-Bo—I even bought myself a nice little sultan with a camel just last week." She paused and tapped her finger on the corner of her mouth. "On second thought, he wasn't worth the tiny island I had to trade for him, and the stupid camel doesn't even fit through the bedroom doorway. I *should* go back to black-mailing men for sex. That's a great idea. Thanks!"

Niccolo swallowed hard. *Cristo sacro! I am going to have to sleep with the crazy she-demon.* Perhaps he could secure the return of her island instead? He, too, was "loaded." *Might even have an additional island somewhere to sweeten the pot.* To keep track of such things proved challenging after a thousand years or so of existence.

"And second"—she held out two fingers—"you're really not my type. I like 'em warm. But I will take that shirt and those pants."

Not her "type"? She is out of her mind. On the other hand, if the goddess merely desired his mud-caked clothes...

"*Bene,*" he replied. He could easily glamour new

garments off a nearby villager later. He slipped off his not-so-white linen shirt and black trousers and stood before her in the buff.

A sly smile stretched across her pixie-like face before she whistled and gave him a leisurely once-over. "I like you, vampire. You have this whole tanned European NBA gladiator *je-ne-sais-pas* man-fusion thing going. I'm totally getting you."

He had no clue what she'd just said, but he did not care to know or to waste more time. He tossed the clothes to her feet. *"Eccolo."*

Still gazing at his nude form, Cimil sighed and then began dressing. "You even smell delicious. Like a hint of chocolate with vanilla, and..."

"Mud?" he said dryly.

"That's it." She slipped on his large shirt and pants. The five-foot woman looked like a child playing dress-up in her father's clothes. "Well, Niccolo, I haven't got all day. Why do you risk life and limb to see me?"

"My freedom."

Cimil froze midway through rolling up a pant leg. "You want to leave the queen's employ?"

He nodded with an uncompromising stare.

"Complicated. Unprecedented. Perfectly insane...I'm in!" She froze for several awkward moments and then sparked back to life. "Wait. Why do you need good ol' Auntie Cimi's help?"

Niccolo hated to air vampire business, but Cimil had to have heard of Reyna, the queen. "There is only one way to be relieved from her service: death. I would like to avoid it."

"I see. You wouldn't happen to have some wildly irrational reason for doing all this, would you? I love acts of futile insolence. They're so whimsical!"

Trying not to sound like a pansy, he admitted, "I no longer wish to kill for her."

"A vampire who doesn't want to ... kill? *You* don't want to—" Cimil broke off, laughing hysterically. "That totally qualifies!"

Niccolo's rage percolated as she clutched her stomach and slapped her knee. How dare she mock him! In truth, he had no objection to killing for the right reasons—for example, to protect the innocent from dark vampires, Obscuros—but for far too long he'd killed simply because he'd been ordered. He needed to be free, to know that every death he caused was justified.

Then there was the small matter of the queen's mental instability, which undoubtedly fueled her unscrupulous behavior. The last straw had been when she demanded he blind the maid because the girl did not curtsy properly. He'd had to quickly call in several favors and get her a position with a respectable family where she'd be allowed to keep her eyes.

Sì, it was as clear as the fangs in his mouth; if there were a Crazy Shrew Olympiad, the powerful queen would triumph.

Upholding the Pact between the gods and vampires, destroying Obscuros, those were still worthy causes, but he needed to get far away from Reyna before he ended up killing her—an act that would have fatal consequences for any vampire unfortunate enough to carry her blood, including himself.

Cimil continued howling with laughter and then suddenly spotted a large black beetle strolling past her foot.

Her eyes filled with horror. "N-n-no. I think you are"—
she swallowed hard—"lovely. I would never say that." She
jerked her head up and looked back at Niccolo. "Okay.
And if I don't help you?"

Is she speaking to me or the insect? "Then I will die,"
he answered anyway.

"Live free or die, is it?" she said, eyeing the bug again.

She is mad. Why did I come here?

"*Sì*. That is correct," he replied hesitantly.

Cimil watched the beetle disappear under a rock. She
sighed with relief and then continued rolling up the other
pant leg.

"You're like a bad bumper sticker," she said.

*Bumper sticker? Why does she insist on speaking in
code?* Niccolo began grinding his teeth.

She stood, grasping the waistline of the pants to hold
them up. "Lucky you, I enjoy a challenge. You'd be surprised what dull, predictable things people ask me. 'When
will I die? When will the world end?' Blah, blah, blah . . .'"

Niccolo released a quick breath. "Will you assist me
or not?"

"Sure, my little cupcake of despair. Now, normally I
charge twelve ninety-nine, plus shipping and handling,
but in this case I'll cut you a deal. You will be indebted
to me, and I will have the right to call in the favor at any
time in the future or past."

*Past? That settles it. I have found another contender
for crazy shrew. Very well, at least I will not have to sleep
with her.* He hoped. He, too, "liked 'em warm" and with
a heart or a soul, for that matter. A little sanity might be
pleasant, too.

"Agreed," he said.

Cimil took several steps forward, closing the gap between them, and stared with her large turquoise-green eyes. "Prophecy time, mighty warrior. Kneel."

Niccolo complied.

Baring a devilish grin, Cimil placed her soft hands on his cheeks and rubbed his unshaven jaw. "Oooh. Just like your eyes. So tough and black. The things your stubble could teach my calluses."

Niccolo cocked one brow.

Cimil frowned. "No? Not into calluses? Fine, then." She took a deep breath and then stared into his eyes before softly kissing his lips. She sucked in a deep breath as if absorbing his scent. "Okay. Up, up."

That is all?

"Well?" he asked.

She turned and pushed through the thick underbrush, uncovering an overgrown path.

Niccolo trailed behind her, thoroughly perplexed. "Where the devil are you going?" he bellowed with his deep, commanding voice. "Tell me what you saw!"

"I was right about you, big guy," she said. "You *are* a challenge, and I'm going to love watching you run this gauntlet. It's a delightfully cruel one, at least for your shallow, undead mind."

What the bloody hell?

She continued talking without slowing her pace. "I saw all possible outcomes of your life, and there is a path that leads to your release from Her Majesty's command."

"Is *not* dying part of the equation?"

She kept up the rapid pace. "You're dead already."

Touché.

Cimil stopped abruptly. Niccolo plowed into her back.

"Ow!" she yelped. A small flock of blackbirds burst from the bush to her side, chirping noisily as they fled to the sky. He winced as the sunlight continued to heat his skin and weaken him.

She spun to face him. "Listen, Hellboy, we need to make this quick. I have garage sales to hit and naughty souls to claim. Decide."

"I do not understand." Was this goddess tormenting him for sport? Why did she call him Hellboy? *How very rude!*

She poked at his bare chest with a razor-sharp fingernail. "You hate taking orders."

Sì, true. After all, I am a vampire.

"And even if you decided to listen like a good little boy, the odds of pulling this off are slim to none."

I happen to excel at all things impossible. I am a vampire!

"So don't come crying if you end up in your queen's dungeon."

Vampires do not cry, silly woman.

"Tortured three times a day for all eternity, which is where you have a ninety-nine point nine-nine-nine percent chance of landing if you don't do exactly as I say."

Actually, those numbers are quite encouraging. He thought his odds were somewhere between pigs flying and hell freezing over. "*Bene.* I understand. Tell me what you saw, what I must do."

"First, you will have to find your true mate. Or, more accurately, she will find you. A human, by the way."

"Human?" *That is disappointing. But, on the other hand, there certainly are more tedious creatures on the planet. Cimil, for example.*

"Yesss." Cimil narrowed her eyes. "And watch your tongue. I happen to be partial to humans—most, anyway. Clowns, not so much. Those evil bastards never stop smiling."

Niccolo didn't know what these "clowns" were, but he made a mental note to stay away if he ever encountered one. Sounded unpleasant.

"I did not say a word," he retorted innocently.

"Good, because I'm warning you, if you're not in this for the long haul, jump off the Cimil Soul Train now and boogie your naked body home." Her eyes quickly shifted to a squawking toucan perched above on a branch. "Who the hell asked you? You can't even dance. I mean, *really*."

Niccolo scratched his chin, ignoring the bizarre behavior and the urge to wrap his hands around her neck. "My resolve will not waver."

She stifled a laugh. "Even though your kind considers such a fate, to be with a human—your food—a curse?" She began laughing again. "This particular female will be disobedient, demanding, and a pain in your cold, old, naked ass. She's also hotter than an apple pie fresh from the oven."

Cimil's description piqued his interest. "You mean to say ... she is beautiful?"

Cimil smiled. "Irresistible. Sharp as a whip. Sexy. Perfect for you in every way."

Niccolo felt his insides twist with anticipation. She would be his? All his? *Hmmm.* "Go on."

She raised her brows. "Before you get all excited, Mr. Studtastic, there are rules. First, you must continue to uphold the Pact. No ifs, ands, or buts. That means you must keep that"—she pointed to his penis—"in your pants . . . when you find some, obviously. And those"—she pointed to his fangs—"in your mouth."

The Pact had many parts to it, and he knew them all since he'd spent the last thousand years upholding its laws. It was central to maintaining the vampires' existence; as long as they followed the commandments, they would be left alone by the gods to live. Rule one: vampires could not kill innocent humans—Forbiddens—although the queen's compliance to this law was highly questionable. In any case, even the most honorable of vampires were known to lose control in the throes of feeding or passion. Therefore, those activities with Forbiddens were strictly off-limits, too. The only exception was for those mated to a Forbidden—practically unheard of—in which case, a careful, consensual nip here or there was allowed, but nothing more.

"Done," he said. "I will refrain from biting without her permission. Nor will I sleep with her until she has been turned."

"Not so fast, tomcat," she added. "No biting, even if she begs. And she *must* be turned *with* her permission on the anniversary of your third month together. That very same day. Understand?"

"Why three months?" he questioned.

"Hey, buddy, my gig is prophecies and hunting for garage sales. I don't make the signs, I just follow them." She shrugged. "Anyhooo, the rest is up to you." She turned and continued marching forward, quickening her pace. "So. You in?"

Niccolo looked from side to side. "In? In what?"

"Yes. *In*. Are you on board? Ready to throw down. Roll the dice. Ride that crazy cow called life and make her your bitch?"

Niccolo frowned. Her colloquialisms were simply offensive. And this coming from a ruthless vampire. "You are asking if I am committed. *Sì?*"

"*Siii.*" She rolled her eyes.

What other choice did he have? Besides, he did not believe in this ridiculous mate business. He had known tens of thousands of vampires over his existence, but only a dozen or so claimed to have found their true mate. It was extremely rare. And for those few, he saw no evidence they were anything more than contented couples who'd beaten the odds. There was no cosmic force at play.

As for his mate being human, he could find a way to cope temporarily. Sure, humans were only a step up from a cow or goat one would eat, or perhaps keep as a favorite farm pet; however, he wouldn't be the first immortal to bear the shame of coupling with a human. It was manageable. Especially if she happened to be beautiful.

Whoever she was, he would woo her, set her up with only the finest of things, and after the three months were up, he'd have her begging to be turned. Once he was free from the queen, he had ample resources to provide his mate with a comfortable, separate life for eternity. Everyone would win. Everyone would be happy.

How doing all this could possibly free him from being that festering bunion of a queen's general, he had no clue. He'd been warned that Cimil's instructions were cruel at best, fatal at worst, and required an extreme leap of faith. But at this point, anything was worth trying. Hell, if he failed, there was always death. He hoped. The queen's dungeons were notoriously hellish.

But he wouldn't fail. He was the strongest warrior the vampire world had ever known. He had fought and won thousands of battles, upheld the Pact, and maintained the peace between the gods and vampires for a thousand years. This would be a stroll through the park...or jungle. Whatever.

"It's much better than I'd hoped for," he stated coolly.

Cimil's eyes lit up. "All right then. Oh, and there's one more thing..."

Cimil waved her hands and watched the vampire collapse to the ground. She poked him several times in the chest, checking to make sure he was out cold.

"*Bene*, Niccolo DiConti," she said, perfectly imitating his deep voice. "Your mate will not be born for, oh, say, about three hundred years, and I have to entomb you in the meantime. Otherwise, you won't live to see another full moon. Did you know your paranoid, sorry excuse of a queen fears your strength and plans to kill you? Crazy shrew. I wish I could take her out myself. But nooo." She shook her head.

The beautiful, naked vampire lay completely oblivious over a bed of leaves.

Cimil sighed. "You are such a scrumptious man treat. How could anyone think of killing you? But I guarantee, after three hundred years, your queen will only be a teensy bit peeved by your absence, and she will have reconsidered her plot to murder you. You can thank me later."

She leaned down and pressed her mouth to his full lips and then ran her finger along his chiseled jaw.

"Come, my handsome vampire. I have a few things I must do to prepare you. Then I'll put you somewhere safe to await your bride. Oh—I know!" She clapped excitedly. "You can stay inside my piggy bank! And I'll create a dramatastic jungle intro to your lady! How about *Romancing the Stone* meets *Apocalypto*?"

She flung the naked giant over her shoulder and gave him a loving pat on his bottom. "Watching you two will be so much fun! I might have to charge the other gods admission to this show when the time comes."

One

⌐

Arms pumping, Helena Strauss chased the smoke-spewing bus down a narrow dirt road through the jungle. "Wait! I'm here! Wait!"

She suddenly sucked in a mouthful of gnats and then gagged and stumbled. She hacked violently, almost losing the remnants of her meager lunch: crackers and apple juice. She doubled over to catch her breath, cursing with every exhale as her ride evaporated right before her watering eyes.

"Dammit. God-effing-dammit! Worst vacation ever!"

She'd left her backpack on that bus—wallet, cell phone, water, and all—with the nice retired Tucson woman with the straw hat and orange muumuu. Helena had clearly told the driver she'd only be *un minuto* before she hopped off at the last second; she needed to use the facilities one

more time before the three-hour drive back to her hotel
south of Cancún. With the sweltering heat and gallons of
water she'd downed to keep cool, Helena had spent more
time seeing the restroom than the ruins. Muumuu Woman
even asked when Helena was expecting.

Seriously?

Okay, she did look a little plumper these days—
comfort food and lots of it—despite all the exercise. But
pregnancy was last on her worry list. *I'd need to have a
boyfriend or, at the very least, have had sex. Once.*

Well, today, that was the least of her problems. Now
she'd been left behind without pesos or bug spray, and that
rotten bus had been the last tour of the day.

Helena looked up. The sun was already seated behind
the thick tree line, and the sky was a deep burnt orange,
veined with shades of purple and gray. *Oh, hell! Almost
night.*

She doubled over again, her head spinning and waves
of nausea washing over her. She'd been feeling odd and
unable to think straight ever since she'd arrived at the
remote ruins.

Montezuma, perhaps?

Everyone kept warning her last night not to have the
mega-margarita with lots of crushed ice, but she figured
the tequila would kill any micro-critters in the water.

Not the mighty amoeba, she reminded herself. *You
studied evolutionary biology. You should know better.*

But last night, she'd already had a few—okay, four—
beers before the Big Gulp–sized margarita came calling and she began howling to the bar crowd, "Who the
heeell is this Montezuma bonehead *anyway*? If he wants
revenge, bring it on!" The crowd cheered as she pounded

down her drink and proceeded to get an apocalyptic brain freeze.

Helena shook her head. *If Darwin were alive, what would he say?*

"Between last night and leaving your backpack on the bus," she mumbled to no one, "you may actually be too stupid to live."

Well, hopefully it was the heat making her woozy and losing her wits, not some Aztec gastric curse.

After a moment, her blurry vision cleared. She slowly stood and then pivoted on her heel several times, turning her head from side to side. The road, encased by two walls of thick vegetation, looked the same in either direction.

Jungle. Jungle. More jungle. But which way is the ...? Oh, hell. This can't be happening. How could she lose her bearings down a single-lane dirt road? The nausea had her completely disoriented.

"This way. The ruins and trinket shack are back this way." She nodded toward the long stretch of road to her right and began walking. Intermittent waves of blurriness struck her as she trudged along the darkening road, twisting her ankle in an obscured pothole every few steps.

She stopped, scratching her sweaty neck with one hand while swatting the unrelenting mosquitoes with the other. "This can't be happening. I think I'm going the wrong frigging way."

Don't panic, Helena. Just go back.

But something wasn't right. She couldn't think straight. And now she was panicking. She'd seen all the Indiana Jones movies, and only bad things happened when he went near jungles and ruins: voodoo priests, giant spiders ... Germans—all sorts of scary things.

As darkness descended, fear continued hammering on the cracks of her rational mind. Even the critters had decided to ratchet up the volume. *Great. A creepy nature soundtrack for my own personal nightmare.*

"How about some *Tomb Raider* music, people!" she barked at the clicking bugs and hidden squawking animals. But only the shadows answered, suddenly taking on a life of their own—engulfing the trees, erasing any distinguishable textures and shapes. Leaves became blackness. Branches became blackness. The length of road disintegrated in front of her. The ominous night swallowed everything but her frantic breaths and the nose on her face.

She ran her hands through her damp, sticky curls.

It could be hours before anyone noticed the missing, slightly overweight twenty-four-year-old from Santa Cruz, California, who was sightseeing alone because her hungover best friends, Anne and Jess, had decided to stay beachside and gape at the Italian water polo team in town for some tournament.

Why did I come on this stupid tour? Because she didn't save her money for two whole years just to get a hangover in Mexico. She wanted to see the remnants of one of the greatest civilizations ever. That's why.

Just then, Helena spotted a glowing light through the dense brush. Was there another road in that direction? Was that a car?

No. Too slow.

She suddenly remembered that the tour guides, mostly locals from a nearby village, had been carrying large flashlights to point out glyphs inside the temples.

Could it be . . . ?

"Hey! Over here! *Aquí!*" The moving light was fading fast. "No, no! *Wait!*" Helena swallowed her fear and pushed through wall after wall of stubborn vegetation, determined to find salvation. "Wait! *Espera!*" she screamed as the light faded to a minuscule flicker.

Helena kicked it into high gear for all of ten steps before she stumbled and performed a belly flop, landing with a thump! Pain ripped through her knee. She rolled over and sat up, wincing as she bent her leg. No structural damage, but a warm trickle of blood slid down to her ankle. Sadly, she'd worn only cargo shorts and her favorite white tank with built-in bra. Otherwise, she'd tear off her shirt and apply pressure.

She waited for the initial sting to subside before she stood up. The light, and whoever had been toting it, was long gone. Now, she was truly screwed.

"*Come to me,*" she heard a deep male voice suddenly whisper.

Helena froze and swallowed her scream. "Wh-who's there?" She held her breath, praying her imagination had conjured the dark, smooth voice. "Who's there?" she repeated loudly. *Crap, I sound like a lame knock-knock joke.*

"*This way. Waited so long for you...*" This time, the voice was hypnotic: raw male strength intertwined with gut-wrenching need. Beauty dipped in layers of savage intent.

Clenching, unfathomable, bottomless desire penetrated her ears. Her mind suddenly felt like ropes of warm saltwater taffy.

"*Come to me,*" he called once again.

Every ounce of tension dissolved from her body. Control went with it.

Entranced, Helena glided effortlessly through the blackness toward the voice. She no longer felt the fear of being lost in the jungle or the pain in her knee; she felt only need. The need to be with...*him*.

"*Sì, sì. I can feel you. This way. Just a bit farther,*" the voice whispered, carried by the humidity-drenched breeze. "*I can feel your essence. Everything I've ever hoped for.*"

When her hands hit a wall of cold, rough stone, she had no clue what sort of structure she'd touched or where she was, but she instinctively knew what to do. Her fingertips traced along the wall until they found a deep groove between the stones. She wedged her trembling hand into the crack and pushed with her index finger. The stones separated with a loud grinding, revealing a narrow, torchlit passage.

She wanted to run, to brave the darkness of the jungle instead. But she couldn't answer the call of her own warning bells or command her very own body.

She crouched through the doorway and stepped inside the dimly lit rectangular passage. Oddly, there were no cobwebs. The torches looked bright and fresh. Someone had been there recently. *Merry Maids?*

Step by step, she made her way. The narrow passage abruptly hooked to the right and then opened up into a spacious chamber with a high ceiling. Towering golden statues of ancient warriors, piles of polished gold coins, and jewel-encrusted treasure chests were heaped in every corner as if hastily deposited by a greedy pirate on the run with a wheelbarrow.

There was a hot-pink flashing neon sign stuck to the wall that spelled Piggy Bank. Right below it was a *Wheel of Fortune* slot machine and a lonely car bumper with two stickers. One read, Live Free or Die, and the other, I Brake for Garage Sales. And was that an exercise cycle next to a Thighmaster?

What the hell is this place?

Then Helena's eyes focused on something else she couldn't quite grasp. In the middle of the room, lying across a stone altar, was a naked man with dark symbols tattooed down the length of one arm. But he was not just any man. He was a male so perfect that words would cat-fight each other just for the honor of describing him. He was a *god*. A bona fide deity. He had to be. Because a normal man wouldn't give her the urge to fall on her knees and worship at his feet. Or drool.

The torchlight licked his sculpted cheekbones, angular jaw, and full, sensual lips. Every capacious curve and ripple of hard muscle looked to be packed with raw power, and his size left no doubt that he'd been built in another time. A time when giant warriors roamed the earth, looking to rescue lame tourists wandering the Mexican jungle at night.

In my dreams. Wait ... this is a dream! It has to be.

"Move closer, my sweet, delicious woman." The deep voice radiated from every direction, filling the room.

Helena's blood pressure crashed to the floor. She gasped as the weight of her body slammed back against the cold chamber wall to keep from falling.

"Hel-hello? Can you hear me?" Fists clenched, Helena waited for a response, her eyes continuing to soak him in. Every inch of him.

Was he real? *No, he must be a statue. Too perfect.* His full lips were built to nuzzle a woman's neck. Specifically, her neck. And that hair—thick, long waves of black satin—was the kind a woman could grab fistfuls of while being driven insane by those lips.

Then there were the diamond-cut grooves of his abs, his perfectly shaped navel, the fine dark hair adorning his lower belly that trailed down to his awe-inspiring man gear. The size and thickness, even in its slumbering state, was something women dreamed of and scores of artists throughout history attempted to immortalize in marble. He was every woman's fantasy, she thought. And by every woman's, she meant hers..._'Cause I'm not gonna share._

"Kiss me, Helena," the seductive voice rumbled.

Had the man said her name? No. Clearly his lips hadn't moved. The margarita amoebas were attacking her brain, and she was losing her mind.

"Kiss me, woman. I command you," the voice echoed, this time compelling her to obey.

Helena's survival instincts gave her a hard kick, jarring her back into the horrific reality of the situation. But as she tried to regain control of her body, her tongue slipped from her mouth and wet her lips.

Traitorous tongue. Backstabbing lips. What the hell are you doing? Her body inched closer.

"Sì, that is it, my love. I can smell your blood."

Blood? What the...? Every nerve in her body fired on all cylinders, but she couldn't run, even if her hair had been on fire. It seemed the harder she fought, the stronger the force controlling her became.

"Brush it against my lips, my love. I want to taste you when you kiss me."

Without realizing it, her hand stretched down to coat

her fingertips with the thick, nearly dried blood from her knee. Trembling, she smeared it over his lips.

"Now, kiss me, my love. Awaken me, my bride."

"No! No! Let me go!" Helena struggled, but her body's betrayal persisted. Her head dipped, and her lips rested on his sensuous mouth. In that instant, the compelling force dissipated and her entire body lit up into one glorious pyre of life.

Had she been asleep the last twenty-four years? Because she could swear she'd just taken her first breath. Ever.

Holy hell, what was that?

The torches flickered, and the wind kicked up around her.

The altar was empty.

She crumpled to the cold, dusty floor. A pair of rough hands touched her shoulders.

"Oh, Christ. You . . . you're behind me, aren't you?" she whispered.

The deep, dark voice replied, *"Sì,* my love. Stand, and let me see my mate."

Helena slowly rose to face the naked god behind her.

Two

Arms limp at her sides, knees shaking, Helena found herself staring straight up a cliff of solid muscles into the face of the most masculine creature she'd ever seen. She'd been impressed by the sight of him lying there dormant. But awake? That was another story completely, one to tell her wine-tasting slash historical-romance book club buddies—the Wino Wenches.

"The expression displayed on your lovely face," he said with a hint of amusement in his eyes, "indicates you are as confused as I. Let us make proper introductions. Then we shall sort through the particulars of our situation." He made a slight bow of his head and then kissed the inside of her wrist. "I am Niccolo DiConti. Very pleased to meet you."

His touch sent a sharp jolt through her arm, causing her insides to liquefy.

She snapped her hand back and scuttled against the

cold, damp wall, trying to assess the situation. She'd never seen a man take up so much space. He didn't simply eclipse her five-foot-four frame; he engulfed her with his presence.

Was he a threat? If yes, then why did she want to throw herself into his arms and treat him like her favorite board-walk ride? *I could stay on that dang Tilt-A-Whirl all day long.*

Her skin felt flushed, the muscles deep inside fluttered and constricted, and her nipples perked. For darn certain, that other sensation (which she was *not* going to think about) was her body telling her the time had come to give away that virginity of hers—just like those size 7 jeans in the back of her closet.

How unkind to keep something someone else could put to good use. Greedy, greedy girl.

But she was *not* going to think about that. She should run. Everything about him screamed danger.

Her eyes made another sweep over his entire bare length. Darn it. She couldn't help herself from looking. She'd never seen a man like him.

His dark eyes twinkled as he crossed his arms over his broad chest and arched one sable brow. "Pleased by what you see, then?"

Oh yes.

"No." She shook her head. "Who the hell are you?" Her eyes continued basking in every scrumptious detail. *Is that? Is he? Oh... yes, he is.* Helena felt her face turn red-hot. She quickly looked away as erotic images involv-ing his erection flooded her imagination. What was hap-pening to her? Her mind wasn't normally in the gutter, or in this case, Lady Pervert Land. On the other hand, this situation felt far from normal. Definitely disturbing. Maybe Lady Pervert Land was her happy place. She'd always wondered where it was.

"Your eyes and body betray your words. Why do you deny your desire?" His dark gaze bore down as he studied her with curiosity.

Dammit. She needed to clear her mind, but who could think with that heavenly smell wafting through the air? She could taste him on her tongue. Was that vanilla? Cinnamon? God save her, the man smelled like cookies. Gooey, warm, fresh-out-of-heaven man cookies.

She had to get a hold of herself. She had to run. Did she have a chance of making it out alive? Something told her no. Definitely no. The chamber exit, a narrow doorway, led to an even narrower passage that would dump her back into the dark jungle. She wouldn't make it two feet before he barreled down on her with those powerful thighs.

Yes, powerful thighs. Ummm. She ground her palm into her forehead. *Tramp! Get a hold of yourself.*

She'd have to find a way out. She had to be strong, keep her wits.

She lifted her chin and glared at him defiantly. The fickle torchlight offered another tempting glimpse of his dark, probing eyes, and in that brief moment, she felt like he was staring right into her very soul.

"You are so lovely." He reached out and brushed her cheek. "Your eyes, they are the color of exotic sapphires." He slid a curl between his fingers. "And your hair is like the sun. I never imagined..."

She didn't recognize the accent. Mediterranean or Spanish, perhaps? No. His name sounded Italian. Regardless of origin, his voice curled her toes, just like the rest of him.

"Imagined?" she whispered.

The corner of his mouth twitched with an arrogant smirk. "You are my mate, *sì*?"

"Mate?" *Like, as in . . . first? Buddy? Other shoe?*

Niccolo took another small step forward, lightly pressing his body, and every hard part in between, against hers. She instantly responded with prickly goose bumps.

"Your mate," he said, then slowly bent his head to nuzzle her neck. "Designed by fate and the universe to be your ideal companion in every way." His breath tickled her neck. He seemed to be completely absorbed in the act of nuzzling. "*Mio cuore*, don't you believe in such a thing?" he continued in a low, seductive voice. "Human women were once enthralled by this notion."

Human? With that word, Helena felt her body knot up with howls of self-preservation. She managed to get a hold of herself and push him away.

He grumbled in protest.

"Why did you just say 'human' like that? And what does *mio cuore* mean?" she asked with a breathy voice.

"My heart. It means, 'my heart'—Cimil did not explain the situation?" he asked.

Helena shook her head. "Who's Cimil?"

"Most interesting." He paused as if about to explain but instead reached out to clutch another lock of her hair. He bent down slowly and inhaled. "What is the date, my golden-haired one?"

This has to be a dream. There's no other explanation. But why does everything feel so real? Why do I feel so alive?

Not knowing what else to do, she simply answered, "August tenth."

His hungry eyes raked over her neck, then down to her breasts. He reached out and grabbed the hem of her neckline. He studied the knit fabric with curiosity, as he'd done with her hair, feeling its texture between his thick thumb and index finger.

"Year?" he asked.

Maybe he was mad and she'd gone mad, too? Or when she fell in the jungle, she'd hit her noggin on a rock? Head injury. Yep, that had to be it.

Again, Niccolo appeared to be amused by her reaction to him.

"Year?" he repeated.

Helena squirmed, sliding sideways against the rough wall to put space between her and the naked tower of muscles with the giant, throbbing man gear she so wanted to inappropriately grope.

"Twenty twelve," she answered.

A blaze of fury engulfed his face. He slammed his fist into the stone wall behind her, causing the entire temple to quake. Dust and small chunks of stone rained down.

"Three hundred years? Three hundred bloody years! *Bloody inferno!*" he roared at the ceiling.

Terrified, she dropped to the floor and covered her head as the structure shook. The mental tug-of-war between her dreamlike lust and survival instincts finally ended. He must be mad. She had to run before he killed her.

When Niccolo awoke, he couldn't have been more confused. He had no clue how he had ended up in that dark, musty chamber with odd-looking objects and priceless treasures, but he knew who to blame.

Cimil.

He recalled her pointy little hand waving in his face.

Next thing he knew, he could sense the human woman. She had entered his dreams like a bolt of lightning. And when she smeared that delicious, floral-scented blood on his lips and kissed him, the world burst to life again. He sensed the pulse of every living creature for miles. And the smells—every leaf, fleck of dirt, drop of rain, and... her—he could smell them all. It was as though he'd been dormant for centuries, suddenly brought back to life by an angel of carnal temptation. The most gorgeous, sensuous female creature he'd ever laid eyes on. Her feminine scent, her warmth, everything about her filled his mind with erotic bliss.

Bravo, buffoon! That is because you have been dormant for centuries, three of them, if anyone is counting. And she is the first warm-blooded creature you have encountered. His body felt famished. She was food. Breathtaking female food with silky golden spirals that framed her delicate sun-kissed face, and a curvy, juicy little body that made his cock harder than the stones that entombed him; but nonetheless, food.

But why put me to sleep for three hundred years? he wondered. *Cristo sacro! Cimil must be mad.* Who had been keeping the population of Obscuros at bay? What had happened to his men? *Bloody Cristo sacro.*

And surely there would be no chance of freedom now. While dormant vampires were like the dead and did not emit any energy, once awake, their blood served as a beacon to their makers. The queen would use their bond to hunt and then disembowel him. Afterward, she would put him back together and haul him off to her dungeon, where she'd deprive him of blood so he would not heal, leaving him in agony for eternity. Death was the only sanctuary for him now. Maybe the female would assist him.

He gathered himself together and looked down at the woman crumpled on the floor. *So weak. Yet so enticing. Just as Cimil had foretold.*

Unexpectedly, something inside him shifted. He could... *feel* her fear. He could taste the acid churning in her stomach and the adrenaline catapulting through her veins. An overwhelming urge to protect her surged deep within.

"What have you done to me?" he whispered.

Her sapphire-blue eyes flashed up at him. "What have I done to *you*?"

"*Sí.* I feel—I feel...you." His mind simply couldn't process the inundation of emotions. Was this some absurd joke? Or could she be...? *Impossible! Mates do not exist.*

"I didn't *do* anything," she responded.

Bloody inferno! There it is again. He could feel her confusion.

He quickly reassessed the situation. If the slightest possibility existed that this mate nonsense was factual, then perhaps Cimil was not so mad after all. Cimil had cautioned he would not so easily accept a human.

True.

But if the prophecy was playing out as she had foreseen, then he still had a chance. Twelve weeks. Could he seduce the female into being turned by then?

Idiota! Of course you can. You are a goddamned vampire. And a handsome one at that—so you've been told. And yes, he agreed.

In any case, he would certainly enjoy conquering her.

Just look at the female. She will make an enjoyable little pet, to be sure. He would not enjoy, however, resisting bedding her or drinking from her. That, he could see, would be a thorn in his side.

He slowly kneeled and placed his hand on her shoulder, trying not to frighten her further. "Tell me, what is your name?"

"Helena," she answered. "But you knew that already."

I did? Why would she think that? She is confused. He mentally shrugged and then repeated her name. Heavens, she was gorgeous. By far the loveliest creature he'd ever seen.

"Let me go. Please," she whimpered.

He swept away the dust from her forehead and then brushed his thumb over her full bottom lip—delicious, pink, supple, and meant for kissing. Just like her golden, smooth as satin skin radiating with life.

"I cannot do that," he said.

Slowly she rose from the ground, still trembling. Her eyes nervously flashed to his swollen manhood, which would only prolong its present state. It aroused him beyond belief when she looked at him with such lust.

"Why not?" she asked in a nervous whisper.

Because I haven't bedded you yet. Would not want to deprive you of such a luxury.

"Apparently," he said, "I have waited three hundred years for you. So I have no intention of letting you go."

He cupped her face and leaned to kiss her.

Three

⌐

Helena's tense body swooned when the force of his lips met hers. He pulled her greedily into his hard frame and moved his strong hands to grip her waist. It felt like he had claimed her as his personal prize. It felt euphoric. *Owned by a sex god!*

Wait! What the hell am I doing? She broke the kiss and pushed him away again. "This is insane. I don't know who you are or how I got here, but you have to let me go. You have the wrong person."

He smiled devilishly. "Afraid not, my dear Helena. Fate has united us."

Helena raised her brow in question.

"However, you are correct, *bella*. This is insanity. And as much as I would like to show you the depths of my lunacy—and the things it is asking me to do to your succulent body at this very moment—we must go. Before they come for me."

That sounded ominous. "Who are 'they'?" Wait. Did she want to know?

"It is forbidden to speak of such things to a human, but I vow the day will come when there will be no secrets between us." The naked warrior held out his hand. "Come, *mio cuore*."

Helena shivered. Something about that explanation left her feeling substantially more terrified. Why couldn't humans know? And what exactly was he? If the scientist in her had no answers, then better not stick around to find out.

Helena nodded. She took his hand—it was cool to the touch, yet heated her skin at the same time—and followed him through the chamber toward the doorway. As they reached the passage, Helena nonchalantly dipped down and grabbed a golden statue. It reminded her of an Oscar. In fact, she could swear there was an inscription on its base.

Sally Field? Too dark to know for certain.

She quickly jumped and struck Niccolo on the back of his head with all her strength. He stumbled to the side. She squeezed past him down the passage.

The moment she burst from the temple into the night, the stupidity of her plan hit home. How far could she get?

At least he was barefoot, bare everything—*sigh*—and she still had on her low tops. That might give her the advantage. Question was, would she find her way back to civilization? She had to try.

Helena pushed frantically with her hands through rough branches and vines. They lashed at her face and scratched her arms and legs. She ran straight into a tree trunk.

She cupped her nose. *Ow! That hurt!*

Thankfully, it wasn't broken.

She slid around the enormous tree, panting and sweating. She continued on with her hands extended, wondering if running through the jungle, unable to see a goddamned thing, was actually more dangerous than trying her luck with that man. Were there any cliffs around here?

Helena tripped and landed on her knees, reopening the cut. "Son of a—" She cupped her hands over her mouth. She quickly picked herself up and slammed right into something hard again. *Another tree?* She probed hesitantly with her hands.

Nope. Not a tree.

"Well, well…What have we here?" said a deep, unfamiliar voice.

Helena screamed.

Two steel hands grasped her shoulders. "Hush, hush, now…" The voice was low and menacing.

She couldn't see so much as an outline of a body or face. "Who the hell are you?"

"I go by Rodrigo. You may call me Lucky. It's been eons since I've dined on such a pure Forbidden, and your fresh blood smells"—he paused and inhaled deeply—"divine."

Yes. Running away had been a bad choice. Helena kicked and fought, but whatever held her was a thousand times stronger. She suddenly felt his hot tongue run down her neck.

"Ummm. Delicious."

He tasted her? *Holy shit!* "Let me go!" Helena shrieked. The man wrapped his unyielding arms around her waist and crushed her into his body.

"Release her, Rodrigo." Niccolo's deep voice sliced

through the night like a welcome knife. "Or I will rip out your entrails and force you to swallow them. Repeatedly."

Rodrigo froze, but did not loosen his painful grip on her body. *Like a caveman trying to hold on to a drumstick,* she thought.

"So, the anonymous tip was right." Rodrigo's voice was filled with arrogance. "You're just the vampire we've been looking for."

Vampire? Did he just say, "Vampire"? Helena's frazzled body took what little energy it had left to resist fainting. She shook her head.

"And let me compliment your fashionable attire, my friend. Is naked the new black?" said Rodrigo.

Apparently, the two men could see each other. *That figures; all monsters can see in the dark.*

"I am uncertain of what happened to the old black while I have been indisposed," Niccolo replied flatly. "But I have no interest in indulging your urges to discuss my legendary body. I do, however, want you to let my woman go."

My woman?

Slowly, the man eased his grip. Helena felt Niccolo reach out and sweep her behind him. She tried not to think about how she was pressed against his bare, perfect bottom.

"Oh, I see," said Rodrigo. "She is *your* meal. I'm shocked. First, abandoning our queen for three centuries and now hunting a Forbidden. And this one is about as forbidden as they come. So innocent." He sniffed loudly. "Just why is that, Niccolo? Perhaps you are unable to perform? Or perhaps she has rejected you and you are too honorable to take her anyway?"

"What the hell?" Helena objected. "And would some-one please flick a Bic or rub two sticks together? I want to die knowing exactly what killed me."

Niccolo ignored her. "What I do with my woman is my business, you dishonorable pile of *merda*. But I am not like you. Nor shall I ever be."

Rodrigo clicked his tongue. "Nobody's perfect."

"*Sì*. You should know," Niccolo jabbed. "After all, you are a shame to both species you have claimed as your own throughout your existence. The queen should never have turned you after I so nearly ended your pathetic human life."

Rodrigo hissed. "I have not forgotten the circum-stances of my demise, and you should not forget my vow to make you pay. I've waited a very long time for this opportunity. I don't care what that whore of a queen says, you'll not be brought back alive."

Niccolo nudged Helena back a few more inches with his hand.

Was he going to fight Rodrigo? What if Niccolo lost? What would happen to her? And wasn't fighting naked sort of dangerous? Not to mention inappropriate? The whole situation was scary. And wrong. What should she do?

"Am I supposed to run?" she whispered to Niccolo.

Niccolo snickered. "Trust me, you are in no danger."

Sure the hell feels like it.

Suddenly, a whoosh of air whipped in front of her. There were grunts and growls and the sounds of tearing flesh and crunching bones.

"Oh, crap!" Helena turned away, unsure who was win-ning or why she was suddenly asking God to make sure

Niccolo, the man she'd been running from only moments earlier, proved victorious. Maybe because the other man wanted to snack on her?

Helena once again found herself charging into the black night, tears of horror streaming down her face. Where was she even going? Helena abruptly stopped, cursing herself for deciding to go on this stupid trip to the ruins. If only she'd stayed at the hotel with her friends, none of this would've happened. Now her life was basically over; she'd end up dinner or a prisoner of some deranged nudist vampire.

Holy hounds of hell! Vampires are real? Impossible! Why haven't any scientists discovered evidence?

Maybe the vampires ate them.

The air kicked up around her. Her heart paused and then slammed into overdrive.

"It is done, my Helena. You are secure now," Niccolo said in a stark voice, then pulled her into his body.

Oh, lucky day. Prisoner of mad nudist vampire it is!

"Who *are* you people?" she asked.

"We do not have time to discuss this now, *mio cuore*. More are probably coming." He grabbed her hand and then yanked her along.

Fab. U. Lous. Can this day possibly get any—

A melody rang out through the darkness, and she felt Niccolo jump. A bright light illuminated the palm of his hand. It was a cell phone playing the Mexican Hat Dance. In any other situation that might be funny.

"Tell me, what is this device?" he demanded, shoving the phone at her.

The glow of the tiny screen sliced through the night, allowing Helena to see him once again. His handsome face was dirty, and he bore a deep scratch down his rock-hard chest. He was now wearing a pair of low-slung jeans. He must have borrowed them from the lovely psycho he'd just offed. Dammit. Despite the pilfered pants and bleeding wounds, he still looked scrumptious.

"Helena, please! We do not have much time," he urged impatiently. "Is it a weapon? What is the meaning of the song?"

Got a sombrero?

"Tell me where you're taking me, and then I'll show you," she replied.

He winced.

She suddenly noticed another deep slice through his side. Blood was running freely. "You're hurt," she commented.

And I care? Okay. It's official. I'm my own species now: pathetic-death-wish-osaurus. I sooo hear extinction calling me.

He made a deliberate motion across the back of his head to remind her that only five minutes earlier she'd hit him. Hard. "Kind of you to suddenly concern yourself," he said.

"I know. Weird, right?"

He growled with pain. "I will be fine once I feed. Been"—he ground out the words—"far too long."

Helena stepped back and covered her neck.

"Not you." He frowned.

"What? Wrong flavor?" She mentally slapped herself. Why was her first reaction to feel rejected? Silly. Although now that she happened to be on the topic, why didn't he want to kill her? The other crazy vampire had called her Forbidden. Could it be something to do with that? Or maybe he was one of those vegetarian vampires like she'd seen in the movies?

With the cell phone still illuminating his face, she could make out his hungry gaze fixed on her neck.

Nope. Not a vegetarian.

Helena's enticing scent was driving him toward madness. It was the most heavenly thing he had ever smelled, and he wasn't certain how much longer he could hold out. He needed to hunt. Unfortunately, leaving her alone in the jungle was not an option. More vampires could be en route, and he knew not if they would be law-abiding.

He looked at Helena and wondered what to do with her. He needed to put her somewhere safe; however, sifting was out of the question. Not only was he too weak, but mortals were not permitted to know their secrets. It was against the Pact. Yes, she now knew he was a vampire, thanks to Rodrigo, but he would have to transport her somewhere safe by whatever means were used in these times.

He would reunite with her once he had gathered the necessary means to ensure her safety. And comfort.

Right. First things first. He needed to find a weapon. He shoved the phone at her again. "What does this do?"

Hand shaking, she took it from him. "Um, it's called a smartphone. You can talk to people or send messages. It's got Internet, too." She pointed to a collection of funny-looking symbols on the glossy surface.

Inter-net. Is that used for some sort of fishing? And why is the phone called smart? Were prior ones stupid?

"Tell me why this communication device is playing that melody," he commanded.

She looked at the phone. "There's a message." She held

it up. It read: Confirm u have him. Then bring him 2 me ASAP. Hz army waits.

The phone made another beep. A new message rolled across the device's surface. If he resists, kill him. Backup is on the way.

Niccolo felt his stomach knot. *Inferno!* More were indeed coming. He was in no shape to fight. On the other hand, the message said he still had an army. Very confusing. "*Bene.* Tell me, who sent this?"

She slid her index finger vertically across the screen to show him the name of the sender. "It says, 'Reyna.'"

Inferno. He was not ready to deal with this predicament just yet. But he must. And oddly enough, the queen's message did not sound as though she was committed to his demise. Why not?

He shoved the phone at Helena. "Operate the device. I must converse with her immediately."

"If I do, you have to let me go," Helena said flatly.

She was making demands of him? No one did such a ridiculous thing without experiencing the severest of consequences. He decided the terms of every action. Yet, somehow, her fearlessness made him proud. *Sì, my mate should be brave. Anything else would bring me dishonor. Nonetheless, she is demanding her liberty. Why?*

Niccolo scolded her with his eyes. "Do you believe I wish to hurt you? After I saved you?"

"Are you really a vampire? Was that…that thing back there really going to eat me?"

Since he hadn't spilled the beans personally, there was no Pact violation on his part. Niccolo nodded. "*Sì* and *sì.* However, *I* will not hurt you. My only wish is to protect you—to see you safe, *mio cuore.*"

Helena cocked her head.

She did not believe him? No one ever questioned his honor! And lived. His pride quickly dissolved into admiration once again.

Yes, of course, my bride should be the cautious type. This will ensure her survival. He smiled inwardly. Perhaps the universe was smarter than he thought. It was beginning to appear that his mate had all the right traits. Physical and mental. He was going to enjoy learning her. Thoroughly.

His cock began to swell once again. *Contain your passion, man. Remember, you cannot join with her until she has been transformed.* His mood instantly soured.

The device made another odd sound. "Here. Push this." Helena demonstrated how to engage the device.

His mood modestly improved; she trusted him enough to help. Very encouraging. Niccolo's attention moved to the phone. "Speak," he commanded it.

A voice came out over the speaker. "Rodrigo! You useless idiot! You'd better have Niccolo on his way to São Paulo!"

Niccolo was amazed by how the small device transported the wretched woman's voice. "I am not on my way anywhere," he answered.

There was a long pause. "Niccolo?"

"Yes, Reyna."

Niccolo held his index finger to Helena's mouth. He did not want the queen finding out about his new human.

"Where the hell have you been?" Reyna barked.

Niccolo shrugged. "Long story. One I do not care to share." Especially not now. His bride was listening, and he did not want to scare her away.

"You refuse to answer?"

"I have not had a meal in three hundred years and must feed. What do you want of me, Reyna?" He knew his attitude might anger her further, but there was only one thing she hated more than impertinence: cowardice.

"Insolent fool! Tell me where you've been," Reyna demanded.

"*Bene*. I'm here now and have taken care of the issue, which detained me. That is all you need to know."

She growled. "Fine. Get your sweet ass down to São Paulo. There's a pack of Obscuros eating tourists—reds and oranges by the handful, like fucking M&M's!"

Niccolo did not want Helena to hear this. It might shock her to know that vampires hunted humans according to the color of their auras. Good vampires preyed only on those with gray or black auras—humans who were beyond redemption. Of course, the sweetest treats were the good apples with red, yellow, and orange auras—Forbiddens like Helena. The only exception was for the queen, who had a pool of willing blood slaves with auras somewhere in the middle of the rainbow.

"São Paulo. As you command," Niccolo responded casually to mask his concern. The queen's reaction was far too...gracious.

In fact, I sense a twinge of...relief? Yes. That is what he felt radiating distantly through their blood bond. What had happened in the world? *Must be bad if she's so willing to take me back.*

He then thought about what it meant to return to her service, a scenario he had not anticipated. *It is merely for three more months, man. You can manage.*

"Go find something to eat," the queen barked. "Sentin

and Rodrigo will be watching your every move. If you even *think* of running again, they will call me, and I will personally deal with you. Understand? Now, hurry the fuck up and get your ass on that plane!"

A plain what?

"And Niccolo . . . after your job is complete, you come straight to me. I'm not done with you yet."

Niccolo looked at Helena. He could sense the turbulent current of fear and confusion coursing through her. He could not help but want to comfort her.

Just as soon as I am certain the situation is safe, I will be comforting you in many, many ways, mio cuore. But for the time being, he could not risk Helena's life; she was his ticket to freedom, though he did not know how this freedom would come about.

"Sentin. Just Sentin will be escorting me. I intercepted Rodrigo in the jungle, attempting to dine on a Forbidden."

There was a long silence. "I guess that explains why you have his phone." Reyna sighed. "Dammit. I had plans this weekend. He was going to cat sit. Well, I guess you've returned just in time. I imagine many of the less honorable men have been bending the rules since you . . ." She screamed loudly, "Took your fucking vacation! Get to work! And clean it up before I change my mind about taking you back!"

The words *Call Ended* flashed across the tiny screen.

Niccolo let out a long, slow breath and then turned to Helena. She was still trembling.

"Please, I only want to go back to my friends."

Niccolo grabbed her hand and planted a lingering kiss on her palm. "That is exactly what I plan to do." He held up the phone. "Give me your coordinates so I may converse with you on this device when the time comes to send for you."

He could sense her emotions. *Deception.* She did not want to return to him. She was afraid. She was also intrigued.

He added, "And do not think of hiding from me, Helena. I am thirteen hundred years old now, and you are my mate. I *will* hunt you. I *will* find you."

Four

~

Three Weeks Later

The nocturnal, salty breeze carried the sound of crashing waves into Helena's second-story window. Although the ocean was a full four blocks away, the soothing crests often sounded as if they were right beneath her window. It was normally her favorite thing about living in the lax beach town of Santa Cruz. But since her return from Mexico, nothing made her happy.

Being alone in the enormous yellow house didn't help either. Her mother was staying at Aunt Rita's in San Diego, her first vacation in a long time.

Helena nibbled her thumb, glared at her cell phone, and then flopped down on her white bedspread, arms sprawled at her sides. It was 8:00 p.m. When would he call? When would he send for her? What would she do when he did?

"You're obsessed! Stop it!" It had been weeks since her return, yet her mind had never left that dark night in the jungle. The memories haunted her every moment of the day and every second of her dreams—when she managed to sleep. Tonight was not one of those nights. Tonight she'd dwell again on his final parting word: "forever."

On that night, after Niccolo surprisingly informed Helena he would let her go, they'd hiked through the jungle for an hour, and he'd asked all sorts of bizarre questions. How did people travel? What weapons were prevalent? Who was currently at war? What form of currency was best?

Helena had explained all about cars, the euro, planes, bombs, and guns. Then the Middle East. Niccolo listened with fascination to every word. When they had finally reached a road, she wondered how he would react to seeing a car. Was he really thirteen hundred years old? How could that be physically possible? He'd also mentioned having waited three hundred years for her. Asleep. The absurdity of that statement swam endless laps inside her head. Not only from a scientific standpoint, but also because she had the worst luck with men. They always seemed intimidated by her independence. To imagine a male like Niccolo waiting around just for *her*? It made her insides liquefy.

Oddly enough, she wasn't hung up on his vampirism. Maybe because her field of study, evolutionary biology, was grounded in the improbable becoming reality. Take the overly endowed Argentine lake duck, for example, with a member the length of its body. Or the Madagascar sucker-footed bat with real suction-cup feet.

When it came to nature's will, wasn't anything possible? Even nocturnal humanlike creatures with super-strength? *Who drink blood, and live for thousands of years, and look like they just walked off the cover of* Hottie Magazine, *and...*

She shook her head. *Okay. Maybe not.*

From another world, then? She *had* witnessed Niccolo flag down a blue pickup that night by merely whispering, "Stop your mechanical carriage."

After the driver had pulled smoothly to the side of the two-lane highway, Niccolo instructed him to take Helena to her hotel and guard her with his life. The driver nodded with an obedient, empty gaze and waited for Helena to get in. As she had been about to step inside the cab of the truck, Niccolo unexpectedly pushed her against the side of the vehicle and slanted his mouth over hers. His hands cradled the back of her head as he deepened the kiss. No one had ever kissed her so passionately, with such desperation.

Before she knew it, she was indulgently stroking his tongue with hers, and within moments, he had her aching. She knew that only the feel of his skin, of their bodies merging, could possibly extinguish that little blaze— okay, forest fire—scorching her insides.

Niccolo broke the kiss, leaving her breathless. "If I don't stop now, I will not be able to. And you must go before they catch up to me," he'd said.

Helena had nodded, her mind a jumbled mess of hormonal overload and adrenaline.

"Helena, remember what I said. Do not think of hiding from me. I need you, and I've never needed anyone."

"I-I don't understand," she'd replied.

He placed a soft kiss on the corner of her mouth. "You

were born for me, to save me from this hell. I will not rest until we are together again and you are safe with me... forever."

That powerful word haunted her every breath, even now as she paced across the hardwood floor of her immaculate room. Why was his life a hell, and why did he believe Helena would rescue him? Did he intend to make her like him? *Forever* carried a lot more weight when it was said by a vampire. Regardless, she knew she wouldn't be content until she saw him again.

I am certifiable.

"Dammit. Where the hell is he?" She glared at her pink cell on the nightstand.

As if magically complying with her wish, the phone suddenly rang, making her jump.

Caller Unknown. Helena's heart nearly stopped. She plucked up the phone and listened for several moments before answering. "Hello?"

"Hey, Lena! What's going on?"

"Anne?" Helena asked, hiding her disappointment.

"Yup! Where are you, girly?"

Helena sighed. *Helplessly pining away at—*"Home. Is everything okay?"

She heard a gasp on the other end. "I'm calling from a pay phone, sitting here all alone with bags of plates and cups. You forgot, didn't you?" Anne was irate.

Helena's mind raced. "Nooo. How could I forget? It's so...important...Okay. I forgot. What are you talking about?"

"Yeah. Weird. Considering the surprise beach party thing was your brainchild..."

Oh, hell! "Jessica's birthday." It was a girls-only bonfire party. She had to go pick up the drinks, logs, cake, everything. And the party started in an hour.

"Be right there." Helena slammed down the phone and scrambled to her closet. *Crap. Okay. Jeans. Find jeans.* She turned and began digging through a pile of neatly folded clothes in a basket on the floor. *Dammit.* She tugged open her top dresser drawer.

"There you are!" Helena had few pleasures in life, but she never skimped on comfortable, well-fitting jeans: classic straight leg, ultra-low waist.

"Helena, my love," she heard a deep voice whisper from behind.

Helena gasped and held on tight to that breath.

Jeans clutched to her chest, she turned slowly toward the voice.

There was no one there.

"It's official. I'm obsessed."

Helena arrived just as the dozen other guests showed up. She'd invited all of the girls from their surf club and a few close friends from the university—mostly Wino Wenches. After summer was over, they'd all be going off in separate directions to start their lives. Jess was taking a job in Seattle, Anne in Chicago. Some of their grad school classmates were going on to doctorate programs out of state.

Helena had planned to live with Aunt Rita and work for an ecological disaster response organization based in San Diego. She had loved her internship, cataloging mutating bacteria last summer and only wanted to get back into the field. She loved learning. She also had a mountain of school debts to pay and wanted to work for a few years before going for her PhD. If she went. For the first time ever, her future felt like a murky pond instead of a wide-open road paved with possibilities.

Helena looked up at Jess, who'd just arrived and realized the event was in her honor. A satisfied grin swept across Helena's face as Jess squealed with delight and hugged everyone while laughing hysterically about being duped.

Helena realized how much she would miss seeing her friends every day. They'd been her rock these last years and filled a void left by not having much family around. And now they would be gone, going off to live their fabulous lives. Not that she wasn't planning to have her own fabulous life, but she wanted them in it. She wanted to be surrounded by friends, find love, get a great job after school—the whole package. Without them, the dream kind of fell apart.

A tiny fissure appeared in her heart and began gnawing away at her.

Helena pasted on a smile. *Don't think about that now. There's a party to throw.*

She passed out sodas for the drivers and beers to everyone else. She then popped in an old Beach Boys CD. Everyone sang and laughed, ate cake, and talked about their plans for the future. Everyone except Helena. She only listened and soaked it all in, knowing it would be the last time they'd all be together.

Life felt so short.

Just after midnight, the party died down and the guests said their good nights. Helena plopped herself down in the sand between Jess and Anne. They stared at the dwindling flames, listening to the low crackle of the logs and the crashing waves in the background.

"Thanks, Lena, that was the best birthday I've ever had," Jess said and squeezed Helena's hand.

Helena put one arm around Anne and the other around Jess. "Love you, guys."

"Love you, too, Lena," Anne said.

Helena wished she could bottle this one moment in time and keep it safe forever.

Forever. She sighed inwardly. *How silly. Nothing is forever.* Change was the one constant in the universe; this much she knew. Lately the air was thick with it, like a sticky mist blanketing everything around her. Even her bones knew it was coming.

Seeking refuge from her dark thoughts, her mind gravitated toward those deep chocolate-brown eyes and thick mane of shiny, black hair. She sighed. Was he her future? Her new steady rock in the endlessly evolving universe?

"Heeey. Got any for us?" a gruff voice spoke out from behind them.

Helena sprang up and turned to find a hulking man staggering toward the fire. He looked disheveled and was clearly inebriated.

"This is a private party." Helena crossed her arms.

The large man stepped into the firelight, providing a better look. He wore only a leather vest and dirty jeans. His heavily inked biceps were the size of footballs, which he made a point to display by crossing his arms over his chest.

"Private? Don't be rude. I don't like rude people." Another six men approached and stood behind him.

Crap! Not good.

The large man moved toward Helena. Sinister intentions flared in his bloodshot eyes.

She swallowed. They were three girls, including her, against seven nasty-looking men. "We're leaving; take what you want." Helena grabbed her purse and tossed it at the man's feet. She needed only her keys to survive and those babies were in her pocket.

Helena glanced at her friends. Jess had her cell casually gripped in one hand and was likely trying to hit the emergency-call feature.

Not going to work. Helena had checked her own cell multiple times throughout the evening, hoping Niccolo might have called, but there was no reception out here. Must have been why Anne called from a pay phone earlier, now that she thought about it. How ironic. They'd come to this beach to avoid being hassled by police or party crashers. Now she'd give anything for the former.

Helena looked at her friends again. The glow of the firelight revealed the panicked looks on their faces. If they stuck together, they'd have a chance.

"Let's go," Helena said to Anne and Jess.

One of the men moved to the path that cut through the sandbank and wooded area to the dirt parking lot. "You're not going anywhere, bitch," the large man said. "We came for a party. You and your friends are going to give it to us."

Like hell we are. I've survived jungles and vampires; you don't know who you're messing with. Helena racked her brain. Jess, Anne, and Helena were in great shape. They ran on the beach every day—okay, three times a week—and surfed all the time. These guys were big but clearly weren't athletes. *Or sober. Or felony-free. We have to run for it.*

At the far end of the beach was another trail that led

back up to the dirt parking lot. If they ran fast enough, they'd get to their cars before the scumbags caught up.

Helena gave a knowing look to her friends. *"Run!"*

As if they'd been thinking the exact same thing, the girls turned in unison and sprinted toward the far end of the beach.

Helena flashed a glance over her shoulder after several seconds.

No! Helena's pounding heart skipped a beat. Anne was missing.

Helena stopped in her tracks and turned. None of the men had followed, but one had Anne by the hair several yards from the bonfire. He was dragging her kicking and screaming.

"Shit!" Helena turned to Jess, panting. "Run, Jess! Get to your car, drive until you have a signal, and call the police!"

"Are you fucking insane, Lena? I'm not leaving you or her."

Helena didn't have time to argue or think through the consequences. She ran toward the sandbank, straining her eyes for anything she could use as a weapon. All they needed to do was free Anne. They could outrun these men again. She hoped.

Ann's scream soared through the air.

Helena and Jess both picked up grapefruit-sized rocks and sprinted toward the fire. All but two of the men were rifling through the ice chests. One of the two held Anne by the hair; the other had thrown himself on top of her.

Helena launched herself and pounded the side of his skull.

He fell to his side. *"Ah!* You *bitch*!"

The other men jumped in and grabbed Helena. She felt a fist slam into her face. Blood poured from her lip as she crumpled. Next, Jess screamed, and then...there were bloodcurdling cries from one of the scumbags.

Helena rolled onto her back to witness the men collapsing one by one, like falling dominoes, landing face-first in the sand around the bonfire, grasping their gushing throats.

"What the...?" She heard a gurgling sound to her right and turned her head. An enormous man held the largest of the scumbags by his neck. Only now that man didn't look so large. He looked like a tiny bug about to be squashed by an angry giant.

Helena gasped. The giant was Niccolo. His shoulder-length black hair was loose, and he was dressed as though he'd walked straight off the Milan runway, wearing a black turtleneck and slacks.

Niccolo snapped the man's neck and threw him like a rag doll. He rushed to her side, immediately reaching for her face. "The bastards! Killing them was too kind!"

"How did you find me?" she whispered, her eyes wide with shock.

Niccolo swept his hand over her forehead with affection. "*Mio cuore*, I will always find you. Forever."

The phone ringing in Helena's ear jolted her from a coma-like sleep. She fumbled with the handset, twice knocking it to the floor before she finally managed to connect it with her face. "Hellooo?" Her voice sounded like she'd eaten sandpaper-covered jalapeños.

Although the curtains were drawn and blinds closed, a

sliver of light sliced through a narrow gap at the bottom of the pane. She glanced at her clock on the nightstand— *2:00 p.m.?*

"Lena. Jeez, there you are! Why aren't you answering your phone? Are you hungover or something?" said the voice on the other end.

"Jess?" Helena's memory jogged. She rocketed from the bed and fell to the floor with a thump. She reached for her lip as she righted herself back into bed. It was swollen and definitely tender. *No, not a dream.*

"Oh my God. Are you okay?" she said into the phone. The last thing Helena remembered was Niccolo holding her.

Jessica laughed. "Depends on your definition of 'okay.' Did you have to bust out the tequila last night, Lena? I've got the worst hangover. We're talking permanent brain damage. I don't even remember going to bed."

Hangover? Jess didn't drink last night, and there was no tequila. Only drunk biker rapists and one very, very pissed-off vampire.

"But I do remember," Jess added, "your smokin' new boyfriend and his buddies! Can you say, 'Yummm'? Why didn't you tell me you were seeing a sex god? In fact, they all looked like they just hopped off of the fabulous-man bus. Can I have one for displaying in the new shrine I'm going to build in their honor? Or a photo? An autographed photo? Naked, of course."

What the hell is going on? "Sorry? But could you repeat that part about..." Helena realized the shower was running in her adjoining bathroom and had just been shut off. *Oh my god...Niccolo.*

"Jess, let me call you right back. I don't feel well," she whispered.

Helena silently put down the phone and tiptoed to the bathroom door. What should she do? Run? Knock? Walk in? Get naked? And...how should she feel? Excited? Freaked out? Angry because he hadn't called for three weeks? Relieved because the wait was over and she could finally start asking all those questions swimming in her head?

The door swung open, and Niccolo boldly stood before her in his birthday suit glory, his unforgettable diamond-cut abs glistening with drops of water.

A whoosh of air left her lungs. *I'm going with...naked and excited!*

His thick black hair dripped as he ran her pink towel over it. She wanted to swoon at the sight of him—there in her room, using her favorite towel. Dreams really did come true. The only things missing were the hour-long foot rub and a happy ending. *Pervert! Stop that.*

The muscles in his right bicep flexed underneath the solid black tribal symbols tattooed down his arm in a neat line. "Helena, love, glad to see you're up," he said all too casually, as if the entire situation were just another day in the life of a domesticated sitcom couple.

"What are you doing here? How did I get home last night? And what did you do to Jess? Hey! And why aren't you asleep in some coffin right now?"

Niccolo looked amused as he strolled past her toward a pile of neatly folded black clothes on the foot of her bed. She tried not to stare at his ass. It was rock hard and perfect. His skin, although slightly pale, had a light golden hue, as if he'd been dusted with cinnamon.

Eyes twinkling, he turned, giving her a clear view of his front.

Her breath whooshed from her mouth again.

The smirk on his face said it all. He was giving her a show and enjoying the reaction.

Well, why wouldn't he flaunt it? Every inch of him was built to please a woman all night long, she thought.

He cleared his throat.

She blinked and looked away from his male anatomy. "Only observing in the name of ... science?" She focused her eyes on the hieroglyphics streaming down his arm instead.

"The tattoo was given to me during my lengthy slumber," he said in a slow, deep voice. "I've been able to decipher only half. 'True to the gods, you shall enter. I brake...' That's as far as I got. But I believe it is a spell of some sort." He shrugged. "I'm here because you are here. I brought you home after you passed out last night. I glamoured Jess—she thinks she had the best night of her life, but really my men took her home. The sun severely weakens vampires, but does not kill us unless we're already injured or out too long." He slipped on his black pants and pulled on his sweater. "And, *sì*, my manhood was created to give you pleasure all night long."

She gasped and covered her mouth. "I said that out loud?"

He nodded.

Oh great. Internal dialogue leakage. Again.

"*Bene*. Any more questions? Wait." He held out his hands. "Hold that thought. We can talk after the plane."

"Plane?"

Niccolo gave a playful smile and crossed his arms over his broad chest. "*Sì*. That large flying machine you humans invented while I was sleeping for three fun-filled centuries."

It was then that Helena caught a mental whiff of something off, some undercurrent of anxiousness and stress.

Must be me. "You're funny," Helena chirped. "I know what a plane—"

"Good because they're quite handy for traveling long distances. Which is what you'll be doing since the home I just purchased for you is in Manhattan, *mio cuore.*"

Whoa. What? Yesterday she'd seriously been thinking about being with him—if he ever showed. Now, she felt like she was being bullied. She hated that.

"Don't you think you should ask me what I want? Shouldn't we get to know each other before living together? How come you sound...different?"

Like a modern guy, but with a hint of "Hi. I'm not from around these parts" and a sprinkle of Italian.

"More questions?" He raised one dark brow. "Fine. Then I shall answer. What you want is obvious: me. Just as I want you. And, no, we should not get to know each other before we live together. Because I plan on slowly savoring that task, learning every inch of you—inside and out—over the course of many long nights for years to come. And like any good vampire, I have spent my time assimilating into this new world. I must blend in. Now, if you're satisfied, I've been deprived for far too long of this..."

Niccolo closed the distance between them with one stride and looked down at her with his dark, delicious eyes before he pushed his lips against hers.

His smell filled her lungs, and his touch made her feel exaggeratedly pliable. *Silly-Girl Putty.*

His tongue slipped past her teeth and stroked the inside of her mouth. Helena leaned into him, her knees undermining her vertical position. She completely forgot about her split lip as her mind drifted into the bliss of his embrace. Once again, being with him made her feel safe, yet vivid and alive—three-dimensional instead of two.

But there was something about him undulating just beneath the surface. Something mesmerizing she couldn't begin to articulate. Like gravity. She could feel his invisible pull as he enveloped her with his entire body. From this day forward, she would do anything to avoid being separated from him ever again. She needed him. She craved him.

What was happening to her?

Her mind was a jumbled mess of fear, lust, anticipation, and other varieties of irrational emotions that radiated from some unknown place in her mind.

As she fully gave in to the kiss, he pulled away. His warmth was replaced with raw determination. "Helena, you are my mate. You must come with me now. I've taken care of everything so you will be safe."

Helena snapped back to planet Earth. She found herself feeling angry and resentful over what was happening to her. Her life was the world of science, where everything had a reason or an explanation. This situation did not.

"Excuse me? Listen, Fred Flintstone, you may have upgraded your syntax and brushed up on modern technology, but you obviously missed one major milestone in social evolution: women are no longer chattel. We make our own decisions and take care of ourselves. Which leads me to my next point—closely related to the 'taking care of myself' topic—I don't know you, and up until three weeks ago, I didn't even know vampires existed. Now you expect me to believe I'm your mate, whatever the hell craziness that really is, leave my life, and run off with you because you tell me to?"

Niccolo appeared to be forcing a polite smile on his face. Perhaps he wasn't used to people not following his orders. Then, without warning, he pulled her body into his once again, making sure she was well aware of his hard flesh. She shuddered.

"No," he said in a low, rumbling voice. "I expect you to come with me because we belong together. Because you will never be content with any other male. And because I am your one true mate. Finally, you will come with me because you are clearly an educated, independent woman who goes after what she wants regardless of the opinion of others." He looked deeply into her eyes. "Now, I believe I've answered your questions and have provided adequate avenues for you to save face. You must now come and do as you're told."

What? She wanted to tell him to take a hike, but the words danced away. There was that crazy pull again. She couldn't think straight.

His voice smooth and deep, he said, "You see, *mio cuore*. You feel the truth. This is why you will come to our home in New York, where you will be treated like a queen. I then plan to marry you and make you mine forever."

Forever? There was that dang word again, and when spoken by a vampire, it could mean only one thing, which ironically didn't frighten her one iota. To the contrary, it excited her.

This was so confusing. Did he really believe she was his mate? He really wanted her? Out of every female on the planet?

Illogical. They were too different.

He was indescribably gorgeous and strong. He was also apparently very wealthy and wasn't lacking in the intelligence department. Or the ego department. Did she mention gorgeous? How about really strong?

She, on the other hand, was an outdoorsy bookworm who actually liked playing with worms. Science, life, understanding how it had all evolved—putting order to it—nothing made her feel more at home.

Helena, you idiot, he said he wants you. Why fight it? Not like you have a chance in hell of forgetting about him. The attraction was undeniable. Like hunger. Like thirst. She felt as though she might simply burst into flames if she didn't go with him. Her need to understand this attraction, the "why," was even greater.

But he was a vampire.

"How do I know you won't kill me?" she whispered, instantly regretting the stupidity of her question. Who would admit to being untrustworthy and murderous? *A vampire might.*

Niccolo frowned. Clearly he didn't appreciate having his honor questioned. Helena felt that odd sensation once again. Anxiety. Stress.

"As you heard from my conversation with Reyna, I slay Obscuros who prey on innocent humans," he admitted freely. "And as you've witnessed, I kill evil men who do the same. However, before you judge, I urge you to recall how my willingness to do so saved your life. Twice. Not to mention your friends."

"Okay. Good point." *He's very honest. I should ask how he is in bed.* She slapped her hands over her mouth. "I didn't just say that out loud again, did I?"

He shook his head no. "But I would appreciate your answer."

"I don't recall you actually asking me anything. It sounded more like a command."

His face turned an angry shade of red. "*Bene*. Will you come with me?"

She wanted to believe in this fairy-tale type of love. So what if the guy wasn't human? Nobody's perfect. Truth was, he was too tempting to resist—a mysterious, strong, sexy creature. And although she couldn't explain what was occurring between them, she knew resisting was useless. She craved to be by his side.

Simply fascinating. Yes, she would go with Niccolo. She would learn everything she could about him, his kind, and this…primal fixation. There had to be some sort of scientific explanation, like pheromones.

She'd kick herself forever if she didn't find out. *Curiosity killed the evolutionary biologist.*

"Yes."

Five

~

Niccolo's dark eyes studied the state-of-the-art GPS inside the sleek black stretch van filled with eight of the queen's finest warriors.

I must buy one of these fascinating "car" machines, he thought to himself. *Just as soon as I learn how to drive.*

Dozens of compact digital monitors tiled one side of the van's interior. Niccolo had never seen so many gadgets and flashing lights, all so they could remotely observe an abandoned military hangar about a quarter mile away. *In the good ol' days, we just hid behind a bush.*

A faint sherbet orange tinted the horizon, and a lonely tumbleweed bounced across the dusty road sprinkled with garbage. This run-down, isolated warehouse district was the perfect place for a rabid vampire coven to thrive and go unnoticed.

For another twenty minutes anyway.

Soon, the foul bastards would be settling down for their naps. A perfect time to attack. Niccolo and his men had accounted for all but one of the coven: their leader. But instead of feeling anxious, he found himself welcoming the time to reflect as they waited. Since his return to duty and to this new, strange world, he'd had little quality "me time," as modern humans now called it. And he was going to need a whole hell of a lot of *that* if he were going to digest the massive transformation the world had undergone.

Big shock number one: over ten thousand vile, blood-thirsty Obscuros now roamed the earth.

Big shock number two: the Obscuro population exploded three centuries ago, about the time he'd vanished.

Perhaps it's not so unbelievable that the world would go to merda *without me. It's not as if the queen could command the army. She can't even tie her own shoes.*

The most puzzling account, however, was bloody, big shock number three: during his absence, the gods had created a new race specifically dedicated to killing Obscuros. They called themselves Demilords.

Ridiculous! As if I could be replaced!

Nevertheless, everyone spoke of their unstoppable strength and ruthlessness. It was said they could take out any vampire, that they'd kill anyone who got in their way. No rules, no Pact holding them back.

Lucky bastards!

But…unstoppable? I'd have to see it to believe it. Lazy seems more befitting. Niccolo saw few signs of these so-called mighty warriors. Reports of new covens, dozens of them, were coming daily. *Where the hell are these Demilords?*

On the bright side, a tiny part of him felt satisfied to be back in the saddle—leading the queen's army, even if only temporarily. Soon the prophecy would be fulfilled, and he would be a free man.

But will you be able to turn your back on the world? Obscuros will still exist after you're no longer the general. And who better to extinguish them than you?

True. He was damned good at it. And yes, the world had changed, as Helena rightly pointed out—women worked and led their households, giant metal birds flew in the sky, and this thing called electricity powered everything under the sun—but killing these cretins was something familiar and noble. He was born to squelch evil. Specifically, Obscuros. *Just like my warriors...*

Through the rearview mirror, he proudly glanced at his men in their black military-style jumpsuits and headsets.

He smiled to himself. Modern technology certainly was a nice perk in these times. For example, he always had the unique gift of sifting long-distance—never knew why—but this used to do him little good when he required an army to take out a coven on the other side of the planet. Months were lost to logistics.

In this new age, everything had changed. Now there were planes and cars to transport his army. Now they had video conferencing and software to share interactive maps and battle plans.

This is...pure awesome.

"Sir," Sentin said, "we have confirmation. Franc, their leader, is on his way. The other members of the coven are in the warehouse all accounted for."

Sentin, with jet-black cropped hair, was his new junior lieutenant from Italy who'd been turned only seventy years earlier, during what humans called World War II. Sentin, who'd been fighting with the English, was barely twenty when Viktor—his right hand and best comrade for over a millennium—found him after a bomb exploded near his bunker. Sentin was braver than most vampires ten times his age. He also had a sense of humor, something rare in the vampire world.

"Ready, sir?" Sentin said.

Niccolo nodded and strapped his swords to his back. Viktor glowered from the driver's seat. Although he was an ancient Viking, Viktor wasn't "old school," as the younger vampires called it. Viktor embraced everything modern and that included automatic handguns with custom-made wooden bullets and quirky sayings like "That's right, bitches! Who's your baddie?"

"Stay close. Remember, the Obscuros have new tricks," Viktor lectured.

Niccolo shrugged. "*Bene*. I'd expect nothing less. Makes for a more challenging fight, does it not?"

Viktor shook his head. "Not."

"Bingo!" Sentin hollered.

Everyone's focus shifted to a monitor. A tall man with slicked-back blond hair, wearing a black tailored suit, glided down the dusty sidewalk with a young woman on each arm. From the look of their attire, they'd just been out at what Viktor called a nightclub—a place where single humans went to listen to loud music, dance, overindulge in spirits, and find sexual partners for the evening. To Niccolo's shock, even the educated females from good families partook in such social activities in these times.

Niccolo's thoughts quickly flew to the angelic, feisty Helena for the fifteenth time that evening. It was increasingly difficult to stay focused. In fact, the Helena channel constantly played in the back of his mind.

Was that normal for a vampire to feel for his mate? He craved her. He wanted to learn her, to savor her scent and bathe in her beauty. But he couldn't. Not yet. Not without derailing the prophecy.

Yesterday, when he brought her to their new home, they spent only a few moments in the same room before he had to run like a weak, pathetic fool lacking control.

The sound of Viktor clearing his throat startled him.

"One moment," Niccolo snarled.

"I think we've waited long enough," Viktor growled under his breath.

He understood Viktor's true meaning. Niccolo's absence had been particularly hard on Viktor, especially having to deal with the queen on his own. Viktor's hide was still chapped—as they liked to say now—even though he understood Niccolo had not intentionally turned his back on him.

"Any day now?" Viktor prodded.

"*Sì, sì.* Do not get your..." Niccolo paused to recall the exact phrase. "Get your balls in a bunch."

Viktor shook his head. "Panties."

Niccolo frowned. "Why would you wear panties? Aren't those for females?"

Viktor growled, "Can we *go* now?"

"Yes, but I insist you tell me more about your man panties later."

The men in the van chuckled under their breath. Viktor's body tensed as though he was about to lunge for Niccolo.

Niccolo shrugged. He supposed Viktor was acting so

irritably because he was anxious to get the job done. This is what he always admired about the man; when it came to killing, he was all about efficiency and execution. That's why Viktor was his most trusted friend and still had a head; no one talked to Niccolo that way, except Viktor. Indeed, Viktor was more like a brother. He was also the reason the queen's army hadn't completely gone to shit during Niccolo's "vacation."

Niccolo straightened his back. "On the count of three. One. Two…" He sifted to the warehouse entrance and then entered the dark, dank building. His senses flared to life immediately. The pupils of his dark eyes dilated on command, picking up every shadow, every movement. His lungs pumped only enough air to detect the smell of his enemies—Obscuros.

He slipped to the side of the door and hid behind a large wooden crate. There was no noise inside the abandoned warehouse except for the nearly silent gusts from the air being displaced as his men swept in behind him, taking their positions. Another vampire would mistake their movements for a mouse skittering across the floor.

Niccolo waited the agreed six seconds, sampling the scents in the air, before deciding the ground floor was secure. Most likely, the Obscuros were in the basement.

Niccolo gave the all clear and motioned for the men to begin searching silently for a door or stairs.

Within seconds, Viktor blew into the air. The signal. To the untrained ear, it was the wind whistling through the gaps under a door.

The men moved with blurring speed toward Viktor and fell in behind him.

Niccolo caught the sound that had drawn Viktor's attention—the low rumble of men talking and ... crying?

Niccolo shrugged at Viktor. No doubt it was odd, but what were they going to do? They were warriors, and whatever was causing a bunch of grown Obscuro males to cry and ... talk—well, they could handle it. He hoped.

Niccolo held up his palm, signaling for the other men to stay put. He quickly found a set of narrow cement stairs and sifted part of the way down, remaining out of sight as he listened to the conversation and whimpering.

One man, whom the others referred to as Luis, was trying to defend his actions. "But as hard as I try, my victims only laugh at me when I show myself," he sobbed. "How can any self-respecting vampire face himself knowing his food doesn't take him seriously?"

There was a low rumble of agreement from several voices in the room.

"Luis!" another male barked. "How many times do I have to tell you? Image is everything! You dress like a biology professor and speak like Mr. Rogers. Of course they don't fear you! You're there to kill them, not ... not teach them the ABCs!"

Another whimper escaped from Luis's mouth. "I know. I know," he whined. "But I can't bring myself to growl or wear leather pants. It's just not ... me."

No. Clearly he's not cut out for such manly cloth-ing. He'd be a disgrace throughout the lands to all vam-pires and other supernatural bad boys alike, thought Niccolo.

"Luis." Was it the leader, Franc, speaking? "Being an Obscuro is an honor. And if you're not going to uphold our ways, then you'll be demoted to a coffin boy or, if lucky, my manicurist."

Niccolo winced. *That sounds low.* A coffin boy was the equivalent of a human's pool boy, but without the sexy connotation. And a vampire's manicurist...well, let's just say that if there were a vampire *Dirty Jobs* show— Niccolo had watched a lot of television recently to acclimate quickly—being a vampire's manicurist would be right up there with vampire dry cleaner.

"No. Please, give me one more chance. I beg you. I can be evil. I can do it!" Luis argued.

"All right, but I want to hear you growl like you mean it this time," said their leader impatiently. "I want to hear you bring terror to my ears like we showed you."

"Grrrr. I'm here to suck your blood," Luis said sheepishly.

Franc growled. "No! That's not it at all. Say it like you really mean it! Grrr! I'm going to *fucking* drink your blood!"

Evil vampire lessons? Niccolo crept up the stairs, shaking his head. He'd never heard such an oddity. He signaled the men to follow him outside. As soon as they'd gathered around, he told them what he'd heard, but instead of being disgusted by the undignified behavior, they looked at each other shamefully.

"Am I missing something?" Niccolo whispered. Several awkward moments passed. "I demand you tell me."

Viktor whispered, "We, um, role-play, too. It's part of our HPT process."

Were these vampire soldiers off their undead rockers? "HPT? What is this?"

"High-Performance Teams. It's a technique to build trust, motivate, and increase output."

"You know, sir," one of the younger male vampires cut in, "we're only as strong as our weakest link."

Niccolo's men grumbled in agreement, nodding.

Oh, for bloody heaven's sake! What had the world of ruthless warrior vampires come to? Where were the ethics from the days of old? Only the strong survive. Dog eat dog. *Carpe diem!*

Niccolo shrugged. "I cannot deny how well the team works together. I must look for the golden lining."

"That's *silver*, sir," whispered Sentin.

Niccolo frowned. This new English was very confusing. Any self-respecting vampire would want his coffin lined with gold—it was worth far more than silver. "Very well. I do not believe in coffins, anyway. On my count, we rush the room and take them out. I heard twelve voices below, evenly distributed throughout the room. Watch out for the humans they brought in earlier. They might be used as shields."

The men nodded. Niccolo counted down. Then they rushed back into the building, toward the stairs. The room was dark, except for a few small candles burning in the center of the room. The two women lay in a dead heap in the corner, and the Obscuros, including Franc, were sitting in a circle on the floor. Something about that visual disgusted Niccolo's inner warrior. Men talking, sitting on pillows...sharing? He shivered down to his alpha male core.

The Obscuros sprang to their feet, and the entire room instantly converted into a tornado of vampires whirling through the air, trying to outmaneuver one another. Blood splattered in every direction and then turned into a gray, sticky ash. They were no match for Niccolo's trained men. The room filled with clouds of dust as the Obscuros were shot with wooden bullets or beheaded with Niccolo's sharp sword. Suddenly, Niccolo heard a cough and a struggle.

"D-don't move. Or, I'll hu-hurt him," someone stuttered.

Niccolo recognized the voice. It was Luis, the one who'd been speaking earlier. He was likely just some poor man who became a vampire against his will and never knew he had a choice to be good or bad.

Niccolo held out his hands. "Put the knife down, Luis. You don't want to hurt him. We're good vampires. You're good, too. I heard you speaking earlier. Drop the knife, and you can work with us."

"No!" Luis began to cry again. "You'll only make me your coffin boy! And there's no such thing as good vampires!"

"Listen," Niccolo reasoned. "I'm over thirteen hundred years old. Viktor, who you're holding there, is almost as old as I am and nearly impossible to kill. He has also been my friend for ten centuries. I would never allow you to hurt him and live. You have no way out but to surrender."

Niccolo saw an easy smile flash across Viktor's face. Viktor was allowing Luis to hold the knife to his throat and giving him a chance to back down.

"Look, Luis. I'm going to count to three." Niccolo smiled calmly at the man. "Then you're going to drop the knife and come with us."

Niccolo saw Luis's free hand reach into his pocket. *Bloody inferno.* "One, two—"

Niccolo rushed Luis with such speed that the man

never saw the sword swipe toward his neck. Luis's head fell to the floor and exploded in a cloud of gray dust.

Viktor shook his head as he looked at the remains and noticed a gun lying there. He picked it up and inspected the bullets. "Wooden. I think that dude was really going to off me."

Niccolo sheathed his sword on his back. He wasn't sure what Viktor expected him to do. Clearly the protocols between males had changed over the last three centuries. Niccolo wanted to be the great leader he'd always been, but this was uncharted territory, completely out of his comfort zone.

A true leader shows no fear when his men need him to be strong. Niccolo closed his eyes and wrapped his arms around Viktor, gently patting him on the back. "There, there, my brother. I am here for you."

Viktor stopped breathing, and Niccolo suddenly heard the other men whispering, shocked. Perhaps even disgusted.

"Niccolo? Why are you ... hugging me?"

Niccolo pushed away quickly. His face burned red-hot. "I thought you might need comfort. You know, like those other..." Niccolo grumbled under his breath and swept up the stairs, barely escaping the humiliation of his men bursting into hysterical laughter.

He sifted off to the van, grumbling and growling under his breath. "Insolent, unappreciative—" He suddenly caught the flicker of movement on the monitor.

Niccolo drew his sword and sifted back into the warehouse. Viktor and the men were emerging from the stairwell, still roaring with laughter as a shadow from the darkness appeared behind Viktor.

Niccolo shoved Viktor out of the way when a thin,

shining blade barreled down on Viktor's neck. Niccolo
kicked the attacking vampire and watched him fall backward. He thrust his sword underneath the male, severing
his head and turning him instantly to ash.

"Ha! Who's the real warrior now?" Niccolo bellowed
as he marched out of the building, chin held high. "That's
right, bitches!"

Six

‑

Helena peeked through the crack of the bedroom door, then quickly slammed it shut. *Damn. The scary blond guy is still there.* Same as the last fifteen times she'd checked.

Eventually, she had to find food and something more than tap water from the adjoining master bath. It had been one entire day since Niccolo dumped her in the posh penthouse. Where the hell was he?

After convincing her to come with him, he put her on a 9:00 p.m. flight to New York, but didn't board. Five nerve-racking hours later, the plane touched down, and there he was, waiting outside the plane doors with an inviting smile on his face.

I guess Homeland Security rules don't apply to vampires.

"We must hurry," he'd said with a wink, "the sun is rising, and I need my strength today."

Ooh. That sounds sexy, she'd thought as he took her

hand, gave it a languid kiss, and silently led her outside, where a sleek black limo waited curbside.

"Oh no!" Helena turned to go back toward the terminal. "I forgot my luggage."

Niccolo patted her hand. "No worries, *mio cuore*. Your belongings are already at our new home."

Our new home? She couldn't quite process that thought just yet. Instead, she asked Niccolo about his mysterious travel tricks.

"There will be time later for Q & A," he'd said.

But there wouldn't be, she'd later realize.

Her jaw unhinged when she saw the opulence of the luxury residential building adjacent to Central Park. It was flabbergasting enough to be in such a big city. And the lobby was downright unbelievable when she saw how posh it was with its übermodern velvet couches and a crystal chandelier the size of a VW Bug.

The doorman tilted his hat as they passed.

Wow, I feel just like Pretty Woman, minus the hooker gig.

"Niccolo?" She tugged at his sleeve after the elevator doors closed.

He looked at her with his large dark eyes and flashed yet another stunning smile. "*Sì*, my love?"

Her heart made a happy little flutter. "You said we were going to talk after the plane ride. Aren't you going to say something?" she asked.

He tilted his head sideways. "What would you like me to say?"

An explanation of why he'd been entombed in Mexico, asleep for three centuries, would be nice. Or how about the nature of his origins? Why were he and she "mates"?

How did it happen? What did it mean? Was happiness a guaranteed part of the package? How about children? Did she need to pass some sort of math test to prove she was smart enough to be his companion for eternity? Not that she was worried, she was great at math.

Helena suddenly felt foolish, like a naive child who required hand-holding. She opted for a question that didn't reflect her eagerness for answers.

She squared her shoulders. "Why did you pick this place to live?"

He frowned for a brief moment. "You are not pleased? You do not like the location? I assure you it is the finest penthouse in all of Manhattan."

She shook her head. "No. The location is ... perfect. But why New York? Is this where you're from?" She didn't think so since he sounded Italian.

He shook his head. "No. I am not from here."

Yep. Stupid question.

The elevator chimed, and the stainless steel doors slid open. They stepped out into a quiet, brightly lit hallway with cream-colored walls, thick floral-patterned carpet, and beveled mirrors on either side of an ornately carved set of double doors.

"Do you work in New York, then?" She had no clue what he did for money.

He turned toward her. His jaw muscles pulsed. Was he frustrated? Had she said something wrong?

"It is simply ... convenient," he replied.

"Why?"

Jaw ticking. "*Bene.* All will be revealed in good time, my bride." The doors swung open, and he tugged her through. "Until then, I'm afraid you'll have to bear with me. There is much I cannot discuss. It is simply forbidden."

"You said I'm your mate. Doesn't that mean I'm allowed to know—"

She suddenly found herself pinned against the wall. He kissed her with such force that for a moment she didn't know if he was attacking her or merely feeling as hot under the collar as she was. His lips pushed and sucked as his tongue invaded her mouth. A jolt surged through her body. The elation was so exquisite, so powerful, that she thought she would either orgasm or pass out if he didn't stop. Either would be just a teensy bit embarrassing at this juncture of their relationship.

She then recalled being whisked away to what she believed was their bedroom. (Who the heck cared?) He pressed his body against hers, continuing to take possession of her mouth. He felt so good, so hard against her softness. A pulsating, sinful warmth pooled between her legs as his hands cupped her ass and pushed her possessively into his erection.

Is there any spot on his body that isn't hard? Tonsils? Kidneys? Oh! His tongue ... silky little devil.

A deep rumble escaped his throat as his hands reached for the buttons of her jeans.

Were they going to do this now? *So soon?*

Hell, who was she kidding? She'd thought about it every minute of every day since she'd met him.

Yiiiippee!

But did he know she wasn't ... experienced? She'd seen him naked and knew his size was not to be taken lightly. *No training wheels on that bicycle.*

How she was able, she'd never know, but she broke the

kiss to warn him and caught a glimpse of his eyes. They were dark abysses that mirrored her own uncertainty, raging lust, and fear.

She gasped. "Niccolo, are you okay?"

A look of frustration— *No. Wait . . . anger. No . . . fear. Oh, hell*—it was a bad, bad look.

"Timothy will watch over you," he scowled before he flew from the room like a wintry gust, slamming the door behind him.

After Helena had caught her breath and splashed cold water—not nearly cold enough—on her face, she attempted to go find him. But instead she found the giant Slavic beast—*Timothy?*—at her door, with a gaze so icy he could freeze a penguin's patootie. That took the wind from her libido sails.

She'd spent the rest of the day unpacking, watching television, and trying to avoid confronting the reality of her situation, though she never ventured outside the room where the scary blond man stood motionless.

Would Niccolo ever return? Damn him. Why did he leave her alone? Perhaps she was a terrible kisser and his eyes were like mood rings that turned black when a science dork touched him?

Ugh! Stop it, Helena. There has to be a rational explanation. He wouldn't bring you all the way here, buy you a home, save your life . . . just to dump you after one kiss.

Helena opened her journal. Yes, she would make sense of everything by separating fact from fiction—aka her deranged imagination—and sort them in an orderly manner, which would lead her to a rational explanation for everything she'd seen, heard, and felt.

Start with the creepy assassin at your door.

Was he a vampire, too? *Maybe.*

Would he hurt her? *Not likely.* Niccolo was überprotective and wouldn't leave her with someone who would harm her.

Okay, that settles it. See? Nothing to be afraid of. Just go out there, introduce yourself, and have him point you to the kitchen.

She peeked one more time outside the bedroom door and shut it once again. *Dammit.* Timothy was too big and deadly looking. He also had the whole supernatural vibe going. It rattled her bones.

She heard a low voice on the other side of the door.

"Ma'am."

Helena gasped and covered her mouth.

"Miss Strauss? I can hear you breathing. I know you're there."

Crap. What should she do? If she didn't answer, she'd look like a coward. For some bizarre reason, images of chickens flashed in her mind. Didn't the stronger hens always peck at the weaker ones until they were sad looking and without feathers? Did vampires think themselves the stronger hens? She couldn't show weakness and let them peck her.

Helena took a deep breath and yanked open the door. "What? What the hell do you want?" she barked.

Timothy took a step back, but didn't appear at all bothered by her tone. "Niccolo told me that I was not to disturb you under any circumstances. But I doubt he anticipated you'd stay in your room without eating for an entire day. So, considering he'll take my head if you suffer under my care, I thought I'd risk it."

"Oh." Helena cautiously eyed him. "Sorry. I didn't mean to be so . . . rude." *But you scare the hell out of me.*

A tick of amusement flashed in Timothy's eyes. "I can see you are not quite comfortable with leaving your quarters yet, so may I order you some food?"

Helena lifted her chin. She was determined to bury her fear and that included her wobbly knees, which seemed to recognize she was talking to a lion who, under normal circumstances, viewed her as a tasty gazelle. "Sausage pizza and . . . Dr. Pepper."

Timothy stared for several moments, fear filling his eyes. "I am certain we can find you a pizza, but I was not aware you are ill and require a doctor. Niccolo will have my head."

This was going to be a very, very long day. "Dr. Pepper is a soda."

"What is a soda?"

"What's a soda? It's a drink. Where have you been this last century?"

"In our queen's dungeon. She only serves pain."

Poor guy. "What did you do to land yourself there?" she asked.

"I did not part my hair on the right side. The queen was displeased."

Jeez. What a psycho. I hope I never have to meet her, especially since I part on the left.

"But," he added, "that is behind me now, and Niccolo will ensure we are all freed from her tyranny forever."

He would? How the hell did he plan to do that?

Eight Sad, Long Weeks Later

Helena stared out the window of the obscenely spacious penthouse overlooking Central Park. In contrast to the stark white walls and white modernist furniture, outside was a vision of drab, sooty gray. The late-afternoon rain pattered against the tinted glass, which partially obscured the breathtaking view, all twenty million dollars of it. Not that she cared.

Sadly, this day was one she'd repeated more times than she cared to remember in recent weeks: alone, waiting, and too much time to think.

Even her thick beige turtleneck and wool socks weren't enough to ward off the coldness lurking in her bones today. Reality had finally sunk in, gonging like a huge bell, really.

I left my home and family for Niccolo.

She still hadn't figured out what she would eventually tell everyone. Right now, they believed she was on the East Coast conducting research for a marine biology outfit in New York. If anyone knew the truth, her best friends Anne and Jess, her mother, they'd all say she had lost her noodle. Helena barely grasped the situation herself, and no amount of journaling could fix the facts because they didn't add up to anything that might be recognized as logical.

Almost three months earlier she'd gotten herself stranded in the jungle, where she met a vampire—irresistibly sexy, yes!—but nevertheless, a real live vampire. She'd then become inexplicably stricken by the urge to spend every waking moment, for the rest of her life and every moment thereafter, at his side. *Like a damned puppy!*

Yes, he had saved her neck, but the intensity of her feelings still didn't make sense. And frankly, she was exhausted from trying to figure it out.

Oh, stop. You sound like a one-woman Maury Povich show titled "Whaa—! I Hooked Up with a Vampire and It Sucks!"

Yeah, but it does kinda suck. Doesn't it?

Keeping up the lies was a full-time job on its own. And she couldn't not answer her cell or ignore texts. People would start to get suspicious. This morning's reply to Anne was supposedly sent from the corner café as she waited in line for her triple skinny venti. Really, she was staring at Niccolo's Nespresso in the kitchen, waiting for the light to turn green.

A burst of cool air rushed through the room. She spotted Niccolo's towering form in the doorway. His gorgeous face displayed his trademark smile: dimpled, arrogant, full of mischief.

Helena sighed. He was so damned beautiful it stole her breath every time she looked at the man. And dammit if she didn't still feel euphoric in his presence. Even now, when she was having such painful doubts about the future, the raw masculine energy he radiated was downright addictive.

"*Mio cuore*, I've missed you," he said, his voice pure decadence. He was wearing his usual black pants. Sometimes they were leather or fine tailored wool, other times linen. But always expensive. Always black. Today, they were snugly fit soft black denim. A perfect choice to go with the tight black V-neck sweater, which accentuated the ripples of muscles covering every inch of his sublime body. A warrior's body.

With his eyes locked on her, he glided over and clasped her hand before he gently pulled her into him. His thick waves of black hair tickled her face as his massive frame melded to her. He raised his strong hands to the sides of her head, buried his fingers deep in her curls, and slowly pressed his lips against hers. His cool touch never failed to ignite a potent explosion of butterflies in her stomach and deeper down.

Yep. No doubt about it, he was perfect in every way. Except he refused to be intimate with her—that was far from perfect.

He gently pulled away and unraveled his fingers from her hair. She looked up at him, wishing he'd keep kissing her.

Instead, he sighed. "Oh, Helena, I can feel it. Something is troubling you. Have my men been unfriendly again? Because if they have, I will let *you* tear out their eyes this time."

Helena winced at the thought and placed her palms against his hard chest. "No, Niccolo."

Amusement sparkled in his dark eyes. "*Bene*. But they grow back." He shrugged.

Ugh, would she ever get used to vampire humor? Or maybe he wasn't kidding. It was hard to tell sometimes.

"What if I were the one misbehaving again?" She wondered what he'd say.

He laughed. "Then I would punish you like last time … in a very cruel way." He gently clasped her hand again and then planted a featherlight kiss on her wrist. "Like this."

Figured. He was always so calculated and controlled around her. She wished she could see the unedited version of Niccolo. She wished they'd have a real fight like a real couple. But he never lost his temper with her. Not once. Not even when she broke one of his many ridiculous rules, rules he'd conveniently avoided mentioning until after she had moved in, which is why she had no qualms about ignoring them. In fact, she began breaking them simply to test him. And even then, his only responses were calm and calculated: "You need more time to adjust to my world," he'd say. Or "I must do a better job of persuading you that my rules are always to be followed." Then he would lean slowly into her, press his full lips to her mouth, and roll his tongue against hers. He wouldn't stop until she was a mindless, gooey puddle. Then he would back away. Sometimes he'd run. Was it because of rule number three? No sex until after the wedding/transformation.

Why? Well, that was rule number six: no answers until, yes, after the transformation. Helena felt the anger and frustration beginning to take hold.

Sentin appeared in the living room doorway with his standard levity. "Is it time to feed our human?"

Niccolo whipped around in a blur. "How many times have I told you?" he screamed. "You are to call her Helena! Next time, you'll pay with your tongue."

Helena grabbed Niccolo's hand and gave it a squeeze. "It's okay," she whispered. "It doesn't bother me." It actually did bother her. A lot. It made her feel like a pet, though yelling and violence bothered her more.

Sentin held out his hands. "Jeez. Touchy, touchy. My apologies."

Niccolo dismissed Sentin and led Helena to the dining room, where there was only one setting. Niccolo sat opposite her across the room-length mahogany table. He'd forgotten to turn on the lights. Again. She could barely see him.

Helena sighed. "Can't you sit closer so I can see you and don't have to yell?"

"I can hear you just fine," Niccolo responded. "And sitting this way is a sign of a distinguished upbringing. I am not a commoner, Helena."

Ugh! "No, it's actually old-fashioned and annoying," she mumbled.

Niccolo stared blankly. "I heard that."

"I'm sorry, but I like having you close," she argued, "and you may not be a commoner, but I am."

Niccolo suddenly appeared at Helena's side, taking her hand and placing a kiss in her palm. "You are anything but common, my bride."

Yes, I'm the lucky acorn who fell from the nut tree.

Silver serving dish in hand, Sentin emerged from the kitchen with what looked like fettuccine Alfredo. She had no clue where the vampire learned to cook, but he had flair except for Italian. He refused to cook with garlic. It was sort of ironic since he was Italian.

Sentin served a heaping pile of creamy, buttery pasta mixed with bits of chicken and red-and-green vegetables—at least she thought they were that color; it was hard to see in the dark.

Niccolo wrinkled his nose and poured himself a glass of red wine from the decanter set out in front of her.

Helena loaded up her fork and took a mouthful of pasta. *Yep. Missing garlic, but edible.* She smiled at Sentin, who was anxiously awaiting her reaction. "Yummm. Really good, Sentin. Thanks."

Pleased with himself, he practically floated from the dining room.

She began attacking her food. God, she was famished! She'd passed on breakfast this morning because she was too busy writing in her scientific journal. She had pages and pages of things she'd learned over the weeks despite the vampires' attempts to be secretive. For example, they were more like wolves—pack animals—than they were the cold-blooded loners like Dracula. And there was a clear pecking order usually associated with age, but sometimes according to physical skills. She'd overheard Viktor telling the other men that Sentin would lead some outing that evening because although he was the youngest, he "moved like a feather." What an odd skill to value.

What astonished her most was how little she really knew about her husband-to-be. He wouldn't tell her a thing: where he was from, who his parents were, if he had brothers and sisters he loved once. How about friends? He had to have some, right?

Helena washed down her bite of pasta with a gulp of wine and noticed Niccolo was observing her eating.

He had a frown plastered on his face. "Hungry?"

She smiled sheepishly and dabbed her face with her napkin. "Niccolo, when you change me, can we have a dinner party so I can meet your friends?"

"You've already met them."

"I have?"

"My men," he clarified.

But she never saw them speak or show any signs of camaraderie.

"However," he continued, "we don't do dinner parties.

Not the kind you're thinking of anyway. I will explain it all...after."

Helena wanted to gag at the thought of a bunch of vampires sitting around drinking blood from crystal goblets. *Ick.* "So, I won't ever bc inviting my girls over, will I?"

Niccolo chuckled. "Not unless you intend on serving them as appetizers."

"Then, that would be a *no.*" Helena frowned and took another mouthful. Was he kidding? Would she really never see the girls again? No. She couldn't let that happen. She'd visit them when they were home for Christmas. Maybe another nighttime bonfire? On second thought, that didn't go so well last time. Niccolo and she never spoke of the incident, but she still had anxiety over seeing those men dead. The degenerates deserved what they got, but it didn't make watching them die any easier. Vampires, on the other hand, seemed at ease with killing. That felt wrong somehow.

"So, what do good vampires do with their time besides buying extravagant penthouses, hunting Obscuros, and saving tourists in distress?" she asked.

His brows pulled together. "I cannot speak about my world. You know this. You already know too much for your own good."

Helena wanted to shout—they needed to talk and trust each other like real people! She needed to be treated like his equal, not kept like a pet. She was about to say so, but the moment she gazed into his deep espresso eyes, her anger evaporated.

His expression had also transformed. He was thinking lusty thoughts. Not sure how, but she could tell.

So, is that what vampires do with their time? Sex?

She swallowed hard and crossed her legs while her mind flooded with images of bed play; shower play; floor, kitchen table, and in-front-of-the-fireplace play. God, she wanted him. She wanted to feel those reams of hard muscles. She wanted him stretched over her naked body. Writhing. Panting. Pumping.

His trademark frown congealed on his face. "I cannot bed you, Helena. It is"—he paused—"for your own protection."

Dammit. He wanted her, too, and she felt it.

Helena didn't believe for one moment that Niccolo would hurt her in the act of passion. She'd witnessed dozens of times how tender he could be with that indestructible, potent body. The way he moved around her, kissed her, touched her—something else was holding him back. It was the same something that caused him to behave as if he were molten lava one second and cardboard the next. And thanks to that effing rule number six—no telling humans about their world—she'd have to wait to find out the truth.

"It's not just that. I want to know *why* it's for my protection. I want to know more about you," she argued.

Harsh emotion flickered in his eyes, and his face drained of warmth. He stood and pulled Helena to her feet and kissed her hard.

Oh yes. This was the sort of explanation she wanted: him holding her, their lips molding together. This was what she constantly craved, so painfully that sometimes she cried. But those were tears she could never shed in front of him. *Rule number two ... or is it number three?*

Ugh! This all felt so wrong. She was never so needy or weak before. She felt like she was on some insane paranormal hormone roller coaster. Or perhaps it was more like *Vampire Price Is Right*. In her right hand, she held her current life, a good deal, but behind vampire door number three was another life. It could be the old donkey with the sombrero—a life filled with darkness, death, no hope of children or even a career. Or the hidden prize behind the door could be eternity with the man she wanted, endless nights of passion. That was the prize she'd signed up for.

Niccolo swept her away to the bed with mind-boggling speed and was suddenly lying at her side. He had already removed his sweater to give her a breathtaking glimpse of his thick, strong arms and powerful chest.

How'd he do that so quickly? Sneaky vampire—oooh.

Niccolo lifted her sweater and began kissing her belly. God, she was so confused. One minute he was pushing her away, chastising her for wanting him. The next he was provoking her, kissing her, and making her melt.

This was all wrong. She had to stop this insane, dysfunctional game they were playing. She needed honesty, and trust, and—

Niccolo unsnapped the top button on her jeans.

"Wait!"

"*Sì*, my love?" He looked up at her with playful eyes.

"Nope. Uh-uh." She pushed his hands away.

"I thought I might try kissing you in a few new places. Is this not what you want?"

You bet your sweet immortal ass I do! "No!" She scooted away and rose from the bed. "You work constantly, but I don't know what you do. I never know where you are or whom you're with. Then you come back for a few hours and then disappear again for days!"

"We have gone over this, Helena. I cannot tell you these things. But I promise everything will be different afterward. Our wedding is in one week. In the meantime, I'd hoped I could make our time together more pleasing for you."

Was it possible he thought that was good enough? Their relationship was seriously lacking any substance. Sure, they were wildly attracted to each other, but lust wasn't enough. Why wouldn't he tell her what she needed to know? She'd put her complete trust in him and left her life behind.

In return, he gave her rules, bodyguards, and material things she didn't care about. *And two months basically living without him...*

"That's not the point. I need—"

"*Bei vestiti?*" he interrupted enthusiastically.

Helena shot him a deer-in-headlights look.

"More beautiful clothes?" he translated. "I can have the men take you shopping anywhere you like. Or do you want me to send a decorator? I'm not so attached to this modernist look, if that's what worries you. You can change the furnishings to any style except Victorian. I'm very pleased to have slept through that frilly mess of an era. However, the penthouse is yours. My wedding gift to you."

Helena frowned. She never cared about material things. Sure, being with a man who wasn't dirt-poor was nice. Not having to worry about a budget or bills, as she had growing up with her working, widowed mother, was a blessing. But Helena had become accustomed to earning the things she wanted. She'd even borrowed and scrapped her way through her master's at UC Santa Cruz.

And when she agreed to live with Niccolo in New York to become his eternal bride, she had no idea it meant she'd be without him all the time. Or that she'd have to be under the constant protection of his elite guards, who were more like eerie Stepford vampires. They silently kept watch over her day and night, allowing her to venture outside only if approved by Niccolo, and even then, only at night because the sun weakened them. She felt like a prisoner, the annoyance only exacerbated by the fact that no one would tell her why she needed guards in the first place.

Helena sat on the bed and cupped her hands over her face. "No, Niccolo," she whispered. "That's not it." She could feel his eyes on the back of her head. "I don't want clothes or new furniture." She slowly turned to him, her eyes filled with tears. *Screw rule number two: no crying. Stupid rules!*

"I want…you. I want to know who you are. And I mean, who you *really* are. I want to know where you go for days on end and why I can't come. I want to know why we can't make love—the real reason—until our wedding night."

He pinched the bridge of his nose. "*Mio cuore*, I know you want answers, but I can only offer you lies. This will not do when I have vowed to tell you the truth. And I will. In seven days, after you've been changed. Understand, I've made other vows, too. Vows that, if broken, would cost me my life. Or yours."

"I won't tell anyone," she argued. "Who'll even know? Don't you trust me?"

Helena suddenly found herself pinned beneath him. A flicker of anger danced in his eyes. Was she finally going to see her unshakable vampire lose his cool?

"I will know," he said. "And it is you who does not trust me, Helena. It is you who asks me to betray you by breaking my vows because you would surely pay the price, just as I would."

Huh? This wasn't making any sense. She looked away from his hypnotic gaze. She knew all it would take was one sweet kiss and she'd be lost again. Lost in his hard body, his powerful arms, and his silky, hot tongue. Then he'd disappear again.

She clamped her eyes shut, feeling the sumptuous weight of his body on top of her. *No. Dammit. Be strong.* She snapped her head toward him and met his eyes. "I don't care what you vowed, Niccolo. I need the truth. Now. So either find a way to tell me or no wedding. No forever."

He pounded his fist into the bed beside her, leaving a gaping hole. Feathers from the comforter rained down on them. In the blink of an eye, he was across the room, standing in the corner.

Against the blond hardwood floor, white walls, and furniture, Niccolo looked like a menacing black panther waiting in the shadows to take down his prey.

"Please." She rose slowly to approach him, but he held out his hands, gesturing for her to stay back.

She suddenly regretted her earlier wish. Watching him lose control was frightening. But she couldn't back down; this was too darn important.

She eased herself on the edge of the bed. "You're being unfair, Niccolo. You're asking me to give up my life to be with you."

"*Sì*, and I value your life more than I value fairness. You will marry me. We will be together. I will not discuss this again." His dark eyes turned into bottomless black pits. "*Capisce*?" he growled.

Barbarian. Or is he a medieval bastard? Dammit, why didn't I pay closer attention to time periods in history class?

Helena sighed. Didn't matter what she called him, he wasn't changing his mind. Not now. Not in the seven days left before their wedding. She would have to follow him blindly into the darkness of his world or leave him. Plain and simple.

So what would it be? She knew what her body said: *stay.*

She knew what her mind said: *leave.*

What did her heart say?

When it came down to it, she really knew nothing about Niccolo. Certainly not much more than the night she'd met him in Mexico. This was not how she wanted to start a marriage, one that would last for an eternity.

"Do you love me?" she asked.

"Love?" he growled. "Vampires do not do love."

"Excuse me?"

He looked at her, his eyes as black as abandoned coal mines. "What does love have to do with it? We are mates. Our bond is eternal."

What does love have to do with it? After everything she'd given up, *that* was his answer? Didn't he feel the overwhelming connection between them? Because she did. She'd completely rolled the dice and had given into it. She'd believed they were meant to be. What other reason could account for the illogical things she felt for a man—*errr*, vampire—she barely knew? So, had she been wrong? Was she the only one with these feelings? Had he just been pretending to care for her? "Love has everything to do with it, Tina! Everything!" She stomped her foot. "We're over! You arrogant vampire, I'm not marrying you. *Capisce*?"

"Why the hell are you calling me Tina? And I thought you wanted to be with me," he said bitterly, but clearly didn't give any credence to her words.

"Not anymore! Who the hell wants a life with someone who doesn't 'do love.' That's...that's...just sad!"

In a heartbeat, he grabbed Helena and held her up under her arms, staring angrily into her eyes. "I know you do not mean it, Helena. Because you love me—I see it in your eyes. And for you, that's everything."

Oh, that does it. Maybe she was human. And a bit smaller. Okay, a lot smaller, but she wasn't afraid of him and wouldn't stand for being bullied. Physically or emotionally. "Unless you plan on killing me, you'd better put me down, vampire! Because I'm not marrying you. In fact, I'm going home! Back to my old life. I don't want what's behind door number three. I don't want your old, stinky donkey! I want my beaches, sunshine, lots of real Italian food"—*God, how I miss eating garlic!*—"I want to start my career and see my mom and friends whenever I want, and..."

She wanted to say something to hurt him, to pierce that undead heart of his and pay him back for not loving her, not trusting her, and treating her like a child. "And men who aren't so bad in bed they avoid sex like the bubonic plague." *Jeez, that was so stupid.* There was no other man on earth who was probably more skilled than Niccolo. She didn't have to sleep with him to figure that one out.

She watched as fury engulfed his face. Still holding her in the air, his voice thundered, "Your old life is over, woman! There is no more mother or friends or sunshine for you! You live in my world now, and if you ever threaten to be with another male, I will chain you to my bed."

"Put me down! You outdated, archaic, crusty, old Italian vampire! And…who the hell doesn't know about Tina Turner?" Helena screamed.

Niccolo cursed at the ceiling, "Why me? I should have listened to Cimil. She warned me that a human bride would only cause trouble." He slowly lowered Helena to the floor and glared down at her. "*Maledizione!* A fucking curse! That's what she said, and I didn't care! I wanted this anyway. But she was right, *Cristo sacro!* It is a curse to be bound to…to food!"

Helena gasped. "Food? Did you just call me 'food'?" She felt her face turn red-hot.

"What the hell do you think vampires eat? Cookies?" he screamed so loud the windows rattled. "And get used to it, because you'll be calling humans food, too! There is no other blood we can survive on. None!"

Helena froze. "None? How about wild game or… bunnies?"

"*Bloody inferno*, woman! You read too many silly books. Those cannot sustain us."

Inferno was right. Helena had never really thought about it. She just assumed she could drink animal blood— no big deal; after all, she was a die-hard meatatarian. Unfortunately, he'd just said, "Humans." If he turned her, she would have to drink…people?

Ick! Ick! Ick! And who would it come from?

Hey, whose blood has he been sucking? It sure as hell hasn't been mine, she thought absurdly. *No. This is all wrong.* What was she doing with him?

"I was a total idiot to ever think I could be happy with you! Your world is dark and miserable. *You* are dark and miserable." She kicked him hard in the groin and bolted for the door.

Helena was seized by two steel arms. She felt Niccolo's heavy breath in her ear. "You go when I say, bride."

"I'm not your bride, you arrogant ass!" Helena squirmed in a futile attempt to break free. "I'd actually have to marry you to be called that, and it's never gonna happen! What the hell was I thinking? I love the sun. I love my mother and friends. I love pizza and Twinkies! I don't love you!"

He turned her so they were nose to nose. His venomous glare burned a hole right through her. "*Bene*, I have news for you, human. I only have to take your blood to claim you, or in your words 'marry,' because you are my mate. We are bonded. I never believed such a thing existed, but now I do! I think of you day and night. I feel every beat of your heart and every breath. I feel every childish, weak emotion! And you're goddamned full of them!" he raged. "Do they ever fucking stop? It's driving me mad! Mad! So, trust me, this, us, has nothing to do with you consenting, or your ridiculous human love, or this...Tina woman!"

He could literally feel her emotions? Could she feel his, too?

Of course. Since she'd met him, she had felt lost. As if there were another dimension to her she couldn't quite articulate. In his presence, she definitely felt more turbulent and amplified. It had to be this bond.

Helena gasped as she realized he was bending his head toward her neck. For the first time ever, Helena caught a glimpse of those long white fangs. She didn't know how vampires were made, but she'd seen enough movies to know that many believed it took just one bite.

Or is that for weres?

Dammit, Helena. Fight, you moron!

Helena kicked and screamed, fighting his unrelenting grip. "No, Niccolo, don't do this! I don't want to be your wife!"

With a shiver, she felt his lips, not fangs, press into the soft flesh at the base of her neck.

"But you already are," he said with an acerbic whisper. "You are my vampire wife. I tasted your delicious blood the night we met, and now we are bound forever whether either of us likes it or not. The ceremony we've been planning was merely tradition, a symbolic gesture to be performed before you are turned."

Sweet immortal pickle! She'd gotten married at the eternal courthouse and didn't even know it?

Niccolo stormed from the penthouse, charging straight for the elevator, and kicked his black leather boot through the wall. It was paper-thin from numerous repairs over the past few months.

"Irrational woman! Who the hell does she think she..." He froze with his finger on the down button, suddenly feeling as though he'd been hit by a blunt object.

He'd actually yelled at her. *Yelled* at Helena? Then he'd left her crying in a heap on the floor and yelled at her again. A few choice words, too. The shameful truth barreled down on him. "I am a son of a bitch!" *I let it happen again!*

Being mated to Helena was worse than a curse. It was an abomination of nature. *Torture!*

For the first few weeks after they'd met, he was in denial. Then he researched his symptoms and came to realize he'd been wrong, dead wrong, about this whole mate business.

Yes, there was a connection the first night they met, but this . . . it was ridiculous. And the connection only grew stronger each day.

Cruel! The desire he felt to take her body was nothing short of unbearable. Torturous images replayed in his mind of her soft flesh writhing beneath him while he pumped himself between her silky thighs. The more he denied himself, the worse his hunger for her became.

Yes. Hungry. So hungry . . .

He'd never been so goddamned famished. Yet he could barely feed. And make no mistake about it, he'd tried. Everyone tasted like putrid trash, including the humans he'd sampled from the queen's pool of willing blood slaves, who were far tastier than his normal fare of rapists and thugs with the blackest of auras. This morning, out of pure desperation, he'd opted for bagged blood—cold, lifeless, revolting. One of his men compelled him to keep from vomiting.

There was no getting around it. He wanted Helena.

One week to go.

Could he make it? Only if he stayed away from her. But if he did that, he'd never have a chance to win her. He was running out of time. He had to turn her willingly, that's what Cimil had said.

Why hadn't the insane goddess warned him that the icing on his frigid misery cake would be exposure to

Helena's emotions—an IV drip filled with concentrated, irrational, human feelings! Distance dulled the effect, as with any bond, but in her presence, he didn't know where she ended and he began.

She got angry; he got livid. She felt lust; he spiraled into a sexual frenzy.

Then there were those emotions that lacked descriptive words. PMS, for example. Helena had it on his last visit, giving him the overwhelming, simultaneous need to fuck her and cry uncontrollably.

The fucking part he could relate to, but crying? Vampires didn't cry!

He could only hope things would stabilize—as others had told him they would—after her transformation.

His hands dropped to his sides as he stared at the open elevator doors. His heart thumped wildly against the walls of his chest.

Anger. Sadness. Guilt. Helena is feeling all these things.

He let the elevator leave and turned back to tell Helena he was sorry. Would it be enough? He still couldn't tell her the truth about his world or how he spent his days.

Bene. To hell with it! I must tell her I'm sorry.

He reached for the front door as Helena screamed from the other side, "You lying leech! And if we're vampire married, then I want a vampire divorce! Do you hear me? I want a divorce!"

Niccolo winced. That was not a good sign.

Seven

Andrus stood in the empty foyer tiled with dingy white marble and illuminated by a lonely, dusty lamp sitting on the floor.

His eyes burned as he ran both hands through the spikes of his hair. It was four in the morning, but he had been summoned by Antonio, who believed office hours were for mortals or the weak.

Andrus snarled to himself. The last time he had come, that bastard Antonio had sadistically dangled the one carrot that could make him hop: he promised their situation would soon be evolving.

Evolving was not a word Andrus would have chosen. It implied a natural order to things. This long-awaited change would come by brute force. Blood. Pain. Souls lost.

No matter. He mentally shrugged. *Life is long. Too long.* Without this coming change, it simply wasn't worth living.

He reached for the tarnished brass doorknob, hoping and praying this would be the last time his shadow darkened the doorstep of the Demilord compound.

He pushed open the heavy oak door and found Antonio in his usual place behind his dimly lit desk, dark eyes buried in the thick leather-bound book.

Antonio had occupied the same Victorian in Sausalito, north of San Francisco, for the last one hundred years. Nothing in it ever changed. Not one piece of dark furniture or the dusty bookshelves that reached the vaulted ceiling. Antonio, too, was trapped in his world, and Andrus knew this was the one reason he could trust his putrid excuse of a leader to deliver what he'd promised: escape.

"You summoned me, sir?" Andrus's tone danced on the dangerous precipice between respect and mockery.

Without lifting his hateful eyes from the text, Antonio said, "You're late as usual. Sit the fuck down."

Andrus took his time slipping off his black leather duster, which matched his standard leather pants and boots, and threw it on the back of the chair across from Antonio's desk before he complied.

Antonio continued scanning the pages, flipping one after another.

"Is that the same damned book you were reading last time I was here?" Andrus criticized.

Antonio's head snapped up. "You idiot. This is the only remaining book of the Oracle of Delphi."

Holy hell. How did he get his hands on something like that? "Didn't know she wrote," Andrus replied, masking his astonishment. According to legend, her books foretold the future, continued rewriting themselves, the words on the pages endlessly shifting as events unfolded, in spite of her death sixteen hundred years ago. But the books were supposedly destroyed by Julius Caesar in the fires of Alexandria.

Antonio ignored Andrus's comment. "I've been waiting for a sign. And it's finally come. The moment we've waited for."

Only the tick of Andrus's left eye alluded to his excitement. "Finally. I was beginning to think I might have to kill you to get you to move." He leaned back into the chair, arms crossed against his chest.

Antonio slammed his fist into the desk, his eyes slowly burning into Andrus.

Andrus was unimpressed.

Yes, like him, Antonio was a large man built for battle. But Andrus had been taking on monsters ten times more fearsome for centuries now. All Antonio ever did was sit behind his goddamned desk, kissing the gods' asses. He'd never once lifted a finger for Andrus or his men while they endured day after day of hell: killing, tracking... killing some more.

Antonio growled, "Anything worth having is worth doing right. So shut the fuck up, and go kill the bitch as planned."

Andrus met his glare. "I'll do my part. You just remember that when I do, justice will come for you. And by justice, I mean me."

Antonio's eyes rolled as he laughed. "The book has spoken. You will not find me here when you return."

A spark of joy lit Andrus's face. "You mean the gods have granted my wish, and you are to be injected with molten lava, then disemboweled?"

Antonio slammed the heavy book shut. "The book says that I am to leave. You now lead the Demilords."

Fucking great. Andrus stood and swiped his leather coat and headed for the exit. "I'll still hunt you down when this is over." He slammed the door behind him.

So close now, he thought.

⌒

Leaning over the white marble sink, Helena stared into the mirror. How could she have let this happen? "You're disgusting!" she said to herself scornfully.

She splashed warm water on her unusually pale face—another irritating reminder of how she'd let Niccolo change her. This time of year, she'd normally have a nice golden glow. She used to spend almost every weekend, well into the fall, at the beach. How could she have given up so much?

Niccolo's arduous words pummeled her mind. "You're already my wife, Helena," he viciously said last night. Why hadn't he told her before?

Cold, heartbeat-less bastard. She'd actually thought he loved her when the truth was he only considered her a possession, something to own and control. How had she not seen it before? Was she living in some delusional trance the last two months? *And he actually had his men take away my laptop and cell! Bastard!*

Helena slipped on her favorite pair of jeans, her Uggs, and low-cut, pink angora sweater.

She made sure the blinds were drawn and then casually strolled to the front door. She took a deep breath and prepared for an Oscar-worthy performance. Her life depended on it.

As expected, she found Viktor at his post, arms crossed, with a bland look on his face. She practically had to unhinge her head to accommodate the upward angle to look him in the eyes. Viktor was at least seven feet tall; had fierce cobalt-blue eyes, chest-length blond hair; and was built like a Viking tank. Like Niccolo, he always wore the standard black clothes. Today it was black leather pants, rich dark brown leather boots, and a thick black turtleneck.

He was almost as breathtaking as Niccolo. *Damned beautiful vampires. Hate them all!*

"Yes?" He raised one golden brow.

Helena spoke in a sugary-sweet tone. "I need your help opening a bottle in the kitchen."

He didn't flinch. "I'm here to guard you, not be your servant."

"No," Helena corrected politely, "you're here to take care of me in Niccolo's absence, which includes ensuring I get fed properly."

Viktor still didn't move. Not an inch.

"Okay. Fine. Let's call him and ask." Helena reached for the cell phone clipped to Viktor's belt.

Viktor gently pushed her hand away.

She shook her head and walked toward the kitchen. It was time to put some of her keen observations to good use. Several weeks ago, Helena had casually commented to Viktor how she missed her mother. His eyes had turned a slightly darker hue. Then he'd responded, "Treasure each moment before they are gone."

Viktor had experienced loss.

Was it because he'd outlived everyone he ever loved? She felt guilty using his pain against him, but it was the lesser evil of options.

"Viktor, come on. Don't be like this. I'm only going to

be human for six more days. Don't I have the right to say good-bye to the things I love? My family? My life? My favorite foods?" She grabbed the can of clam chowder, clamped the opener down, and began turning.

Viktor was suddenly at her side, towering over her. "What do you need?"

It worked. Her eyes flashed to the bottle of wine on the counter.

"Cocktails before noon?" he questioned.

She shrugged. "It's always happy hour somewhere in the world. Right now, that somewhere is here. Niccolo only has those weird corkscrews they use in restaurants." She continued opening the can.

From the corner of her eye, she watched Viktor swiftly remove the red foil and effortlessly pluck the cork from the bottle.

She ran her finger over the sharp edge of the soup can, letting the jagged edge make a deep slice. She waited one second to allow the blood to pool so it would permeate the air and then said, "Ouch, son of—"

As if she'd been bulldozed by a ton of bricks, she found herself smashed against the wall. Viktor's eyes had turned from a brilliant blue to a bottomless black. His chest was heaving as he gazed hungrily down at her.

She was right; her Forbidden blood was unusually tempting to vampires, just as Rodrigo had said.

"Viktor! Let me go!" She struggled, hoping her plan wouldn't backfire; he could actually decide to drink her— a bad choice considering she was Niccolo's wife. On the other hand, hungry men had been known to do stupider things.

She bent her head and bit down on his right arm.

The moment he jerked away, she snagged Viktor's cell from his belt. "What do you think you're doing?" she barked. "Niccolo will kill you! You're here to protect me!" Helena did her best to rattle the fearless Viking.

She grabbed a kitchen towel from the counter and wrapped it around the phone along with her bleeding finger. "Get out! Get away from me!"

Viktor looked as if he'd been kicked in the pants by an angry, large man. "I'm ... uh, sorry, Helena. I really—"

"Just get the hell out!"

With her breath held tight, she watched Viktor turn and leave the room.

Helena tiptoed around the corner to the bedroom, pulled out the phone, and dialed 911. Carefully and quietly, with her most convincing damsel-in-distress voice, she alerted the operator to a nonexistent fire raging in her bedroom. She included the erroneous fact she was trapped in the bathroom.

She rushed back to the kitchen, placed the phone on the floor near the wall where Viktor had plastered her, and then went back to her soup.

Within seconds, Viktor was standing at her side, glaring. "Where is it?"

She clutched her cut finger, feigning fear. "Get away from me!"

Viktor took one step closer, hovering over her. "Nice try, human. You trying to get me killed? You're not allowed to have a phone any longer. Where is it?"

Helena shrugged. "What?"

"My phone. I know you took it."

"You mean the phone on the floor right behind you?" She nodded toward the wall. "You're damned lucky I didn't see it because right now, I'd be calling Niccolo and telling him you tried to gobble down his wife!" Pretending to sob, Helena stomped to the bedroom, slammed the door shut, and then waited. She couldn't believe she'd succeeded, and hopefully, Niccolo would never know she had pulled one over on Viktor. She didn't want him punished, and if her plan worked, no one would get hurt, least of all herself.

Toting her backpack, Helena nonchalantly glided past the panicked doorman talking via radio to someone on her floor about the false alarm. The commotion caused by the team of firemen had been the distraction she needed to break into Niccolo's desk—where she'd seen him stash her cell—and slip past Viktor.

She burst through the revolving glass door onto the bustling street, her heart galloping. If the doorman now knew the fire was a hoax, then Viktor knew, too, and would be hot on her trail. Thank goodness the bright and sunny day would slow Viktor down.

She glanced over her shoulder, weaving between busy tourists and shoppers carrying bags. She made her way to the corner. *Almost there!*

She lifted her head to scout out a cab and noticed a man standing across the street, staring at her.

Creepy.

Distracted, she tripped and stumbled, catching herself before she nearly plowed into a parking meter. She righted herself and paused for a double take. What caught her eye wasn't so much his staring, but it was the *way* he looked at her—as though he'd been expecting her.

His gaze silently sliced through the flowing crowds, through the rumble of traffic, and straight through her. He was extraordinarily gorgeous and loaded with menacing, powerful muscles. He reminded her of Niccolo, was even dressed like him—black leather pants and a long leather duster. But this guy had spiky, dark hair and wore dark shades.

He slid his glasses down his nose and locked his golden eyes on Helena.

A cold shiver ran through her body. Who was he? Better yet, what was he?

He casually stood on the sidewalk in full sunlight. Sure, Niccolo and his men could do that—the sunlight only weakened them—but they wouldn't stand in it, bathe in it.

Not sticking around to find out. She'd had enough of this strange world she'd been pulled into.

Helena threw her hand in the air as she reached the corner. A yellow cab screeched across several lanes, cutting off a bus, limo, and two delivery trucks.

The cab skidded to a halt directly in front of her, a trail of burning rubber following closely behind.

Too panicked to play the "Is this really safe?" card, Helena jumped in, frantically glancing over her shoulder at the strange man through the back window.

"Oh, boy. What a tasty man treat!" said the female driver, who noticed Helena watching the man. "He gonna chase us? 'Cause I love a good game of cat and mouse! Raarrr."

Helena's mind took a second to register the driver's bizarre question. "Sorry. What?"

The redhead didn't turn around, but through the rearview

mirror, Helena noticed the woman had thick black eye-liner chalked around her turquoise eyes.

"Nada, enchilada. Where to? Wait! Let me guess!" The driver bounced excitedly in her seat and clapped. "I love guessing games! Ummm...You're running from a man who's so dang hot, he scorches the lace trim from your panties. And you think you can get over him if you run, but you're like a stray dog that's found a giant cow patty! You won't be happy until you've had a good roll." She cackled. "Did I nail it? Did I? Did I? Huh? Huh?"

Helena sneered. *Great. Just what I need.* "Amsterdam and West Ninetieth, please."

The driver nodded. "Sure, baby cakes."

As soon as they were ten blocks away, Helena released her breath. The man had made no attempt to follow her.

The cab abruptly hooked right.

"Hey. Where are you going?" Helena didn't have time for this.

The driver shrugged. "Amsterdam and West Hundred and Seventh. Just like you said!"

Ugh! "No. I said Ninetieth."

"Tsk-tsk." The woman shook her head. "Everyone knows that place is a rip-off."

"Dammit! Just pull over." She'd walk the rest of the way.

The driver huffed. "You're a stubborn little thang, aren't you? Look it, I guarantee this other guy will give you top dollar. If he doesn't, then I'll take his soul and the ride is free."

Helena smothered her sparks of frustration. "Fine." *Wait. Did she just say she'd "take his soul"? What a whack job.*

The driver nodded. "Here we are!" she sang out.

"I'll be right back." Helena slid from the vinyl seat.

"You won't regret it! And don't settle for anything under four hundred!" the driver screamed out the window as Helena reached for the front door of the shop.

Helena glanced back, but the driver quickly turned away, preventing Helena from getting a good look.

Whatever. All that really mattered was being free. Now she'd have to figure out how to stay that way.

Cimil watched Helena disappear into the pawnshop. "Ha! Did I tell you this was gonna be dramatastic or what?" she said toward the roof of the car. "Just wait till you see what I have coming next! That vampire's gonna be so jealous, his head's going to spin like a Beyblade."

Cimil howled with laughter, then whipped out her phone and began texting: Vampy bride just went into pawnshop, corner of Amsterdam & 107th.

She knew Andrus would assume one of his men had sent the text from the blocked number. They'd been watching Helena's every move for weeks via satellite. (The gods personally had the system installed for the Demilords; it was a much more efficient way to keep tabs on people...or naughty vamps.) That said, Cimil wasn't leaving anything to chance. Not today. This particular meeting was critical.

The door of the cab suddenly flew open. A tall man in a gray suit hopped in. "University Medical Center, please."

Cimil turned her body to get a good look through the Plexiglas. "Oh, hey there, naughty boy. Isn't this convenient? I was about to come for you! Ah, fate...what would I do without her?"

The man shot Cimil a confused look.

"Hold on, honey. It's going to be a bumpy ride! Hope you like Twister and molten lava. 'Cause that's how we roll where you're going."

"I don't have time for this crap," the man mumbled and tugged on the now inoperable door handle.

Cimil cackled loudly, then cranked up the radio. "Oooh! Lucky day. Neil Diamond."

The cab screeched away from the curb.

Eight

The full-bellied man wearing a beige, grease-stained sweater stared impatiently at Helena across the glass counter. The grainy picture of a foreign soccer game flickered on the large-screen TV behind him.

"What do you mean fake? That can't be right." Her blood pressure hit the floor. She'd been free from the penthouse only twenty minutes and already hit a snag in her plan?

No. She could figure this out. She was smart, resourceful, and pissed as hell about how Niccolo had treated her. In short, she wasn't even close to giving up. She was getting her life back!

The merchant handed her the large solitaire engagement ring. "Listen, lady," he said with a thick, indistinguishable accent. "I do dis my whole life. Is fake. No worth five dollar." He picked at his molar with his pinkie finger to remove whatever horrible fishy thing he'd been eating when she entered the pawnshop.

Lord love a duck! She only had eighty bucks on her and zilch in her bank account. After graduation, she'd been planning to start working right away, to begin saving again and paying her student loans. Then, well, Niccolo happened.

As much as she'd protested, Niccolo insisted she wasn't to worry about such trivial human things anymore. She hadn't even known he'd paid off her student loans until last week, when she'd received the closing statements forwarded in the mail. She'd made a mental note to talk to him about finances as soon as possible, including her plans to go back to work.

If Niccolo was wealthy, why would he give her a fake engagement ring? It made absolutely no sense...unless... he wanted to keep her resources limited? Maybe he feared she'd leave, and if he knew about her student loans, he probably knew how much money she had in the bank. He wanted to keep her from getting far.

Damned sneaky vampire! If it was the last thing she did, once she found a way to "divorce" him, she'd pay him back every cent he had spent on her. She didn't want to owe him anything.

Helena noticed an odd pang in her stomach when she thought about life without Niccolo. It felt...uneasy, somehow. She still craved him, his addictive scent, the endless depths of his dark eyes. *But dammit! He is so closed off and controlling. And so, so strong and sexy.* She stopped herself. *And arrogant! And controlling! And don't forget...he said he doesn't "do love." He will never, ever love you.*

Helena swallowed the dry lump in her throat and then eyed the intricate filigree gold ring on her right middle finger. It had been her great-grandmother's and was the only thing of value she owned. She slipped it off and placed it on the counter. "How much?"

The man wiped his greasy palm on his sweater and popped the jeweler's loupe to his eye. "Two hundred."

"What?" Helena's mom once had the ring appraised; it was an antique worth a thousand. *Darn it!* She needed to make it to Chicago, where she could stay with Anne until she figured things out. "Five, or I go down the street."

The man blinked. "Four. That's my final."

Helena's mind boggled. Hadn't the crazy cabbie said something about four hundred? *Weird.*

"I'll take it." Helena only hoped she'd be able to buy the ring back somehow. Her mother would be devastated to know she had sold it.

A few minutes later, Helena emerged from the pawnshop, and there, standing across the street, was the same man she'd seen outside Niccolo's building minutes earlier.

She froze.

His lips twitched with a predatory smile.

How had he found her? Who the hell was he?

Once again, he slid his dark sunglasses down his nose and drilled into her with his fierce golden eyes.

Helena's body stiffened. "Darn it," she spoke under her breath. Where had the crazy redhead cabbie gone? Helena hadn't even paid her.

With no time to lose, she raised her arm and flagged down a new yellow chariot.

Again, the stranger made no movement toward her as she loaded herself in a cab.

Andrus smiled to himself as he watched the bus, bound for Chicago, pull into the rest stop as it entered Ohio. He'd been leisurely following in his black Hummer the last six hours, ensuring none of the Executioner's guards had followed the female out of the city.

They had not, but that didn't mean they weren't coming. Like him, they had their ways of finding people.

Andrus parked across the lot from the silver bus and waited for the passengers to unload. He immediately spotted Helena peering out the dusty window, looking side to side. She rose from her seat and came down the steps of the bus. This was it.

He quickly left his vehicle and stalked toward her, summoning shadows to camouflage himself until he was on her heels.

"I think you lost this," he said and then held out his hand. She pivoted and gasped. He quickly grabbed her arm to keep her from fleeing. "It is your ring, yes?"

Helena looked at the ring, then up at his face. Was she frightened or confused? *No…relieved. Wait. No… angry?*

"I'm not going to hurt you, you have my word," he said in a low voice. His eyes suddenly felt dry. He blinked several times.

"That might actually mean something if you were someone I trusted or knew," she replied.

"Andrus Gray. I am a scientist—the paranormal kind." *Lie.* "I just want to speak with you." *Another lie.* His eyes felt drier. Why did that always happen?

Helena jerked her arm away. "Speak to me about what?"

"Your fiancé."

Helena frowned. "He's not my fiancé, and why the hell should I trust you—you've been following me."

Andrus nodded. "He's your boyfriend then?"

Helena didn't respond and turned to get away.

Andrus had to say something fast to gain her trust. "Okay. His kind"—Andrus rubbed the stubble on his chin—"does not ... appreciate the work my organization does. If we are spotted, it often ends poorly. This is why I've been following you, waiting until it's safe to talk." *All true.*

"Not my problem." Helena looked at his closed hand at his side. "I can't afford to pay you back, and I don't take charity. So, your little plan was a waste of time."

Andrus's lips curled into a smug smile. He liked this beautiful woman's feistiness. *Lucky vampire.* "I propose an equitable exchange: a few hours of your time for the ring."

She paused, considering his offer, then narrowed her eyes and shook her head.

She didn't trust him.

Smart woman.

"I can't do that," she said. "The bus leaves in twenty minutes." She turned toward the convenience store. Andrus moved quickly, blocking her way.

Helena slammed into Andrus's chest. "Wha—what are you? Another effing vampire?"

I'm something far worse. "No. Like I said, I'm a scientist—or, more accurately put, a student of the paranormal." *Lie.* Blink. "I've learned many of their tricks over the years and can teach you. You'll need my help if you really want to run from him."

He watched intently as her radiant blue eyes locked on his face. She was still afraid.

Time to close the deal. If she resisted, he'd have to take her and risk witnesses or police being called. That would leave an easier trail for the vampires to follow.

"Look. I know you're afraid, but I'm your only chance. Vampires never let anything get between them and their mates. He'll go after the people you love if he has to. He won't rest until he gets you—"

"He says we're married," Helena interrupted, her eyes filled with anger. "That it happened when he took a drop of my blood. Do you know how I can break the bond?"

"I do not," he answered. "But I can teach you how to evade him. I can even keep him from sifting you away if he gets close."

"What's sifting?"

He's never sifted in front of her? Idiot, Andrus thought. *He's probably worried about using his vampire talents in front of her because of that idiotic Pact.* Well, he could give a rat's ass about the Pact. Besides, what could the gods do to him that hadn't been done already?

"It's how vampires travel. They can move from one place to another using their minds. Although they cannot travel far, it burns up too much energy."

"Crap. Then there's no way for me to outrun him?" Helena's face showed her desperation.

Andrus suddenly found himself feeling sympathetic toward the poor woman. Like him, she felt trapped.

Stay focused. "We rarely do this, but we have an archive. It's the only one of its kind—centuries of texts and artifacts. Perhaps we can find an answer for you there."

Was that a flicker of hope in her eyes? Today was turning out much better than he'd planned.

"Where?" she asked coldly.

"North of San Francisco." The Demilords' archives were in fact there, but the records were mostly profiles of vampires on their watch list or documents they'd confiscated. Fact was, Demilords didn't care much about history, just killing vampires. Preferably Obscuros. Now, if a good vamp or two—or three or four—got in the way ... oh, well. No loss.

Three hundred years ago, the vampire queen's army began failing at containing the Obscuros as the Pact dictated. It was then that the Demilords were created, and it was then that Andrus's hell began.

"Okay." Helena nodded. "I guess I don't have a choice. But if you lay a hand on me, I'll make sure Niccolo finds out."

Oh, I hope he does.

"She *what*?" Niccolo screamed at the top of his lungs into the phone from his lavish 180-degree Strip-View Suite at the Four Seasons in Vegas. "How could you let her leave? You had two orders: keep her safe and don't let her leave! How hard is it for five vampires to keep an eye on one tiny human?"

What if something happened to her? He would never forgive himself. He hadn't even had the chance to apologize for their fight or to make it up to her. This was horrific! *He* was horrific. He'd made her feel so bad that she had fled him.

He wanted to wretch. Thank goodness she couldn't get far; she had no money or anything much of value. *Yes, thanks to you, you evil bastard.*

"I'm sorry, Niccolo," Viktor explained with a hint of humor in his voice, "but your human is"—he paused—"sly. A very fitting mate for you. Speaking of, how are the wedding plans coming along? Are you going with the *Gone with the Wind* or the *Star Trek* theme?"

Niccolo cringed. He was, as Viktor would say, "Busted." Attempting to make amends, the fiercest vampire in the world thought to surprise Helena with an extravagant theme wedding in Vegas, a suggestion from Sentin, who insisted she'd enjoy the "hip scene."

"Do you find this humorous? Do you?" He paused and took a breath. "Truth be told, my primary objective here is to conduct a little cleanup."

Niccolo suddenly felt sick again as the fresh memories assaulted him. The carnage left behind by the Obscuros was ghastly. They'd attacked a large group of humans at a *quinceañera*—a fifteenth birthday party for a young woman—and slaughtered children, expectant mothers, the elderly . . . they spared no one.

"My apologies, Niccolo. I was only trying to lighten the mood. Has the team been able to bring Las Vegas back under control?"

Niccolo and the local team who were permanently stationed in Vegas—it needed constant monitoring—had mowed the vile Obscuros down, but he didn't feel like reliving those memories. He knew Viktor would understand if he diverted the conversation.

"Control, no. This place, I simply do not understand it. The humans here wear giant cocktail glasses around their necks and insert exorbitant amounts of money into little machines that light up. I still cannot figure out why they call them 'slut machines.' Is it because they steal your money?"

"I believe the correct name is slot machine. They're kind of fun..."

As Viktor spoke, Niccolo's mind involuntarily shifted back to the topic of Obscuros. According to his calculations, he'd personally executed two hundred rogue vampires in recent weeks; over a thousand had been killed by his soldiers, yet the list only grew longer each day. Niccolo needed to make a bigger dent. He'd heard all about the Demilords, who had supposedly been put in place to control the outbreak during his absence, but where were they? From what he could see, no one had been keeping the Obscuros in check. Suspicious to say the least.

"It matters little what the machines are called," Niccolo interjected. "This place is loathsome. But if a wedding here will please Helena, then I shall do this for her. Please tell me one of your men is tracking her."

A long silence ensued before Viktor replied, "Not exactly. She...slipped away too quickly. We couldn't pick up her scent—it is pretty sunny today."

"*Inferno!* I am in no mood to blindly sift all over the goddamned—"

"Don't go ballistic," Viktor added. "I gotcha covered with GPS tracking. I had it added to her phone. She busted into your office and took it back. I've been watching her movements via Internet. You can use the live satellite map to find a safe place to sift nearby—away from any structures—then boom. You're there."

Thank the gods for her thievery and for this "GPS."

"Where is she now?" Niccolo asked.

"Heading west toward the Windy City. I'll send the link to your phone and get you hourly updates."

"*Bene. Grazie.*"

Niccolo hung up and rubbed his hands over his face. He had to get her back quickly and make amends. He had only six days left until their three-month anniversary. She had to be turned willingly or the prophecy would not be fulfilled, and Niccolo's one opportunity of leaving the queen would be lost.

That meant he'd never have the chance to know peace or a day of freedom. He'd never know Helena's sweet body inside and out. His mind toggled through the catalog of fantasies awaiting their day in the spotlight. His standard: taking her for the first time over a bed of velvety, red rose petals, the midnight crackle of a fireplace, the sweet scent of her arousal filling his lungs as he plunged himself repeatedly inside her. Then there was the fantasy of taking her in the shower, pinning her against the wall, her legs wrapped around his waist as she panted his name in his ear.

Niccolo grew hard for the fifth time that day and shifted himself.

Gods, he could not wait to bed her, and he needed to buy looser pants. Otherwise, his cock might not make it to their wedding night. Or perhaps he needed to stop thinking about her.

Idiota. You realize that's impossible. Any second now you're going to get the itch. You won't be able to resist wanting to feel her with your mind.

His attempt to fight his craving for her indeed lasted all of one glorious second before he gave in. He focused to catch a whiff of her mind in the atmosphere. Distance dulled the connection, but it was always there.

Ah, Helena. Right now, she's annoyed, but no longer angry. In any case, the guilt was almost unbearable;

he'd caused her pain. Thank the gods he didn't love her. He couldn't imagine how miserable he would be if they shared more than a powerful bond and insatiable lust.

For a moment he considered using his gift to sift to her, but blind sifting was extremely risky. And sifting toward a moving target was unthinkable. He could end up landing inside a steel girder, slab of cement, or being hit by a semi. No. He'd have to wait until she stopped moving and then do as Viktor suggested.

Niccolo suddenly flinched and released a growl from deep within his chest. He sensed a burgeoning lust radiating via their connection. *She'd better be thinking of me.*

Nine

⌒

Helena stared out the dust-coated window of the black Hummer speeding west on Interstate 80, watching the sherbet sunset and chewing her thumbnail to the nub. She'd already surveyed everything inside the enormous tough-boy vehicle twice. A waste of time. The interior was spotless except for several discarded candy wrappers on the floor. There was nothing to tell her who this dark, brooding man truly was.

She quickly stole a glance at Andrus, whose gaze was fixed on the road, sunglasses covering his eyes despite the darkening sky.

Of course he can see in the dark, she griped to herself, *all monsters can.*

Earlier, he'd pulled off his leather coat and was now wearing a plain black tee and leather pants. With both hands firmly gripping the wheel, the thick muscles of his forearms flexed enough for her to see every menacing rope. She noticed his appearance the first time she'd laid eyes on him. What woman wouldn't? He was unusually handsome—in a dangerous-to-your-heart kind of way—and built like a brick house.

Problem was, he reminded her of Niccolo. *They could be brothers,* she thought.

So who was he really? More importantly, what was he? She didn't buy his scientist story one bit, but she did buy the part about him knowing how to keep Niccolo away. Something about Andrus screamed, *"I am lethal!"* Yeah, he'd had lots of practice keeping people at a distance.

Helena was a trained observer, a scientist; she knew how to watch and learn. She was good at it. This was how she noticed the pain undulating just beneath the surface of this man's menacing shell. Maybe it wasn't obvious to the average Joe or Jill on the street, but this creature was a walking contradiction. Even his short dark brown hair—recently cut and deliberately mussed—was a clue. Cold-blooded men didn't care about styling their hair in a way that advertised they were dangerous. Truly lethal men tried to hide what they were. The element of surprise was more important. No, he was trying to look more dangerous than he really was—which was still considerably dangerous.

"Where are you from?" she suddenly blurted out.

Andrus didn't acknowledge her question.

Helena was growing seriously impatient with the secretive act.

Suddenly her phone beeped. It was a message from her mother. Baby, you okay? No response on my e-mail. Are you coming home for Christmas, or am I coming to see you? Airline tickets are on sale, want to buy now.

Crap. She had no idea when she could go home. She needed to end things with Niccolo first. Otherwise, he'd find her and take her. The situation stank.

Helena quickly replied: Sorry. Been swamped w/ work. Yes, coming home for Xmas. Got ticket already. Love u. Miss u!

She'd have to figure it out later. Dammit, she hated all these lies!

She turned to Andrus. "Look. You can cut the crap right now. I know you're not a paranormal scientist."

A hint of a smile, the frightening kind, touched his lips. "Then what am I?" he said, his voice low and crawling.

Helena thought for a moment. "You're not a vampire, but you're no human, either. I can tell."

No response. His eyes remained locked on the road.

"I think you're a...demon," she guessed.

Demon? That sounded silly. Helena chuckled inwardly. She had read way too many novels. Her favorites were the ones where the heroes were dark, brooding demons. She had never actually seen one, or truly believed they existed, for that matter. But up until a few months ago, she would've said the same thing about vampires.

"Sorry. Not a demon," he said coldly, scratching his rough jaw, obviously not interested in discussing the matter further.

"Fine. I don't care. Just promise you'll hold up your end of our bargain and not bully me like Niccolo and his buddies."

Andrus removed his glasses and flashed a glance her way. "They've treated you badly?"

The surreal golden color of his eyes startled her. She lost her train of thought for several moments until she realized he was waiting for a response. *Speak, dum-dum.* "No. Not badly, but like a redheaded stepchild. It's not only annoying, but hypocritical. I mean, if I'm so lowly, then why did he want me?"

Andrus did not respond for several moments. "Even a dog is missed by its owner when it runs away. But it's still a dog."

Did Niccolo really think of her as his dog? *Christ, he probably does.* "I'm not some vampire pet."

Andrus stifled a laugh. "No, but can you blame him for trying? You look like the kind who might incite frequent stroking."

"Sorry?" Helena snapped. Had he just flirted with her?

"Forget it. I will not treat you like a dog, I vow it," Andrus mumbled, returning to his icy demeanor.

So then, what *was* he going to do to her? Was she safe with this stranger?

Unlikely.

With the way things were going, Andrus would turn out to be the Grim Reaper.

In fact, now that she was in feeling-sorry-for-herself mode, why not move the needle to a full-fledged pity party? That's right. Because her life had always been a struggle. Why should now be any different? For years she worked hard, helping her mother make ends meet. It had made her into a workaholic, worrywart control freak. Her life became all about the future, avoiding a repeat of her mother's mistakes. That's why she'd never had a boyfriend; friends and school were way safer bets.

Helena's mom, Laura, had married young. She was from Kansas City and dreamed of the California life—endless sunshine, beaches, and being carefree. When she met a young man, a corporal traveling through town who'd stopped at the local bookstore where she worked, it was love at first sight. At nineteen, she left her life behind in the middle of the night—her hard-core religious parents would have never approved of a church "outsider"—and traveled with him to San Diego, where they were married. He was redeployed shortly after, but never returned. A freak, unexplainable disappearance during a routine patrol somewhere in the Philippines.

Devastated, pregnant, and unwilling to crawl back to her family, her mother moved north to Santa Cruz, where she did her best to make a home for Helena and herself. But despite her mom's affection and hard work, Helena always knew something important was missing: her father, her mother's laughter. Family.

When Helena became older, she secretly hoped her mother would move on and find another love. But Helena's mom swore she'd never love another. To this day, she wore her wedding ring and reminded Helena every chance she got of two things: make sure she could always take care of herself, and if the universe blessed her with the gift of knowing her soul mate, she should love him with her entire heart, no matter how much time they were given.

That was Helena's big mistake. In a moment of weakness, she'd bought into her mother's romanticized version of the world and had forgotten the pain and sacrifice accompanying it. She fell for Niccolo—or perhaps she'd fallen for the dream of Niccolo. Reality, as she'd discovered, hadn't stacked up.

Because he didn't love you back. She would never, ever, ever make that mistake again.

Helena again glanced over at the menacing-looking man who could have been Niccolo's long-lost cousin, except for his golden eyes. He was a painful reminder of what she'd left behind and wanted so desperately to forget. And like Niccolo, she knew she couldn't trust him; no man with that much darkness clinging to him was meant to be trusted. But what choice did she have? He was right; Niccolo would not stop until he got her back. Life would be running and hiding until she found a way to free herself.

Pang. Again that stupid pang when she thought of life without Niccolo.

Her cell phone suddenly vibrated again. She dug it from her front jeans pocket, expecting another text from her mother, but instead saw: I warned you, Helena. You cannot hide from me. I will find you. I will always find you. You are mine.

Helena fumed. "Arrogant son of a …"

She texted in reply: Not yours. Never was. Never will be.

He replied: I'm sorry for what happened. Please, come back.

Too late, vampire. It's over.

Several moments passed before he replied: Tell me where you are before someone gets hurt.

Her heart sank. Was he really threatening her?

Andrus glanced at her several times before saying, "It's your vampire, isn't it? He's threatening you."

"He's just mad. It's the bond, that's all. He'll get over it once it's broken." Ironically, she felt embarrassed by his behavior.

Andrus raised one brow. "I'm sorry. I know your situation is not easy."

Helena shrugged. "I'm sorry, too. I wish things had ended differently." She ran her hands through her tangled curls and flipped down the sun visor to inspect her face in the mirror. The bags under her eyes said it all. "So, which airport are we going to? Midway or O'Hare?"

Andrus smiled at her unexpectedly. "We are driving. I don't fly."

"Don't fly?"

He shook his head. "No. It is…unnatural."

Okay. That was strange coming from someone who was obviously so…unnatural or, well, supernatural. "Driving to San Francisco will take days."

"Yes," he said firmly. "This will give us plenty of time to talk. I will teach you what you need to know, and you will answer my questions."

Why did Helena suddenly feel like she was betraying Niccolo by spending several days alone in a car with a devastatingly gorgeous man? Her mouth went dry. She turned her head toward the backseat to grab her water bottle from her pack. "Oh, come on! I left my backpack on the bus."

According to Darwin, you're a prime candidate for extinction. Too stupid to live! Could she be any more forgetful and ridiculous? How about predictable? She let out a long sigh. *Cut yourself some slack. You've gone through some major trauma.* Well, what did it matter? She was going to have to leave her life behind anyway. Again.

As if reading her thoughts, Andrus said, "Material things are replaceable, Helena. You can always start over as long as you have control of your life."

He was right. That's what she needed, to be in control

again. She wasn't a helpless victim of this bond she now shared with a vampire. She was smart. Yes, yes, forgetful at times, too, but she was also resilient, resourceful, and determined.

"What do you want to know first?" she asked.

Helena was beginning to notice how everything Andrus said was devoid of emotion. He'd asked simple questions about Niccolo and Helena's day-to-day life—not much to tell. He asked about Niccolo's work patterns, how many men guarded her, and if she'd ever heard any particularly strange conversations.

"Am I boring you?" she finally asked.

Andrus made a little shrug.

"Well," she said, "I never promised you any juicy information. It's not my fault they wouldn't tell me anything."

Andrus nodded. "It is strictly forbidden for humans to know about their world. Leaking such information is punishable by death."

"Why can you tell me everything, but he can't?"

Andrus answered, "I tell you what you need to know, not everything."

"Even so."

He shrugged. "There is no punishment anyone can inflict worse than what's already been done."

His answer made Helena's skin crawl. "Done?"

Andrus turned his head, his golden eyes reflecting the hatred lurking inside him. "They stole something from me."

Who's they? she thought. Helena asked him to elaborate,

but he ignored the question. She let it go. Clearly, talking about it pained him.

After several quiet moments, Andrus abruptly turned off the highway and insisted she buy supplies. Their first stop had been the drugstore for toothpaste and other toiletries. Now he wanted her to buy clothes.

Helena reluctantly took the roll of bills from Andrus as he ushered her toward the front door of the trendy-looking boutique just east of Chicago, in the burbs. "I'm paying you back for this—"

"No need," he objected. "You're doing me a favor. Three days in a car together, remember? Please, the store is closing in fifteen minutes, and more importantly, it is now dark. I do not know how closely they are following behind, nor how many he'll send." Andrus's voice held no hint of concern. He was merely stating the facts.

Andrus crossed his arms over his broad chest and turned his back to stand guard in front of the store. She then noticed how tall he was, maybe six three? The heavy leather boots he wore made him appear taller.

"My boyfriend loathes shopping, too."

Helena turned and saw a thin brunette with heavy, black eye makeup standing behind the counter. Helena chuckled nervously. "Oh, he's…" *Not my boyfriend*, she was about to say. *Never mind, doesn't matter.* "Yeah, he's completely allergic to shopping."

The clerk smiled. "The shop closes in ten. But if you need a few extra minutes, I'm just straightening up, so no problem."

Helena nodded and headed straight for the stack of jeans and tees. They had a small selection of sexy, little lace bras and thongs. Right now she'd give anything for a pair of comfortable grannies and cotton tank bras, but there were none. She shrugged, added a black 34C push-up to the pile in her arms, and then followed the sign to the dressing rooms.

She hung the items on the hook, removed her sweater, and tried on the bra. It was just like one she'd purchased recently, hoping Niccolo might see her in it. But he never had. Technically, they'd barely been to first base. That was outrageous considering they were also technically married in vampire world. And weren't vampires supposed to live for seduction? Maybe she wasn't good—

"That bra is delectable on you."

Helena jumped. Niccolo stood directly behind her, elegantly poised against the full-length mirror, arms casually crossed over his powerful chest. He wore plain, low-slung jeans—blue for once, not black—and a snug light gray sweater. His thick black hair was loose, slightly wild, and hanging below his collar. He looked incredibly sexy. And angry.

"How—how the hell did you find—"

He lunged forward, grabbed her by the shoulders, and gave her one furious shake, making her teeth clack. "*Inferno sacro,* woman!"

Before she had a chance to protest, he moved his hands to the sides of her head and took her mouth in a possessive kiss. Helena's toes instantly curled. Every muscle in her body devolved into ebbs and flows of warm molasses. His lips were like two demons of temptation sent to coax all rational thought from her mind and replace them with hard, hot lust.

His rough hands slid down to her bare neck and shoulders, to her waist, and then slowly raked their way back up over her stomach to cup both breasts. His thumbs toyed with Helena's nipples through the thin black lace of her bra. His touch was like being struck with a searing bolt of erotic electricity.

Stunned by her body's potent reaction, Helena broke the kiss and sucked in a sharp breath. Their eyes locked, and in that fleeting moment of silence, something happened. A wordless exchange of raw emotion. Acknowledgment of their connection. Time seemed to stand still as she felt his light—his soul—mingling with hers. She was inside him. He was inside her. For that one fragile instant, everything between them was pure, honest, and strangely primal. Two living creatures connected.

The bond.

Then, like a dust storm whipping through the wide-open desert, the moment of clarity was swept away. Her mind fogged with a blaze of raging lust.

Niccolo, as though caught in the same mindless storm, effortlessly lifted her and plastered her to the wall with his body, wrapping her legs around his waist. The hard ridge of his erection pushed against her. He growled and ground his hips between her thighs, sparking bursts of flutters into the depths of her core.

He took her breath away.

Oh, God, now she couldn't remember why she'd ever left him. She needed him. More than air, or sunlight and beaches, definitely more than garlic. Hell, she just needed him. She flung her arms around his neck, silently inviting him to take everything from her.

"Please, Helena," he panted in between smoldering thrusts of his tongue, "I'm sorry...for the way I behaved...I wasn't...myself. Please come back. I promise...everything will make sense." He continued rubbing his thick erection through her pants, thrusting his tongue into her mouth in time with his hips.

His rough touch and grinding through her jeans almost pushed her over the edge. *What does he do with those hands to make them so rough?* she wondered in a fleeting thought. *Ask him later. Yes, later.*

"Don't stop...Please, don't stop," she moaned with a breath.

His pace quickened. She couldn't believe it, but she was so close, almost there...Something about this man drove her insane. He was a walking aphrodisiac.

"Yes!" she gasped, nails digging in deep through the fabric of his sweater into his shoulders. Pulses of ecstasy ripped through her body.

Niccolo's solid frame suddenly froze, his whole body taut and straining against hers, still pinning her to the wall. He groaned loudly, clearly lost to the thunderous release crashing through him.

Absurdly, Helena felt proud. She had been able to push this experienced, sexy vampire over the edge. They weren't even naked.

Brow glistening with sweat, he made a soft chuckle in her ear and peppered her cheek with light kisses. "Not once in my entire thirteen hundred years has a woman turned me into a raving, hormonal lunatic such as you've done to me." He slowly released her, and she lazily slid down the length of his solid frame. He bent his forehead to hers, cupping the back of her head. "What you do to me, woman. *Santo*, you're addictive."

Ditto. "How did you find me?" she whispered.

"I will always find you, Helena. You are mine now. Not

just by vampire law. We are connected by the same bonds that forged the universe. Do you not feel it?"

She sucked in a breath. Yes, yes, she did. What did it really mean? "Please, tell me what's going on. What just happened?"

He pulled his head back. Hardness struck his eyes. "I will tell you everything I know after your transformation, I promise. Please, come back with me now. We'll still have the wedding ceremony in six days."

Helena felt as though she'd been slapped by reality's cold, unwelcome hand. She was such an idiot! He had no intention of telling her anything. Nothing had changed.

Helena let out a quick huff and bent down to grab a T-shirt from the rainbow-colored pile. She slipped a pink tee over her head, grabbed the clothes, and slipped her feet into her Uggs. She pulled the latch to one side and stepped out of the dressing room.

"Helena," he scolded in a whispered voice, "where are you going?"

Someplace where you can't hurt me again. She turned on her heel. "I told you. I don't want to be with you, so don't even think of following me again. It's over."

She suddenly found herself caged between two arms, the same ones she'd been helplessly clutching in ecstasy moments earlier.

Niccolo was staring down at her with pure frustration. "You do not mean that, my sweet. I know you are lying."

Yes. Maybe. Crap! I don't...

"No. You're the one hiding behind wall after wall of rules and vows and I-don't-know-what-other-crap excuses."

"I've never lied to you, Helena. Never. I simply cannot

tell you what you want to know, but that doesn't mean I do not care for you. What do I have to do to prove myself? Why don't you trust me?"

"Trust you?" She wanted to scream. "Trust *you*?" Oh, wasn't that nice? He wanted her to trust him, yet...

Helena paused for one short moment. "If I'm so god-damned important, break one of your stupid rules!"

"I cannot. There would be—"

"Consequences? Shocking answer." Helena rolled her eyes, then snapped her arms away. "Good-bye, Niccolo. It's over. You and I aren't even the same species, and we're definitely not meant for each other. The universe made a mistake."

Niccolo snarled, "The universe does not make mistakes."

"Oh yeah?" Helena retorted. "Tell that to the...to the..." *Oh, heck. Why can't I think of anything?* "The dinosaurs!"

Niccolo frowned. "You compare our relationship to—"

"Ma'am? Were you calling me?" the store clerk called out, approaching quickly.

Niccolo squeezed his hands on Helena's shoulders, but his look of anger turned to confusion.

Had he just tried to sift her away?

"Ma'am?" the young woman came around the corner as Niccolo disappeared.

Helena placed her palm on her flushed cheek. "Um—no. I'm good. If you don't mind, I'm going to..." She paused, realizing how strange her words were about to sound, but she hadn't had time to put her own garments back on. "Wear the T-shirt and bra now. They're really comfy." She handed the rest of the new clothes to the clerk and tried to pull herself together.

Helena chucked her overflowing shopping bags in the backseat and then slammed the door shut.

Andrus turned the engine on and gave her a suspicious look. "You smell like..." He shifted into drive.

"What?"

"Nothing, but— Did something happen inside?"

Could he really smell...*that*?

He crinkled his nose. "Your face is red, and your scent is..."

Oh, God. He can*! Kill me now! Giant bomb, falling tree, spontaneous combustion...anything!*

Even worse than her embarrassment was the fact that she herself couldn't understand what happened. Her soon-to-be ex-accidental vampire husband had just appeared in the fitting room. They went nuts, dry humped like a couple of wild, horny bunnies, he tried to sift her away, and then she told him to pound sand.

Yes, a proud, proud moment in my life. If only that could go on my Facebook timeline!

She had to find a way to undo this...this thing between them before his emotional grip tightened further. With Niccolo she was exposed, vulnerable. She'd fallen for him hard and taken an enormous leap of faith. But like everything in her life, it hadn't turned out. No father, no husband...no true love.

Going back to the pity party again, are you? You should be grateful. Life had given her some very wonderful people—her mother, her friends—and a great education with a bright future.

But that man...he just gave you a taste of something

more. Are you forgetting the connection you felt? Could she really live her life without experiencing it one more time? She craved it. She craved him.

She brought her fingertips to her lips and savored the memory of his delicious kiss.

He doesn't love you. He'll hurt you, she reminded herself. *He's controlling, arrogant, and too closed off. Not what you want from a man.*

"Niccolo tried to take me," she finally confessed after a few seconds of stewing.

Andrus slammed on the brakes and reached for something below the seat. Helena threw out her arms to avoid slamming into the dash.

"He was here? Now?" Andrus screamed.

Helena grumbled and slid back into her seat. "Yes! But he's gone. Okay? And did you have to do that? I'm mortal, remember?" She pulled the seat belt strap across her chest and buckled in.

"What did he say?" He released his hand from whatever was under his seat.

"Nothing. He wants me back. I said no. It's over." But it wasn't. She knew it. He was not the sort of creature to give up. *Bonds forged by the universe . . .*

She sighed loudly. Andrus needed to drive a whole hell of a lot faster to that archive if she was going to find a way to divorce this vampire and break the connection between them.

"And he tried to sift me, but it didn't work for some reason."

Andrus's cold demeanor returned, and he went back to driving. Several moments passed before he finally said, "The ring. I gave it an upgrade."

Helena looked at her grandmother's gold filigree ring on her hand. "Sorry?"

"I've…" He seemed to be searching for the correct word. "…Treated the ring. You cannot be sifted while you wear it."

"How?"

"Trade secret," he replied curtly.

"Thought you were going to share your secrets."

"I said I would teach you how to evade him and how to not be sifted. Lesson number one: wear the ring."

He was going to be that way, was he? *Great. Just what I wanted, out of the secretive-man frying pan…*

"And the evading part?" she asked.

He scratched his stubble-covered chin. "I'm working on it."

"Care to elaborate?" Helena asked.

"Bonded vampires, or vampires and their makers, can sense each other's presence. It's like a compass, and there are only a few ways to 'go dark,' so to speak. Being asleep or unconscious, for example. They probably evolved that way since a sleeping vampire who can be found is vulnerable. You're human, so I don't think that applies to you."

"Great. So he's got Helena GPS even when I sleep. What am I going to do?"

"We could still give it a try. I can knock you out."

Helena huffed. "Don't even think about it. And if you try anything, I promise Niccolo will find out. I doubt that was the last time I'll see him."

The corner of Andrus's mouth curled for a quick moment. "So then, we keep moving. Get off the main roads and make it harder to be followed."

"Wait! I know this really great invention that can get us to San Francisco quickly. It's called an airplane."

Andrus shot her a warning with his eyes. "No airplanes."

"Fine." She crossed her arms. "But I don't get it. I'll still answer all your questions. You'll get everything you want from me."

"Everything?" Andrus flashed a smile her way, then turned his focus back to the road.

Had he flirted with her again?

Helena was up to here with wicked men; she chose to ignore the comment. "That man is downright determined."

"So am I," Andrus stated coldly.

Helena rolled her eyes. "Do you really think we'll make it all the way to the coast before he finds a way to nab me?"

"Yes," he said starkly. "I never fail."

"Nice to see you're confident, but it's my life you're gambling with."

He blinked multiple times in rapid succession, which struck her as odd. "No airplanes," he said again.

Helena suddenly felt exhausted. Being around stubborn men was like rolling a giant boulder up a never-ending hill, or in this case, rolling a giant domineering man up a hill.

Wait. She didn't have to stay with this guy. He hadn't guaranteed she'd find the answers in his archives. She was smart, independent; she could figure this out on her own. "Pull over. I've changed my mind about our little deal."

Andrus laughed. "Not going to happen."

"Oh, I get it. I'm *your* pet now. I don't know who or what you really are, but you're worse than a vampire!

At least they keep their word. They believe in honor. You— You're—"

Andrus growled, then pulled to the side of the road. "Watch your tongue, human. And anytime you want to leave, be my guest. I give you one hour until they snatch you up."

"Fine!" Helena reached for the door handle, but inexplicably found herself whiplashed into Andrus's lap.

Helena was now nose to nose with the snarling man. He smelled surprisingly sweet. She suddenly became all too aware of the powerful arms encasing her, and the part of his body positioned below her bottom. *God, he smells incredible!*

Dammit! What's wrong with me?

"Who the hell are you?" She was not about to capitulate and cower to another...whatever he was. "You stalk me, tell me you're going to help free me in exchange for answering a few questions, and now I'm your hostage. You vowed not to treat me like a pet, but here I am... woof!"

Andrus stared into her eyes, giving her a look somewhere between hunger and frustration. His eyes shifted down to Helena's lips and froze for the length of several slow breaths. As if catching himself doing something wrong, he pushed Helena back into her seat.

He gripped the steering wheel, his chest rising rapidly. "You win. We'll take a plane."

Ten

⌒

Following hot on Helena's heels, Andrus slammed the hotel room door behind him, grumbling something about whiny women.

"Hey, don't blame me!" Helena barked. "Not my fault there aren't any flights until morning. What's the big damn hairy deal anyway? I'm the one who should be complaining; I have to share a room with Mr. Unknown Species, who might feed on my soul while I sleep."

Andrus glared at Helena and threw his black duffel bag on the bed. He was about to retaliate with a cruel rebuttal—that much she knew—but instead pinched his lips together for a moment before saying, "I'm going to take a shower. I suggest you take this opportunity to think about curbing your snotty comments."

"Or what?" Helena perched her hand on her hip.

Andrus pulled his black T-shirt over his head and snapped it off his wrist onto the bed. Helena's mouth fell open. His pecs where chiseled, rounded curves, headlining the ripples of perfection that cascaded down his stomach to form the only other ten-pack abs she'd ever seen in her life besides Niccolo's. They were hard, deep, and tanned. Was he showing his powerful body to scare her? Wasn't working.

Her eyes lingered over every splendid inch until they snagged on the trail of dark hair that ran under the waistband of his black leather pants. There, her eyes involuntarily stuck. She recalled how Niccolo wore a similar pair of pants two weeks ago.

She'd had to bite her tongue, almost drawing blood, to keep from licking her lips when she saw the distinct outline of Niccolo's large bulge thrusting against the zipper. Andrus wasn't aroused, but suddenly she was.

Andrus's angry glare morphed to something more mischievous. He cocked one brow. "See something you like?"

Busted! Helena frowned and turned away to search for a pretend missing object in her shopping bag. "Not even."

She held up the charade until the bathroom door closed and then smacked her forehead with the heel of her palm. *Dork!*

Niccolo's boots thumped across the hardwood floor as he paced the spacious penthouse bedroom—*Helena's abandoned penthouse*, he chastised himself—bathing in her luscious, fading scent while he considered and reconsidered what to do. He quickly realized that reshuffling the deck of options didn't change "squat" since they all "sucked ass," as Viktor would say.

Sì, maybe I should consult Viktor.

Niccolo pulled his phone from his pocket. His fingers jabbed at the miniature text pad with frustration. H asked me 2 break 1 of my rules. Then I should sleep w/her. Yes? Niccolo hit Send.

Viktor responded immediately. U mean sexting, right?

Niccolo: Sexting?

Viktor: Sex+texting.

Niccolo: Idiot. Real sex.

Viktor: Dumbass! Then u lose chance 4 freedom.

Niccolo: Have lost it already. I think.

Viktor: K, then tell her who U R instead, ass.

Niccolo frowned. Why did Viktor, and modern humans, for that matter, always speak of beasts of burden? Ass this and ass that. Hungry as a horse . . .

Niccolo punched in his response. Am killr. Queen's murdering slave. H will reject me, loathe me.

Also, breaking the Pact, which he'd upheld for over a thousand years, wouldn't do at all. Telling her all about vampires and the laws that governed their world would make him a "lame ass."

Viktor: Tell her WHOLE truth. She'll b pist as balls but whtver. She's UR mate. Honesty is best.

Niccolo shook his head. She would think he'd been using her to gain his freedom, that he didn't care for her. Well, maybe he didn't. It was impossible to say what was real. Did he want her, need her, because of their bond? Or was there more between them? He wished he knew, but more than that, he wished for the luxury of time to find out.

Niccolo ran his fingers through his hair. If he were going to do something to cause Cimil's prophecy to go unfulfilled—breaking the Pact, biting or bedding Helena before turning her in six days—well, bloody hell, he didn't want Helena to end up hurt or hating him. It was also very likely, according to Cimil, that he'd die or end up in the queen's dungeon. At least sleeping with Helena would give him one fantastic, perhaps final, memory to cling to.

Dammit. He couldn't give up. Failure wasn't in his nature.

He picked up a hardback from the nightstand and was about to hurl it across the room, when he noticed the title. "Bram Stoker's *Dracula*?" He grunted. It was Helena's book. She based her opinion of him on this?

Niccolo's phone buzzed.

Viktor: U still have 6 days. Too early to throw in towel.

He was right; however, there was no way to win her back without sacrificing something that would also mean sacrificing his chance for freedom, according to Cimil's prophecy.

Niccolo: This is a fucking karmageddon. The universe's payback for my sins.

Viktor: Calm urself, vampire. She's human. Use your charm.

Niccolo released a slow breath. "*Bene.* And if that doesn't work, then I will still seduce her. At least I will see some satisfaction come from all this before my demise."

⌒

Helena sat tightly wound on the edge of the queen-size bed, staring at the dark carpet while listening to water hum through the pipes as Andrus showered. Now alone, that pang—*stupid goddamned pang!*—was too notice-able to ignore.

It was silly to feel a sense of loss for something she never had, but she couldn't ignore it. Absurdly, she thought about how perfect her life would be if she could combine Niccolo's strength and looks with someone more open and caring. Maybe once upon a time, he'd been that man. He had a mother, right? He probably loved her with tenderness and compassion before he'd been turned. Maybe Helena could help him remember those lost pieces of his humanity.

"Hopeless." She sighed. "I'm totally hopeless! He wants to turn me into a vampire, and I want to turn him back into a human."

Helena quickly slipped off her jeans, thinking to take advantage of Andrus's shower and change into the baggy tee and yoga pants she'd bought at the clothing store.

"I see I'm just in time," Niccolo said, suddenly appear-ing in the corner of the room. He took several rapid steps toward her and cupped her cheek. "To lovingly wash every square inch of your creamy skin."

"Niccolo. How the hell do you keep finding me?" Hel-ena hissed, but her heart rejoiced. "I told you to leave me alone, and I meant it." *Sort of.*

His dark eyes narrowed. "I cannot do that, *mio cuore*. We are bonded, and until my last breath, I will think of nothing but you."

"Good for you, vampire, but not my problem, and con-sidering you don't love me, not sure it's yours, either."

He frowned. "Please, my bride, let me explain. My heart is blackened by my world. It barely beats now, but you, you bring light to the darkness I've endured for over a thousand years. It is the closest thing to love I will ever know, and this has to be enough for you. You must—" He froze.

The water stopped running.

Oh, hell! Andrus! She'd almost forgotten he was there. What would Niccolo do if he found out she was sharing a room with another man? She hadn't wanted one room, but Andrus insisted and made it clear he'd be sleeping on the floor. No biggie. Until now. Niccolo would kill him.

"Go! Now!" she screamed at Niccolo.

"You . . . you . . ." he growled. It was a dark, deadly growl that made Helena shiver down to her bones. "Someone is here with you?"

Helena made a jerky nod. No use in lying. Niccolo could probably smell Andrus. What the hell was she going to do?

Wait! He has no right to be here. He's the one who threw your heart under a bus.

Suddenly, the bathroom door burst open. Andrus stood firmly in the doorway, wearing nothing but a scowl and a white towel around his waist. He gripped a sword in each hand. Had he been carrying them when he'd entered the bathroom? Helena wondered. She didn't recall seeing any swords. And who took showers with weapons? What the hell *was* Andrus?

Helena wedged herself between the two men, holding out her arms. She swiveled her head in Niccolo's direction. "You have no right! I don't belong to you!"

Niccolo, too, held a sword in each hand.

Where did he get those?

"Move, Helena," Niccolo ordered. "I'm going to kill the son of a bitch. No one touches you and lives to take another breath."

"Bring it, vampire!" Andrus's jaw flexed. "I've been hoping for another head—or in your case, ball of dust—to add to my collection."

Helena noted that whatever Andrus was, being afraid of vampires wasn't on the list. That only meant one thing: He was more dangerous. Or believed he was. In any case, Helena felt 100 percent bona fide pissed off. How dare Niccolo act as though he had a right to her after he treated her like a child, manipulated her, and refused to trust her!

The two men raised their arms and weapons high in the air, closing in—despite Helena acting as their buffer. At any moment, one of them would toss her aside and begin brawling. She had to think of something fast. Yes, she was angry at Niccolo, but she didn't want anyone dying on her account.

Stupid men . . . males . . . dudes. Heck, whatever!

"Niccolo! No! Stop. Andrus isn't . . . He's . . ." She paused for a moment. "I may share a bond with you, but it isn't real because my heart wants him! Don't be such a sore loser."

Her strategy was a huge gamble, but playing the one chord he valued—honor—might just get him to take a hike. She only had to convince Niccolo that Andrus had won her fair and square.

Arms still stretched, holding the two men at bay, Helena glanced at Andrus. His golden eyes were locked on Niccolo like two heat-seeking missiles. Would Andrus blow up her lie? She turned her head toward Niccolo, who visibly seethed with anger.

Did he buy it? "Please, Niccolo. We're through. Just go," she begged.

Niccolo's already dark eyes turned into pits of blackness. "Who the hell are you?" he asked directly to Andrus.

With a slight bow of his head, Andrus said, "I am the man who is going to collect your soul and fuck your woman. Not necessarily in that order, but both will involve screaming."

Helena's eyes went wide. *What the . . . ?* Not only wasn't Andrus going to blow up her lie, he was going to run to the hundred-yard line, spike the ball, and call it his very own touchdown. Christ, he had a nasty streak.

Niccolo's fangs stretched into tiny daggers that protruded from his mouth. "The only thing you will be doing is dying."

"Well, Niccolo, the Executioner, I have yet to see a vampire best a Demilord." Andrus smiled coolly. "Face it, asshole, your minutes are numbered, and I am the one with the stopwatch. Ticktock. Ticktock."

With that, Niccolo shot a glare at Helena. His expression had moved from furious to betrayed.

He vanished.

"What the hell is a Demilord, Andrus? What. The everloving. Godforsaken. Hell. Is a damned . . . *Demilord*?" she half screamed, half blubbered. Anything that could scare Niccolo away certainly scared the bajeebers out of her. What had she signed up for?

"We must go. Quickly! Before he returns with his men. I can't fight off more than a few at once." He ignored her question, instead focusing on repacking his duffel bag.

"Who said you need to defend me? Niccolo doesn't want to harm me. He wants me to be his submissive, obedient immortal wife. And why did you call him 'the Executioner'?"

He ignored her, continuing to zip up his bag.

She tugged at his arm, forcing him to drop it. "What the hell is going on? Who are you, Andrus?"

"You…" He turned and gripped her shoulders. His eyes silently warned her not to push him any further. "All you need to know is that you're not safe with him." He stalled for words. "They are violent creatures. We need to leave."

She nodded stiffly. She had no idea what was happening, but she now knew she didn't want to be a part of Niccolo's world. Or Andrus's. Too violent. And yet Andrus was her only chance at an out from the stickier of the two situations—that much was clear.

Was she safe with Andrus? She wasn't sure at all, though she felt strangely unafraid. The darkness he projected was some sort of armor he wore to hide his true nature.

"Okay. But you're explaining everything in the car."

The gentle glow of the dashboard illuminated Helena's delicate face. He wanted to concentrate on the road, but it was impossible not to steal a glance or two of those pink, plump lips or those sky-blue eyes. They were mesmerizing. No wonder the vampire was crazy for her. Andrus didn't even have a bloody bond, yet he found himself feeling drawn.

Maybe that's why he'd blurted out what he had about taking her along with Niccolo's soul. Something about her felt calming, and right now, he needed it. His mind was like a fucking Ferris wheel—thoughts, emotions going round and round. Anger, that was a big one.

Fear of failure was another. And now there was a new one: guilt.

Helena didn't deserve her hand in life, as Andrus didn't deserve his. They'd both been misled into believing they were getting something worth fighting for, but instead found themselves fighting to get their lives back.

"I don't know what's going on, Andrus." Her hand shifted to the armrest between the seats, lightly covering his. "But I promise you can trust me. I'll help you any way I can."

She wanted to help him? She felt sorry for him? Figured. The guilt factor turned up ten notches. "Why? Why do you care?"

She shrugged. "I see it in your eyes. They didn't just take something from you, they hurt you. Didn't they? No one hates as much as you do without a reason, and I saw the look in your eyes. You really wanted to kill him."

Smart human. Andrus would have to do a better job of keeping his emotions hidden.

"The only thing I'm asking, Andrus, is for the truth. I can't take any more of this…these secrets. My heart's been broken. My life—the one I wanted, anyway—is gone. Now I feel trapped. All because I made one reckless choice to love someone I shouldn't. It was one stupid mistake, and I want my old life back. I only want out."

Andrus nodded as he contemplated what he should share. Too much information and the human might put the pieces together on her own. She was extremely bright. Not enough information, she might not trust him. Then she might try to escape or derail his plans some other way. If he could win her sympathy, that could come in handy later on. A tiny twinge of guilt spiraled through his gut.

Helena squeezed his hand gently. "Please, tell me."

The simple gesture and sweet tone of her voice made him feel worse than a vampire for what he'd planned to do to her, but there was no turning back now. Life was full of injustices. The way of the world. His story was no different.

"Fine. I will tell you what's going on, but don't blame me if you don't like what you hear."

Eleven

⸻

The Story of Andrus

When she came to him on their very last night together, three hundred years ago, it had been a night like many he'd spent with her—filled with sweat-slicked skin, words of raw passion, and endless fucking. There was never any shame or hesitation with her. She gave herself willingly, in every possible way a woman could physically give herself to a man. And he took. And took.

It began when Andrus saw her standing in the dark corner of the lavish, crowded ballroom at his uncle's estate during another stuffy formal ball in Paris. Their eyes met, and in an instant, a smoldering connection formed.

When he took her to bed that evening, he knew he'd never want to stop gazing into her large mahogany eyes, running his hands through her vibrant red hair, tasting her smooth skin and every part of her body in between.

She tasted like wildflowers and sweet vanilla mixed with the forbidden. He found it simply addictive. He didn't know why. Didn't really care. He wanted her so badly it scorched his soul.

Months of passion-filled nights flew by, yet his craving for her would not abate. He came to realize that it wasn't her full red lips or her generous, round breasts that he burned for. It was that hidden corner of her soul she refused to open to him.

Each night, with his sweet words and passionate bed play, he tried to coax from her that which she kept locked away. Her heart, perhaps. Yet no matter how hard he tried, there was no emotion when she said she loved him. Nothing he did truly made her vulnerable to him as he was to her.

But he was determined. He would not relent until she was fully his. Being the son of a powerful family from eastern Russia—a country plagued with war and corruption—taught him all about persistence and pain, especially how to endure it, which was ultimately his downfall.

Their nights of passion turned into demented one-sided quarrels filled with his irrational accusations. "You love another!" he would scream. "You are using me for my money!"

She would demurely sit on the edge of the bed while he hurled the delusional insults. Her dark eyes would remain sterile and untouched until she'd finally say, "Are you going to calm yourself and take me to bed or not?"

Eventually, he would. He had no choice but to give in to his lust, to feel her velvety skin writhing beneath him as he pumped his hard flesh into her.

On the last night, he went to her lavish apartment in Paris. He was broken beyond repair from the torment of being unable to conquer her heart. She was the one woman he loved and held above all others. He would do anything for her. Anything.

"Anything?" she asked. Her red silk dress hugged her tempting curves and full breasts as she strolled across the polished marble floor of the rococo-style bedroom. Red velvet cushions topped the ornately carved couches and chairs. Exotic floral arrangements and expensive cognac sat on the side tables. She'd never told him how she came into her money, but he didn't ask—what if she had once been married or had lovers? He couldn't bear the thought.

She stopped in front of the fireplace, staring into its glow. It was winter now, and the snow fell in a soft, thick blanket outside. She stretched out her pale arms to warm her hands.

"Yes," he answered coldly. "*Anything.* Just say you love me and mean it. Truly mean it!" His long, dark hair was a disheveled mop. His shirt was rumpled with several buttons missing. "Money, my horses and homes, I don't give a shit. Just say the words and mean them. Give me this one thing, that is all I ask."

Boldly, she turned. "I want your sworn loyalty. Forever."

He didn't bat an eyelash. To devote himself to her forever? He could ask for nothing more. "It is yours. Always has been." At the time, his heart filled with the deepest joy, believing that she truly loved him but had been simply waiting for him to declare his undying love. *So simple,* he thought. *So damned simple!*

"Are you certain, my precious Andrus? Because there is no turning back."

Oh, God, yes. He marched across the room and claimed her soft lips. Like the rest of her pale face, they were warmed by the fire. "I said *anything*, and I meant it. Now, tell me. Say the words," he demanded. His heart pounded with anticipation.

She pulled away from him enough to see his eyes. Her face was filled with sorrow. "Hold still, my love. I'll try to make it quick."

Confused, Andrus attempted to pull back, but she immobilized him in her iron grasp and tugged him close to her body . . . before sinking her teeth into his neck. She drew deeply from the gash. Andrus jerked and flailed against her impossible strength until he was too weak to move.

Finally, she dropped him like a sack of wet sand to the floor and bit down on her own wrist, drawing her blood into her mouth. Slowly, she bent to him, then kissed him hard, letting her blood spill into his mouth. A trickle escaped down the side of his cheek as he hacked and sputtered.

Andrus stared up at her, his eyes burning with confusion and betrayal, his heart pumping wildly. "What did you . . . you . . . do to me?" he gasped.

She hovered over his paralyzed body, the life slowly seeping from his muscles. Her eyes were cold as ice. "Andrus, I love you and only you. I'm sorry." The words did not touch her eyes, and he screamed as the darkness took hold of his soul.

Helena covered her mouth and pushed back the tears of sympathy. "Sh-she made you into a vampire? That…bitch!"

Andrus's lips curled for a fraction of a second. "Yes, she's a bitch."

"So, you're a vampire?"

He shook his head and continued staring at the road. Clumps of snow pelted the windshield. "Not exactly."

"Then what 'exactly'?" Helena's phone suddenly beeped. "Oh, jeez. Not now."

She glanced at her phone. The message was from Jess. Hey Lena, WTF? Ignoring your day-turnal frenz again?

Helena froze for a fraction of a second. *Jess knows about vampires? Wait…*

She had texted them while on the bus earlier that day, saying she'd be working nights for a while so not to call during the day. She thought it might cut down on having to lie so much.

Helena released a breath and responded: Can't chat now. K? Catch u ltr.

Jess responded: Loser!

She glanced apologetically at Andrus. "Sorry. My friends. I don't want them to worry and say something to my mom."

Andrus nodded, but didn't continue speaking.

"Please, I want to hear the rest." Helena thought her head would spin off if he didn't tell her.

He shot her a look.

"Please?" she whined.

His jaw worked for several moments before he spoke. "Days later I woke and was a vampire. Thirsty and cold, I could think of nothing but killing. Women, children, I didn't care who—I just wanted blood and lots of it."

Helena's eyes were wide. "You ate ... children?" *Please say no. Please say no. Please say—*

"She was there to stop me. The queen's final trap. Reyna knew how much I hated her for what she'd done. But I hated myself more for what I craved. I didn't want to kill innocent people for survival. Yet that was all I could think of doing. I was a depraved monster. So instead of informing me that I could learn to control the thirst, she offered me an out."

Helena didn't move or breathe.

"Reyna said if I did what she asked and served loyally, I would never thirst and, therefore, never kill a Forbidden, an innocent soul."

Helena looked down at her hands, fully comprehending his situation. "So, you agreed?"

Andrus nodded. "Yes."

"What was the deal? What did she make you do?" Helena almost hated to ask. His story was already too hard to hear.

"Reyna locked me in an iron box and shipped me off. I didn't know where I was going or if I'd survive the madness from the hunger. It was months of hell, unimaginable pain. When the box was finally opened, I found myself in the jungle, somewhere in Mexico. That's when I saw them." He shook his head, clearly pained by the memory. "They were so beautiful, I thought they were angels coming to save me." He stopped talking for several moments.

Helena was filled with anguish. "Andrus?" she prodded.

He didn't respond, his jaw grinding again.

"Who were they?" she pushed.

He continued on, "They threw me into a cenote,

an ancient Mayan ceremonial pool, their portal. They dragged me to the other side to make me like them. Well, half anyway."

Helena was thoroughly confused. Why wouldn't he tell her? "Who were 'they'?"

"The gods. They put their light inside me," he said, almost sounding ashamed.

Gods? What the...? No way! "Sorry? Did you say, 'Gods'?"

"Yes. Obscuros were out of control because that bitch of a queen is useless. The gods were finally fed up, about to kill her. So she offered up an alternative to save her skin: to help them create a powerful race that could kill Obscuros and whom they could command—the Demilords. She bartered our lives for hers."

Wow! First vampires. Then gods. Now...vampire gods? What's next? Werewolves? Smurfs? Were-Smurfs?

"Do you have any powers?" she asked.

"I possess certain talents."

Her eyes popped open. "Can you sift?"

"I track and kill. I have the skills necessary to be good at both. That's it."

"Oh." Helena sank into the seat, digesting for several moments. Even for her, a relatively open-minded woman who'd studied science, this was a bit much. But regardless of how she felt, Andrus had done the honorable thing. He loved—albeit in an obsessive, stalker-like fashion, but he loved. Then he was betrayed. Afterward, he'd tried to make the best of it and not eat children. Where was the shame in that?

She twisted in her seat to fully face him. "Andrus, I realize we don't really know each other, but you should believe me when I say it's not your fault. You loved her. She screwed you over. You tried to do the right thing. End of story."

Andrus quickly slammed on the brakes. With the snow blanketing the concrete, the Hummer skidded. Several cars honked and flashed their lights as they passed by.

"No! That's the fucking point! It's not the end of the story. If the gods ever feel like it, they can remove their light. They can turn me back into a vampire, and I'd binge until I've made up for every day I haven't fed. I'd become a depraved, bloodthirsty monster. So there is no fucking end! Not unless I make one."

He turned his head left toward a driver who had slowed to dish a healthy portion of glare. "What the hell are you looking at? *Huh?*" Andrus screamed. The offended driver, who thought twice about provoking Andrus, sped off.

He turned his attention back to Helena, who'd plastered herself against the passenger door. She held out her hands defensively. "I'm sorry, Andrus. I'm sorry this happened to you."

Andrus regained control. "No," he mumbled, his head hung low. "I shouldn't yell at you like that."

She nodded cautiously, now understanding why he was so volatile. He was broken, just like her. But he had no intention of hurting her. He was good. Dark and neurotic, but good. "What will you do?"

"For starters, I'm going to kill Reyna." There was no shame in his voice that time.

Definitely dark. So, this was as much about revenge as it was justice. But she couldn't bring herself to condemn Andrus, although she didn't believe that killing the

woman he once loved, who sold his soul to the gods—
there are really gods?—was going to heal him. Like Helena, he needed his life back.

So where did Helena fit into all this? Was Andrus
really trying to help her? Doubt swirled in the back of her
mind.

Something was...not right.

Regardless, she had no other choice but to continue on with Andrus and hope the Demilord archives
held the secret to her own freedom. No turning back.
Not now.

"Andrus, I really think you should—"

This time, it was his phone that beeped.

He held the device up and then growled at Helena.
What could possibly be wrong now? She leaned in to
catch a glimpse of the message.

"It's not my fault!" Helena barked. She could practically see the steam rising from Andrus's nostrils despite
the darkness inside the vehicle.

He glared down at his smartphone, then at her.

"What? Stop looking at me like that!"

"Then whose fault is it?" he growled, showing her the
ten-day weather report on the tiny screen displaying little
clouds with snowflakes and rain.

She crossed her arms over her chest. "Not mine, snow
happens. Where the heck did you say you're from again?"
*Wasn't it Russia? They had lots of snow there, didn't
they?*

"Fine," she conceded, throwing up her hands. "The
snow is all my fault. The canceled flight is all my fault.
I'm so sorry, my gracious Demilord. Please forgive the
poor, stupid human for the weather-related travel delay."

He let out a breath, and his body softened. "That was uncalled for. I'm sorry."

She turned her head toward the window and then waved her hand, sighing. "Forgiven. Just stop making a habit of yelling at me—that's twice in one night."

"I am not used to being around others," he said quietly.

Her anger softened, too. How could she possibly respond to that?

"All right. What next?"

"We drive," he replied.

In the back of the limo, Niccolo slumped against the black leather seat, staring at the tablet screen as the dot slowly flickered across the map. Helena, or at least her cell phone, was moving south, away from Chicago and the storm.

His fingers curled into a tight fist. In less than an hour, the sun would be rising, and he and his men would have to find shelter. Unpleasant, angry thoughts moved through his mind. How to kill a Demilord was one of them. It had never been done, but he'd find a way. More pressing, however, was how to get her back.

There were only five days left. And—perfect—he was unable to sift her away! Likely thanks to the Demilord. What had she called him? *Andrus.*

He imagined that pretty-boy head of Andrus's sitting high in the sky on a five-meter spike. *Sì, just like the good old days, when they knew how to do things right.* At this very moment, only the gods knew what lies that cretin was telling his sweet, trusting bride.

Where is he taking her? Niccolo resisted the urge to sift to Helena while she was on the move. Too dangerous.

And yet Niccolo felt overcome with the primal urge to protect her. The pull was almost as bad as the night when he'd saved Helena from those men on the beach. Her fear had created an agony so intense that his body felt like it might be ripped in half. When he arrived and found the vile males, auras completely black, attacking the women, he'd turned into a blood-crazed demon. Luckily, his men weren't far behind and were able to help with the cleanup. Niccolo had never told Helena, but they'd been in the area for several days, killing Obscuros. He visited her every morning before the sun rose and watched her sleep. She was so beautiful. He wanted her near him—had purchased a home for her even—but he wondered if he'd be able to keep his hands off her if they shared the same roof.

Everything changed after that night. What if the bikers had been Obscuros? He would never be so careless again. He'd take her to their new home, have her guarded 24-7, and ensure she'd never be in danger again. After all, she was his mate, for better or worse. Human or not, it was his job to protect her.

Well, he'd failed miserably at that task, hadn't he? Now she was with one of the most dangerous creatures in the world, and they had only five days until their three-month anniversary.

Do you really care about fulfilling the prophecy anymore?

He sat, quietly pondering the question. The answer was a shocking surprise.

No. He didn't care. He merely wanted her safe.

His chest tightened. *You idiot! Admit it, You care for her. Don't you?* There was no denying that he did. Seeing her pretend to want another had pushed him over the edge. He felt wounded. Truly and painfully wounded.

So what did it really mean?

For starters, he was a damned fool to continue ignoring the powerful bond between them. Out of billions of living creatures, her soul was bound to his. It was a connection more powerful than hunger or the need to survive.

Niccolo didn't know why or how, but there it was: Helena now meant more to him than anything.

Do you love her? He still didn't know. Perhaps that was because love was so foreign to his cold heart.

Niccolo looked up toward the front of the car. "How much time until sunrise, Viktor?"

"Forty minutes," Viktor replied without looking at his watch. "With the polarized glass, we can follow her for another two hours before I'll tire."

"Do it. We'll go as far as we can, then find a hotel to bunker down."

Viktor nodded. "Then what?"

"I don't know. Pray they stop soon—somewhere I can safely sift to and get a chance to steal her back."

"What about the Demilord?" Viktor asked.

Niccolo growled. Why the hell did the Demilord want Helena anyway? At first, he'd surmised that Andrus wanted to lure him to his death. Niccolo wasn't an Obscuro, but that didn't mean the gods couldn't find offense with something he'd done; however, if that were the case, Andrus would have killed Niccolo on the spot in the hotel. According to what Niccolo had been told, once Demilords located their target, they'd stop at nothing to finish the job. Collateral damage, loss of innocent human life, wasn't a concern. They claimed their actions were justified because they served the greater good. Just like those idiot gods they obeyed, the Demilords lacked any sense of compassion. That's why Niccolo had fled the hotel; he didn't want Helena to get caught in the middle.

So now, in retrospect, he knew the Demilord's speech about coming for Niccolo's soul was a lie. The other part about fucking his woman? *He wants Helena for himself. I must kill him but how?*

Rumor had it that no Demilord had ever been killed by a vampire; they were a hardy breed. But Niccolo was well trained. He could take him; he knew he could. Helena would simply need to be out of the way.

Viktor smiled. "Are you sure she's worth it? The queen will have your head if she finds out you're picking a fight with the gods' guard dogs."

Niccolo looked out the window toward the glowing horizon. "I'm sure."

Twelve

———

Andrus glanced in the rearview mirror at Helena curled up on the backseat. God, he was tired. This was the longest he'd ever gone—two weeks without sleep and a proper meal. Yes, he was immortal and part vampire, but his body functioned best with natural foods. Easy, convenient energy, such as Snickers and Pop Rocks, his favorites, could only take an angry warrior so far.

He glanced at his watch. The sun would be rising in twenty minutes. He'd drive all day to put distance between them and the Executioner. Then he'd find somewhere safe to stop and sleep for a few hours before driving the rest of the way. No doubt the world's most deadly vampire and his guards were right behind them. Andrus, like all Demilords, knew Niccolo and his men were a force to be reckoned with. He'd never have a chance fighting so many well-trained warriors at once. Especially since Andrus's abilities were geared toward hunting, not being hunted—a tiny detail he'd failed to share with Helena. He had already summoned backup, but they were dispersed around the globe and would take a day or two to catch up with them.

Heading southwest, eyes fixed to the rain-slicked road, he leaned to his right and grabbed another Snickers from the glove box. Two more days and they'd be there. Then he'd play out his next move and Reyna would finally be his. Perhaps after three hundred years, he'd finally see an emotion touch her eyes. Terror. Yes, even the coldhearted queen would feel *that* when he took her head.

Helena sensed the faint hum of an engine as her mind slipped out of a deep sleep. If it weren't for the discomfort of a seat belt digging into the top of her head, she might have slept for a whole week. She wiggled her toes and lethargically sat up.

"Good morning, Helena," Andrus said in a groggy, deep voice. "Or should I say afternoon?"

"What's good about it? I feel like the world just sat on my head and kicked me in the stomach."

Andrus did not respond.

"Hey, are you okay?" She leaned between the driver and passenger seats to look at him. His eyes were glued to the road, but his lids were at half-mast.

"I am . . . tired."

Helena noticed the pile of candy bar wrappers on the floor of the passenger side. "I hope Demilords have a good health plan."

"I only wish I could get sick. Then maybe I'd die."

"Jeez. Morbid enough?"

"Sorry," he said. "I'm tired. That's all." His eyelids notched down another fraction of an inch.

"When's the last time you slept?"

"Two weeks ago."

Lord love a duck! Even Niccolo slept daily, and he was tough as nails. "Pull over. Let me drive."

Andrus shot daggers with one glance. "No."

"Oh, I get it. Only big, strong men know how to drive a Hummer?"

"What car do you drive, California girl? Wait. Let me guess. A convertible VW or a Prius."

Ha, was he going to feel stupid! She was one of the lucky ones who commuted less than five miles each way to school. So when Ann's brother wanted to sell his truck for the bargain price of two g's, she pounced.

"A 1974 Bronco."

Andrus's head swiveled. "Windsor V-8?"

"What else?" Helena loved that frigging gas-guzzler. The hard top was a bear to put on in the winter, but in the summer that truck was a little slice of heaven. She felt strong and free riding that beast down the highway along the coast.

"Fine." Andrus pulled off at the next exit, into the gas station.

As soon as Helena topped off the tank and hit the freeway, Andrus was sawing logs in the backseat. For her, the seat had been spacious, but for a man his size, he looked like a bear crammed in a shoebox. As soon as she found a good spot, she'd pull over and rent a room so he could stretch out. In all honesty, she could use a hot shower and bed herself. Helena flicked on the radio and picked an oldies station. The Beach Boys came on, and it suddenly reminded her of the night Niccolo saved her.

She changed the station. She didn't want to think about him; she wanted to think about going back to her old life with her mom and friends.

But they're moving on with their lives. Shouldn't you?

She'd spoken to Jess and Anne the week before. They'd already moved away to start their careers. Her other friends had gone off to get their doctorates. What was she really going back to? Just a place with lots of memories of surfing at sunset and running on the beach?

What about your mom? She's still there.

Even her mom had her own life now that Helena was grown. Helena hadn't really left anything behind in Santa Cruz.

Well, there's your career. You had to give that up.

Actually, Niccolo never said she'd have to give it up, only that she didn't need to worry about money.

So that left the question of what was behind door number three? What would her world be like if she had to live as a vampire? She knew it was a must if she wanted Niccolo; otherwise their relationship would always be about him trying not to hurt her. They'd never be intimate, either. Total deal breaker. Could she handle living in his dark world? It seemed so violent and cruel.

He said things would be better after your transformation. Don't you trust him? He saved your life.

Yes, she did. But *he* didn't trust *her*. That hadn't changed. He also said he didn't love her and never could. That mattered.

So does the fact you want him. And…with time, he

might learn to love. Look how long it took you. It was true; Helena had never tried to open her heart to anyone until Niccolo came along. It wasn't for lack of trying, either; she'd simply never met anyone who sparked the desire, who stimulated her imagination, and challenged her.

Helena glanced at Andrus through the rearview mirror. His head was propped against the door, arms crossed against his chest. God—*oops*—gods, he was beautiful. His thick dark brown hair swirled in random spikes. His dark lashes fanned out along the slit of his closed eyes. His lips had a slight fullness to them, making him appear as though he were puckering for a kiss.

Helena shook her head. *He's still not Niccolo.*

There was also something about Andrus she didn't trust. Maybe that dark cloud following him? Whatever it was, she still couldn't resist wanting to help him. He was in pain and alone. She could relate.

Thirteen

~

"Crap!" Andrus sat up in the backseat of the vacant Hummer. It was parked in an empty lot behind a hotel, under a shedding tree. Yellow-and-brown leaves covered the windshield along with a light sprinkle of rain.

He jumped out and scanned the area. Where the hell was Helena? There was no trace of her smell. The rain had washed it away. Could she have gone to the hotel?

Dammit. He couldn't lose her now. Without her, his plan completely fell apart, which meant he'd be fucked. How could he have been so stupid to let her drive? Sure, he'd felt tired, but he was a Demilord, a hardened assassin who could live an eternity without sleep or food. Not that he would want to do so; he had so few pleasures in life as it was. But Helena's quirky humor and propensity to trust blindly, her compassion for others, had made him let his guard down.

Idiot. Keep your eye on the fucking ball. He could only pray he hadn't blown the game already.

He charged toward the side of the building and found the entrance to the reception area. A young woman with short strawberry-blonde hair stood behind the counter. The moment she looked up, her smile melted away.

"May I help you?" she asked with a shaky voice.

Andrus leaned over the counter, his height and size easily bringing him a foot from the woman's face. "I am traveling with a young woman. She has shoulder-length blonde hair. Where is she?"

The woman smiled nervously. She handed him a small envelope with a card key. "The young woman was just here and asked me to direct you to your room."

Andrus let out a sigh of relief. "Thank you. Where the hell are we?"

Confused, she answered, "Amarillo, Texas."

He nodded and turned toward the elevator.

"But," the clerk added, her voice barely a whisper, "she also asked me to tell you that she'd gone for food."

"Where?"

The woman backed away from the counter and pointed across the street.

Seriously? Is this the only place to get food? What a nasty dive, Helena thought as she pulled open the stainless steel door of the roadside bar.

The parking lot was littered with Harleys, beat-up trucks, and, well...litter. The building was worn and nondescript except for a crooked, washed-out sign over the entrance that read: Bar.

As soon as she opened the second set of doors, her heart stopped, and so did every leather-clad man in the cesspool. Each face—unshaven, bearded, or just plain dirty—swiveled toward her.

The inside mirrored the outside decor—floors and walls painted black, no windows, and one neglected pool table in the corner.

Not exactly an OpenTable.com establishment, is it? Neither open nor any tables.

Helena's eyes migrated to the only splash of color and light in the entire establishment: a giant neon rainbow over the cash register behind the bar. Lynyrd Skynyrd's "Freebird" played on the jukebox.

She sighed with relief. *Gay bar! Sweet Lord, thank you.* She lifted her chin and smiled. "Where can a girl get a killer mojito around here?"

A few of the men smiled at her and turned back to their conversations. One man, who was wearing leather chaps, jeans, and a leather vest, pointed toward the bar. "Fernando there makes the meanest mojito this side of the Caribbean. Just hope you're a fan of hangovers."

Fernando—a lanky man with short brown hair— looked up from behind the bar, shaking a martini, and gave her a wink.

Helena bellied up to the only open space at the very end of the bar. For a middle-of-nowhere gay bar, the place was packed.

"Mojito, sweetheart?" Fernando asked.

Helena paused, rethinking her choice. "Actually, make it a double Don Julio, and keep 'em coming."

Tonight she wanted to forget. Forget that a vampire had broken her heart. Forget that there were gods abducting vampires and making them into Demilords to kill Obscuros. Forget that she was "married" to a vampire she hadn't actually married and who didn't love her. God-effing-double-dammit, life bit hard!

Pity party again, Helena?

Yes! Okay? Yes, I am having my pity party, so get out the pity piñata and the pity pretzels!

Fernando slid a thick tumbler her way. Helena caught it and threw it back. She wiped her mouth with her hand and nodded to Fernando. He raised one brow and returned to refill her glass.

"Man problems, honey?" Fernando asked as he refilled her glass.

Helena sneered. "You could say that."

He rested his hand on top of hers. "Let me give you a piece of advice: none of them are worth it. They'll say anything to get in your pants—promise you the stars—then leave you the minute they get bored. Save yourself the trouble and take up tennis or yoga."

"Oh, put a clamp on it, Fernando," said the redheaded man next to her. He was wearing black jeans and a wife-beater. "Don't listen to him, honey. He's just bitter because Pepe dumped his ass for a stockbroker."

Helena's chest buzzed with warmth as the second double shot took hold. She hit her palm on the bar and said, "That's because men are pigs! What do you expect?"

Fernando laughed. "See, Joe? She gets it."

"Maybe the problem isn't the man, but the toy. I've never been dumped," Joe bragged.

Fernando rolled his eyes. "You're in denial." He moved down the bar to fill empty beer glasses.

"Really, honey, don't you listen to him," Joe said. "You get what you deserve in life and that includes your relationships."

Helena snorted. "Maybe." But what the hell did she do to deserve this paranormal soap opera? "Maybe not. Sometimes life isn't fair."

The man chuckled. "What's your name?"

Something about the redheaded man seemed vaguely familiar, but Helena couldn't put her finger on it. "I'm Lena." She threw back the third glass. "Recently broken-hearted and currently drowning her sorrow in the finest tequila money can buy."

The man nodded. "I'm Joe."

Helena smiled. "Well, Mr. Never Been Dumped, what's your secret?"

He took a sip from his frosty mug. "Simple. I'm a man; I know what they want," he said with a wide grin.

Helena laughed. "I'm pretty sure that even if I nailed that part, things wouldn't change for me."

Joe raised one brow. "It's not so hard to figure out—all starts with the kiss. It's your lover's calling card. Get that right . . . and a man will follow you to the ends of the earth no matter what happens."

"Ha!" she snorted. "Am I drunk, or did you just tell me I have relationship problems because I can't kiss?"

Helena noticed the room starting to swirl. On her empty stomach, the tequila had traveled at supersonic speed to her bloodstream. *Hiccup!* Helena covered her mouth. "Okay, maybe I am a teensy bit drunk. But you're crazy if you think a kiss could get a man to love you."

Joe chuckled. "The kiss is the most powerful tool in your box. In fact, I bet I can teach you to kiss so hot you'll set lips on fire and even a gay man would pay *you* for lessons."

Helena laughed. "What the hell. I'm in."

Andrus charged through the parking lot, anger spilling from every pore. What the hell was the woman thinking, going into a dive like this? Images flowed through his mind of finding Helena screaming as some man roughed her up, intending to do vile things to her innocent body.

Andrus raised his arm and slid his hand under the neck of his leather duster, readying to pull the sword strapped to his back. He yanked open the first set of doors and then stopped dead in his tracks.

On the other side of the second door, he could hear men screaming loudly. *Shit!* He swung it open.

Like the lethal assassin he was, his mind quickly went to work assessing the scene. He efficiently identified all of the exits, how many people were in the room, and which individuals were possibly concealing a weapon—which was, yep, just about every guy in the joint.

Great choice, Helena. Well, at least they all smelled mortal. Then again, the sun was about to go down, and this looked like the exact kind of place an Obscuro would go for their next meal.

Andrus's eyes zeroed in on the opposite end of the room, where the men were gathered around someone, cheering wildly, raising their glasses.

Helena. They must have her. These foul males would pay for touching her. First, he had to get her to safety. Then he'd return to exact justice.

Andrus frantically pushed past several large, leather-clad men who protested as they fell to the side, but immediately backed down once they caught a glimpse of him.

"Hi there! What's your name?" said a large man in a leather jacket.

The other man to his side gasped and smiled. "Oh my. Look what my fairy godmother dragged in. Yum."

Andrus frowned. These men were... extremely friendly for such rough-looking types. He ignored them and kept moving. As he reached the last barricade of bodies, he spotted a large redheaded man facing the crowd, holding up a hundred-dollar bill.

Then he saw Helena.

His vision dotted with red. A young, shirtless man wearing only jeans and chaps held Helena in his arms and was leaning in to kiss her.

Bastard!

Andrus would take his head first.

He pushed the man away. "Get the hell off her!" If the sleaze bucket had a shirt, Andrus would be holding him up by it. However he didn't, so Andrus would opt for ripping off his arms instead.

Helena stumbled back. "Andrus! Hey, honey!" She flung her arms around his neck. "Nice to see you, but you'll need to wait your turn."

Andrus surveyed the rowdy crowd surrounding them. They were laughing and smiling. *And winking?*

"You're not... in distress?" Andrus asked.

The redheaded man looked at Helena. "This must be the asshole who broke your heart."

Helena wobbled and poked Andrus in the chest. "This guy? Nooo, but he's a lying pig just the same."

Was she drunk?

Andrus took a whiff. *Holy cocktail! The woman smells*

like she's about to vaporize. And why does this place reek
of Polo cologne mixed with gasoline?

"What the hell is going on, Helena?"

She stepped forward and jabbed him in the chest again.
"I'm having a little fun! If you wanna play, you'll have to
pay, bub! One hundred buckaroos, like Ricky boy here."
She flicked her thumb toward the shirtless guy she'd been
about to kiss.

Helena stumbled to the side. Andrus caught her arm
and frowned. She was wasted.

"What's gotten into you?"

Helena laughed. "Jealous?"

Was he? He certainly wasn't happy to see her about to
kiss a stranger. He grabbed her, pulled her to the bar, and
then sent the onlookers a warning with his eyes and mind.
They obediently returned to their conversations.

He stared deeply into her blue eyes. "Maybe."

"And what can good old Fernando get you this evening?" the bartender asked with an eager smile.

Andrus noticed that Fernando had on the same leather-
pants-and-black-tee outfit.

Nice look. Andrus swiped the small Plexiglas freestanding menu from the counter and then asked for a
Guinness and chicken fingers. "You need to eat something," he said to Helena.

"Are you over her?" Helena asked. "Really, reeeeally
over her?"

Andrus knew immediately to which "her" she was refer-
ring. The answer wasn't so simple. How could he be over
the woman who'd not only broken his heart, but his spirit,
too? She changed him into a monster, and he had to look at
himself every day, a constant reminder of her betrayal.

"No. I will not be over her until justice is served," he said coldly.

Fernando returned with a thick, frosty mug of dark brown beer, smiling. "On the house."

What friendly service. Andrus nodded and threw down a twenty anyway. Fernando winked at him.

Yes, very friendly.

"So, you still love her, don't you?" Helena asked.

No. He hated that demon with every fiber of his being. He wanted to take her head and put it in his trophy case, though that wouldn't be possible—vampire bitch couldn't even do that much for him since her head would turn to ash.

"I'm half vampire; I love nothing and no one. I want her dead so I can forget her. And what about you, Bride of the Executioner?" he asked.

Helena winced. "Oooh, God." She punched Andrus in the arm. "Don't say that! Sounds like a horror movie."

Andrus smirked.

"Why do you call him that anyway?" she asked.

Should he tell her? It might make it easier for her to move on when Niccolo died, given every vampire with the queen's blood would perish along with her. Yes. Knowing she was bound to a killer could prove helpful.

"He's the queen's right hand, Helena, the general of her deadly, immortal army. A ruthless, bloodthirsty assassin."

Andrus watched her face fill with sorrow. His gut churned with guilt.

She gave an empty nod. "He never told me what he did all night long or where he went. I figured he had some kind of dangerous job. But her general? Her right hand? She's so evil."

"I'm sorry."

Helena raised her hand. "Fernando, can I get another?"

"Don't you think you've had enough?" Andrus objected.

"I want to forget him, Andrus. He kept the truth from me, except when he said he could never love me." She laughed. "How ironic! I'm not even good enough for the Executioner!"

He reached out and pushed her hair behind her ear. "Helena, he can't love you because he's a vampire. You, you're perfect."

"Andrus! Are you flirting with me?" she asked, amused.

Andrus looked down at his feet, shocked to realize that in fact he was. He thought that Reyna had destroyed that part of him—the part that felt affection. Go figure it would be the Executioner's wife who'd bring him back. But there was no denying it. Helena had an easiness about her. Since she'd entered his life, he could breathe again, just a little.

"Yes, you are perfect except for your secret fetish: getting stinking drunk and trying to kiss strange men in seedy bars."

She laughed and socked Andrus in the arm. "Nuh-uh! That red-haired guy bet he could teach me to kiss so well that even a gay man would pay for a lesson. I was about to make my first hundred."

What! She was kissing men for money? He growled and then froze. Wait. They were in a gay bar? Andrus's eyes swept the room, and he realized the truth. Ironically, he fit right in with his leather pants. That might explain why women steered clear of him. Or perhaps it was because he was a dark son of a bitch who always had a cloud of shadows lurking near him.

In any case, he'd have to rethink his wardrobe choices. *Aw, fuck it. I like my leather pants.*

He looked down at Helena with amazement. How come she didn't mind his dark side? In fact, despite his snapping and barking, she still wanted to help him. She was strong, smart, and honorable in addition to being beautiful.

Lucky damned vampire. She was an extraordinary woman who could have any man she wanted. How could she, of all people, think she wasn't good enough for that lowly Executioner? He suddenly realized how badly he wanted to kiss her, for her to want him instead of that vile bloodsucker.

He looked into her eyes. He was going to tell her exactly what was on his mind, "Helena, I—"

Helena turned and did a little jump. "Oooh. I love this song!" She looked at Andrus. "Hold that thought, Andrus baby! Helena's gotta go get her Pet Shop Boys on."

Helena scuttled across the crowded room and pushed her way into a line of fifteen men, locked arm in arm, singing at the top of their lungs and swaying in unison. "Whooo! That's right, baby!" Helena howled as the men on both sides hooted and jeered in response. "You are always on my miiind! You are always on my miiind!"

She sounds like a bloody drowning cat. Andrus winced as her off-key voice carried through the bar. *And that song, bloody fucking awful, but dammit, she makes me laugh.*

The tune ended, and Helena staggered over to Andrus, giggling. "No encores. Please. I know how much you want one, but the diva Helena needs more tequila."

He reached into his pocket, pulled out a silver money clip loaded with bills, and slipped out a hundred.

Helena's eyes lit up. "Oooh. You buyin' me another?"

"I think you've had quite enough, but how much did you say it was for a lesson?"

Helena's eyes went wider, but before she could say a word, his mouth was over hers.

Her lips softened immediately, and she opened her mouth to him. He instantly felt himself grow hard as her sweet tequila-tainted taste filled his mind, and her warm body leaned into him. Gods, she was irresistible.

Damn ... this woman can kiss.

He felt a euphoric rush. He could feel again! He instantly knew this wouldn't be enough. He wanted her. All of her.

His passion took over. He snaked one hand behind her back, the other to cup her head. He dipped her to deepen the kiss. It was nothing like the lust he'd had for Reyna. Helena's spirit elevated him; she chased away the dark clouds and replaced them with warm, radiant light.

A tiny moan escaped her throat and reverberated in his ears. Gods, she was amazing. He broke the kiss for a moment. "Definitely worth a hundred."

She smiled and reached her arm around his neck. "I think you've still got a balance left on your tab."

She reached her lips to his and pulled him back into the kiss.

Legs dangling over the edge of the full-size bed, Niccolo stretched, slowly coming out of his deep sleep as the sun set. Heaviness filled his chest.

They'd had to stop at a hotel early in the morning to rest instead of tracking Helena as he'd wanted. He couldn't risk his men's safety since driving in daylight was too risky; any one of them could fall asleep behind the wheel, and there were four vehicles in their caravan.

He slid the tablet from the nightstand and turned it on. He anxiously waited while the screen refreshed. He hoped Helena's signal was still there or, even better, close by. When he finally caught up to her, he'd do something he personally objected to; he would glamour her into coming with him quietly.

Glamouring a human was considered socially acceptable only under very specific circumstances—like covering up an accident or wiping the mind of a human who'd discovered their existence. Only a low-class vampire, unable to depend on his or her charm or wit, stooped to glamouring a love interest. It was considered unsportsmanlike. When it came to mates, it was a reproachable act of deception that brought the highest dishonor to a vampire.

He'd simply have to make an exception. After all, it was not as if he could keep her glamoured forever. Eventually, he'd have to find a legitimate way to convince her to stay. He'd start by explaining why being in the company of a Demilord was dangerous even on a good day. Unlike vampires, Demilords held the reputation of having no honor. They only cared about killing whoever was on their hit list. Innocent bystanders were of no concern. Then there was the fact that every vampire on the planet hated them for being such arrogant bastards. It said a lot to be thought of as arrogant by his people—the official sponsors of arrogance.

The page loaded, and the blinking dot suddenly appeared on the screen.

Thank the gods. She was only a few hours ahead. She'd stopped to rest! He drilled down on the map, and a huge smile swept across his face.

"The Bar!" He'd been there before. He could sift to her!

His smile dropped off a cliff. *Vergine sacra!* What the hell was Helena doing in that dive? He'd been there just last month trying to track down an exceptionally violent group of Obscuros. He'd managed to catch and kill only five of the thirteen. His cold heart turned to ice, then to fire. If that bastard Demilord had anything to do with her being there, he'd not only kill the son of a bitch, but he'd pluck out his eyes and break every bone in his body first.

Niccolo picked up his cell. "Viktor. Get up. It's time for me to kill a sacred cow."

"You want to kill a cow?" Viktor said with a groggy voice, half asleep.

Niccolo growled. "I'm going to kill Andrus tonight after I get Helena somewhere safe. I'm sifting ahead. I'll see you there."

"Yes, sir," Viktor responded. "I'll try and catch a few non-Forbiddens on the way. I have a feeling you're going to need blood by the time I get there."

Niccolo winced. He did need to feed, but bagged blood was all he could stomach, and barely. Perhaps his body would return to normal once he drank from Helena and turned her.

"No, thanks. Just get there as quickly as you can; I don't know what I might find when I arrive."

Niccolo grabbed his two ancient swords and criss-crossed them over his back under his duster. He closed his eyes and visualized the alley behind the dive bar, where he'd killed a few contemptible Obscuros the month before. As his feet materialized on the wet asphalt next to the overflowing Dumpster, his senses shifted to warrior mode, ready for anything. He was grateful that the trip had not entirely purged him of his waning, precious strength.

Suddenly, he heard the loud roar of a crowd. Maybe there was one of those football games on tonight? Silly humans with their mock battles. If they wanted real excitement, they should hunt Obscuros. Now, *there* was something worth cheering for.

He pushed his finger through the heavy dead bolt of the back door and yanked it open. He could hear the crowd more clearly now. They were chanting... "*Lena*"?

"Helena!" He bolted through the dimly lit, long hallway that led past the bathrooms, into the main room. There, in the corner, was Helena passionately kissing...

"That fucking Demilord. I'll kill him!" His fist balled tightly as he captured the unmistakable emotion of lust radiating from Helena.

Bloody hell! This couldn't be happening! She was his mate. They were bonded. There was no possible way she could ever want another as long as his heart still beat—some said even after that.

And why the bloody hell are these men chanting her name?

Fourteen

⌒

Helena's mind swirled with tequila as Andrus embraced her in a soul-clenching kiss. His warm, strong muscles were hard against her soft body, and from the moment his lips touched hers, she almost felt the crater-size hole that Niccolo had left behind filling up. Almost.

From the corner of her mind, she suddenly heard Joe and his friends howling and cheering. "That's it, Lena! Take the bull by the horns, girl! Show him who's boss!"

Boy, Joe had been right. There was kissing, and then there was kissing. Joe showed her how to put her whole body into it, to make love to a man's mouth with her tongue. Joe was a genius. No wonder he'd never been dumped.

I can't wait to try this out on Niccolo.

Dammit! She just couldn't stop thinking about Niccolo. Not even the top-shelf tequila dulled her feelings. It was so damned frustrating! Well, once the bond was broken, she'd be free to make out with any man, and her heart would be free to enjoy it. Andrus was first on her list. He was a great kisser.

Yeah, but he's no Niccolo, is he? In fact, you're so sick in love with Niccolo that right now, your mind is making you believe he's standing next to you while you're kissing his enemy.

"Lena!" Niccolo barked.

Andrus released Helena and spun her behind him.

Niccolo's nostrils flared, his chest heaving. He took a step toward Andrus, snarling, putting them face-to-face. Helena noticed that Niccolo was about four inches taller. It was odd thinking of Andrus as the smaller one when he was absolutely huge.

"I will not let you take your anger out on her, Executioner," Andrus said.

Niccolo raised a brow. "The name is Niccolo. And I could never hurt my bride. You, however…"

Andrus laughed right in his face. "Anytime, leech."

"Take it outside, you two!" Fernando called out from behind the bar while pouring a beer. He didn't look at all worried. With this crowd, maybe brawling was the norm. It would explain why there were no tables; they'd just get in the way of a good Texan leather-daddy catfight.

Niccolo nodded. "You heard the human," he said, his whisper so low that only Andrus and she could hear.

"Wait!" Helena begged. Every set of eyes in the room followed as she trailed behind the two seething warriors. They huffed and cursed at each, soaring past the bathrooms and disappearing out the back door.

"Wait! Niccolo! Andrus! Stop! *Please*," she pleaded again.

She caught the heavy door with her palms before it slammed closed in her face. She pushed hard and spilled outside into the dimly lit alley. Her heart skipped as her eyes registered a sight she wasn't expecting; instead of facing off with each other, the two enormous warriors were staring down a gang of savage-looking men dressed in torn jeans and mud-caked leather jackets.

There must have been more than twenty monsters, although Helena found her counting skills sorely lacking at the drunken moment. They were lined up in a loose formation, each brandishing a sword or a stake. Some were blond, some had black hair, but each had eyes that were pits of evil.

A shiver climbed up her spine.

"Go back *inside*, Helena!" Niccolo yelled.

"That would be an awesome choice, but I can't seem to move my feet." Helena was surprised she was even standing—seemed like a great time to pass out.

Andrus, not taking his eyes off the small army of ... whatever the hell they were, barked at her, "Do it now!"

Helena glared down at her Uggs. Maybe the tequila had pooled inside them and they were too drunk to move. "Nope. Feet still not moving," she whispered.

She heard the two warriors groan.

"Bloody hell, woman!" said Niccolo.

Helena suddenly felt herself shoved through the back door. It had been Niccolo. The door slammed shut behind her, and the loud clank of metal and grunts of combat filtered through.

Help. She needed to find help. She ran toward the crowd inside the bar, panting.

Fernando instantly spotted her. "Everything okay, honey? Those two slugging it out like the big, gnarly, sexy, manly men that they are?"

She pointed toward the back door. "They...they... There's...um..."

What if she lost Niccolo? Or what if Niccolo killed Andrus? She didn't want anyone to die because of her.

Her head began to swirl violently, and then the room went black.

⌒

Andrus studied Helena, who was stretched out on the bed and finally beginning to come back to life. Despite her run-over-by-a-bus hangover appearance, Andrus couldn't help but stare. She was gorgeous even in her worst state.

Andrus sat down in a chair beside the faux-wood table near the window that glowed with full sunlight. He bent down and pulled off his boots.

"Where are we?" she asked, her voice gravelly with sleep and her golden curls plastered to the side of her head.

"Super 8. And before you say anything, you're lucky not to be dead."

Helena nodded. Her head plunked down onto the cushy white pillow. "Okeydokey. Super 8. Great."

She rolled over, putting her back to Andrus, and then pulled the floral comforter up over her head.

Andrus couldn't help but smile. After Niccolo's unexpected appearance last night, he'd thought for sure his plan was out the window. Niccolo had caught him locking lips with his bride, so that meant there'd be a fight to the death. So when those Obscuros showed up, he'd never been so happy to see the vile, despicable creatures. The perfect diversion.

As soon as Helena was inside the bar, the Obscuros attacked from every direction. Andrus could hold his own against a gang of Obscuros; nonetheless, he couldn't help but be awed as Niccolo sifted repeatedly, taking down one vampire after another with ease. His motions were fluid and fast. He was completely silent except for the sound of his sword slicing through the flesh and bone of his victims.

Andrus finally understood how Niccolo had earned his nickname. The Executioner was indeed a killing machine.

Andrus was tempted to take advantage of the diversion and leave with Helena, but he couldn't risk anything happening to Niccolo, either. The general was essential if he wanted Reyna. Andrus masked himself with shadows and inconspicuously took heads as Obscuros swooped by. He heard the faint rustle from above and turned in time to see two more vampires jumping from the roof toward Niccolo. Andrus leaped and swung. He hit one but missed the other; they were too far apart.

"Behind you!" Andrus screamed.

Niccolo swung his sword in time to take the Obscuro's head.

Down to a handful, the remaining vampires suddenly vanished.

"Oh, come on! Can I get a goddamned break?" Niccolo screamed at the fleeing vampires, "Get the hell back here and die like real vampires!" He turned toward Andrus. "I must go after them."

Andrus nodded. "I'll go back inside and check on Helena."

Niccolo knew Andrus would take her again, yet he chose to go after the bad guys? He put his duty before his own personal needs?

Had he misjudged the general? That was no good. He was banking on Niccolo behaving like a possessive, obsessed jealous mate.

"Make no mistake, Demilord," Niccolo added, "I am coming for you, and I will take back Helena. Then I will take your head next."

Andrus smiled inwardly. *That's more like it.* He dipped his head. "Until we meet again."

With a blur, Niccolo dashed off in the direction of the Obscuros.

Andrus released a sigh. That was too close. He'd have to be more careful. But how was the sneaky bastard finding them so quickly? Vampires didn't have such precision. It was like he had Helena GPS, like she'd said.

He closed his eyes and shook his head. *Of course.* He reached in his pocket and stared at the GPS app on the screen of his smartphone.

Sneaky bastards.

After that, he'd gone inside, retrieved a passed-out Helena, dumped her phone, and hit the road. He'd driven well into the afternoon.

Now he looked down at her snuggled in the large bed. If only he had someone like her to come home to every day. Andrus's shaft stirred again as he remembered kissing Helena's sweet lips. Would he be able to give her up when the time came? Would he be able to betray her to get his hands on the queen? Would she ever forgive him for killing Niccolo?

Does it really matter? There is no choice, he reminded himself.

He only hoped that someday Helena might forgive him. For now, he wanted to savor his last days with her as his ally.

Fifteen

———

Niccolo was astonished by how easily he'd been able to sift to Helena by merely opening his mind to her presence. Their bond was incredibly strong now—unlike any he'd ever heard of. But his satisfaction over this discovery quickly dissolved into rage. Bloody fucking rage.

He stared down at Helena nestled in the arms of another man. A fucking Demilord—a dog of the supernatural world. Not good enough to be a god and certainly not good enough to be a vampire. Something in between.

He ground his teeth so firmly he could taste the char from the friction. In one fluid motion, he flung Helena over his shoulder like a sack of grain and carried her out the door with blurring speed.

He continued down the road at a pace so rapid that the ordinary human eye would never spot them.

Niccolo finally stopped under an old oak tree in a heavily wooded area backing up to a green pasture. It was far enough away that Andrus could not track them for several minutes without luck or help.

Clutching the sides of her head, Helena scowled as he set her to her feet. "What the...*Niccolo*?"

Niccolo frowned. "Did you really believe that demon would keep you from me? Not even the loss of your phone or the sun will stop me."

"You have no right to snatch me away like that. You have no right to me at all!" She stomped her foot. "Ow!" Her hands returned to the sides of her head.

Niccolo grabbed her shoulders. "Did he hurt you?"

Her eyes darted to his face, then narrowed into tight slits. "No. You did...and the tequila."

"I have tried again and again to explain—to apologize for my words. I am not the one being unfaithful, Helena. You are my wife, yet I find you kissing another man! In bed with him! A Demilord, no less!"

Helena winced. "I don't belong to you, Niccolo," she whispered acerbically. "I don't care about your vampire rules. We. Are. Not. Married."

Niccolo felt his chest cave. "You really want to be with him?" he said, his voice serrated.

"No! The kiss was— I was drunk, and he was...I don't know why I kissed him."

Was that the truth? Niccolo recalled feeling her lust when she was kissing Andrus. He reached with his mind into hers. He sensed no deception from her, only confusion.

He pulled her to him and whispered, "Helena, I'm begging you to stop this madness and come back with me."

"Don't," she hissed. "I gave you everything. My trust. My love. But instead of returning it, you ridiculed me for my feelings. You hid the truth from me! And don't tell me it was all for my safety because Andrus was more than happy to share his story, and I'm just fine!"

Niccolo froze. "He told you of his origins?"

Helena nodded.

"Then you know about"—he looked up at the sky—"them."

She nodded. "I know."

Niccolo's mind windmilled. Cimil had been very clear that in order for the prophecy to play out, he had to follow the Pact to the letter of the law. He couldn't tell her anything about their world. Technically, mortals weren't even supposed to know of their existence—his or the gods'. They believed it would cause chaos if humans discovered they weren't at the top of the food chain. Secrecy was therefore written into the Pact.

Niccolo shook his head. *Bene, all is not lost. I didn't break the rules, Andrus did.*

He brushed her lower lip with his thumb. "Then I must tell you that they could be watching, my love. And they will not be pleased of your knowing about them. It is forbidden."

She swatted his hand away. "Oh, I get it. Now you're going to tell me that the only way for me to live is to become like you?" She turned away and began marching barefoot through the thick brush. "Nice try, Niccolo."

With lightning speed, he scooped her into his arms and pulled her back into the shade, tightly against his body. "I would never lie to you, Helena." His dark eyes stared down at her.

Her head was tilted up as she squirmed against him. "Let me go!"

"No!" Niccolo roared. "I will not permit you to go back to that beast. I will not permit him to touch you again."

"You can't sift me, and you can't travel far during the daytime, so you can't make me go anywhere with you."

"Then I will wait here until he comes for you, and I will fight him."

Helena screamed, "No!"

She wanted to protect Andrus? He swallowed hard as doubt filled his mind again. Had he misread her before?

"You love him?" he asked.

Her eyes narrowed. "No. I don't love him. I just don't want anyone to die, especially over me. But I do want to be free, and Andrus is my ticket."

Her ticket away from him. The words stung. Maybe he should let her go, but...

"The Demilord's intentions cannot be honorable; they have no honor. They are nothing but hired guns."

"Okay, Executioner, why don't you tell me all about that? How you're not the hired gun for your queen? Or how you haven't killed anyone because you were ordered to?"

That bastard Andrus had told her, and now Helena was disgusted. So that was it. That was the reason she was rejecting him. And it stung like hell.

Then it hit him. Hard. *You love her.* It wasn't jealousy or his male ego. *Impossible! I'm in love with a human?* Sure. Before, he'd wanted her. He felt endless lust for the woman. After all, they were bonded. But now...he loved her? He truly loved her.

He clutched at his chest. It felt warm for the first time in thirteen hundred years.

"Helena, I have something to tell you, and you will

listen without uttering one word until I have shared what I need to say."

She huffed.

He took that as a yes.

"First," he announced, "I am going to tell you my story, and then I am going to tell you how you've changed my life, and how much I love you."

"You— You love me?" she muttered.

Smiling warmly, he nodded and stroked her cheek. "We are not to that part of the story yet, my love. But be patient."

The Story of Niccolo

He hadn't always been the coldhearted vampire known by his closest and dearest friends as Niccolo the Executioner. Roughly thirteen hundred years ago, he'd been a soldier and the fifth son of a nobleman from the coastal town of Genoa in northern Italy. The country was divided, at the time, into the Lombard Kingdom and the Byzantine Empire. His eldest brother was in line to inherit his father's title and lands.

So like his brothers, Niccolo chose a soldier's life. War was plentiful, and they were constantly fending off attacks from the Franks to the north. By the time he was thirty-two, he'd fought hundreds of battles and earned a fierce reputation. Some said the gods protected him, that he was indestructible. For this, he was feared by all and his men were loyal.

When he received word that his father's lands had been repeatedly raided by Vikings—yes, Vikings, of all bloody people—he headed home immediately with half his regiment, leaving the other half behind with his third-eldest brother to protect the border.

On the second bone-chilling night of the journey, he and his men awoke to the horrible cries of a woman. Niccolo gathered his sword and charged into the darkness of the grassy hills, only able to see the gray shadows produced by the moon on that overcast night. Before he knew what hit him, he was knocked off his feet and plucked from the dirt. His body, immobilized by something powerful, moved through the air with such speed that he was sure the devil himself had taken him, intending to drag him all the way to hell.

He wasn't far off.

After several moments of being hurled through the air, his head landed on a sharp rock. The pain ricocheted through his skull. The silhouette of a woman appeared over him, and even in the shroud of darkness, he could see she wasn't of this world. Before he had a chance to cry out from the crippling pain, she clamped her cold mouth over his sweaty, dirty neck. He was instantly catapulted into the bliss of her bite.

When he awoke several days later, it was only miles from where his voyage had been waylaid, but it was leagues past his old life.

"Who are you?" he'd asked, unable to wiggle more than a finger. The pain was unbearable, like shards of glass flowing through his veins.

She was lying next to him and staring at the stars above. "My sweet man, how refreshing you are. It is not so much about who I am, but who you will become."

From those first moments, he recalled how something about her was ominous yet magnetic.

Days later, when he awoke a second time, he learned the raw, despicable truth. But nothing mattered aside from pleasing her. He'd forgotten all about his beloved brothers and loyal men, his father's plundered lands. Like a moth to a flame, he was under her spell, blind to the undeniable wrongness of what she'd done to him—she'd stolen his life.

Years later, he'd discover he was compelled to obey her—partly because of their blood bond, partly because she was skilled at the fine art of glamour. Eventually, through pure grit and toil, he would build a tolerance to her will. Before that day took place, centuries would slip through his fingers in an endless blur. So many god-damned years. So many battles. So much death by his hand. He was darkness and savored the awesome power that came with it. He was a vampire. The queen's general.

One evening, near the border of Scotland, in the queen's castle—a recent acquisition from a mysteriously deceased lord—the axis in Niccolo's world tilted once again. Niccolo had been ordered to kill an entire village.

"My queen, surely those people do not need to be eliminated. They have done nothing wrong except refuse to bow when you rode through."

And merely called you the bride of the devil a dozen or so times and instructed the children to pelt you with rocks. Where's the harm in that?

She sauntered over to a plush red velvet chair by the fireplace and flopped down, throwing her legs over the armrest. "They've disrespected me, the queen, and for this, they must die. I want them taken care of before I depart for Paris."

He felt the strength of his will snap into place for the

first time in centuries. He did not stop to ask why or reflect upon the dark path he'd been treading. He simply basked in his regained free will, straightened his back, and said, "I will not kill innocent people simply to stroke your ego."

Before he blinked, the queen was on him, gripping his throat, gleaming white fangs exposed. "Then I will go to your pretty, little Italian village and kill the whole lot of DiContis. Even the children. I'll suck them dry and make you watch your grandnieces and -nephews wither into nothing. I seem to recall there is one young woman who is the exact likeness of your sweet, dead mother."

He growled as he saw the truth in her eyes. She would follow through.

With a grunt of frustration, Reyna released him. "Niccolo, do not force my hand. It is such a crude way to gain compliance, and think of the consequences. In the end, you will be compelled to do my bidding, and not only will your descendants die, I will see justice served to the clan that has assaulted my honor."

Niccolo finally understood; he would do her bidding, or she would kill the people he cared for. When they were long gone and dead, she'd find some other leverage. Perhaps an orphanage. Or ten. There was no threat beneath her. Nothing she wouldn't do to prove her power.

It was astounding that the gods continued to let her live on.

"Then kill me. Though the thought of displeasing you pains me, committing such an atrocity would pain me more." He stared boldly into her eyes. He was prepared for the likely outcome of losing his head. *So be it.*

"Ugh!" She rolled her eyes. "You're a vampire, Niccolo! Killing is what we do."

"Vampire, yes. Ruthless as well. Monster, I am no longer. I will not kill an entire village, children included, just to please you." His eyes did not waver from her glare, and she seemed to understand that her power over him, her ability to glamour him, had dwindled.

She stomped her foot. "You are so stubborn, Niccolo. Fine. Be so goddamned honorable." She waved her pale hand through the air and walked over to a small table in the corner of her chamber to pour a glass of red wine. "Very well, you win. Be off with you, and check to be sure my carriage is draped properly."

Niccolo felt as though the wind had been knocked out of him. He knew this wasn't over. The queen never backed down. She was merely reformulating her strategy.

A chill that would stay with him for the next millennium embedded in his very soul.

"*Sì*, my queen."

"I really hate her," Helena said. "It almost makes me want to become a vampire just so I'd be strong enough to take her down myself. What an evil, horrible woman!"

Niccolo nodded. "So you see, Helena, why I did not tell you of my history. It is full of shame and darkness."

"What? Are you joking? She used your goodness against you! End of story. You can't possibly blame yourself."

Niccolo couldn't begin to convey the depths of his guilt for the things he'd done. In fact, he never understood why the gods permitted him to live, considering he'd blatantly violated the Pact dozens of times. In any case, after his moral reawakening, he vowed to make amends for the past.

"So, what happened? What did she do when you disobeyed her?" Helena hadn't moved an inch the entire time Niccolo spoke.

"She'd anticipated my reaction. Several days earlier, she turned a man I'd left for dead. He was a self-proclaimed demon hunter who killed not only a fair amount of vampires—innocent ones who were living in accordance with the Pact—but also a large count of humans...anyone believed to be a demon or otherworldly creature. His aura was one of the blackest I'd ever seen."

"Why would she do that?"

"She needed a henchman to do her dirty work. Rodrigo executed my entire village right after he took care of the clan in Scotland. The queen told me that if I served obediently, she'd keep Rodrigo on a leash. Yet if I tried to end my life or disobey or escape her, she'd let him roam free until the gods stopped him. That could equate to a very long time—they seem to have a different sense of urgency."

"Oh," was all Helena could manage to say for several moments. "I guess I never thanked you, did I?"

"For what, my love?" Niccolo scooped Helena's hand into his.

"For saving my life in the jungle that night. Rodrigo would have killed me."

Niccolo pulled Helena close. "I should have killed him a long time ago. And it is I who should thank you."

"For what?"

Niccolo held her tightly. "That is the second part of my story. It was the goddess Cimil who first told me of you. I thought the idea of having a mate was a myth, certainly a joke. But the moment I saw you, I realized how wrong

I was. And now, for the first time in a millennium, I have love in my heart. You are a miracle."

Niccolo bent his head and took her lips hard, the burst of emotions—his very own—gripping him in a vise. He could still feel Helena, her light trickling through him like a quiet stream. But his own light roared—a river, powerful and unstoppable. It plowed through centuries of desolate stone mountains of despair and hate, sweeping away the bleakness in its currents.

Helena tensed for a moment. Then her body melted against his. Her soft lips parted as he slid his tongue into her mouth. A tiny moan accompanied her breath, sending Niccolo over his last remaining edge of control. He wanted her. He loved her. He could not bear waiting to take her any longer. He needed to touch every inch of her. He wanted to taste her skin. He wanted to feel her writhe beneath him as he pumped his hard flesh between her thighs.

"I love you, Helena. My life means nothing if you are not happy and alive. I will tell you anything else you want to know. Today. I vow it. But I must have you," he whispered.

Helena flung her arms around his neck and pulled herself deeper into his ravenous kiss.

That must mean she agrees.

"Let me take you somewhere private," he panted.

Helena nodded. Her eyes said she was just as hungry for him as he was for her.

Niccolo's heart continued pounding, and his breathing was hard. He pulled away, breaking the kiss. "Tell me what to do, how to sift you."

Helena's eyes were wild with passion. She shook her

head for a moment, trying to get a hold of herself. "Oh. Sift. Right." She reached for the gold ring on her finger and slipped it off.

Niccolo quickly took her free hand and tried to sift her, but nothing happened. "It's not working."

Helena still held the ring in her hand.

"Give it to me. I will hold it." Niccolo gestured frantically.

She eagerly handed it to him. He grabbed her with his other hand, but again, nothing happened.

"We must leave the ring," he concluded.

"Wait! No. It's my grandmother's. I don't want to lose it."

Niccolo cupped her face and gazed into her eyes with affection. "Of course, I understand. I will bury it here and send someone back for it."

Andrus opened his eyes at sunset and immediately knew something was amiss. The door to the room was ajar, and Helena was gone. How could he have slept through the woman being taken? Which obviously she had. Her little slipper boots were still bedside.

"This isn't over, vampire," he growled under his breath as one single thought plucked like a sour chord in the back of his mind. *Mine, she's mine.*

Why? Because he needed her to exact revenge on the queen? Because Helena was the key to leaving him free from the vampire blood that flowed inside?

Or was it because she brought him a sense of warmth and peace and maybe he wanted her for his own? No. Impossible. Yes, she was an irresistible mixture of sweet and sour, kindness and combustion. But Andrus was incapable of love. Reyna had murdered that piece of him.

He wanted to kill the queen. He had to see this through, rid himself and his brothers of this cursed vampire blood. One measly human woman, no matter how pure and kind, could not stand in the way of having justice for so many.

He would not allow himself to think of the possibility of having her as his own, no matter how sweet her kiss had been or what it made him feel. Besides, she was blood bound to Niccolo the Executioner.

Yes, but once the queen is gone, Niccolo will be dead, the bond broken. She will be free to love another.

And then the truth hit Andrus. It would be impossible for Helena to want him; after he betrayed her, she would never forgive him.

He slid on his jeans, pulled on his tee, and grabbed his cell from the pocket. He dialed and held the device to his ear, hand trembling with anger. "Are the men ready now?" Pause. "Good. Because our human got away."

Sixteen

Helena blinked, literally blinked, and found herself standing in a hotel room wrapped in Niccolo's arms. She jerked her head back, noticing she was now standing right beside the bed. A big empty bed. "Wow. That was impressive."

Niccolo released her, a hungry look in his dark eyes, and took several steps back. He began slowly peeling off his light gray sweater. "I am older," he said slowly, his voice gruff, "and therefore more gifted than most. And there are many..." He paused and made a low growl as his eyes moved over her body. "Many things I can do, which you have yet to experience."

The muscles of his thick arms flexed as he revealed the solid ripples of his impossibly strong chest and perfectly sculpted abs.

Helena gulped. This man completely undid her. Just looking at him made the sexual tension pool in the depths of her core, flutter between her legs, and then radiate out, touching every inch of her skin like tiny shards of mind-numbing tingles. It was as if she'd plugged herself into Niccolo's mind and felt every flicker of emotion, every pang of sexual desire, every impulse to take her completely. She swore she even saw images from his mind of him drinking from her.

Helena shivered, trying to gather her thoughts. "What's happening, Niccolo?"

Now shirtless, he slipped off his boots and carelessly tossed them aside, and then approached her slowly, popping the top button of his faded jeans.

If it weren't for the fact that she knew something even more pleasing to the eye awaited her, she'd be feeling an extreme sense of loss for not being able to see him wearing those pants. The way they hung low on his hips, giving her a peek of those wicked ropes of muscles that ran under his abs and disappeared down into the front of his jeans...

Yum! She licked her lips.

Niccolo seemed to feel her every thought, too. He paused in front of her so she could continue admiring him.

He cocked one eyebrow. "Do you want to see the rest?" he asked teasingly, ignoring her earlier question completely. He slowly began opening the fly. She could see the dark patch of masculine hair above his cock. He was commando. She loved that.

Helena's core clenched hard as she thought about tasting him there. She remembered with perfect clarity how the rest of him looked. That image of him lying nude on the altar in Mexico would forever be seared in her mind.

"Yes." Her voice was scratchy and rough. "I would."

Her eyes traveled down as he shed his pants. His legs were tight and muscular, with a light dusting of black hair; his thighs were powerful like a champion stallion, and his cock could equally be described. Large and thick— it begged to be put to hard work. Again, Helena gulped. Her mind had forgotten all about the reasons she'd left him. Right now, the only thing that mattered was how she wanted him in the worst kind of way.

He slowly lowered his head and took her mouth with a leisurely, controlled pace. Yet she could sense the tension undulating beneath the surface, ready to explode. All he needed was one little push, and she'd feel the full force of his passion; nothing would be held back. Was she strong enough to take him? She could feel his concern; he was quite sure he would break her.

His rough hands slid under her shirt and briefly stroked the curves of her waistline before pulling her shirt over her head, his gaze languishing over her bare breasts. He kneeled down slowly, his eyes never breaking from hers as he pulled down her pants and panties, leaving her just as bare as he was.

Niccolo's body was so large compared to hers that she felt like a doll. His strength excited her.

His face was level with her midriff, but he bent his head to place leisurely kisses over her lower belly, grasping her hips with his large hands.

Helena gasped. The touch of his lips only made her need painful, unbearable, as they slowly worked their way up the center of her stomach to her breasts. She ran her fingers through the thick wave of midnight-black hair while he kissed the underside of her breast, massaging the skin with his tongue. He continued placing kisses over every inch of her skin, except her eager, hard nipple. Was he teasing her?

"Please, Niccolo, I can't take any more."

He looked up at her, his eyes filled with primal lust, like a lion hovering over a fresh kill. "I'm just getting started." He pushed her back, and she fell into the bed. Niccolo's enormous body pinned her onto the mattress. "Do not say anything, Helena, not a word. The sound of your voice will send me over the edge, and I do not want to lose control."

She was about to protest, but he covered her mouth quickly with his hand and shook his head. "No, my love, I must go slowly." He paused, his lungs heaving. "I cannot risk hurting you."

Helena gave a nod, still feeling shocked by the raw emotions she felt deep within him. She'd never slept with a man, but she imagined that this connection was far more intimate than anything she could experience from having sex with any other.

He cautiously slipped his hand away from her mouth, replaced it with his full lips, and returned to the task of savoring her body. Helena tried to relax, but feeling his hard muscles and velvety skin blanketing hers was too much. His strong thigh rested in between her legs, and his erection pushed against the inner side of her hip bone. That was not where she wanted it to be.

His hand slid down her neck, raked over her breasts, down her belly, until his fingers met her cleft. She gasped as he ran his finger up and down the center of her folds, pressing lightly on that sensitive spot aching for him. Helena's mind tumbled to a place it had never been...pure pleasure.

He worked his thick fingers faster and deeper, coaxing from her body the eruption she craved. Her hips rocked toward his hand, and suddenly she exploded.

She heard her cry simultaneously through her own ears and his. She felt her moans vibrate through him like a violent earthquake, shattering the fragile veneer of control he was trying to maintain.

Her own mind scrambled.

She'd just released the ferocious beast inside Niccolo. In the space of a heartbeat, he had thrust her thighs apart and positioned himself at her entrance, his mouth had moved to the base of her neck, his fangs about to pierce her skin.

She froze with fear as all tenderness evaporated from his mind and was replaced with savage emotions: hunger, lust, possession. His fangs pricked her skin. She felt the sting. She realized that he was right; he would break her. The primal instincts within him were too strong.

"No, Niccolo. Wait!" She pushed him back with all her force, but it was no match for his power. "I know you love me. Stop! Goddammit!"

The head of his hard cock was wedging its way inside her, and a part of her couldn't believe she actually wanted him to stop; he felt so good, so right. But her fear of being sucked dry and broken as he unleashed his lust for her blood and body was stronger.

"Please," she whispered, stroking the back of his head and those thick black wavy locks. "You can stop. I feel you love me. You don't want to hurt me."

Against her naked chest, she felt his heart hammering.

His fangs suddenly retracted from her skin, and he pulled out.

Helena sighed. *Thank God.*

Now that he'd regained control again, Helena felt sheer frustration. Yes, her mind was filled with fear—both his and hers—but her body craved him.

"I'm sorry, my love," he whispered against her neck, sending shivers down her entire body. "I should not have thought I was strong enough to resist you. I haven't fed for many days now. And even if I had, I wonder if it would change anything. I crave you."

He rolled off of her and pulled her head to his chest. She could feel his emotions. Failure. Shame.

"Niccolo? It's okay. Really." She looked up at his sublime face. The masculine features triggered her neediness all over again. His angular jaw—rough with black stubble—his dark lashes and thick, straight brows were works of art.

Eyes closed, he nodded. "I am very sorry for hurting you, my love. Please forgive me."

She smiled and snuggled into his chest. His heart was beating so loudly now. "Don't worry. Everything will be different after you've changed me."

Like a bucket of ice water poured over his head, Niccolo cringed inwardly at her words. The thought of changing Helena was absurd. He loved her. Truly loved her.

She was right when she'd said before that his world was dark...that *he* was dark. Dammit, he was also an arrogant, stubborn, deadly bastard, and he always would be. She deserved better. It didn't matter if he found a way to be free or not; he'd still be who he was, and killing was as much a part of him as anything. He understood that now after seeing the wake of destruction the Obscuros left behind. So many innocent lives were prematurely snuffed out every day. The Obscuros' numbers were growing, and they had to be eliminated.

He would always be the Executioner, queen's general or not.

Then another horrifying notion struck him...*Reyna's dungeon*. Cimil had mentioned that would be his fate if the prophecy went unfulfilled.

Cristo sacro, what a mess!

Helena could feel his emotions. She probably had all along, but hadn't realized exactly what they were. Now, she'd opened her mind and heart to him, she could feel him like he could feel her.

Bloody fucking mess!

If he ended up tortured by the queen, she'd be tortured, too!

And if by some odd chance he didn't end up in the bowels of the dungeon, he still couldn't be with her. He'd kill her. She'd driven him past the brink of madness with her satin skin infused with her sweet, feminine scent. When he'd brought her to release with his hand, it was the silver straw that broke the hungry vampire's back. His mind became permeated with her rapture.

It took every ounce of willpower he had to deny his primal instinct to devour her, mind, body, and soul— well, mostly body, to be honest. Then the trickle of blood from her neck pooled in his mouth, shocking him back to reality. That was odd; the taste of her blood should have sealed her fate. Perhaps his love for her was stronger than he thought. But would he be so lucky next time? Not likely. That meant he'd have to transform her. *Not happening. Back to square one.*

He tipped her face toward him and brushed the hair from her face. "Helena, we need to talk. I—"

The door burst open. In charged Andrus, flanked by five Demilords. Each wore black leather dusters and leather pants. Niccolo jumped from the bed, wedging himself between them and Helena.

"I'm wondering why you were foolish enough to get a room in the same hotel as us?" Andrus asked.

Helena gasped, and everyone looked at her. "You were about to take my virginity in a Super 8? You and I are going to have a long talk about that!"

Niccolo shrugged. "Figured the last place he'd look for us was the room underneath his. I also thought it would be easier for me to kill him at sunset, when my strength returned. My gamble might still pay off."

Andrus crossed his arms. "Sorry to disappoint you, but I'm not planning on staying or dying." He tilted his head to look past Niccolo at Helena. "Get dressed."

Helena pulled the sheet from the bed as she rose. "Andrus, thank you for coming to rescue me and for everything you've done, but I've decided to stay with Niccolo."

His eyes narrowed. "I said . . . get *dressed.*"

She stepped beside Niccolo and looked up at him with her large doe eyes, then back at Andrus.

Niccolo suddenly realized the ugly truth: Helena's only means of salvation was to be free of him. That meant she'd have to go with Andrus.

He didn't want to do this to Helena. But he had to.

Helena frowned at Andrus and his men. "Andrus, I'm sorry if you got the wrong impression last night. I was drunk. I know it's no excuse, but it's the honest truth. I love Niccolo. I want to stay with him. But that doesn't mean I don't want to help you." She stepped forward and placed her hand against Andrus's chest. "What was done to you was wrong."

It was the hardest thing Niccolo had ever done in his thirteen hundred years, but he stepped back, away from Helena. Every cell in his body screamed for her, to take her away. He forced himself to bury his true emotions so she wouldn't catch on. He'd have to carefully choose his words now. He needed to extinguish any hope she might ever have of him changing his mind. She needed to go with Andrus. If there was any hope for breaking the bond, the Demilord's archives were it.

He crossed his arms. "If he wants you, then he can have you. I cannot afford a war with the Demilords right now. My men's lives are too valuable to lose. We have important work we must carry out." Niccolo died on the inside—again—as he spoke the lie. He dipped his head toward Andrus. "She's all yours."

He tried not to look at her. He knew the pain on her face would be too much to stomach—worse than the torture likely awaiting him in the dungeons, worse than the thought of eternity without her. But this was the only way to truly save her.

"You're a bastard, Niccolo. I hope you rot in hell." She picked up her clothes from the heap on the floor and marched toward the door, pushing the enormous heathens out of the way. They snickered.

Andrus looked angrier than he had when he'd entered.

"You're a bloody fool, you know that? And yet I'm glad you are."

Niccolo nodded and then sifted away back to the darkness of his life, hoping that Helena would find a way to break the bond soon. He couldn't bear to feel her pain in addition to his own for very long.

Seventeen

~

Niccolo stared out the second-story window of Reyna's Paris town house at the streetlights below. Couples strolled down the cobblestone sidewalk at a leisurely pace, enjoying the unusually warm evening. After leaving Helena, he'd sifted to his queen, hoping secretly she'd simply end his suffering and kill him; Helena's anger and despair were like sharp knives jabbing at his heavy chest.

"Niccolo!" Reyna screamed as she stormed into the house.

He rolled his eyes. What idiotic request would she have this time? Maybe he should end everyone's suffering and kill her instead. But that would never happen. The universe's cruel joke. Although a well-trained vampire might be strong enough to kill her, no vampire would dare because if the queen were to die, any vampire carrying her blood would perish along with her. It was plausible that this meant the entire race. And *that* was why he suspected the gods had ultimately spared her; they believed the Creator would punish them if they wiped out one of his creations.

According to lore, the first vampires, or the Ancient Ones, were created in approximately 2600 BC, at the same time the Mayans began to flourish and the Egyptians built Giza. The gods, at the time, had become drunk with arrogance as humans made it their primary goal in life to worship them and pay tribute to their greatness. Humans built pyramids and made sacrifices; they would do anything for the gods. As the gods became fat with vanity and arrogance, they began to neglect their true purpose: protecting the Creator's children and their earthly playground. Evil among humans began to flourish.

The Creator, wanting to teach the gods a lesson, plucked out a piece of light from each of the fourteen gods. He then chose three human women and three men. The six humans inherited a piece of the gods' strength, immortality, and their gift of manipulating the physical realm—giving them the ability to sift, control minds, and see human auras. To keep the six Ancient Ones from growing too arrogant and powerful, as the gods had, he bound the Ancient Ones' strength to the night.

Finally, many believed that the Creator gave the Ancient Ones the thirst for evil humans' blood, as they were flourishing due to the gods' neglect of their duties.

An elegant solution for a simple problem.

Yet somehow the vampires evolved and developed a taste for innocence. The Pact was then created, though no one knows the exact date, to remind vampires of their true calling and purpose on earth. If they did not stray from the path of righteousness, their souls would be spared.

"Niccolo! You useless lump of medieval crap!" Reyna called out, snapping Niccolo from his thoughts. Oh, hell. Who was he kidding? If all vampires were truly related to her, they'd all be going straight to hell in a handbasket.

"I am here, my queen, and there is no need to yell. I am quite capable of hearing you." What he wouldn't give to become deaf.

She charged into the room wearing hot-pink overalls and leopard high-tops. "I order you to do something about this atrocity immediately! Immediately!" She stomped her foot. "Do you have any idea how much I just paid to fill up my gas tank?"

Niccolo sighed. "No, my queen—"

"One hundred and six euro! This is outrageous! Nobody—and I mean nobody—rapes the queen's wallet. Despicable humans!"

For once, Niccolo could actually see her point. There were certain elements of the human world that were out of their control: war, inflation, *American Idol*—all things that could cause major irritation to a vampire's daily life.

"What do you propose I do, Your Majesty?" *And why the hell doesn't she save gas and sift anyway?* Like him, she had the gift of being able to sift long distances.

She huffed and waved her hand through the air. "Fig-ure. It. Out. What do I pay you for?"

Niccolo swallowed a laugh. "You do not pay me, Reyna. I am your unwilling slave, remember?"

"Well, I..." Flustered, she paused. "I pay you by allow-ing you to live. So don't make me regret it. Kill whoever is running up the prices."

Niccolo bowed his head. "*Sì*, Reyna. I'll get right

on that. But first, I need to notify you of a new coven of Obscuros reported near San Francisco. We've got a report that an unusual amount of day laborers have gone missing."

This was always one of the metrics Niccolo and his men watched. Day laborers were easy prey because no one really tracked them. They often lived under false identities and roamed from state to state.

"I must investigate and handle the situation. Then I will"—he cleared his throat, finding it difficult to say the words—"handle the issue of high gas prices."

She narrowed her eyes. "Fine and I want hourly updates. Got it?"

Niccolo had to do what he could to appease the queen and avoid the dungeons for as long as possible. He only hoped Helena found a way to break their bond quickly.

He bowed his head. "As you wish."

He sifted to the New York penthouse to prepare his weapons. He'd promised himself he would stay away, but he could not resist. He missed Helena so badly that he could not feed—not even a drop of flavorless, bagged blood. Nor could he sleep. It had been just two days since she left, but it felt like an eternity. He felt her sorrow and pain twenty-four hours a day. Could it be that she wept even in her sleep? The thought drove him mad. He hoped she'd find a way to break from him—not that it would stop him from loving her, but at least he didn't have to feel her pain, too. At least she might be free to move on and find another worthy of her.

He lay on the bed in a plain white T-shirt and worn jeans, using her favorite cream sweater as a pillow so he could wallow in her scent. He stared at the ceiling, hands folded neatly over his stomach, wondering where he'd gone wrong in life. What had he done to deserve such a miserable fate?

Sì, he had a dark past, but he'd learned the error of his ways and fought ruthlessly to protect the innocent. Countless lives—children, mothers, sons, and daughters—surely the tens of thousands he'd saved meant something? Was it really so much to ask for a life wrapped in the loving warmth of a good woman? Helena had brought the light back into his soul. How cruel the universe was to give him something so spectacular only to make it impossible for him to keep her without destroying her.

The doorbell rang to save Niccolo from his personal pity party. He lethargically climbed out of bed and made his way to the door. Gods, he was so hungry. So weak. Useless now.

Viktor would have to do the Obscuro hunting tonight.

He slowly opened the door. He peeked through the crack to see a young man standing in a Windbreaker and long bicycle pants.

"*Sì?*"

"You Niccolo DiConti?"

Niccolo nodded.

The guy slipped an envelope through the crack. "I've been told I gotta wait for a reply."

Niccolo tore open the letter. His eyes took only one second to register the words. His heart stopped beating for the length of one breath, and then his blood began to boil.

Bastard! Andrus would die after a very, very long visit to Niccolo's secret cavern in the bowels of Barcelona. No one there would hear the screams as he took the flesh from his bones nick by nick.

"Ain't got all day, man. What's the answer?" asked the courier.

"Tell him I will rip his balls off, stuff them in his mouth, then tear off his head while I make him masticate!"

The courier raised one brow and stepped back. "'Kay, dude. Whatever." He pulled out a walkie-talkie from his pocket. "Hey. Found Mr. DiC..."—dramatic pause—"onti. Says he accepts." He looked back up at the seething Niccolo. "Don't worry about the tip, man. And you should try laying off the 'roids and coffee. Not a good combo for you."

"You're a total ass. You know that, don't you?" Helena barked at Andrus from across the deep cherry antique dining table. The room was well lit by a large, but neglected crystal chandelier. Several corners of the spacious room hosted dusty marble statues of toga-clad men cupping handfuls of grapes raised toward the sky. Post-its, displaying words such as *douche bag* and *imbecile*, adorned the statues' surfaces. Helena surmised these must be statues of the gods. *How mature.*

Five of the six Demilord warriors sitting around the table snickered as Helena dressed Andrus down.

Helena's eyes darted furiously at each of them, dishing a helping of shut the hell up.

They returned to quietly eating their steak and potatoes but maintained healthy smirks.

"I suppose you think that vampire mate of yours is an angel. Right?" said Andrus.

Helena grumbled and looked down at her untouched plate. "No. He's an even bigger ass than you are if that's possible."

"I'll take that as a compliment," Andrus replied with a grin. His men chuckled.

She was appalled by their glib dispositions. "You think this is some kind of joke?" She snarled at each of them.

Their smiles melted away.

"Sorry," Andrus said quietly. "I understand you are upset, that you feel I betrayed you, but that's no reason to not eat. It's been two days."

Helena simply wasn't hungry. "I know how long it's been. The question is, when are you going to let me go home?"

Andrus shrugged and picked up his fork to spear a chunk of baked potato soaked in butter. "Not until I know you're safe from him."

Helena suddenly noticed how Andrus did the quick blinking thing with his eyes when he said that. If memory served right, he'd done it the day they'd met, too. *His poker tell.*

"You suck at that, you know," Helena said.

The men stopped eating again and watched intently for Andrus's response.

Andrus chewed slowly, then swallowed. "At what?"

"Lying. And you know what kills me? I would have done anything to help you if you'd just had the courtesy to ask. But you decided to pull this. Why?" Helena stood up and pounded her fist on the table, sending her fork flying. "I wanted to stay with him! We could have had a chance if you'd left us alone! Why, Andrus? Why did you show up? Why did you come looking for me?"

Andrus winced. "I-I can't…"

"Is this some kind of punishment? Because I didn't give up on Niccolo after one kiss from you?"

His men exchanged astonished glances.

Andrus's face flushed. He rose from his seat, walked over to Helena, and yanked her hand.

She popped out of her seat and pulled her hand back. "Fine! You wanna talk? Let's. Because I've got plenty to say!" she yelled.

She followed him into the empty kitchen.

Helena was first shocked by his rude behavior and then by how run-down the kitchen looked. Some of the white tiles were missing from the walls. The white ceramic sink and tiled counters were chipped and cracked. An old refrigerator groaned in the corner. In fact, the entire mansion looked like the inside of a forgotten Victorian-era museum. This was the home of a person, or group of people, who'd clearly given up on life.

Fists clenched tightly, Andrus paced across the kitchen. "No," he finally said in a hushed voice. "I would never punish you for something like that. You should actually be thanking me for showing you what he's really like. He let you go without batting an eyelash, and you were ready to spend eternity with him. He's not the one for you."

"What are you saying? That you are?" she asked bitterly.

He growled, "I am not worthy of anyone, least of all you."

"*Whatever!* Then why are you doing this?" she screamed.

He ran his hands through his short, dark spikes. "You would never understand the truth, but this isn't about revenge—not against you anyway."

Helena's mind began sliding the pieces into place.

Andrus was using her for revenge. Against who? Couldn't be Niccolo. If that were the case, Andrus would have killed her. Or killed Niccolo that first night in the hotel. So if not Niccolo, then who?

Lightbulb. "Dammit, Andrus! This is about *her*! Isn't it?" Helena gave him an ineffective push.

Andrus's face went from flushed to pale.

She was right. Helena wondered if maybe he still desired Reyna. Sometimes the lines between love and hate blurred.

"I've never met the woman. What possible use could I be?"

He cleared his throat and stared down at Helena's feet. "I've sent a letter to Niccolo, advising that you will be executed unless he brings Reyna to me tomorrow evening."

"*What?*" she screamed.

Andrus sighed. "I will not harm you, I vow it."

Helena huffed. "Too fricking late." Then a thought struck her . . . The queen was extremely powerful and dangerous. And bonkers. "Niccolo will be killed if he tries to take her on."

Andrus shook his head. "The Execution —"

"Niccolo! His name is Niccolo! And if you knew anything about him, you'd realize he's no different from you. He didn't want to become a vampire any more than you wanted to be a Demilord." *Why am I defending him? The jerk told me he loved me, tried to sleep with me, then abandoned me.*

Andrus cleared his throat and nodded. "Niccolo is quite intelligent; he will bring her to me. I would go after her myself, but she's impossible to track. This is the best solution."

Helena hissed. What a total dirtbag! Was there no end to the parade of big, mean, untrustworthy immortal jerks?

"So you planned this all along? How did you even know about me in the first place? What are you going to do once you have the queen? You know I totally hate you, right?"

Andrus frowned. "Yes, this has been my plan all along. The Demilords have been watching Niccolo's place for a while; they found out there'd been a wedding dress maker visiting—a lucky discovery given how powerful of a bargaining chip a vampire's bride can be. That is between her and me. And... yes. I know you hate me. Although I hope you will forgive me."

"Have I told you lately that you are a complete and utter—"

"Ass?" he cut in. "Easy on the compliments. You might overinflate my ego."

Helena sizzled with anger. He'd never cared about helping her. "It was all a lie, wasn't it? Everything you told me about yourself was just to get me to feel sorry for you so I'd come quietly, wasn't it?"

Andrus stepped in closer. "No. Everything I told you was real, except... I do not know if our archives hold the key to breaking the bond with Niccolo."

Jerk! How could she have been so stupid to trust this man? "So, you lured me here, intending to do what exactly?"

Andrus sucked in a breath. "Niccolo will bring me Reyna and get you in return."

"Jeez. Thanks, Andrus. He's going to come and save me—which I highly doubt, since he made it clear he doesn't want me; but if he did, then I get to face the man who just broke my heart again. Thanks bunches!"

He closed the gap between them and looked down at her, his golden eyes filled with powerful emotion. "I, too, was surprised. If you were mine, I would not have let go so easily. But it was the best outcome—better than we hoped for. He was weakened from being out during the daytime, and with you in the room, we suspected he would not risk a fight. He had no way of winning."

"Oh," Helena responded. Was that why he let her go so easily? No. If that were the case, she would have expected Niccolo to say something like, "This isn't over; I'll get you back." But no. He told her to go. She'd been dumped cold.

Andrus gripped her shoulders. "I'm sorry."

Helena jerked away and stepped aside. "I don't want to hear it. Just tell me what to do so we can get this over with. Then I never have to see you or him again."

He looked away. Was that regret in his eyes?

Oh, for heaven's sake! Did he expect her to feel sorry for him? "I need you to be honest with me now. Is there any chance I might be able to break the bond?" She watched closely to see if he'd do the blinking thing.

"I do not know." He did not blink. *Truth.*

"If Niccolo doesn't come for me, will you let me go?" she asked.

Andrus nodded. "Sure." Blink, blink. *Lie.*

What purpose could there be for him in keeping her? She would never trust him. There could never be anything between them. *Oh no!* "Are you going to kill me?"

His head snapped up, his eyes wide. "Gods, no! How could you speak such words?" No blinks.

Relieved, Helena mentally sighed. "Show me where the archive is."

Step one: find a way to break the bond. Step two: find a way to escape before Niccolo shows up with Reyna. She was done with them all!

⌒

Andrus silently led Helena back through the now empty dining room, through a large formal sitting room, to a hidden staircase behind the bookshelf. It was all too *Scooby-Doo* for her liking.

Andrus swiped the cobwebs from the doorway and hit the switch at the top of the stairs. An old, dusty bulb flickered on. Was the key to her freedom really down there? She sucked in a lungful of air over her shoulder, reacting to the stale, dank odor wafting up from the stairwell.

Unaffected, Andrus descended quickly. Helena, not wanting to be left alone, scurried close behind down the creaking stairs. They reached another doorway at the bottom, where Andrus hit another light switch.

A long string of bulbs, which ran the length of the ceiling, illuminated the room. "It's the size of an airplane hangar," Helena mumbled under her breath.

Shelves, which covered every square inch of the brick walls, ran the length of the room. Freestanding wooden shelves, which nearly touched the ceiling, ran down the center of the cavernous room like stacked dominoes, leaving passages on either side.

"There must be hundreds of thousands of books," Helena said, still unable to believe all this space was hidden beneath the Demilord mansion.

Andrus charged on, not bothering to look at her. About

fifty yards later, toward the center of the library, the room opened up. Andrus stopped. "I'll be back to check on you in a few hours. I'm locking the door so you don't get any ideas."

"Can you at least point me to the right shelf, for crying out loud?" she asked.

Andrus's cold expression didn't change. Was he upset because Helena had told him to pound sand? Wasn't she the injured party?

He replied, "That wall contains records of vampires and other creatures we've extinguished. That wall..." He pointed behind him. "...has all the vampires we've been watching with the potential to turn Obscuro." He pivoted on his heel and walked toward the nearest freestanding shelf. "The rows here hold the records on the queen's guards."

Helena's curiosity peaked. What information would there be about Niccolo? "And the DIY section?"

Andrus looked confused.

She elaborated, "Do-it-yourself? As in divorce."

He looked around the room and pointed to a shelf with twelve inch-thick books. "Those are the legends of the Ancient Ones. Start there." He turned away coldly and left.

Bastard. For as long as she'd live, she would never forgive him. His plan was to swap her for the queen or keep her. Helena didn't like either of those lame plans.

She turned toward the shelves that held the information on the queen's guards and stared at the books, thinking.

She stepped closer to the shelf and cocked her head to one side to read the bindings. They were organized by dates—*2000 BC to 1000 BC?*

"Christ! Oops, before Christ! How old are these books?" she mumbled to herself. *If Niccolo is really thirteen hundred years old, it would mean he was born in . . .* She counted backward in her mind. *The seven hundreds? No wonder he didn't know who Tina Turner was. To him, Bach and Mozart were wild pop stars.*

She reached for the book marked "First Century ~ 1000 AD" and eagerly carried it back to the desk. She flipped open the pages. It contained page after page of names in alphabetical order. She flipped until she reached "DiConti, Niccolo." Her eyes locked on the page with his name in bold print at the header and began absorbing the words. Part of her felt like she was spying; the other part hoped she'd find something that would magically make her hate him; loving him wasn't working out so well.

The first few pages detailed his hometown near Genoa, Italy. Like Niccolo had told her, he'd left home at a young age to fight in the north with his brothers. At the age of thirty-two, he'd disappeared from the human world, but reemerged by the ninth century. Niccolo's reputation in the vampire world was well established as a brutal, savage, unbeatable warrior.

The thousands of accounts of his battles and extermination of rogue vampires were legendary. In one particular battle during the twelve hundreds, Niccolo had been taken by surprise when he and his men arrived in the Amazon expecting to find a group of thirty Obscuros who'd been snacking on the local population. Sadly, communication in those days was slow, and word had not reached Niccolo until twelve months after the outbreak. When they arrived, he and his men found that the Obscuros had been busy creating an army. They were confronted by over three hundred vicious vampires. They were outnumbered with reinforcements months away. He instructed his men to retreat into the jungle. There they would regroup. But Obscuros seized two of his men before they could get away.

"You may take me in their place, and I will not fight you," Niccolo said, according to witnesses. "If you keep them, I will leave here now. But I will return with an army of one thousand, and you will not be killed. We will remove your limbs and let you experience the excruciating pain of your body being bloodless and helpless. Then we will transport you to the queen's dungeons, where you will live for an eternity deprived of blood so you will not heal."

His threat worked. The Obscuros agreed to the swap and released his men. The story said that Niccolo spent the next few months being tortured and drained repeatedly by the Obscuros, who used his blood to become stronger. Helena cringed. She couldn't imagine enduring so much pain. When reinforcements finally arrived to rescue Niccolo, the Obscuros were a hundred times stronger than before. The battle between the queen's army and the evil vampires raged on night after night, each side retreating during the day to recover.

On the sixth night, Niccolo, who had been entombed underground, finally escaped. Witnesses said he clawed his way from the ground, sifted behind the leader of the Obscuros, and took his head. The entire army of Obscuros turned to ash within seconds.

"Why would they die because their leader died?" Helena wondered aloud. She quickly flipped through the pages to find another story, then another and another. All three were accounts of battles where Niccolo had won by capturing and killing the evil vampires' leaders.

That's it! Helena gasped. "Oh my *God*." Andrus hated the queen. He'd told her once that he planned to kill the evil bitch. Crap, Andrus was going to kill Reyna, and with her, every vampire she'd ever made would die.

She hopped up from the desk and ran down the side of the library, up the stairwell, and then pounded furiously on the door. "Andrus! Open this door! I won't let you! Open the goddamned door!" She kicked and threw her fists at the thick wooden door for over ten minutes, but no one came. Finally, she sank to the step.

Eighteen

⌐

The car radio was hammering some odd house music, when Viktor noticed Niccolo clutching the sides of his head in the passenger seat. "Are you all right?"

Niccolo shook his head. "She's in so much pain, I can't think straight."

"Oh. Thought you were going to lecture me again about the timeless, soul-enriching traits of Bach. Or as I call him, Baaalılılıhch." Viktor made a sour face.

Niccolo did not laugh.

"You need to feed, my friend." Viktor handed him a bag of cold blood from a small cooler in the backseat. "Here, this will help you keep up your strength."

The thought of tasting anyone but Helena made his stomach churn. Yet drinking her blood, changing her into a vampire, made his heart crack in two. What on earth was he going to do? Focus. *Bring her back safely first,* he reminded himself.

"I will be fine."

Viktor shook his head. "You are far from fine. As your friend, I am telling you that you are a liability. You couldn't even kill an annoying cocker spaniel. You're too weak."

Viktor was right. Always the voice of reason. But it was Niccolo's decision to defy Andrus's instructions. Niccolo wasn't stupid enough to hand Reyna over. If anything happened to that crazy shrew, he and his men would die. Niccolo also didn't believe for one moment that Andrus would kill Helena as the note said. Not after he'd seen Andrus kissing her so passionately in the bar a few nights ago. The memory made him grind his teeth.

Andrus likely wanted her for himself once he got Reyna and Niccolo out of the picture. How could he have let Helena go off with that cretin? Yes, Niccolo felt devastated by what he'd almost done to her in bed. Yet his need to keep her safe caused him to overreact, a fact he sorely regretted.

Niccolo turned his head and stared out the window toward the wrought iron fence that surrounded the entire Demilord compound. Somewhere on the other side of the thicket was their mansion. And Helena. No vampire had ever successfully penetrated the grounds. It was warded in every possible way. Some said even mosquitoes could not enter.

"I cannot let you go in alone." Niccolo groaned, barely able to speak from the throbbing pain in his head. "She is my bride. My responsibility."

"I won't be alone. We are twenty." Viktor sighed. "My friend, over the centuries you have saved my life in battle more times than I care to count. You kept my family safe so that I could watch my children and grandchildren grow. You stayed by my side when I had to watch each of them die from old age, unable to comfort or help them. You saved me from a life of darkness. Please, brother, it is my time to do this one thing for you."

Niccolo knew Viktor would go regardless. Once he'd made up his mind, he didn't change it. Stubborn bastard. That's why he liked him so much.

"*Bene*, be careful. If anything happens, we shall rendezvous at our meeting spot."

Viktor nodded. "I hope this works." He glanced at Niccolo's tattooed arm.

Niccolo lifted the sleeve of his black T-shirt. "What else could it be for?"

"A useless decoration?"

Niccolo shook his head. "No. Cimil is known for pulling this kind of crap. Did I ever tell you how I found her? About the legend of the Spanish monk I uncovered in an old text?"

Viktor's brow furrowed. "Not sure I want to know."

"Word had traveled to the church about a Mayan legend of a powerful seer in southern Mexico. The monk had been plagued by years of violent dreams of his brothers turning on one another in a murderous rampage. Desperate to stop his nightmares from becoming reality, the monk traveled for months to reach her. And when he finally did, she merely said, 'Sorry. Can't give you the time of day.' But the determined monk wouldn't give up. He stayed in the jungle, living at the edge of the cenote— her portal—waiting for her to pass through, which she did on numerous occasions. Each time, she simply repeated her words."

"I'm guessing the story doesn't end well." Viktor frowned.

Niccolo's eyes grew darker. "The poor monk died of a fever, but the local priest documented that there was a date tattooed across the monk's chest. At his burial, an agitated, strange redhead appeared out of nowhere. She said, 'What the hell happened to him? I gave the guy the date of the massacre so he could stop it! I tattooed the goddamned thing on his chest so he wouldn't forget. I mean, really, just because I didn't know the exact time of day. Men!' "

Niccolo paused. "I'm guessing Cimil gives people help when they ask, but doesn't provide detailed instructions. Either that or she simply enjoys watching them squirm."

Viktor nodded. "Well, now that I'm feeling inspired by your uplifting story, I guess we should test your theory."

Niccolo nodded and reread the tattoo on his arm. It translated as "True to the gods, you shall enter. I brake for leather pants and garage sales."

Niccolo once again felt his stomach churn. Cimil had a cruel sense of humor to create a spell using those words, but she was beyond twisted for tattooing the damned thing on his arm. He focused his thoughts away from throttling her. If luck smiled upon him, there'd be time for that diversion later. For the moment, he had no choice but to trust that she'd carefully planned this moment.

"Are you certain you translated the symbols correctly?"

Niccolo nodded. "*Sì*. And when I see her again, she's going to pay. Especially if I find out her little spell doesn't work."

Viktor opened the car door and stepped onto the dark

street. The other men, who'd been eagerly waiting in a row of black vans behind them, exited their vehicles and melted into the night.

For the first time in a millennium, Niccolo prayed. May his men return unharmed with Helena safely in their possession.

"True to the gods, you shall enter. I brake for garage sales and leather pants."

Dea pazzesca, Cimil. This better work.

Slumped against the locked door, Helena sobbed for over thirty minutes before her wits returned. She couldn't give up. Not yet. Not when Niccolo's life was on the line. It didn't matter what he'd done or how badly his rejection hurt. She still loved him and had to do something to keep Andrus from killing the queen—and, therefore, Niccolo. Sooner or later, Andrus would return to check on her, and she was going to be ready.

She marched back down the stairs and began searching the library for a weapon.

Books, shelves, a desk, and lights. Nothing useful. She did another lap around the enormous room to make sure she didn't miss anything.

She sighed loudly. There had to be another way to warn Niccolo! If he could feel her emotions, could he hear her thoughts, too? Anything was worth a try. *If you can hear me, Niccolo, Andrus wants to kill the queen. Don't come for me. Don't bring Reyna here.*

"He can't hear you, ya know."

Helena jumped. There was a petite woman with long red hair standing in front of her. She wore pink leather hot pants and a half tee with "My Unicorn Poops Rainbows" written in hot-pink glitter.

The woman winked. "But I can."

Helena hated to ask; the woman radiated hazard. "And you are?"

The woman lifted her pasty hand over her heart. "You wound me. I am Cimil, your divine cheerleader and sponsor of chaos. And you are a very, very naughty human." She shook her finger.

"Sorry?" The woman seemed vaguely familiar, but she couldn't quite put her finger on it. "You wouldn't happen to drive a taxi or have a gay brother who gives kissing lessons, would you?" Helena asked.

Cimil pointed innocently at her own chest. "Me? Nooo."

Helena frowned. "Sorry, but who are you again?"

"You should be sorry! You've totally ruined my fun. You just had to make the one choice that would tip the scales of fate toward the bad guys so when the apocalypse comes, they win."

"Apocalypse?"

Cimil perched her hand on one hip and shook her finger again. "Now the other gods are totally peeved at me, and I have to do all the cleanup to set everything on the right path again."

Gods? Cimil? The name suddenly clicked. "Oh my God, you're the one who put Niccolo to sleep."

"First, it's...oh my *goddessss*. Get it right. And second, thank you for finally joining me in the Land of Nooo, Really?" Cimil said.

Helena, who wasn't sure how to react, stared blankly while her mind raced.

Cimil then closed her eyes and took a slow breath. "I am a good goddess. I am kind. I am a good goddess. I am kind." Her eyes flipped open. "All better. Where was I?"

Helena was about to say that she had no clue, but Cimil jumped in again. "Ah yes! I was explaining how you've totally mucked everything up, and now I have to fix it—you can thank me later." She waved her hand through the air.

Helena had the urge to run to the door and begin screaming again—this time for help. Cimil was scary.

"First," Cimil said, "you are correct that Andrus plans to kill Reyna, and therefore, any of her disciples would automatically perish. What you *don't* know is that if the good vampires die, we won't have enough soldiers to fight on our side when the Great War comes. It's the reason we didn't off the queen ourselves. 'Cause she's one crazy bitch I'd like to take down."

Mrs. Kettle, meet your long-lost redheaded step-child...Ms. Pot.

"But you're a goddess. Can't you step in and do something to stop Andrus?" Helena asked.

Cimil rolled her eyes. "Hellooo. What does it look like I'm doing? Does this not scream 'divine intervention'?" She made two fists and started air boxing.

Helena stepped back again. "No, I meant, just go upstairs and stop Andrus and his men from killing Reyna. Lock him up or something."

Cimil froze. "What? Am I speaking the wrong species again? I thought I had that glitch all fixed."

She held her hand to her throat. "Testing. Testing. Nope. I'm speaking human." She began speaking loudly.

"Let me turn up the volume so you understand. Is this better?"

Helena nodded cautiously.

"Good," Cimil bellowed. "If I could stop them, don't you think I would? I can no more intervene with their free will than I can yours." Cimil leaned over and pointed up. "It's against the rules," she whispered, "a major no-no. And the last time we pissed off the Creator, he took away some of our powers."

It was all becoming too much. Vampires, gods, Demilords, and a Creator. What next? Aliens? Vampire aliens? Vampire alien gods? Helena shook it off. "Didn't you put Niccolo to sleep for three hundred years?" she asked.

"Sure, but he asked for my help; that's allowed. Check the rule book." She pointed to a twelve-inch-thick book on the shelf behind her, titled in black, bold letters *RULE BOOK*.

How odd, Helena hadn't noticed that book there before.

"Now, listen up," Cimil snapped. "We haven't got much time before the big apocalyptic kickoff." She looked at the extra-large rhinestone-encrusted watch on her wrist. "Our tasty little warrior cupcake, Niccolo, is supposed to lead the army. Without him, we cannot win. So, not only must the queen and he survive, but the entire queen's army, too."

Helena listened carefully, but didn't know what to say.

"Don't you get it, stupid girl? There is only one person in this story who is not central." Cimil's eyes bulged toward Helena.

Helena hesitantly pointed to herself.

Cimil jumped up and pointed. "Ding, ding, ding!"

"I planned to break our bond. Then he can go on to..." Helena swallowed. "To save the world. And I can"— *try not to die from a broken heart*—"figure out how to move on."

Cimil laughed. "Oh, sweet child. That's where you've taken a wrong turn. You cannot leave him. There is no way to break a bond forged by the universe herself. It's like asking the moon to leave its orbit around Earth, or the cream filling of an Oreo to stop living between those crispy, chocolaty cookies." She licked her lips. "That's just wrong."

"I don't follow."

Cimil shrugged. "They never do. Only the bugs get it, but they are sooo needy. And vengeful. You have no idea." She paused for several awkward moments, rubbing her bottom. Then her head suddenly fell back, and she began staring at the ceiling. She rolled her eyes and shook her head as if listening to someone speak. "Okay. Okay. You win." She looked back at Helena. "Here's the deal-ee-o, baby. Only death will break the bond."

Helena gasped. *Death? That sure was one hell of a way to get a divorce.* "Are you sure?"

"Surer than a cheerleader drinking Four Loko on prom night. If it'll make you feel better, I'll read your future."

Helena stepped forward. What did she have to lose? "What do I need to do?"

Cimil's smile was nothing less than devious. "You must ask for my help."

Helena knew she would regret this, but with so few options at her disposal, what else could she do? "Will you help me?" Helena's voice was filled with dread.

"Thought you'd never ask!" Cimil stepped forward and

gripped the sides of Helena's head and stared deeply into her eyes. Helena could swear she saw fear flicker across Cimil's face.

"Well, that was . . . interesting."

"What did you see?" Helena asked.

"I didn't know you liked garage sales. I love them, too! How exciting." Cimil's joy melted away when Helena didn't share the enthusiasm.

Cimil sighed. "Okay. We'll save the girl talk for later. As I mentioned upon my glorious arrival a few moments ago, the path you are on will result in Niccolo's death. That's bad news for everyone. You must save him, throw yourself in harm's way, be the heroic female. Got it?"

Cimil's words were like a stab to the heart, what was left of it anyway. Could things possibly get any worse?

Sure they can, she reminded herself. An apocalypse sounded pretty darn awful. An apocalypse that the good guys lost sounded worse.

"Did you see anything else? Any other way to save him?"

"Changing your mind about wanting that vampire divorce, are you?"

Helena nodded, but her mind raced. Was she really going to die? There was still so much she wanted to do.

Cimil looked around the room at the books. Several moments passed again.

"Hello?" Helena cautiously waved her hand at Cimil to get her attention.

"Hi. I'm Cimil." She held out her hand.

Helena wanted to scream. Cimil just said that she needed to die and then zoned out. And this was one of the beings who supposedly controlled the world? No wonder it was so messed up.

"Am I really going to die?"

Cimil's face lit up with shock. "Jeez. What kind of goddess do you think I am? We just met, and I only kill people I know."

Yikes. "I have to die in order to save Niccolo so he can help win the Great War. Remember?"

Cimil looked Helena up and down, and then her gaze turned to the book on the desk. "Have you read page five hundred and two?"

"Why? Will that tell me what I need to do?"

"No, but it's a fab story. Reminds me of the time you were marching in the jungle and I lured you to Niccolo." She made a deep voice that sounded like Niccolo's. "*'Come to me, Helena.'* You were so adorable, falling and crying, trying to follow my flashlight through the jungle like a little moth. And wow! The look on your face when you saw him lying there naked. He is one yummy hunk of burning love. Think I can have a go at him? When you're gone, of course."

Helena wanted to pummel Cimil. So it was Cimil who'd orchestrated her encounter with Niccolo. And now she wanted him?

"Why, Cimil? Why go through so much trouble to bring us together only so we'd end up with our hearts shredded to a pulp?"

"That's easy. Your scrumptious vampire asked for my help. He came to me all whiny. 'I don't like the queen. I don't want to kill for her anymore.' Blah, blah, blah," she blathered mockingly. "So, I read his future and made sure he set his sails on the right course—a course where he lives, leads the army, and still has you."

So there was a time when things would have worked

out. Where did she go wrong? Could she fix it? "What did you see when you saw his future?" Helena asked.

"Hmm. Let me see." Cimil tapped the side of her cheek. "You were frolicking on a beach at night—Mexico, I think—splashing and playing in the waves. He was kissing your face and smothering you with love. I've never seen a happier mated pair in all my existence."

Helena felt as though she'd been punched in the stomach. She'd given up her winning lottery ticket to true love and happiness with Niccolo. "What did Niccolo need to do in order to be on that path?"

Cimil replied, "There was a high probability he would have been murdered before you were born—I had to stop that from happening. Then there was the matter of accelerating his falling in love with you." She sighed. "He's such a workaholic. Never stops to reflect, smell the roses. It's just kill, kill, protect, protect with that man. If I hadn't intervened, it would have taken him years to not only take your blood to create the bond, but to truly realize his love for you. So, I set the stage. He wanted his freedom from the queen. I told him you were the key. I also threw him a few curveballs. Told him—and you're gonna bust up when you hear this—he could not bed you, bite you, yada yada." She roared with laughter. "That way he'd focus on getting to know you as a person and not the sexy tigress...grrrr"—she clawed at the air—"that you are."

She snickered and slapped her thigh. "It was hysterical watching him keep his hands off you! OMGsss." She shook her head. "Good times. Good times. Oh! And I told him you needed to be made a vampire, willingly, on the day of your three-month anniversary. That was a big must—or is a big must. Yeah. That one was right...I think. It's hard to keep this stuff straight in my head."

It all explained Niccolo's bizarre behavior. "So you lied to him? It was all a plan to get him to fall in love with me quickly and then lead the army for your war?"

Cimil flashed a devilish grin. "Yes? And...yes again? Protecting one's true love makes for an excellent warrior. Didn't you see how he slaughtered that creep Rodrigo the night you met? Brilliant move on my part, by the way, tipping off the queen—I knew she'd send that loser to check things out, and I was itching to collect his soul. Cha-ching!"

Damn her! This was all some cruel joke. But on the bright side...

"He really does love me?"

"Of course. Weren't you listening?" Cimil pointed up. "The universe herself has destined your joining. You were meant for each other."

"Then why can't it still work out?"

"Looks like your boy Andrus there has taken a liking to you. Totally unexpected, you know, and it will all end terribly. He kills Niccolo. You kill Andrus. And we're left with that crazy cow, Reyna, and lose the Great War." Cimil made a sour face and turned her thumb down. "Booo. Terrible ending."

"Why does Andrus try to kill Niccolo? I thought he was after Reyna?"

Cimil shrugged. "Ask him. Likely some competitive, jealousy bull crap. What do I care? He's not nearly as entertaining as Niccolo. Especially with that bond you two share—it's the most powerful I've ever seen. Oh! How about the time he was PMSing? Does it get any better than that? PMSing vampire men! Hysterical!"

A blind rage flew over Helena. "Glad to see the destruction of our lives is so damn amusing to you! You know what? Maybe the world is better off ending in a giant apocalypse! At least we won't have to put up with your insanity!"

Cimil shrugged. "Hey, I've been alive for a very, very long time. Boring," she sang out. "Gotta do something for kicks, and a good apocalypse every now and then fills the cracks. It's like the Super Bowl for us gods . . . but without the beer and everyone could die. Fun, right?"

Helena wanted to strangle Cimil. It really *was* all just a big game to her, but Helena would lose everything, including her life. At least she could save Niccolo; that was something. And she'd die knowing he really loved her. And hopefully the good guys would win, saving the people she loved, too. But what if this was another lie? She just told Helena that she'd lied and manipulated Niccolo. The woman was obviously insane. But was she evil? Were there bad gods? Helena had no clue. Christ! This sucked!

"I hope the universe has a big payback planned for you, Cimil. I hope she mates you to a toad and he gets eaten by some animal so you can suffer a broken heart for eternity."

Cimil frowned. "Oh, believe you me. I've starred in that movie four times! Hey, what made you such a bitter pill?"

Helena had never been so angry and heartbroken in her entire life. "I don't know, maybe it has something to do with you telling me I found the love of my life and now I have to die to save him. Could also be that there's an apocalypse coming so everyone I love is in jeopardy? Take your damned pick!"

"Isn't it so exciting?" Cimil clapped and jumped as if on a pogo stick. "You're going to love it! Did I tell you that your auntie Cimil is also Goddess of the Underworld? We're going to be together for a very, very long time."

Underworld? "You mean—I'm going to hell?"

"Silly, where else would a vampire's bride go? Heaven?" Cimil burst out laughing. "You're a riot, girl!"

Nineteen

Niccolo pressed the heel of his palm to his throbbing forehead. In his other hand was a bag of ice-cold blood. His brain felt like the victim of a bear trap.

Helena. She's afraid. She was also feeling loss and love, the sting of betrayal and rage, all at the same time.

Then suddenly, it melted away. He felt nothing. *Bloody inferno!* What was happening to her?

He clutched the bag firmly in both hands. *I must go to her. I must be strong to fight.* He thrust the bag to his mouth and pierced the plastic with his fangs. The blood slid down his throat. *I will not retch, I will not retch...*

His stomach churned painfully. The air seemed to swirl violently around him. He was going to either pass out or vomit.

Think of Helena. Think of Helena.

He swallowed hard and managed to hold it down. He felt his strength returning immediately. He grabbed another bag from the cooler behind the passenger seat and drank it down quickly.

He lifted the sleeve of his black tee and recited the annoying words etched in his skin. He knew the phrase actually worked because he'd watched his men slip over the gate and into the stand of trees. Niccolo moved out of the vehicle and strapped two swords over his back. He gave the leather straps crossing his chest a quick tug and then turned to the iron fence.

There, standing just out of reach on the opposite side of the iron slats, was Andrus. His face was all smiles, smug and mocking.

Niccolo unsheathed his swords and approached with deadly determination. He would take Andrus's head if it was the last thing he did. If he had to gnaw through the metal fence, he'd goddamned do it.

The Demilord held out his palm. "Don't go there, Executioner."

He threw something metallic and large over the fence. Viktor's sword landed at Niccolo's feet.

Andrus blew on his fingernails and then buffed them on his dark shirt. "We've got your men locked up in our dungeon. You did a piss-poor job of training them, you know. Taking their weapons was like taking candy from a baby."

They are still alive. Thank the gods. Niccolo only needed to buy a moment and think. "You speak from experience. Why am I not surprised you pick on babies?"

Andrus frowned. "Funny. Let's see if you're in the mood to crack jokes tomorrow after we stake your men to the ground and let them bake in the sun until they wither and die. I think one is named Viktor, is he not? Your right hand for almost a millennium? Then there's always Helena... I bet she'd make a nice snack for a few of your hungry vampires."

"They'd never touch her. In fact, they'd give their lives to protect her."

Andrus laughed. "Not if I drain them to the point where their hunger overshadows their loyalty toward you."

Fury engulfed Niccolo's mind. He stepped toward the fence, reaching for Andrus.

"Uh-oh," Andrus snorted. "You're angry and aren't thinking straight. Remember, you can still save them all if you bring me Reyna."

"Do I look like a fool, Andrus? You'll kill the queen, and we'll die anyway."

Andrus shrugged. "But you'll have saved Helena."

"I'll be dead. You'll have no reason to let her go. Gods only know what you'll do to her. After all, didn't you say you like to hurt babies?"

Andrus growled, "Don't be vile, Niccolo. That's even beneath a bloodsucker like you. I'll forgive you anyway. I'm in a gracious mood today. I'll give you a chance to take Helena somewhere safe before I take Reyna's head."

Niccolo did the mental math. This was not a simple choice. If Niccolo somehow managed to hand Reyna over to the Demilords and they killed her, any vampire with her blood—which was likely the entire population—would perish. On the bright side, that population would include Obscuros. With them gone, hundreds of thousands of innocent human lives would be spared.

If he brought Reyna to Andrus, he could also save Helena. He could sift her away somewhere safe—his island in Greece. He'd show her where his treasures and money were hidden. There was enough wealth for her to buy a new identity and stay away from Andrus for the rest of her life. Perhaps after Niccolo was dead, her heart might heal and she'd find love again. She could be happy.

As much as he loved her and wanted the Obscuros dead, could he bear the guilt of letting so many good vampires die? There were a lot who had not asked for their fate, and yet they accepted it and chose to fight for good.

No. He could not make this choice for so many. He would not play gods. There had to be another way. He needed to buy time.

Niccolo nodded. "I will bring you Reyna, but I need a week to get her here."

Andrus shook his head. "So you can gather your forces, attempt another rescue, and save Helena? Not happening."

"Reyna is powerful. I cannot force her to come. It will be a question of persuasion, and with her, this is very difficult. I need time."

Andrus turned his back to Niccolo. He began strolling casually away through the woods. "I want her here before sunrise tomorrow. If you don't show, Helena will become food. And your men...toasted leeches."

It was almost midnight in California. He had about seven hours to figure this out.

⌒

A loud commotion from the top of the stairs woke Helena. The clank of metal and then the unmistakable sound of muffled screams echoed down the stairwell into the basement library. The door flew open, and a body tumbled down toward her. Then another and another. She stared with disbelief as she recognized one face in the tangled mess of arms and legs covered in black leather.

Viktor. "Oh my God!" She jumped forward to the heap of bodies spilling onto the floor from the stairwell.

She tugged at an arm on the top of the heap and slid the giant man to the side. His long black shaggy hair covered his face. She rolled the next man off the top of the heap and kept rolling him. It was Sentin! The next was Viktor. They were all unconscious.

She gently slapped Viktor's cheek. "Can you hear me? Wake up, Viktor. Are you okay?"

Suddenly, Viktor's bright blue eyes slammed open. With vampire speed, he was up with his back against a bookshelf in a defensive posture. His face softened immediately when he recognized Helena.

He rushed to her. "You are alive!"

Viktor's eyes locked on Sentin and the other man. He rushed over to check them. "They'll be okay," he said. "We were hit from behind. We're lucky they didn't take our heads."

Viktor swept up the stairs and returned to her side in the blink of an eye. "The door is warded. I cannot pass."

Helena began to babble hysterically. She told Viktor about her conversation with Cimil, including her instructions to read the story, which she hadn't done. He listened carefully, then finally responded, "Did she indicate how you must die?"

Helena stepped back. *Nice to see you care, buddy.* "No. Are you going to kill me?"

Thankfully, Viktor looked horrified by the thought. "Niccolo is like a brother to me. I would give my life to save him or his mate."

His words touched her. "Cimil was pretty clear I have to die."

Viktor paused for a moment. "Cimil is crazy and manipulative. We should question everything she's told you. Show me the book."

She walked to the desk in the middle of the library where the text was set out. Helena picked up the thick leather-bound pages. It was as light as a feather despite its size. Her fingers instantly began to tingle.

She dropped it onto the desk and looked at Viktor.

Viktor studied it for a moment before deciding to open the cover. "It says it's written by the Oracle of Delphi."

Helena vaguely remembered the stories of the oracle from history class, but nothing about any books.

She watched as Viktor thumbed the page. "There! Did you see that?"

The words on the pages faded one at a time and were replaced by new ones every few seconds. "Holy *crap*! What is that?" Helena sputtered.

"The legends are true," Viktor whispered. "They say the book tells the future. As the future changes, so do the words."

Helena stared at the book in silence.

"What page did Cimil instruct you to read?" Viktor asked.

She didn't want to answer his question. She didn't want to know the future. What if she found her worst fears written on the pages? "I can't remember."

Viktor gave her hand a gentle squeeze. "Helena, don't be afraid. I'll do everything in my power to turn the tides in your favor. As you can see, the future is not unalterable."

Helena looked up into his deep blue eyes glowing with determination and sincerity. She finally understood why Niccolo cared for Viktor like a brother. He was a good man. Or vampire—whatever.

"Five hundred and two."

Viktor flipped to the page.

They both gasped at the same time.

"Helena, don't even think about it," Viktor barked. "I'd rather face the fires of hell than do that."

Helena looked at her watch—12:01 in the morning. *So ironic. I met Niccolo three months ago today.*

"But Cimil said I have to die to save him! And look at the goddamned book, Viktor! Look at it! You can, and you will."

Twenty

Niccolo rang the red call button at the front gate of the Demilord compound—*Camp Fucktard*—and groaned as the sun hit his back. It would drain what little energy he'd managed to gain from the small sips of blood he'd kept down.

A deep voice answered over the speaker box. "Wait there."

"Before I turn to ash, if you don't mind."

The sun fully emerged over the horizon just as Andrus appeared a moment later with a large sword strapped to his back.

"Where is Reyna?" he barked through the wrought iron gate.

Niccolo crossed his arms over his chest. "I'll take you to her once Helena and my men call me from somewhere safe."

Andrus raised his dark brow. "Nice try, vampire. How

do I know you really have your queen and won't double-cross me?"

Niccolo reached into his pocket, punched the speaker button on his cell phone, and then held it out for Andrus.

Reyna's voice roared through the phone. "Niccolo! I can hear you. Untie me immediately! You worthless pile of dog—"

"As you can hear," Niccolo said coldly, "she's ready and waiting for you."

Reyna continued to scream obscenities as Andrus paused, thinking it over.

"Three hundred years, right? That's how long you've waited for your revenge," Niccolo urged Andrus.

"Sift her here," Andrus demanded.

"She's bound with silver chains; I cannot. You'll have to go to her."

Andrus's eyes narrowed. "Where?"

"Somewhere in Europe. I'll sift you there," Niccolo responded.

"I understood vampires could only sift a few miles at a time."

Niccolo smiled with a cocky grin. "What can I say? I'm awesome."

Andrus cocked one brow, turned his back, and pulled out his cell. "Let them go." He paused and listened. "Then open the hidden door so they can sift away with the girl." Andrus hit the face of the phone and shoved it deep in his black leather pants before he turned to Niccolo. "It will be a moment."

"How were your men able to capture them so easily?" Niccolo asked.

Andrus shrugged. "What can I say? I'm awesome."

Niccolo laughed. "Come, come now. I'll be dead within the hour. What's a little sharing amongst friends?" In truth, if he survived this, it might be useful information.

Andrus paused for a moment, still standing out of arm's reach on the other side of the gate. "Let's just say the gods gave us more than their blood."

"Divine weapons?"

Andrus shrugged again. "Something like that. We were created for the sole purpose of taking out vampires. Got to have some tools."

"I sometimes wonder," Niccolo said with regret, "what we could have accomplished if we'd worked together."

"You're partially to blame for my life being taken."

"I'm quite certain I am not responsible for your situation in any way."

"Where did you go, Niccolo?" he drawled scathingly. "You disappeared off the face of the planet, and without you leading the army, everything fell apart; the Obscuros began multiplying like cockroaches. Humans would have ended up enslaved if the gods hadn't stepped in and created us."

Niccolo debated telling Andrus the truth. Would it change his desire to take Andrus's head? No. Andrus had used Helena's life as a bargaining chip for the queen. Andrus wanted to kill Reyna and end all vampires, even those who lived according to the Pact and served a crucial purpose in this world—culling the evil human population. Yes, perhaps a bit of the truth is what this man needed.

"My absence was involuntary."

Andrus snarled. "What do you mean?"

"Divine intervention is what I mean."

"I don't believe you," Andrus growled.

"Ask Cimil yourself." Niccolo crossed his arms. "It's also clear the Demilords can't handle the job alone. The world needs good vampires."

Andrus laughed. "Can't handle it? I think we can."

"Really? When I was taken by Cimil, the planet was in fairly decent shape. I returned to an Obscuro"—*oh, what's that phrase Sentin likes? Ah!*—"cluster fuck. Makes me wonder. Whose side are you really on?"

Andrus growled, "My side. We gave up killing Obscuros. It was futile. We'd kill one, three more would pop up—like fucking immortal Whac-A-Mole."

Niccolo's phone rang. He looked at the number. Viktor. "Are you with Helena?"

There was a pause. "She is here." Viktor sounded distraught.

Niccolo stared directly at Andrus as he spoke to Viktor. "Are you on your way to the safe house? I don't want those bastards to find her."

"Yeah, but there's something I gotta tell you," Viktor said.

Niccolo nodded. "I will call you very shortly, Viktor." He hit End. Unfortunately, whatever Viktor had to say needed to wait. Right now, everything hung in the balance.

He turned his attention back to Andrus, who seemed hell-bent on finishing his point. "As you can see, we found a much better solution to killing Obscuros. We'll just kill your queen and watch your race dwindle to nothing. The vampires who remain will be hunted. Ah, the smell of retirement grows near." He took a stoic breath. "All right, then. I held up my end of the bargain. Now take me to Reyna."

The gate creaked open, and Andrus stepped out. "No tricks, Niccolo. There is nowhere you or your men can hide from us. And don't think we can't get our hands on Helena again if we wish. We have friends in very high places."

Niccolo swallowed his anger. "Are you certain you wish to do this? You are half vampire. This could end badly for you, too, if Reyna dies."

Andrus stepped forward. "I'm willing to take the chance that my other half saves me."

"So be it." He grabbed Andrus by the shoulders. "Hang on."

Andrus blinked and suddenly found himself in a long, dark tunnel. A wave of dizziness struck him, and he stepped to the side, his feet landing in a shallow puddle.

A hand grabbed his shoulder to steady him. "The effect will wear off in a moment," Niccolo said.

"Where the hell are we?" Andrus asked, sliding his sword from his back. The tunnel looked like a sewer, but the smell did not match. It was dank and moldy, but not overly offensive.

Niccolo turned and began walking. "Barcelona. These are ancient catacombs built by the Christians in the thirteen hundreds. The Obscuros used them for hiding during the daytime." Niccolo continued marching at a fast clip. "They kept humans down here for food, too. I obviously put a stop to them some time ago."

That explained the bones he'd just stepped over.

"Soon the world won't need to worry about such things." Andrus's nerves sizzled with anticipation.

After several minutes of trudging in the darkness Andrus barked, "Where the hell is she? You better not be fucking with me, vampire. If I don't call my men within the hour, they'll recapture your Helena."

He wanted to brag about how he'd made certain Helena had a phone before she'd left the Demilord compound. Like the one she'd carried before, it had GPS.

"I have Reyna restrained with silver in a cell," Niccolo answered dryly.

Andrus's ears perked. He suddenly heard the faint sound of Reyna screaming to be untied. It was like nails on a chalkboard. He hated the sound of her voice. He'd had nightmares featuring the sound of it for centuries.

They marched on until Niccolo suddenly stopped and turned to Andrus. "This way." Niccolo leaned into the stone wall of the tunnel. A doorway ground open. It led to a long, narrow passage. Reyna's raging voice poured through the air. "Enjoy, my friend."

"Where the hell do you think you're going?" Andrus growled.

Niccolo turned to leave the way they'd come. "If you don't mind, I'd like to spend the last few moments of my long existence with the woman I love."

"Is it that you really care for Helena, or is it simply the bond?"

Niccolo's eyes flickered. "She is everything to me. I only wish I'd realized it sooner. It is my only regret."

Life was full of regrets. Some things simply could not be helped.

"Niccolo! You fucking idiot! I can smell you. Get your ass in here and untie me, or I'll have your head!" Reyna screamed.

"Good luck." Niccolo was gone in the blink of an eye.

Andrus turned his head toward the sound of Reyna's voice. This was it. The moment that would change the world.

The narrow passageway was dark and long, but there was a tiny flicker of light ahead. Sword drawn, his hand trembled with anticipation. He hadn't seen Reyna since the night she'd shoved him into a steel box and shipped him off to Mexico to be transformed by the gods.

With each step, his heart thumped louder and harder. It was as if the vampire blood in his veins—her blood— was calling out to its maker. Thoughts of Helena suddenly entered his mind once again. When he'd met the spirited young woman, she was so desperate to divorce Niccolo and start her life over. She'd asked him how to break the bond with the vampire. Now he suddenly knew the answer to her question.

There's only one way to rid yourself of a vampire— death, preferably the vampire's.

He reached the end of the passageway. There was a narrow steel-plated door. Light poured from a gap along the side with the hinges. He pushed. The door swung open, and Andrus lunged into the small, dark chamber. Several candles were burning in the corner, and there in the middle of the room was a small table and a chair.

Empty.

Andrus's heart stopped as he spotted Reyna standing to his side. She grabbed him, threw him onto his back, and pinned him to the floor.

Reyna straddled him, a wide, evil grin stretched across her face. "Hello, Andrus, honey. You and I are going to have a long, long talk, and then I have a little revenge of my own to dish."

Niccolo was surprised by how well his plan had worked. It actually seemed a little too easy. Initially, he'd debated whether or not to tell the queen about the Demilord's plans to assassinate her. Reyna was known for being hot-headed and vengeful. But he figured if he could convince her to play this out his way, she could stop Andrus and save Helena and his men.

He slipped his phone from his pocket.

"Yes?" Viktor answered.

"It's over, my brother. My plan B went off without a hitch."

It was one of the reasons Niccolo never lost—he thoroughly planned elaborate contingencies for multiple scenarios.

Viktor let out a long breath. "I knew you wouldn't let us down."

"There is more," Niccolo added. "The queen granted our freedom in exchange for delivering Andrus."

What I do not know yet is my fate. Will I still end up in the queen's dungeon as Cimil predicted?

"You, we, are free. If you choose to fight Obscuros, it will be your choice. It will be on your own terms."

"Thank you, Niccolo. I'm speechless."

Niccolo had spent so long dreaming of the day he would be free from Reyna, and yes, it felt better than he'd imagined—even if he did not know how long that freedom would last since he'd not fulfilled the prophecy—but giving his men this gift was an even greater joy.

"Are you and the men in the safe house? Is Helena all right?" Niccolo asked. The safe house was a location they'd prepared ahead of time with supplies—extra weapons, a medical bag, and bagged blood—before they went into any risky situation. They sometimes used one of Niccolo's homes since he had one in almost every major city, but many times, they'd rent a room at a hotel within sifting distance for the other men.

Today they didn't want to take any chances. The Demilords knew too much about Niccolo, so they'd rented the penthouse at the Fairmont in San Francisco. "Yes, she's shaken up, but otherwise"—Viktor paused—"intact."

He registered that something was wrong. "I'll be right there."

"Niccolo, I-I will not be here."

Had his ears heard correctly? "Sorry?"

"I have something I need to do ... something which has waited much too long."

Niccolo did not want to pry, but Viktor was like a brother. "If there is anything I can do to help, don't hesitate to ask."

"Thank you. You have always been too kind to me. I hope someday to pay back the favor."

In all his years, Viktor had never behaved in such a sentimental manner. It was odd, to say the least, but perhaps he was simply overwhelmed with joy. Or maybe...

"You're going to look for *her*, aren't you?" Niccolo asked.

Viktor had dreamed of a blonde woman every night for the last five hundred years. On several occasions, Niccolo had prodded Viktor to look for her. There was a reason for everything, and there had to be a reason this strange woman haunted Viktor's slumber.

There was a long pause before he answered. "I haven't decided yet. I have other demons to put to bed first."

"*Bene*. Be safe, Viktor. If you need anything, call."

"Good-bye, Niccolo. Forgive me."

The signal dropped.

Forgive him? For leaving? Viktor's sense of loyalty knew no boundaries. He'd have to make sure Viktor understood how grateful he was for his friendship. Later, of course. Because right now, it was time to reunite with Helena.

Niccolo hadn't had much time to think about what he would do when he finally saw her; there was so much to say. Should he start with how sorry he was for not giving her his heart from the first moment they'd met? Or perhaps ask her forgiveness for being so selfish and thinking only of his freedom and the prophecy? What about his insanely stupid move to let her go with Andrus so she could be free from him?

No, he would start with saying how much he loved her. He quickly sifted back to the penthouse in New York to get the ring—the real one—he'd had made for her months earlier. The one he'd first given her was a fake. What an idiot he'd been. He'd thought to limit her means until her transformation in case she tried to run. Without money, she wouldn't have gotten far—or so he thought. What he'd ended up doing was putting her in more danger by pushing her into the arms of Andrus. Now he would make everything right. The three-carat stone had been in his family for generations before it had come to him. It was the one item he'd kept from his mortal life. Now he would give it to the woman who made his existence mean something.

He sifted to the posh hotel suite—their safe house for this mission. It had rich green carpets and drapes, a spacious living room with a big-screen television, a full bar, and several large bedrooms. He glanced around the room, but the place appeared empty. Where had everyone gone?

There was a note on the table from Sentin: *Thought you might need some privacy. Went fishing.*

Niccolo knew that meant they were halfway to Bacalar, Mexico, by now. He had recently acquired a villa on the lake just for them after his return from hibernation. Niccolo liked the idea of giving the men a place that was warm and peaceful where they could fish at night— merely for sport, of course. But there was also something about the area where Cimil's cenote stood that called to him. Perhaps because it was the very place that his fate had taken a turn toward his beloved Helena.

With Niccolo's sensitive hearing, he realized that Helena was in the shower. He thought about joining her, but she might not be ready to forgive him yet. He sat on the couch and waited anxiously; he paced and sat again, returning to a pace while he practiced his forgiveness speech.

Finally, the water shut off, and he heard the bathroom door creak open. The scent of Helena, shampoo, and soap filled the air.

"Is someone there?" Helena called out from the bedroom.

Here goes. "We are alone, *mio cuore*," he responded from the living room.

Helena quickly appeared in the doorway wearing nothing but a plush white towel. Her large blue eyes immediately widened when she saw Niccolo. She had a bandage on her wrist, and he could see splotchy deep black bruises running up her arm. She must have fought Andrus. She also looked thinner and pale, as though she hadn't eaten or slept in days. Had Andrus chained her up or hurt her? Niccolo pushed away his thoughts of taking Andrus's head for mistreating her. *Andrus is dead by now or soon will be. I need to be content with that.*

He slowly stood, but did not approach. He needed to look at her, soak her in.

Despite the apparent fatigue, she was more glorious and beautiful than he'd remembered. Her plump lips, her full breasts, her curvy hips...she was almost too beautiful. His heart wanted to jump from his chest and weep with contentment. Helena was everything to him. How could he have been so foolish to think he could let her go?

He would find a way to keep her human and safe from his world. *Even if we only have hours or days left together.*

But what was she thinking and feeling? Did she hate him for all that he'd done to her? He reached out with his mind to sample her emotions. Anger. Pain. Fear. And...love.

A wave of relief washed over him. She still loved him.

"Helena, I know you have no reason to forgive me, but I hope you will." *While there is still time for us.*

Helena fidgeted with a corner of the towel near her bare knee, exposing her upper thigh. Niccolo balled his fists to keep from pouncing. He wanted to take her to bed more than he'd ever wanted anything in his entire existence.

"I heard the good news about your freedom," she said in a quiet tone. "Congratulations. I guess the prophecy wasn't right after all."

Niccolo winced. So she knew about the prophecy. "Cimil?" he guessed.

Helena nodded. "She paid me a visit while I was with Andrus."

"What did she say?"

Helena looked down at her feet. "Nothing coherent, really."

Niccolo felt relieved. He was not going to tell Helena how the likely outcome of his story was ending up in the queen's dungeon—*ninety-nine point nine-nine-nine percent, according to Cimil*—which he would do everything in his power to prevent since Helena would feel his pain, too.

No. Death would be the answer. This way, Helena would be free from their bond.

Before I go...

"Cimil was right. You are my one true love." Niccolo continued to hold back. He needed Helena with every cell in his body, but he wanted the choice to be hers. He listened carefully to her heart. It was pounding furiously in unison with his own.

"Niccolo, I want you to know something." She stepped toward him from the bedroom doorway. Drops of water slid down her shoulders from her damp hair. "I know you pushed me to Andrus because you thought you were trying to protect me."

"You're not angry with me?"

She was angry at someone. He could feel the emotion radiating from her. Andrus was the likely answer.

Helena shook her head and took another step. "Not anymore. I'm just grateful to see you again. I love you."

Niccolo could no longer refrain from touching her. He closed the remaining gap between them and pulled Helena into his arms. She looked up at him, her eyes filled with so much affection he thought he would die from joy.

"I love you, Helena. I will love you until my last breath. Please forgive me. I thought if Andrus had a way to break our bond, I should give you that chance."

"No. I'm afraid you're stuck with me, vampire. Until... until death do us part."

Maybe she did know about the consequences of the prophecy going unfulfilled? Didn't matter now. They had this moment. He'd take it.

He dipped his head and covered her mouth with his. The sweet scent of her clean, warm skin filled his lungs. His groin swelled instantly. Every fantasy he'd ever had of her flashed in his mind. He must have her.

He slid his hand through her damp curls to the back of her head and deepened the kiss. Over thirteen hundred years of living, and he'd never felt anything so euphoric.

He kissed down the side of her neck. "Ask anything you want of me, Helena. Anything at all. Your own island. A small country. Anything. It is yours."

Helena whispered, "I want... you. Just you." She dropped her towel onto the floor.

Niccolo's breath escaped him. She was so beautiful. So perfect. The soft curves of her hips. Her silky, creamy skin that glowed with life. Her round, full breasts. The golden-brown curls between her legs. He would sample every inch of her tonight. He would savor every moment. Because whatever change she'd provoked inside his heart had affected his body, too. He longed to be inside her, to make love to her.

Yet his savage vampire side that called for her sweet blood was now completely under control. *The power of love.*

Niccolo dropped to his knees, wanting to worship at her feet as though at a sacred altar. He nuzzled her stomach. He spread kisses over her hip. He moved his hands up the back of her thighs and cupped her round bottom. Like him, she seemed to be lost in the moment of their bodies touching, the sensation of lust running between them. His erection throbbed painfully, but there was one thing he wanted to do before sweeping her into his arms and taking her to bed. He pulled her real engagement ring from his pocket.

He gently took her hand and trailed kisses down her wrist before sliding the ring on her finger. He looked up at her face.

A glorious smile swept across it. "What's this?" She held out her hand.

Now the moment was perfect. "This is the ring I should have given you—a priceless family heirloom. I still want to complete the ceremony with you so that you feel like my real wife."

She tilted her head to one side. "I don't need a wedding. I am already yours, vampire. Forever."

He smiled. He knew they wouldn't have forever, but he'd savor every moment.

"In that case, there is one last thing we must do to make it official. I must take you to bed."

Helena laughed. "What are you waiting for? I'm not getting any younger."

Twenty-One

⌒

Niccolo was going to die.

And Helena had to stop it. Not just because she loved him, but because the lives of everyone she'd ever loved were at risk, too.

Yes, it was possible Cimil could be wrong, but who in their right mind would roll the dice on something so important? Maybe that was the reason this was her destiny; she understood and respected the impact one life could have on the other billion life-forms on the planet. One life-form, a virus, could kill millions. Another life-form, a scientist in a lab, could save millions. The power of one should never be underestimated.

She chuckled to herself. If she survived, she'd have to change her official career from evolutionary biologist to evolutionary paranormal spiritual scientist. *Sounds like a perfect new religion for California.*

Speaking of the impact one could have, she looked up

at Niccolo and wondered how many specks of dust, how many millions of stars, drops of rain, births and deaths, flakes of snow, and days of sunshine it all took for the world to evolve in such a way for the universe to bring her the one person who'd changed her life. And now, the two of them were together in this perfect moment.

He's evolutionary perfection. She didn't want to waste any more time thinking of the task to come and all that was riding on her. Niccolo loved her. She loved him. They had this moment together. It had to be enough.

He studied her briefly. Then he scooped her into his arms and carried her to the king-size bed. The room glowed softly from the muted sunshine filtering through the thick curtains. The bed linens were her favorite: soft white sheets and a fluffy down comforter. If they had actually had a human wedding today as planned, she would have picked a hotel and a room just like this one for their wedding night.

Niccolo laid her gently on the bed and began peeling away his own clothes while his thirsty gaze raked over her naked body.

Perhaps as a sign that he, too, had changed, she noticed he wasn't wearing a stitch of black. He wore a soft white linen shirt and faded blue jeans. She sighed. He was so sexy that her mouth literally watered.

My tasty man candy. His broad shoulders were twice the width of hers. He was larger and stronger than life.

What she loved most, aside from the depths of his soul-filled eyes, was the sleek, hard lines of his stacked muscles and the slight golden glow of his skin. Okay. She had to admit there was one other part of him she might like better. And that part was currently hard, ready, and bulging against the fly of his jeans.

She stared at him as he slowly unbuttoned his shirt and let it drop to the floor. His thick black waves of dark hair hung just past his shoulders, giving him a wild look. His stomach rippled as he reached for the top button of his pants.

Dark eyes twinkling with passion, he released his pulsing erection. It was long and thick, and Helena had dreamed for months of how it would feel when he slid it inside her.

For weeks, he'd been part of her mind and heart. But her body had been missing out on the fun, and that was just wrong. *Poor, poor body.*

The moment he shed his jeans, she reached to pull him on top of her. She pushed her lips to his and glided her fingers down, letting the back of her hand graze his washboard stomach before gripping his solid cock.

He gasped and pulled her hand away. "I'm not sure I'll be able to contain myself if you do that."

She smiled. The thought of bringing him over the edge almost made her burst. "I know what you mean."

He slowly moved over her, nestling himself between her legs. He kissed her with a wild frenzy while grinding himself against her. It wasn't enough; she wanted him deep inside.

She broke the kiss. "What are you waiting for?"

Niccolo smirked and ran his hand over the side of her face. "Patience, my love, patience."

He slid down her body, trailing kisses over her neck and breasts. He lovingly savored each nipple, paying respect to each before continuing the journey down, down, down. *Oh, okay. Maybe I can wait a few more minutes.*

He stopped.

Oops, belly button detour? Would he ever get to the other place? She was ready to explode. She ached for his touch on her soft flesh. "Please, Niccolo."

"Please what?" he asked with a wicked smile, gazing up at her with his dark eyes.

"Please, please...please me." *Wasn't that a Beatles song?*

"I love the sound of you begging," he said, his voice deep and velvety.

"How about the sound of me crying hysterically if you don't—*oooh*," she moaned as he moved his mouth between her legs and plunged his tongue inside.

She shuddered as she instantly found her release. He didn't relent as she grabbed fistfuls of sheets beside her and quivered under his tongue. Her chest rising and falling rapidly, all she could hear was the thundering sound of her own heart. "That was... It was... amazing."

"Only a warm-up, my bride." He crawled up her body like a predator ready to pounce. "Just relax. We'll take it slow."

She shook her head. "Not slow. Fast and hard."

Niccolo didn't bother questioning. Maybe he couldn't. Maybe her command was all he needed to lose the tender restraint he'd been showing her. He positioned himself at her entrance and brought his mouth to hers once again, lapping and panting as he slowly sunk his hard flesh down her passage. She felt a twinge of pain as he pushed deeper. She let out a moan she wasn't expecting, and he eased back.

"You're so tight and slick. So warm," he said in a husky voice saturated with sex. "It's like my cock died and went to heaven."

She stifled a laugh.

"The smile on your face is almost as good as the other expression you just had," he said.

"Which was?" she whispered.

"Pure pleasure." He thrust deep inside her again, taking her breath away.

The sting subsided almost immediately. Now all she felt was the delicious friction of him pumping into her, filling her over and over again. She moved her hands over his back, feeling the solid muscles work beneath his smooth skin. Everything about him liquefied her. Suddenly a scream escaped her mouth as he sank deeper, sending her over the edge once again. A moment later, he followed her with one long, hard, final push.

Panting, he collapsed on top of her, burying his face in her neck.

It was done. She was no longer a virgin, and Niccolo was truly her vampire husband.

Until death do us part.

Nearly comatose with euphoria after three more hours of wild lovemaking, Helena stared at the ceiling, realizing why vampire divorce was unheard of. Because if the other vampire males were one-half the lover that Niccolo was—well, why would any woman leave? Then there was that whole death-is-the-only-way-out thing. That made it a little harder to call it quits. She wondered what the human divorce rate would be if they faced the same circumstances?

"Thank you, Helena," Niccolo finally said after a few silent moments and squeezed her close in his arms.

Eyes closed and barely able to move from absolute bliss overload, she asked, "For?"

"Forgiving me. You have brought me more happiness in one day than I've known my entire existence."

Helena's heart fluttered with guilt. *Oh, gods. If he only knew.* "Niccolo, there's something we need to discuss."

"What, my love?"

Could she tell him the truth about what had happened at the Demilord compound? Viktor swore that Niccolo would never forgive either of them.

"You want to know what happened to Andrus, don't you?" he growled.

"No. I was going to..." He'd piqued her curiosity. What had happened to Andrus? Yeah, he betrayed her, lied to her, and held her prisoner. But nonetheless, she still cared about him. She knew what it was like to do stupid, irrational things when backed into a corner. "You didn't kill him, did you?"

Niccolo snarled. "How can you care after what he did?"

She sat up. "What he did was wrong, but he didn't lay a finger on me."

Niccolo looked confused. "Then who hurt you?" he demanded. "There are bruises on your shoulders, you look like you weren't fed, and there's a bandage on your arm. Somebody sure the hell did something to you. Which one of his men was it! Who hurt you?"

Could she tell him the truth? She had to try. She had to tell him everything. "Viktor did it, but—"

Niccolo flew from the bed and slid on his pants.

"Niccolo! Wait! Where are you going?"

"I'm going to find him and kill him," he screamed.

"No, you don't understand...He..."

She blinked, and Niccolo was gone. Just like that.
"Holy hell. What have I done?"

Holy hell! How the fuck did I end up here?

Andrus stared past the scowling Reyna at the flickering candle on the stone floor, trying to calm himself. Panic was for the weak. And weakness for idiots. But... holy hell!

He'd been so blinded by his need for revenge that the thought Niccolo might recruit the queen to help never occurred to him. Hell, it was a risky move even he wouldn't have attempted. Reyna was crazy and unpredictable.

Guess the son of a bitch got lucky. Because Andrus was now tied to a chair in the dark, dank room deep in the bowels of Barcelona.

He looked up at Reyna's smiling face. "Don't be so fucking pleased with yourself," he growled. "You might kill me, but you'll still be a crazy, useless bitch and the worst ruler the vampire world has ever seen."

Reyna backhanded him with such force that he was sure she'd fractured his jawbone. She cackled. "Oh, shut it. I'm not going to kill you."

Not. Good. That meant she was going to torture him. Best provoke her and pray she lost her temper.

A quick death. There was also the off chance that if she killed him—a clear violation of the Pact—it would displease the gods and they might off her themselves. Of course, he had been plotting to kill her, also a violation of the Pact. Oh, well. It was worth trying at this point. What did he have to lose? Death really was the best option.

"I'm adding stupid to that list," he said. "You keep me

alive, and I'll find a way to get loose. Or my men will come for me. I will find a way to take your head, Reyna."

Reyna's smile melted away. "Such cruel, cruel words, Andrus, dear. But keep it coming. It will make your screams that much sweeter to my ears."

With slits on either side, her long black dress didn't impede access to her usual arsenal of weapons strapped to her thighs. What tool would she choose? The small jewel-encrusted blade he'd given her as a gift when they were lovers? Or her favorite machete she was rumored to carry these days? Today, she also had on leather thigh-high boots. She could be carrying a shotgun, too. He had to keep pushing her, make her furious so she'd kill him now, or he'd end up filleted, diced, and then charred daily for an eternity. Demilords were extremely resilient.

Andrus resisted the urge to squirm in the chair even though the ropes were burning his wrists. "Let's also add delusional to that list. Shall we? Or how about disgusting, evil, unfit to rule, vindictive, and..." He could see his words were not having an impact. In fact, she seemed bored by his tactics.

"Are you getting fatter?" he threw out.

Reyna's eyes bulged with anger.

He wanted to laugh. Some things never changed. She was anything but fat. In fact, Reyna's body was sleek and muscular. The memories of what he'd done to that delicious body flashed in his mind. He flinched. He didn't want to think of those days. The days when he worshipped her, loved her. The days when she drove him mad because she refused to love him back.

Think of the day she betrayed you, he told himself.

Think of how she turned you into a vampire and then tricked you into becoming a Demilord.

He said, "It's amazing. Really. I didn't know vampires could put on weight, but you've managed to be the first. Yes. Let's add fat pig to the list of Reyna's marvelous traits."

Reyna snarled. She wrapped her fingers around Andrus's neck and gave it a squeeze. The pain rippled down his spine. "Nobody calls me fat!"

Andrus closed his eyes. He prayed she'd keep going and take his head cleanly off.

Suddenly, she let go. "I suppose," she said with an optimistic, perky tone, "everyone's entitled to their opinion."

Dammit all to hell! There has to be something I can say to push her over the edge.

"Oh, trust me," he said, his voice raspy and low, "everyone's got one. You should hear what your men say behind your back. They think you're incompetent—"

"Enough, Andrus! It's not going to work. You will be tortured. And I will enjoy every second."

She bent down slowly and placed her hand gently to his cheek and kissed the corner of his mouth. "But first, I thought I'd enjoy that body of yours one last time, you know, before I slice it up into luncheon meat."

She gripped his arm and snapped her fingers. They were suddenly in her town house bedroom in Paris. He recognized it because it was the very same one he'd been in when she had taken his human life. This didn't surprise him, but what did was how she could sift such long distances. Like Niccolo. So what other things had he been wrong about?

With vampire speed, Reyna tossed him like a rag doll

onto her plush red velvet bed and tied him to the wrought iron headboard. Before he blinked, she was tugging at the top of his black leather pants. With ease she slid them down.

"Just as I remember you," she whispered, sliding her red fingernails up his thighs, "strong and lean." She paused, staring at his flaccid penis. "What's the matter, Andrus, honey? You used to love it when we played this game. Don't you recall?" She ran her hand over his groin.

Andrus stared blankly at the ceiling. Oh, he remembered all right. But there was no way in hell he would allow himself to forget how she'd betrayed him. He would not think about those endless nights of marathon sex when he bent her luscious body every which way possible and took her. He would not think about how much he enjoyed pounding his cock into her. He would not give her the satisfaction of watching him grow hard for her—

"Oh yes. Just like I remembered." She began stroking him vigorously.

What? He looked down. *Dammit!* He was getting hard. This was not going well. If he kept this up, she'd keep him around for a millennium chained to her bedroom wall. "It's only hard because I was thinking of Helena."

The queen's hand suddenly froze on his stiffening member. "What did you say?"

Andrus instantly regretted his words. He should have simply said "another woman." The name Helena had slipped out.

The queen flew into a rage. "Impossible! You could never love another woman! Never."

Finally. He found the key to provoking her. Who knew she would be the jealous type? It would be a risky game, this one. The queen might go after Helena. He didn't want that.

"Who said anything about love? She's just a hot piece of ass. I find a new one every week," he lied. "And trust me, compared to you...let's say age is beauty and the bloom fell off your two-thousand-year-old rose about, well, two thousand years ago. Frankly, fucking a woman that old is pretty disgusting. I'm amazed you still get any."

There. That ought to do the trick.

In the blink of an eye, Reyna was straddling him, her hand wrapped around his neck. "You'll regret saying that, my love. I promise."

She leaned down and sunk her fangs into his neck.

Twenty-Two

Helena frantically paced across the living room of the lavish hotel suite. What was she going to do? She had no way of calling anyone for help or stopping Niccolo. He was hunting his best friend and would likely kill him before she'd had a chance to explain. Yes, Viktor had hurt her; however, there was more to the story.

She had to do something. She was even considering calling Andrus at this point. He might help her—*oh no.* Her heart suddenly sank. What had happened to Andrus? Niccolo never answered her question. Not that she had any feelings for him, and technically, she should hate Andrus for everything he'd done, but she couldn't. He was just another soul caught up in this mess.

"Ha! I knew it," a female voice blurted out behind her. Helena swiveled on her heel to find a gorgeous red-headed woman in a long black dress with side slits and thigh-high leather boots. "So predictable, my boy

Niccolo. He said he was going to San Francisco. I picked the most expensive room in the most expensive hotel." The woman looked around the room. "I can smell him. Where is he?"

Helena wished she knew, especially now. This woman screamed danger. Was she another crazy goddess?

"He left a while ago. Didn't say where he was going." Helena tried to sound nonchalant.

The woman huffed. "When you see him, tell him to get his ass back to my place."

"And you are?" Helena asked.

The woman blinked. "Who are *you*?"

Helena swallowed. *Why do I have a feeling this day is about to get a lot worse?* "Helena."

"You!" The woman lunged and grabbed Helena's neck. "Little bitch!"

Helena coughed and sputtered while she clawed at the woman's icy, steel hands. "Reyna?" Helena croaked.

The woman smiled and released her. Helena tumbled to the floor.

"I hope they told you all of the wonderful things about me," Reyna said proudly.

Helena rubbed her neck. "Not really."

Reyna shrugged. "Good, because I'm a heartless shrew who doesn't know the meaning of mercy."

Helena couldn't argue with that.

"Especially for you," Reyna added.

"Why did I figure that?"

Reyna's eyes narrowed. "I see why he's so fascinated with you. You are a spunky one. But a puny little human like you could never compete with the love he has for me. A true mate's bond is eternal."

Helena suddenly forgot all about her aching neck and her fear of this woman. She stood boldly and faced Reyna. "I thought vampires only have one mate?"

"Oh, silly girl." Reyna flicked her finger at Helena as if she were a fly she was shooing away. "Did he say you were his mate? Did you fall for that old trick?" Reyna cackled at the ceiling.

Helena couldn't believe it. Reyna was mated to Niccolo? No. That couldn't be right. "I feel the bond."

"Silence!" Reyna screamed so loud the windows flew open. A gust of crisp afternoon air burst into the room. "I am the one who paid the price! I am the one who gave up my sanity to be mated with a human. Andrus could never love you!"

Helena's mind clicked. *"Andrus?* You're mated to *Andrus?"*

Holy crap! Poor guy. No wonder he was crazy. No wonder he wanted to kill her so badly—even if it cost thousands of good vampires' lives. If Helena were in his shoes, she'd do the same damned thing. Poor, poor Andrus.

Reyna stopped and sniffed the air. "You...are..." she hissed. "You are Niccolo's mate! Aren't you? You smell like him!"

Helena stepped away. She had no idea what sort of politics and plots lurked in their world. Niccolo had never told her anything other than he wanted to be free, and now he was. Wherever this conversation was landing, she didn't think it would lead to her happy place—the one with a naked Niccolo in it.

"It all makes sense now!" Reyna began stalking across the room. "Niccolo wanted to be with you. That is why he asked for his freedom. And somehow, Andrus has taken a liking to you. Oh! This is a lucky day. I will get my revenge and get Niccolo back. He'll have no use for his freedom once you are gone."

Helena eyed the window. Could she survive the fall? Because there was zero point zero-zero-zero chance she'd survive the queen. Maybe the door was a better option. Helena made a run for it.

A hand appeared out of thin air and slapped her on the arm. "Come."

Before Helena could blink, she found herself transported to another room. A log crackled in the fireplace, and the darkness of night peeked through a narrow slit between the burgundy drapes. She guessed she was in another time zone since it was now nighttime.

Reyna instantly released Helena and marched to the large bed in the middle of the room. She pulled down the blankets to reveal Andrus's face.

Helena covered her mouth. What had Reyna done to him? His face was pale and thin, as though he'd been partially desiccated. *Guess his plan to swap me for the queen didn't go so well.*

Neither had Helena's plan to save everyone. So far, she'd managed to drive away Niccolo—who was going to kill Viktor—Andrus was about to die, and so was she. Once Niccolo realized Helena had been murdered by the queen, he'd kill the queen himself, thereby ending his own life.

Apocalypse. Boom. Everyone dead. Good job, bonehead! Wanna take up another cause before you die? How about global warming? Maybe she'd end up getting the planet cooked before they all died in the apocalypse.

Reyna jumped on the bed and straddled Andrus. "Wakey, wakey! I have a surprise for you, my love!" she sang out and slapped his face a few times. There was no movement. Maybe he was dead? "Oh, for the love of gods, wake up. I need to get this over with so I can go to my lambada lesson." She bounced on his stomach like a child riding a rigid merry-go-round horse.

No response.

Reyna moved her wrist to her mouth and bit down. She opened Andrus's mouth and let a few drops of blood dribble in. A moment passed, and he suddenly jolted up. Reyna flew to the floor.

"Finally." She stood and dusted herself off. She then pointed to Helena. "See? I brought you a gift."

Andrus's face looked as if he'd been run over by the Reyna bus. He suddenly looked horrified, too. Then a sour calmness washed over him.

"Oh. It's her." He lay back down on the bed and pulled the covers up.

Helena, standing toward the foot of the bed, glanced at Reyna. She was no longer smiling.

"You're going to play it that way, are you?" Reyna asked.

Helena instantly felt Reyna grasping her throat from behind. Helena's arms thrashed as the air was cut from her lungs.

"Yes. Fight my dear." Reyna snickered. "It will make it so much more enjoyable for me. Andrus doesn't love you, but he does care for you. I can feel it. I can feel every pathetic emotion running through that thick skull of his."

Andrus suddenly lunged from the bed and slammed

into Reyna with such force that she flew across the room and hit the wall. Plaster crumbled as she slid to the floor, moaning.

"Leave her out of this, Reyna! This is between you and me!" he screamed.

Helena crumpled into a ball on the floor. She grasped her own neck, struggling to let the air back into her lungs. Andrus rushed to her side. Somewhere in the back of Helena's mind, she registered the fact that Andrus was nude.

Had Reyna forced herself on him? *Poor Andrus.*

Reyna began crawling in their direction. "You do care for her! I knew it!" she hollered. "I don't know how it's possible, but if you value your life, you best remember that I am your mate. Me! You cannot love her! You are not destined to be with that wretched mortal."

Andrus turned in Reyna's direction. "What the hell are you talking about?"

Mingled with bloody tears, black mascara ran in thick, clumpy rivers down Reyna's pale face as she cried. If Andrus didn't hate her so much, he could almost feel sorry for her. "What are you talking about?" he repeated.

"Mate! You idiot." She chuckled psychotically under her breath. "Three hundred years, and the thought never occurred to you?"

Reyna slowly rose. If he didn't know better, he'd say there was a look of remorse in her eyes.

"I didn't want to turn you," she said. "I fought it off as long as I could. But there was no other way. The legends were true."

Though her words were frantic and thoughts incoherent, there was a harsh churning in his stomach as his mind began shuffling the pieces of the puzzle.

No. It can't be. No! "What. The. Hell. Are you talking about, Reyna?"

Her face twitched. "Did you not hear me? You are my mate, Andrus. My. Mate. And vampires mated to humans slowly go insane if their mate is not turned."

Andrus shook his head. How could this be possible? Mates were supposed to love one another, protect the other at all costs, have a connection. He hated her with every fiber of his being. He'd dreamed of nothing but killing her for centuries. Surely, this had to be another one of her many delusions. "I don't understand."

Reyna's eyes continued pouring pink tears. She began pulling at her hair. "I can't think straight. Your emotions... are like cancer!"

Andrus grabbed her shoulders. "You're lying! You're fucking crazy! I can't be your mate. You never cared for me. I saw it in your eyes."

Her eyes darted wildly from side to side. "No! That's not true. I did everything to shield you from the truth. I was prepared to do anything to keep from turning you; this was not the life I wanted for you."

"And this one was okay? *This!* You turned me into a vile, bloodthirsty vampire. Then you blackmailed me and traded me away to the gods to save your own ass. You betrayed me! Twice!"

"No! It wasn't supposed to turn out that way. I wanted to keep you human. I only cared about being with you, even if it meant I'd go insane and have to end my life. You were everything to me!" She pounded her fist into the side of her head, her words flowing frantically. "I had Niccolo to keep the order—to keep the Obscuros in check. But when they began taking over, I realized he was gone. The gods demanded I be punished. They demanded I make you into a vampire and hand you over along with my best men."

Bastard gods. Andrus recalled Niccolo's story. It was Cimil who had taken Niccolo out of action for three centuries.

That meant the gods caused the outbreak of Obscuros, then demanded action from the queen. In the end, the gods got their own race of soldiers—the Demilords. Was that what they were after all along?

Andrus stood in shock, digesting her words while attempting to sort through centuries of memories tainted by erroneous assumptions. A tiny voice of reason chimed in his head. Reyna was telling the truth.

Bloody goddamned hell. It just couldn't be right. But it was. The gods caused this mess. And...Reyna was in fact his mate.

Flashes, moments in time, hundreds of them, shuffled through his mind like a revolting slideshow. Images of lying in bed at night, feeling Reyna's light hovering over him. Irrational feelings and thoughts bombarding him for no good reason. That horrid darkness plaguing his heart day after day. His inability to move on and forget her. She'd never left him. That godforsaken black cloud following him was her. Her darkness.

Andrus tried to take it all in, but it was too much. All this time he figured she'd just thrown him away. That she didn't love him. In fact, she'd been trying to mask her pain and was going crazy. He felt her insanity, her loneliness and regret. Her hate for the world.

"Why didn't you tell me? We could have found a solution."

She stood, her hair wild about her face, and cupped her hand to his cheek. "Like what? By the time I realized my mistake, it was too late. Fate had decided for me, and the gods had spoken. I tried to bargain. I even offered myself, but they said I had to be punished for neglecting my duties and allowing so many Obscuros to roam freely. They decided I would live an eternity knowing my mate was somewhere in the world—also immortal—paying for my sins and far from my reach."

"Three hundred years, Reyna. You could have told me."

"No. There was to be no contact. If I broke my word, the gods would punish you somehow." She fell to her knees and wrapped her arms around his legs. "Forgive me, Andrus. I tried! I did. The only concession they gave was to allow me to keep my best soldiers to fight the Obscuros."

Reyna mumbled on and on about how she'd offered up their descendants. Unbeknownst to everyone, she had made it a habit to track her best warriors' bloodlines. Eventually, she would turn the cream of the crop into vampires. That was how she first spotted Andrus.

"I don't understand." Andrus's brows pulled together.

"Andrus, you and the other Demilords are all descendants of my best warriors. Like the others, I'd been watching you since you were a boy. You are from Niccolo's bloodline. There are dozens of his ancestors in my ranks."

Andrus felt like he'd been hit upside his head. Niccolo was his great-great—okay, he didn't know how many greats, but *that* vampire was family? And his men were related to other vampires who worked for the queen? Andrus felt sick. Reyna thought of these bloodlines as her own private breeding stock of warriors. Did her men know she'd been plucking out males from their families and turning them into vampires without consideration for the lives she was stealing away? Reyna truly had no heart.

Andrus gazed into her eyes and realized the truth. Some part of him did still love her. Yes, it made no sense. Yes, it was pathetic and twisted. But . . . it was what it was.

Maybe he'd known all along she was his mate. It would explain why time couldn't mend his broken heart and why she occupied his thoughts constantly—except when Helena was near. That was his attraction to Helena; she gave him peace, even if for only short moments. And as badly as he might hope to someday truly love again, it wasn't in the cards for him. Reyna had been his destiny, and it was time to end the suffering. His and hers. He and Reyna were not meant to be a fairy tale. They were not destined for happily ever after. But he could still save Helena from the queen and hope time would heal her broken heart after Niccolo turned to ash. Helena might have the chance he never got.

Andrus looked down into Reyna's icy green eyes. "I understand now." He leaned down, kissed her lips, and slid his hand from her waist to her hip. He was about to go for the knife strapped to her outer thigh, when—

"Nice try." She slipped the dagger from its sheath and held it out in her hand. "Looking for this?"

Andrus tried to swipe it from her hands. Reyna lost her grip. The knife fell to the floor.

A deep voice suddenly howled with rage from the corner of the room. "Reeeyna!"

Niccolo.

His eyes flew to Helena, who was still on the floor, struggling to breathe. "Why is she here? Who did this to her?" He then looked at Andrus, bare in the middle of the room, pointing at Reyna as the culpable party. "I'll fucking kill you," Niccolo said to Reyna. "Nobody touches my mate."

Reyna took a few steps back and smiled. "Well, what can I say? I had planned to kill her so you might work for me again. But what the hey, since you're here"—she pulled a long, razor-sharp machete from her thigh-high boot—"welcome to my party. Who's up for a round of piñata?"

Helena fought to suck the air into her lungs and push it out again through her scorching throat. The pain was excruciating.

In the back of her mind, she could hear the conversation between Andrus and Reyna, and for a moment, she believed things might end joyously for the two. In a dysfunctional, warped kind of way. Clearly, there was a valuable lesson to be learned in all this: Couples, no matter what species, should have open communication. Honesty was the key to happiness. Yes. She felt the makings of a good self-help book in all this. She could gear it toward immortals and put her academic background to use.

Andrus suddenly turned on Reyna, and the two were at it again. Helena felt another book opportunity: *The Art of Letting Go of the Past for Immortals.*

Then her knight in shining armor, Niccolo, appeared in the room. She'd thought her vampire would sift her away to safety and that she would finally get to tell him the truth about what had happened with Viktor. But hope was short-lived when Niccolo announced his intention to kill Reyna.

"I vote you and I kill Reyna together. I was about to do so myself," Andrus suggested to Niccolo.

Niccolo pointed one of his two gleaming swords at Andrus. "Stay where you are. I handed you over to Reyna, hoping she'd kill you. So I'm pretty damned sure you and I are not on the same team."

"Got me there," Andrus replied with a grin.

Helena's senses heightened to a level she'd never imagined possible while she watched the three facing off. She inched across the floor, scooting several feet to the knife. She didn't know what she'd do with it. Nevertheless, having a weapon seemed like a good idea.

"How about I kill you?" Reyna pointed to Andrus. "Then you." She pointed to Niccolo. "And that little blonde slut last."

Had the queen just called her a slut? That was like calling a Twinkie "a healthy snack." Or like calling Cimil "well-balanced." It wasn't even in the ballpark.

"At least I'm not a psycho immortal spinster," Helena retorted with a low, gravelly voice, purposefully baiting the queen to pull her attention away from Niccolo.

Reyna's eyes flared. "You die first!" She jumped at Helena.

Andrus was on Reyna's back in the blink of an eye.

Reyna turned, machete in hand, but Andrus hung on. If it weren't a life-and-death battle, the scene of a naked

Andrus clinging to the queen's back like a rabid monkey might actually be funny.

The queen swiveled on her heels back and forth, trying to shake Andrus off. She moved so fast, Niccolo had no choice but to stand back. Andrus suddenly lost his grip and tumbled to the floor. Reyna turned, but instead of going for Andrus, she lunged at Niccolo. He sidestepped her, and she flew past him, skidding across the floor.

A look of unrelenting rage in his eyes, he raised his sword.

Time stood still.

Helena watched the blade barreling down like a hammer hell-bent on slicing the world in two. How Helena did it was a mystery, but she moved herself between the blade and Reyna, hoping to stop the queen's death. Without Reyna, there was no Niccolo. There was no world. This was it.

Horror overtook Niccolo as he stared down at Helena's wide blue eyes, her body draped over Reyna like a shield. His sword had plunged straight into Helena's abdomen. Blood poured from the gaping wound.

"No! Helena!" He slid her off Reyna. His entire world shifted on its axis.

Niccolo had lived an obscenely long time, and he'd made his fair share of miscalculations. Regret was no stranger to this immortal. But if he gathered up every moment of remorse, sadness, anger, and pain and then condensed them into one, it would represent only a fraction of the despair that struck him down.

Nothing in the past, present, or future would ever matter as much as this very moment, for if she died, he'd destroy the entire fucking world, down to the last blade of grass, with his own two hands to take his revenge on fate.

This. Isn't. Meant. To. Be.

Blood flowed like an unstoppable river over his lap, forming a crawling puddle on the floor. She could not survive such a wound. And if he tried to turn her now, his blood would simply run right out of her.

Despite the odds, he could not stop himself from hoping, trying. "Please, Helena. Drink."

She pushed his hand away. "You're too late," she whispered.

"No! Helena! Drink!" He refused to let her give up.

Again she shoved his dripping wrist away.

"Why?" He felt his soul sinking into an abyss, into hell. "Why did you do it?"

Her hand trembling, she managed to raise her arm and stroke the side of his face. "To save you. Why else? If you kill her, you die. Everyone dies." Her sky-blue eyes were filled with such love. And pain.

"I don't care about everyone! *You* are all that matters," he bellowed.

Helena smiled gently. "That's very sweet, vampire. I love you."

Her eyes slowly closed. Niccolo heard her heart rate slow to an almost undetectable murmur.

No! He had to save her. There was still time.

He could stitch her wound and fill her full of his own blood. He scooped her in his arms and lifted her. His mind flipped through every memory of every hospital he'd ever been to. He was about to sift when he suddenly noticed the room was silent. Too silent.

"*Cristo.* No!" He'd been so wrapped up in Helena he hadn't noticed that his sword had run through his beloved, right into the queen's heart. His sword was forged with a silver alloy, especially designed to kill vampires. A direct hit to the heart was as fatal as decapitation.

Reyna. Was. Dead.

No! No! No!

But there was no denying it; her eyes were as cloudy as a week-old fish, and her body was disintegrating.

"Gods, no!"

He couldn't care less about Reyna, but how would he save his woman? His body now felt as though he'd been submerged in hot liquid metal. Reyna's blood—the blood flowing through his veins, which had kept him immortal all these years—was withering away. In a matter of moments, all that he was would be no more.

Helena...

Clutching his beloved like a cherished broken doll, his knees buckled. "I love you, Helena. Love you like no other man has ever loved a woman in the history of the world." He brushed the tendrils of her honey locks from her forehead. "I know a part of you still hears me, and you must know that you've meant everything to me. You are the light I've been deprived of for thirteen centuries. Do you hear me, woman? I love you!"

With those solemn words of desperation, he realized her heartbeat was gone. He never knew so much pain could be possible for one being to bear. What had he done to deserve this? Wasn't it enough that he'd had his human life, a life filled with love for his brothers and family, ripped away? Wasn't it enough that despite his loss, he hadn't crumbled? That instead, he'd chosen to dedicate his existence to protecting the innocent and killing Obscuros? He'd asked for very little in return: his freedom, which he no longer cared about, and now, for his mate to live.

Despair filled every crevice of his soul as he sat on his haunches, paralyzed, while Helena died in his arms and his own life slipped slowly from his body, preventing him from saving her. "I will find you in another life, my love. I will always find you. We are meant to be together… forever."

A small chuckle came from Andrus, who was curled up on the floor, writhing in pain. Niccolo had almost forgotten about him. Black splotches covered Andrus's body. The spots were turning to gaping holes, some the size of a grapefruit. He groaned as the holes seemed to be filling in with new pink flesh. The vampire blood in his body was dying, and the light of the gods was repairing him. Andrus's gamble had paid off.

"I'm finally free." He laughed quietly, his eyes empty.

Niccolo gathered up his strength and walked slowly to the bed with Helena cradled in his arms. He laid her down on the soft velvet comforter before taking his place beside her. The last memory he wanted was of sweet, beautiful Helena.

He stroked the loose strands of hair from Helena's face. She was so beautiful. He couldn't have imagined ever loving anyone so much. But he had. He still did. And he was grateful for it. He was grateful for every moment they'd had together.

I will find you in the next life, my love. This I vow.

He looked at his hand. The flesh melted away, leaving giant holes filled with ash. He gripped Helena with his last ounce of strength, hoping their souls might travel together to the next place, wherever that was.

"I love you, my bride."

Too overcome with pain as the queen's blood died inside him, his body gave out.

Twenty-Three

⁓

"Bravo, people! Well done! That was fabulous!"

Gripping Viktor by the arm, Cimil appeared at the side of the bed and began clapping and jumping as if she'd just won a shiny new car.

"I can't remember how long it's been since we've seen such a fab show! This was dramatastic! Better than *Romeo and Juliet*. Better than *The Sound of Music*, *South Park*, *True Blood*, *Dexter*, *My Little Pony*, and *Shrek* put together!"

"Cimil, shut it!" Viktor barked. "You're a sick, sick goddess, and I sincerely wonder why the gods haven't locked you away yet."

Cimil's bright red lips puckered into an exaggerated pout. "I'm wounded, Malibu Beach Vampire. I thought we had something special, you and I. Now I feel like a razor head, toothpick, dental floss, Q-tip, gallon of gas, paper plate, plastic fork, space shuttle, baby seal soul, cruise ship, Swarovski crystal, and Fabergé egg."

"Huh?" Viktor's face twisted.

"Yunno. Things you use once and throw away. Did someone forget his vampy oatmeal this a.m.? Jeeeez," she spouted.

Viktor snarled. "Yeah. Whatever. And for the record, you *made* me sleep with you. Blackmail sex does not constitute 'something special.'"

Cimil coyly chewed her index finger and shrugged. "Well, you wanted to find out who the blonde wench from your dreams was and why she haunts you. I saw an opportunity to get a taste of that manly body of yours. What can I say? I'm an opportunist—or a total whore. Gods, it totally rocks to be me!"

Viktor shook his head and stared down at Niccolo and Helena. "Are you going to help me move them or not?"

Cimil sighed. "I suppose. Do you think Niccolo will ever forgive you for turning Helena into a vampire?"

Viktor growled, "*You* told me he would because I saved her. Since Reyna wasn't my maker, Helena will live on. Do you think he'll ever forgive *you* for turning him into a Demilord before you put him to sleep in your piggy bank?"

She shrugged. "Oooh. I hope not. I love conflict— World War Numero Dos...fucking awesome! Can't wait for number three! BTW, I wonder if we can come up with any new twists for these two lovers. Oh! How about *Immortal Survivor*? We can put them on an island with only each other for food. See who holds out longest?"

Viktor growled, "Don't even think about it, you crazy shrew. They've been through enough." Viktor scooped up Niccolo's limp body, which was already healing.

Cimil shrugged and picked up Helena, whose wounds were now also closing.

"I guess we'll come back for the other one," Viktor commented as he glared at Andrus, unconscious on the floor.

Cimil narrowed her eyes. "That one is gonna need a little therapy after his ride on the crazy-Reyna bus. I'll have to take him back to my realm and see if that puts him right."

Viktor cocked his head. "You can take other beings back to your world?"

Cimil looked confused. "Nope. Private club. Gods and demigods only."

The realization hit Viktor. He looked down at Niccolo. "You mean, now that their vampire blood is dead . . . ?"

Cimil nodded. "I know! It's fabulous, right? I love when we get new members!"

Helena's awareness of her own thoughts washed over her like an unrelenting fog. In the distance, birds chirped and a gentle breeze wafted through the treetops, penetrating the sanctuary of her deep slumber. The air was thick and warm, like a soft, soothing blanket.

She was dead, right? Because she didn't feel alive, and she was certainly somewhere peaceful and quiet.

To her side, the fluid sound of gentle breaths swept in and out of her ears. In and out, coaxing her to fully awaken and open her heavy lids. What was missing were her own breaths. And her heartbeat.

Yes. Heaven.

Her eyes crept open. Her blurry vision cleared instantly,

and her gaze gravitated toward the sublime male specimen sleeping at her side.

"Oh my God!" She flung herself over Niccolo's body unable to believe he was truly there. Was he a dream?

"Oh, God. Niccolo, is it really you? Wake up. Please, wake up." Cupping both sides of his immobile face, she smothered him in kisses—cheeks, earlobes, lips, brows, not one centimeter was left untouched.

He remained peacefully resting, unaffected by her touches. Helena quickly looked him over, her hands frantically hopscotching over each of his limbs. Was he injured?

He seemed intact. He was dressed in all-white linen, looking tanner than usual. Almost golden, in fact. His long dark hair was pulled back into a low ponytail.

No, he didn't look simply intact, he looked magnificent, and she could hear his heart steadily drumming away. He was alive! Definitely alive.

She moved her mouth to his and kissed his lips, face, and neck. Then she stopped to inhale his scent.

Man! He smells so good! Like a delicious bouquet of chocolates, vanilla, and spice. Her mouth watered. She licked her lips as her eyes zeroed in on the pulse of his neck. Fangs painfully popped from her gums, along with the irresistible urge to bite him. Hard.

"Crap!" She covered her mouth and scrambled away. *I want to eat him, and not in a naughty kind of way.*

His eyes flew open, and he sat up. A large, glowing smile swept across his face the moment he recognized her.

"Helena!" He jumped from the bed, grabbed her, and clutched her tightly to his body.

"Oh my God, you're okay!" she screamed.

Niccolo kissed her with such passion that her toes curled. Every nerve tingled; every cell ignited with his touch. He electrified her body.

"Wait." She pushed hard and broke his grip. She was much stronger than before.

"No," he said in a low, desperate voice. "I need you. Now. I never thought I'd see you again. I died. You died. I don't know how or if this is just a dream, but…" He pulled her into him again.

This time she didn't resist. He was right; she needed him as badly as he needed her. She really didn't know how they'd survived, but there would be time for answers later. Right now, they were together…somewhere tropical maybe? Who cared? Could be a damned Super 8 in Podunk, and it still wouldn't matter.

Helena looked down and noticed she was wearing a gauzy white dress that matched Niccolo's white outfit.

She pulled the dress over her head and flung it to the Saltillo tile floor.

Niccolo smiled as his eyes wandered over her naked flesh.

Turquoise! Oh my God. "Niccolo…your eyes! They're—"

"No talking! Kiss me. Now!" His gorgeous, new turquoise eyes gleamed with desire and joy. The handsomeness of his face stole her breath.

"How did I ever think I could live without you?" she asked. Her heart fluttered, and the sensation jarred her. She quickly removed the clothes from his body and shoved him down on the bed. The new power surging through her veins only heightened her arousal.

"I have absolutely no idea." He snickered.

"I'll never leave you again," she promised. The steady

gaze of her eyes held the conviction of her words. She would never again separate herself willingly from him. "Until the world ends, I'll stay by your side."

Niccolo grinned from ear to ear.

Something about seeing this man genuinely happy felt... magical. As though the universe was finally set right. The raw edges of his personality, the darkness, had lifted.

She loved this man's soul with every fiber of her being.

And his body... was it custom-made for her? It was even more glorious than she remembered, with sleek and hard curves of muscles everywhere she looked. His stomach was chiseled from pure steel. His erection was thick and hard waiting for her.

A million emotions bombarded her mind, but only one was worthy of her attention: she needed him. Yes, they'd made love in the hotel, and it was fan-frigging-tastic. But at the time, this epic connection hadn't been fully forged; she hadn't committed her entire soul to him just yet.

She slowly moved toward him with her trembling hand. She let her fingertips gently float over the ridges of his sculpted abdomen.

His gaze smoldered with ravenous intensity as she lowered her head and sampled his lips.

It was a kiss unlike any other, like lightning bolts of euphoria shooting into her core. Before her mind could process the flood of raw lust crashing into her, Niccolo had her pinned under his weight.

Sexual hunger shined in his dark eyes; he, too, was overcome with this animalistic drive. He plunged his head and took her mouth with fury, gripping her hair tightly with one hand and cupping her cheek with the other. He held her still as his tongue thrust deeply in her mouth. He panted and groaned with each sharp breath.

His hardness pulsed against her hip, and he thrust his thigh against her juncture, undulating and pushing in time with the movements of his mouth. Helena wanted to touch him, to stroke his velvety hard cock. She wanted to taste him on her lips, to lick and savor every inch, but she couldn't muster the will to stop their momentum. The weight of him, the urgency and hunger in his touch and kiss, they were rapidly taking her to the place she wanted to go.

Lady Pervert Land? Oh yeah...Happy place, here I come!

Helena's mind barely registered the sensation of his strong, calloused hand sliding down her neck, over her breast and stomach, until his touch reached between her legs. His fingers delved into her cleft, and Helena moaned.

"You are so silky and hot, Helena," he whispered into her ear.

She wondered if she would ever want this man to take his time with her. Foreplay simply felt like a waste. He had only to look at her, and she was ready.

She flipped him on his back and straddled him. "I want you...*now*."

Niccolo's head flew back and his lids clamped tight as Helena bore down on him. Once he was deep inside, she ground her hips at his base to savor the fullness of him inside her. Every inch of him drove her mad. Every. Thick. Inch. Was made just for her pleasure.

"Yes, it is," he replied with a breathy voice.

Helena laughed. *Internal dialogue leakage. Again?*

Oh, well. Any second now, she was going to scream much naughtier things.

Niccolo pulled her close to his warm body slick with sweat, and Helena couldn't think of a better place on earth. If a comet struck her down at this very moment, she'd die with a dopey grin on her sated face.

Her fingers lazily rode the waves of his ripped stomach. Every inch of him drove her mad, but now his smell . . .

"I can't believe what you do to me. Right now, I want to fuck you, lick you, and drink your blood. All at the same time."

His eyes opened wide. "You want to what?"

Helena, unable to believe what she'd said—so vulgar—clapped her hands over her mouth. "Oh my God. I'm so sorry. I don't know why I just spoke to you like a dirty truck driver. It won't happen again."

"No! The dirty talk is great. But the drinking blood part . . ."

Oh. That. Did they really need to talk about it right now? The ache to have him inside her again was unbearable.

She stood up and began to pace at the foot of the bed. Niccolo was propped up on both elbows staring at her. "Answer me."

There was no way around it; they had to have this conversation. She threw up her hands. "Viktor turned me while we were captured at the Demilord compound."

"He did what!" Niccolo sat up and looked as though he was about to leave her again in order to go hunt and kill Viktor.

Not gonna happen! She jumped to his side and pushed him down.

Vampire strength was cool, but this new body of hers was going to take some serious getting used to. Luckily, she knew a few people who could help figure all this out.

"You're not going anywhere until you hear me, Niccolo. I went through a lot to save you; it's the least you can do."

Niccolo huffed and then nodded.

"Good." She sat next to him and relaxed. She told him all about the conversation with Cimil and how Helena was destined to die.

"Why didn't you tell me?" he asked, clearly disapproving of her scheme.

Helena remembered her own snarky little thoughts about honesty when Andrus discovered Reyna's dirty little mate secret. "Stupidity, I guess," she replied.

"I would have warned you not to take Cimil's word. She has a way of telling the truth and lying at the same time."

"Her skills at the art of manipulation put vampires to shame, but Cimil..." Helena paused. Should she tell Niccolo about all of the phony rules Cimil had made up—no bedding Helena, no biting, etc.—just so Cimil could watch Niccolo suffer? *Naah. Some other time.*

"I wonder about her," Helena said. "If she hadn't helped me, I really would have died. She was the one who told me to read the stories in that weird book."

She could see that Niccolo was growing impatient. Was he still thinking about hunting down Viktor? Likely. She had to hurry while she still had his attention. "The pages were filled one second, empty the next. Hundreds of blank pages. Except for the last one—the ending to your story."

"What did it say?" he asked.

"That your vampire bride saved your life, but it was her belief in your goodness, her love that made you the one man with the strength and conviction to save the world."

She held back her tears as she thought about how those words humbled her. "I thought, *What if?* What if Cimil really had told you the truth about the prophecy, that I had to be turned on our three-month anniversary? Which was, in fact, the day of her visit. What if she'd also told me the truth—that I had to die to save you? Becoming a vampire is dying. Right?

"So, I begged Viktor to turn me. What did I have to lose? When he refused, I jumped him—I was desperate— and tried to force him to bite me. I wouldn't give up. Finally, he gave in when Sentin woke up and convinced him I was right."

"I didn't sense any change in you when we made love at the hotel."

Helena wasn't sure why. "Too soon maybe? Viktor had given me his blood. He said it would take an hour or two for it to work its way through and then stop my heart." She sat down at his side and brushed a stray lock of hair from his cheek. "He saved me. He saved you, too."

Niccolo nodded solemnly. "I'm sorry you had to make this sacrifice for me, Helena. I didn't want this life for you."

"It was inevitable, Niccolo. Reyna told me vampires cannot be mated to humans; they go insane after a few months, and our time was up." She gave his hand a consoling squeeze. "There was no other way."

Several moments of silence passed while Niccolo stared at their joined hands. He made tiny circles with his thumb over hers. A look of aggravated acquiescence washed over his face.

That's my warrior. She smiled inwardly. It was her latest observation about the general, Niccolo DiConti—sure, he was physically strong, but his secret to being undefeated and thirteen hundred years old was that he never wasted time brooding over things he could not change.

Case in point, once Reyna had made him a vampire, he moved on and found another way to honor his beliefs; he became the fiercest warrior the world had ever known. He saved countless innocent lives from becoming an Obscuro meal. So while Niccolo was no doubt unhappy about Helena's fate, what was done was done, and the alternative would have been death for both of them, possibly for the world, too.

His eyes gently lifted to meet her patient, loving gaze. "I guess that explains why I didn't want to bite you when we made love at the hotel."

"Huh?" she said.

Niccolo shrugged. "Vampires don't crave vampire blood."

"They don't?"

He shook his head no.

"Then why are my fangs aching to make you my first snack?" she asked and then opened her mouth to reveal two gleaming white fangs.

Niccolo's expression soured.

"What?" Helena asked. "Is it my fangs?" She cupped her hand over her mouth. "Do I look that bad?"

Niccolo shook his head. "No. You look stunning and delectable. It's just—Reyna is dead."

Helena frowned. "So why didn't you die?" She suddenly gasped and covered her mouth. "Oh my gods. Your eyes!"

"What about them?"

She was about to answer when he sprang from the bed. "Did you hear that?"

Helena and Niccolo cautiously walked through the enormous Spanish-style villa. As they followed the voices, Niccolo told her that this was his most recent acquisition. They entered the brightly lit modern kitchen—stainless steel appliances, polished granite countertops, and built-in brick oven—and were shocked to find Niccolo's team, including Viktor, Sentin, and Timothy, sitting around a large table. Cimil sat at the head, wearing a visor, dealing cards. An unlit cigarette hung from her mouth.

"Pony up, bitches! Auntie Cimi's got some garage sales to hit this weekend."

The men grumbled and threw their multicolored plastic chips to the center of the heaping pile.

"She's cheating, dammit," Sentin said. He tossed his watch on the table anyway and lifted his cards. "But I'm not giving up until I kick her ass."

Cimil cackled. "Bring it, vamp! I've got all day. Those two lovebirds won't make their appearance until—"

Niccolo cleared his throat. The men and Cimil jumped from the table and stared at him.

"Guess your fortune-telling abilities aren't so sharp after all," Sentin goaded.

Cimil shot him a quick glare. "Hey. I haven't gone in for a tune-up lately. Been too busy coddling your ass. Really, how many Swedish massages can a vampire need in one day?"

Sentin smiled sheepishly and shrugged. "It's a fair trade since you keep making me sleep with you."

Niccolo stalked toward Cimil. Helena was certain he was going to throttle her. "What the hell happened, Cimil? What have you done to me?" he snarled.

She pointed to herself. "Me? I delivered! That's what I did. You are free from the queen, you remain immortal, and Helena is also immortal and yours for eternity." She threw up her hands. "Touchdown, baby!" She did a quick little disco dance that seemed to only enrage Niccolo further.

"And what exactly am I if Reyna is dead?" he asked. "What did you do to me and my men?" Niccolo turned and looked directly at Viktor. "And Helena."

The thought had not occurred to Helena, but he was right. If Reyna was dead, then how come they were all alive?

Cimil smiled coyly and exchanged glances with Viktor, sitting at her side. "This hunky bunch"—she pointed to the ten men around the table—"are still vamps. Their maker was not *la señorita* Reyna."

"Of course she was. We all remember her turning us," Niccolo argued.

Cimil held up her index finger. "*Au contraire mon frère!* Reyna may have drained these scrumptious bounties of masculinity, but her partner in crime, el Grrran Vampirrro Roberrrto Xavier the Second—let's call him Bob, Bob the Ancient One—actually donated the not-so-fresh-squeezed juice for her army."

Cimil buffed her nails on her T-shirt. "No one ever remembers that part, ya know." She chuckled. "Bob is like the ultimate vampire baby daddy! Oh, wait. No. He's a deadbeat dad!" She howled with laughter. "Get it?" She turned to Sentin, who just looked... annoyed. "Get it? I said 'deadbeat dad.' Because he goes around making vamps, never sends money or birthday cards..." She noted no one was laughing. "And you are all... dead. Okay, never mind. Point is, except for Niccolo, her second-in-command, none of you could be from her bloodline. You know why, right?"

Everyone exchanged glances, but did not respond.

"Oh, come on! It's a vampire law older than the Pact—the ruler cannot make the army. Too risky. I mean, what if the ruler dies? Can't lose your warriors. Didn't you know that?" She looked around the table. Still no response.

Cimil clapped loudly. "Come on, people! Wake up! Get those hamster wheels moving! You mean to tell me no one ever noticed they don't have Reyna's gifts? Reyna's peeps—may they rest in peace—could sift long-distance. Bob's peeps come with built-in stealth, which is why they're fantastic warriors. And then there is the father of the Obscuros..." Cimil's eyes went dark and her face blank.

"Cimil?" Helena snapped her fingers.

Cimil lit back up. "Wow! Now that was wicked hot." She fanned herself with her hand. "So, where was I?"

Helena jumped right in. "You were going to tell us which Ancient One is making the Obscuros."

Cimil frowned. "Was not! Besides, it is forbidden to speak his name." She crouched under the table and then popped back up. "I was going to tell our ex–fanged friend,

Niccolo, that he's now an ex-Demilord. Or as we like to call them, a demigod." She clapped.

Niccolo growled. "You turned me into a Demilord?"

Cimil replied, "Yippee?"

Helena's mind did several somersaults. She was transported back to the moment she saw Niccolo in the tomb. Her first thought was that he looked like a god, not a vampire. At the time, he was actually both. She also remembered how Andrus's vibe reminded her of Niccolo's.

"But how? When?" Niccolo asked.

Cimil winked. "Oh, come on. I saw your future. I knew you would kill Reyna—the gods thank you for that, by the way. What a show! We watched every minute with popcorn, Funyuns, pineapple mojitos . . . the works! We've been waiting eons for that horrible monster to go down. None of us were allowed to touch her, though." Cimil pointed up and whispered, "Consequences."

"You must be joking. Since when have you cared about consequences?" Viktor said under his breath.

Cimil perched one hand on her hip. "Reyna was the Creator's creation—she was an Ancient One. We aren't allowed to touch any of them. Now, vampire-on-vampire action, well, that's a whole other enchilada. I think it's also a kinky website but don't quote me."

So Cimil had lied. Again. The gods hadn't spared Reyna because they thought her death would exterminate the good vampires needed to win the Great War; they were forbidden to kill an Ancient One.

"You used me to do your dirty work. Fucking gods," Niccolo growled.

Cimil sucked in an impatient breath. "Well, no duh! I also just plain used you. Wink. Wink. How could I not? Looking at your splendid nakedness standing in the jungle only inches from my sizzling goddess body... ummm." She licked her lips. "That kiss, I can still taste you on my lips, my little ex-vampire."

Helena gasped. "Niccolo! Please. Tell me you didn't!"

"Dammit, no! Never. I gave her my clothes before she put me under that sleeping spell..." He frowned and then glared at Cimil. "You didn't...with me...I mean, while I was asleep, did you?"

Cimil winked. "That's my dirty little secret, and I don't kiss and tell...without a royalty deal."

Niccolo looked like he wanted to retch. Helena's fangs popped out of her mouth.

The men around the table all stood slowly, seething and glaring at Cimil.

"Yikes! Down, boys. Down," Cimil barked. "Just a little joke. I didn't touch him!" She put her hand to her mouth. "Much," she whispered.

The men shook their heads and sat.

"Oh!" Cimil added. "You'll like this! I did leave your vampy powers intact so you wouldn't notice the change. You earned it with all that heroic behavior. You're very trusted among the gods, you know. But boy, it took you forever to realize your body didn't want blood. Old habits, I guess."

"Trust! Trust! You put me through hell! For Christ sake! I've been trying to survive on blood for three damned months. No wonder I'm starving! Why didn't you tell me the truth?"

Helena tugged on Niccolo's arm. "Please, Niccolo, leave it alone. We've been through a lot. Let's settle this later." She tugged him back toward the bedroom. "Please?"

Niccolo's expression softened. "You are right, my love. There will be time later for settling scores."

"Tsk-tsk, my little man cake." Cimil clicked with her tongue. "Is your bad attitude any way to show gratitude for saving your existence, your mate, and planning your wedding?"

"Wedding?" Helena asked.

Cimil nodded. "Everything is ready outside."

Helena looked down at her clothes and Niccolo's. She realized the entire crew was dressed in white linen. Cimil hopped up from the table and led them past two French doors, onto a large deck overlooking the water.

The sun was nestled just below the horizon, and the water of the lake glowed with turquoise hues. White garlands were intertwined with small white lights that ran the length of the rail down the dock, stretching twenty meters into the water. At the end was a thatched-roof structure. It was breathtaking.

"Is this for us?" Helena asked.

Viktor moved forward. "It was my idea. I knew Niccolo wanted a real wedding for you, but never had the chance. I also thought this would be preferable over the Klingon monstrosity Niccolo booked for you in Vegas."

Sentin snickered.

Helena flung her arms around Viktor's neck. The only thing that could make it better would be for her mother, Anne, and Jess to be with her. But they were better off being protected from this new world of Helena's until she could find a safe way to be a part of their lives. "Thank you, it's perfect. You're the best vampire daddy ever."

Viktor laughed and gave her a tight squeeze. She knew he wasn't pleased about making her immortal, but hopefully now he realized it was all for the best. As she let go, there was a brief moment when she could feel his guilt, joy, and relief.

"Oh! Was that... you?" She took a step back.

Viktor nodded.

Niccolo slipped his arm between them and pulled her close. "You may have a blood bond with him as well, but I'm not sharing you. With anyone."

Cimil chimed in. "Ha! With anyone? The boat set sail on that minutes ago. Where two lie to sleep, three wake up! Where three sleep, they all wake up wet!" Since no one understood, they didn't respond.

"Okay, then. Let's get rolling." Cimil snapped her fingers and was instantly at the far end of the dock, dressed in a mariachi outfit. A full ensemble of mariachis holding trumpets, violins, and guitars were behind her.

Helena turned to Niccolo and whispered, "Please tell me she's not marrying us."

Niccolo shrugged. "I don't think we have a choice." He looked back at his men standing behind them with proud, cheery faces.

Helena looked into Niccolo's eyes. "I love you."

Cimil clapped, and they began to play a slow, romantic version of the Mexican Hat Dance.

"They're playing our song, my love," Niccolo said. "Are you ready?"

Helena took Niccolo's arm, and they marched down the dock.

Epilogue

Six Months Later

Helena sat curled up against Niccolo on a plush velvet cushion in front of the fireplace of their Manhattan penthouse, staring at him with large doe eyes.

Niccolo glanced down at her with a knowing smile. "Helena, you must stop looking at me like that. I'm going to end up with an enormous ego."

Helena laughed. As if his ego could get any larger.

But she wouldn't have her arrogant ex-vampire any other way. She reached up and pecked him on the cheek. "Can't help it. I still don't believe I'm married to a real live deity. And your new eyes are . . . wow. Just wow."

Niccolo raised one brow. "I'm a demigod. Not a deity. And other than the fact I now eat normal food and can stay in sunlight all day, I am no different."

Helena smirked. Maybe he didn't think so, but the

change was like night and day. She didn't know if it was Reyna's blood that always made him so grumpy and brooding, but that side of Niccolo was gone. Arrogance, confidence, raw power—those were all traits he still carried, naturally, but his transformation gave him the ability to connect with others in a way he'd never been able.

He now had upward of twenty thousand men—vampires, demigods, and ... others—under his command. Helena knew the clock was ticking, but she tried not to think about the apocalypse. It was Viktor's job to monitor the book of the Oracle of Delphi since Antonio had disappeared without a trace.

Niccolo's turquoise stare was intense as he sensed Helena's emotions. He slipped his large hand to her belly and gave her a comforting pat. "All will be well, my little vampire," he said.

Helena's gaze moved to the glowing embers of the fire. "I can't help but worry. I'm the first vampire to ever have a baby. With a demigod, no less. And although they're completely unaware, there's her human grandmother, two human aunties—Anne and Jess. Then there's also her three dozen vampire uncles who kill Obscuros for a living, and—"

"Don't forget Auntie Cimi, Goddess Delight of the Underworld! And baby's other godparents! Get it? God ... parents!"

Helena and Niccolo looked up at Cimil standing next to them decked out in a bright yellow Southern belle dress, holding a frilly matching parasol.

Niccolo grumbled in Helena's ear, "Will she ever learn to knock?"

"Well, I never!" Cimil feigned a Southern accent. Her eyes locked on Helena's stomach, and she froze.

Helena still couldn't get used to Cimil's odd quirks. Even though Cimil had shockingly gifted them with a baby—*"where two lie down, three wake up"*—and permission to let her mother and two closest friends in on their secret world, though Helena was still waiting for the opportune time to break the news about everything, there was always something about the crazy goddess Helena couldn't trust.

"Cimil? Hello?" Helena called out.

Cimil rebooted and put her ear over Helena's round belly. "What's that, my sweet, sweet little dumplin'?" she asked Helena's stomach.

Niccolo and Helena watched nervously as Cimil listened to the baby.

Helena's brows knitted together. "Is something wrong?"

Cimil laughed and shook her head at Helena's baby bump. "Oh, you sneaky little girl! Yes. Auntie Cimil will buy you a puppy, pony, turtle, jumping bean, and whale! But you must promise not to eat them."

Whale? Oh, for heaven's sake. Where the heck would they put it?

"Cimil," Niccolo said, "while we are eternally grateful for your gift, the sun will be rising soon, and Helena needs her rest. Is there something we can help you with?"

Cimil cocked her head to one side and began clapping and jumping. Her hoopskirt swayed like a giant bell. "Oh! Oh! I wanted to tell you I found the perfect nanny to help out while Dad is...you know...saving the world!"

"Nanny?" Helena didn't want to ask. Would it be a talking chipmunk? Or perhaps a bag of chips? Maybe a bug of some sort?

Cimil snapped her fingers, and Andrus appeared in the room.

Niccolo jumped up and lunged, but Cimil wedged herself between the two men. Despite her waifish appearance, Cimil was a full-blooded goddess and much stronger than both men.

Helena jumped up. "Andrus! Is that you?"

Andrus leaned to the side, looking around Niccolo's hulking, seething body, and smiled. "In the flesh." He gave a quick wave.

Helena rushed around the tangle and threw her arms around him. "I never got to thank you for saving me from Reyna! Where have you been?"

Niccolo took a step back from Cimil. "How could you?" he screamed. "How could you bring this vile, deceitful cretin into our home?"

"Now, now." Cimil shook her finger. "Andrus was in a very bad place. The queen was bonkers, and it wasn't his choice to be bound to her any more than it was yours to become her general. But he's all better now."

"Leave! Both of you!" Niccolo barked.

"Niccolo? What's gotten into you?" Helena whispered.

Andrus's eyes were also a sparkling turquoise. His skin glowed with a healthy golden hue. He, too, looked transformed by the death of Reyna. "I didn't want to listen to Cimil when she first told me about the"—he swallowed—"job, but I owe you, Helena." He turned toward Niccolo. "And you, too. I know what I did was unforgivable, but I *am* changed."

Niccolo growled, "Good. Good for you. Now go before I tear your head off."

Cimil clicked with her tongue. "Sorry, bub. Not gonna

happen. I've foreseen the future, and while you're away on a mission, your home is attacked. Andrus is destined to save Helena and your little girl. So, Auntie Cimil says he stays."

"Absolutely not!" Niccolo roared. "I'll guard them myself."

Helena held out her finger to silence Cimil. "Give us one sec. Why don't you and Andrus help yourselves to some cookies I just baked in the kitchen?"

Niccolo's anger flared even hotter. "My cookies, too? You're letting him eat my cookies?" he grumbled as Helena pulled him aside.

She looked up at Niccolo with loving patience and waited for him to meet her gaze. She knew this would soothe him. "Honey," she said, "you can't stay and protect me. When the time comes, you have to lead the army. Otherwise, what kind of world will we have for our baby?"

Niccolo grumbled at his feet.

"Cimil is crazy," she added, "but if she's seen it happen, then Andrus will protect me, and he is your family."

"Family?" Niccolo's dark brows lifted.

Helena had not wanted to tell Niccolo until the right time—which ironically never came—but she thought he had a right to know.

She told him how Reyna had abducted dozens of men from Niccolo's bloodline to turn into vampire soldiers.

Helena nodded. "Yes, he's a descendant of your eldest brother."

Niccolo brushed a stray curl from her face as he mulled it over for several moments. "Fine, if he lays one finger on you, though—"

Cimil appeared close behind Niccolo, chewing an

extra-large chocolate chip cookie. Crumbs tumbled down her dress. "Funny you should bring that up. Because fate has spoken, and Andrus will have another chance at love now that Reyna is dead. No worries, though. Helena's off the table."

Niccolo glowered at Cimil. "Thanks for clearing that up. Now, if you don't mind, we are trying to talk, Cimil."

Cimil strolled away, mumbling and chewing. "Fine... but don't say I didn't try to warn you ahead of time. His son and your daughter's wedding will come faster than you realize, and making a bridesmaid dress for a whale is no easy task."

Niccolo and Helena swallowed hard as they realized what Cimil was trying to say. Andrus's future son and her baby?

"I'm going to kill him!" Niccolo flew from Helena's grasp, but when he reached the kitchen, it was empty.

Cimil's laughter echoed from some unknown place in the room. "See you at the big kickoff!"

THE END (Not Really)

Hey there! If you enjoyed this novel and want to let me know, just click those fantastic little stars on the retailer's website, write a review, or ping me directly! (Contact info is below.) I see every note/review and do a little disco dance when they're good. Helpful feedback also welcome! (Sorry, Mean People. You'll just be ignored because Mean People suck. Yeah, you know you do.)

Mimijean.net
Twitter @MimiJeanRomance
Facebook.com/MimiJeanPamfiloff

Backlum Chaam, the God of Male
Virility, wasn't always such a bad
guy. He was compassionate, loyal,
and dedicated—before his heart
turned black and his biggest goal in
life became destroying mankind.
Where did it go wrong? Well, it was
all about a woman…

Turn this page for
an excerpt from

Accidentally… Evil?

One

⁓

There has to be evil so that good can prove its purity above it.

—Buddha

November 1, 1934. Bacalar, Mexico

Why is that man...naked?

Dazed and flat on her back, twenty-one-year-old Margaret O'Hare observed the man's bare backside as he stood on a nearby weather-beaten dock, toweling off. Her vision, at first a groggy mess, focused to a machete-sharp point, the pain in her forehead equally knifelike.

Yes. Naked. Really. Really. Naked. She'd never seen such a large, well-built man or such a perfect backside—hard, deeply tanned, and worthy of a marble sculpture. Maybe two. Or five. Too bad she was a painter.

Hold on. Where the ham sandwich am I? Margaret's eyes, the only body part she could move without experiencing pain, whipsawed from side to side. *Jungle. Dirt. Lake. Okay. I'm lying near the lake.* Yes, this was good. She recognized the place. Sort of.

Am I near the village dock?

Her peripheral vision said no; this dock had a tiny *palapa* for shade at the very end.

Then where?

She made a feeble attempt to lift her throbbing head, but her body rewarded her with a spear to the temple.

Ow. Ow. Ow. She took a slow breath to allow the skull-shattering jab to dissipate. *All right. Relax and think. What happened? What happened? What happened? And who is Mr. Perfectbottom over there?*

A sticky blanket of gray coated her thoughts, but she did recall swimming that morning. Maybe she'd slipped on the village dock and fell into the lake. Maybe Mr. Perfectbottom had been bathing down at the shore and rescued her.

Or not.

Her clothes were bone-dry except for the sweaty parts. Come to think of it, she felt like a mud pie, soggy underneath and dry on top, baking in the sun. It didn't help that someone—maybe the man?—had placed a warm fur under her head and neck. God, it was itchy.

She willed her hand to make the painful journey behind her ear to give it a good scratch. Her fingers brushed the soft, silky hairs of the makeshift pillow.

How odd. People in these parts don't wear mink.

The mink coat purred.

Maggie sprang from the moist grass and scrambled back a few feet against a thick tree trunk. "Ja-ja-jaguar!"

The glossy black cat didn't budge a paw. It simply stared, its eyes reminding her of two big limes—wide, round, and green. Then the damned thing smiled right at her like some real-life Cheshire cat. Goddamned disturbing.

"You! Cat!" The man barreled down the dock, each heavy step thundering across the creaky wooden planks. "Leave! Do not return until I call you."

Maggie should have been frightened by the boom of the man's tone, but instead, his rich masculine timbre soothed her aching head.

"Raarrr?" the cat...

...*responded? I must be hearing things,* she thought, her eyes toggling back and forth between man and beast.

"Do as you are told," he said to the animal, "or the deal is off."

The black cat hissed, whipped its shiny black tail through the air, and dissolved into the shadows of the lush vegetation surrounding the small lakeside clearing.

This is too bizarre; I need to get out of here. Maggie turned her wobbling body to seek shelter in another dream.

"Where the *hell* do you think you're going?" said that deep, rich voice that wrapped her mind in ribbons of warm dark caramel and exotic spices.

Before she could mutter a word, her head cartwheeled and her body tipped. Two firm hands gripped her shoulders and propped her against the tree. "Close your eyes. Breathe."

She suddenly wanted to do just that. And only that. The man's voice was...compelling.

As she sucked in the dank, thick, tropical air, her mind slotted missing memories back into place.

How had she gotten there?

She recalled searching for the path to the ruin where her father spent his days. Little Kinichna'—or Little House of the Sun—as he called it, was the biggest find of his career, the one that would put his name on the archeologist's map. Ironically, this dilapidated and historically uninteresting pile of rubble had been known about for years, but when her father's colleague asked that he decipher etchings from a rare black jade tablet found not too far away, he'd realized they were directions, an ancient Mayan treasure map. Said map led to a hidden chamber right underneath Little Kinichna'.

"You are now well. Open your eyes," the man's husky voice commanded.

She took a moment to survey her body.

Miraculous. Her pain *was* gone. In fact, she felt downright euphoric and tingly. Especially in the spots where he touched her. Maybe in a few other spots, too. *Margaret O'Hare! You dirty trollop!*

She slid open her lids. Two icy turquoise eyes, just an inch from her face, sliced right through her, their raw, unfathomable depths filled with stark, primal desire.

Applesauce! She jerked her head back and knocked it on the tree. "Ouch!" *Great. Now I have a lump on the back to match the front.*

The colossal man straightened his powerful frame and towered over her like a giant oak, but he didn't release her from his fierce gaze.

Well at least he'd put a socially acceptable distance between their heads. The same could not be said for their bodies; the heat from his heaving chest seeped right through her. And thankfully—or was it regrettably?—or perhaps magically, since she didn't know how he'd had the time?—he now wore a pair of simple white linen trousers. No. It was a definite "thankful." The moment was awkward and unsettling enough without the man being naked *and* staring. Which he was. Still staring, that is. Silent. Suspicious. Studying her with his beautiful turquoise eyes dressed in a thick row of incredibly black lashes.

Why the deviled egg is he looking at me like that?

Maybe he thinks that giant lump on your forehead is about to give birth to an extra head.

"What happened?" she finally asked.

"I'll ask the questions," he said. "Who are you, woman?"

Not the response she'd expected. "Ducky. I'm lost in the jungle with a half-naked rake."

"Rake?" Dark brows arching with irritation, he planted his arms—silky milk chocolate poured over bulging, never-ending ropes of taut muscle—across the hard slopes of his bare chest. Maggie meticulously cataloged the man's every divine detail, like she would for each precious artifact from her father's dig, from his long, damp reams of shimmering midnight hair falling over his menacingly broad shoulders; the cords of muscles galloping down his bronzed neck into said broad shoulders; and his sinfully sculpted abdomen tightly divided into rounded little rectangles which reminded her of an ice cube tray—a fancy new invention. *God, I miss ice cubes.*

But as impressive as his raw, abundantly masculine features were, it was his height that most bewildered her. People from these parts were not known for stature. In fact, at five-foot-six, she had a good six inches on the tallest men in the village, and her father, Dr. O'Hare, an entire foot. No. This giant man most certainly wasn't from the sleepy little pueblo of Bacalar or anywhere in the Yucatan, for that matter. But then, from where? His exotic, ethnically ambiguous features didn't provide any clues. He could be a Moroccan Greek Spaniard or a Nordic Himalayan Kazak. *Hmmm...*

"Yes, rake, as in cad? Or if you prefer, savage," she said.

"Hardly. Savages don't save women in distress. They create them."

True. They also don't have wildly seductive, exotic accents. Like one of her parents' Hollywood friends.

Light bulb.

"Oh my God. You're a picture film actor, aren't you?"

Yes. Yes. It all made sense now. The locals in the village had been talking about a film crew for weeks. Word on the street—errr, word on the pueblo corner next to the stinky burro—was that a famous Russian director was making a movie about Chichen Itza and filming historical reenactments in the area.

"An...actor." His icy, unsettling expression turned into a charming smile inspired by the devil himself. "Yes."

She sighed. "That explains the trained cat. Where's the crew?" She glanced over her shoulders.

"Crew. Errr." He raised his index finger as if to point somewhere, then dropped it. "My crew will be here in a few days."

"Getting into character! Right." Maggie had heard firsthand how actors prepared for their roles. Fascinating business. Of course, acting had never really interested her. Nothing that required work ever had, which was why she'd taken up painting when her parents pestered her to do something productive. Going to parties and dating famous, good-looking men apparently weren't worthy pursuits.

They were right. If only her mother had lived long enough for Maggie to tell her so.

"Now," he said, "will you tell me who *you* are?"

She held out her hand. "Miss Margaret O'Hare of Los Angeles."

"You are a very long way from home."

No. Really? "I'm here working with my father. He's a professor doing…ummm…research."

A teeny fib. Or two. Who's gonna know? Truthfully, her father wasn't researching doodly-squat; he was secretly excavating. And the "work" she was doing? It didn't amount to a hill of pinto beans; her father wouldn't let her anywhere near the sacred structure. "No place for a young lady," he'd said. Well, neither was this slightly lawless, revolution-ravaged Mexican village, where electricity was considered a luxury—as were beds, curling irons, and those blessed ice cubes.

And chicken coops. Don't forget the chicken coops. The village was plagued with wretched little packs of villainous roaming chickens. *Like tiny feathered banditos who leave their little caca-bombs all over the damned place.*

You'll survive. Some things are more important.

"Well, Miss Margaret O'Hare from Los Angeles, very pleased to meet you." The man bent his imposing frame, slid his remarkably-rough-for-an-actor palm into hers, and placed a lingering kiss atop her hand.

An exquisite jolt crashed through her, causing her to buck. She snapped the tingling appendage away. *Wow. That kiss could combust a lady's drawers like gunpowder. Poof! Flames. No drawers. Just like that.*

The residual heat continued spreading. *Please don't reach my drawers. Please don't reach my drawers…*

He frowned and dropped his hand. "So tell me, what were you doing in the jungle, Margaret?"

"Jungle?"

"Yes, you know that place where I found you unconscious. Barefoot. All alone. It has many trees and dangerous animals." He pointed over her shoulder at the lush forest filled with vine-covered trees that chirped and clicked with abundant life. "It's right behind you, if you've forgotten what it looks like."

"Yes. That." *Thinking, thinking, thinking.* She wiggled her bare toes in the mushy grass and looked out across the hypnotic turquoise waves of the lake. Funny how the man's eyes were the exact same color right down to their flecks of shimmering green.

An early afternoon breeze pushed a few dark locks of hair across her face. *Still thinking, thinking, thinking.* She brushed them away and then focused on the grass stains on the front of her white cotton dress. Darn it. She loved this dress, with its tiny hand-stitched red flowers along the hem. Her father had had it specially made along with a beautiful black stone pendant the week they'd arrived. He'd said the gifts were in celebration of his find; everything was exactly where he'd thought, including some mysterious, priceless treasure that would "change their lives." He'd said he couldn't wait to show her when the time came.

"I'm waiting," the man said with unfiltered impatience.

"Waiting. Oh, yes. I was in the jungle because…" *Still thinking…*

Fear. Yes, fear was the reason she'd been capering about. Her mother's recent death had left her plagued with the corrosive emotion. She feared she would never make right with her past. She feared opening her eyes to the present. She feared the future would bring only pain and suffering because eventually anyone she cared for would leave. Fear was like an irrational cancer that ate away at her rational soul.

It was why, when her father began acting peculiar back home—disappearing for weeks at a time, mumbling incoherently, obsessing over that tablet—she came to Mexico. She feared he might simply disappear in this untamed land, evaporate into nothing more than a collection of memories—just as her mother had.

And now she feared that she had failed; her father had not been seen for three days. But she didn't dare articulate this distressing, gloomy thought aloud.

"Because...I am a painter!" she said. "I went exploring for new scenery. I got turned around, and then that giant cat of yours appeared out of nowhere and chased me." She rubbed the gigantic lump on her forehead. "I fell and hit my head. You didn't happen to find my sandals, did you?"

One glorious turquoise eye ticked for the briefest moment. "Searching for scenery?"

"You don't believe me?"

He shook his head and grinned with a well-polished arrogance only found on the face of a Hollywood actor. She quickly wondered if he'd ever met her mother but then dismissed the thought. She didn't want to think about her mother; the pain was simply too fresh.

"No. I do not believe you," he stated dryly.

The nerve! "You did find me in the jungle, didn't you? Wasn't I unconscious?" She pointed to the large lump on her forehead. "And wearing this?"

"Yes, but I believe you were searching for something else."

Nosy rake. "Well, it's been a pleasure, Mr.…" *Arrogant Nudesunbather? Mr. Nomanners Perfectbottom?*

"Backlum Chaam."

Backlum? What an odd—oh! He's in character. "Sure, Joe. Whatever blows your wig, but—"

"The name is not Joe, it's Chaam. I just said it."

Margaret blinked. *Deep, deep into character.*

"And I assure you, I do not wear a wig. This is my real hair." He gave his shiny black mane a proud tug.

"I meant—oh, never mind. Listen, it's been great, Mr. *Chaam,* but I gotta skedaddle; my father is probably wondering where I am." She wished. Her father was likely dead. Or injured.

Stay calm. You'll find the ruin. You'll find him…

If only she'd insisted on knowing exactly where the excavation site was hidden. Instead, she'd done what her father had asked—fearing his anger—and stayed near the village, spending her days painting, learning Spanish from the local children, or swimming with a friend she'd made: a young woman named Itzel who didn't speak a lick of English.

"Have a lovely afternoon." She flashed an awkward grin and turned toward the shoreline.

A firm grip pulled her back and twirled her around. Two powerful arms incarcerated her body and smashed her against an astonishingly firm, naked chest. His touch instantly ignited that gunpowder, and…

Combustion!

A wave of carnal heat ripped through her body. *Oh my God. Oh my God. Oh my Gooood…*Margaret felt her face turn a lascivious red. Beads of volcanic sweat seeped through her pores. Every muscle in her body wound up with merciless unchaste tension, like ropes anchoring a massive sail, a sail blowing her ship toward the most delicious place ever. And then...

Release.

Maggie braced herself on the man's bountiful biceps as the tension snapped and silent fireworks exploded throughout her body.

Oh my God. Had she just...had she really just...?

He cleared his throat. "Was it as good as it looked?"

She let out an exaggeratedly long breath. *What the flapdoodle?* "You're not an actor, are you?" she asked, unable to keep her voice from quivering.

He shook his head from side to side. "No. And you are no human."

Dr. Antonio Acero is a world-renowned physicist whose life takes a turn for the worst—and the bizarre. In southern Mexico, he finds an ancient Mayan tablet that is said to have magical properties. But when he puts the tablet to use, he discovers that Fate has other plans. And her name is Ixtab.

Turn this page for
an excerpt from

Vampires Need Not... Apply?

Prologue

⌒

Near Sedona, Arizona. Estate of Kinich Ahau, ex–God of the Sun

New Year's Day

Teetering on the very edge of a long white sofa, Penelope stared up at the oversized, round clock mounted on the wall. In ten minutes, the sun would set and the man they once knew as the God of the Sun would awake. Changed. She hoped.

Sadly, there'd been a hell of a lot of hoping lately and little good it did her or her two friends, Emma and Helena, sitting patiently at her side. Like Penelope, the other two women had been thrust into this new world—filled with gods, vampires, and other immortal combinations in between—by means of the men they'd fallen in love with.

Bottom line? Not going so great.

Helena, the blonde who held two bags of blood in her lap, reached for Penelope and smoothed down her frizzy hair. "Don't worry. Kinich will wake up. He will."

Pen nodded. She must look like a mess. Why hadn't she taken the time to at least run a brush through her hair for him? He loved her dark hair. Maybe because she didn't truly believe he'd come back to life. "I don't know what's worse, thinking I've lost him forever or knowing if he wakes up, he'll be something he hates."

Emma chimed in, "He doesn't hate vampires. He hates being immortal."

Pen shrugged. "Guess it really doesn't matter now what he hates." Kinich would either wake up or he wouldn't. If he didn't, she might not have the will to go on without him. Too much had happened. She needed him. She loved him. And most of all, she wanted him to know she was sorry for ever doubting him. He'd given his life to save them all.

Tick.

Another move of the hand.

Tock.

And another.

Nine more minutes.

The doorbell jolted the three women.

"Dammit." Emma, who wore her combat-ready outfit—black cargos and a black tee that made her red hair look like the flame on the tip of a match—marched to the door. "I told everyone not to disturb us."

Penelope knew that would never happen. A few hundred soldiers lurked outside and a handful of deities waited in the kitchen, snacking on cookies; new vampires weren't known to be friendly. But Penelope insisted on having only her closest friends by her side for the moment of truth. Besides, Helena was a new vampire herself—a long story—and knew what to do.

Emma unlocked the dead bolt. "Some idiot probably forgot my orders. I'll send him away—" The door flew open with a cold gust of desert wind and debris. It took a moment for the three women to register who stood in the doorway.

The creature, with long, matted dreads beaded with human teeth, wore nothing more than a loincloth over her soot-covered body.

Christ almighty, it can't be, thought Pen, as the smell of Maaskab—good old-fashioned, supernatural, pre-Hispanic death and darkness—entered her nose.

Before Emma could drop a single f-bomb, the dark priestess raised her hand and blew Emma across the large, open living room, slamming her against the wall.

Helena screamed and rushed to Emma's side.

Paralyzed with fear, Penelope watched helplessly as the Maaskab woman glided into the living room and stood before her, a mere two yards away.

The woman raised her gaunt, grimy finger, complete with overgrown grime-caked fingernail, and pointed directly at Penelope. "Youuuu."

Holy wheat toast. Penelope instinctively stepped back. The woman's voice felt like razor blades inside her ears. Penelope had to think fast. Not only did she fear for her life and for those of her friends, but both she and Emma were pregnant. Helena had a baby daughter. *Think, dammit. Think.*

Penelope considered drawing the power of the sun, an ability she'd recently gained when she had become the interim Sun God—another long story—but releasing that much heat into the room might fry everyone in it.

Grab the monster's arm. Channel it directly into her.

"Youuuu," the Maaskab woman said once again.

"Damn, lady." Penelope covered her ears. "Did you swallow a bucket of rusty nails? That voice...gaaaahh."

The monster grunted. "I come with a message."

"For me?" Penelope took a step forward.

The woman nodded, and her eyes, pits of blackness framed with cherry red, clawed at Penelope's very soul. "It is for you I bring...the message."

Jeez. I get it. You have a message. Penelope took another cautious step toward the treacherous woman. "So what are you waiting for?"

"Pen, get away from her," she heard Emma grumble from behind.

Not on your life. Pen moved another inch. "I'm waiting, old woman. Wow me."

The Maaskab growled.

Another step.

"Don't hurt my grandmother," Emma pleaded.

Grandma? Oh, for Pete's sake. *This* was Emma's grandmother? The one who'd been taken by the Maaskab and turned into their evil leader? They all thought she'd been killed.

Fabulous. Granny's back.

For a fraction of a moment, the woman glanced over Pen's shoulder at Emma.

Another step.

Penelope couldn't let Emma's feelings cloud the situation. Granny was dangerous. Granny was evil. Granny was going down.

"We wish"—the old Maaskab woman ground out her words—"to make an exchange."

Penelope froze. "An exchange?"

The woman nodded slowly. "You will free our king, and we will return your prisoners."

Shit. Free Chaam? The most evil deity ever known? He'd murdered hundreds, perhaps thousands of women, many his own daughters. His sole purpose in life was to destroy every last living creature, except for the Maaskab and his love slaves.

No. They could never let that bastard out.

But what about the prisoners? She debated with herself. In the last battle, the Maaskab had trapped forty of their most loyal vampire soldiers, the God of Death and War, aka Emma's fiancé, and the General of the Vampire Army, aka Helena's husband.

Dammit. Dammit. Crispy-fried dammit! Penelope had to at least consider Granny's proposal. "Why in the world would we agree to let Chaam go?"

"A bunch of pathetic...little...girls...cannot triumph against us," the Maaskab woman hissed. "*You* need the vampires and your precious God of Death and War."

Penelope's brain ran a multitude of scenarios, trying to guess the angle. Apparently, the Maaskab needed Chaam back. But they were willing to give up Niccolo and Guy? Both were powerful warriors, perfectly equipped to kick the Maaskab's asses for good.

No. Something wasn't quite right. "Tell me why you want Chaam," Penelope said.

Another step.

"Because"—Granny flashed an odious grin—"the victory of defeating you will be meaningless without our beloved king to see it. All we do, we do for him."

Ew. Okay.

"You, on the other hand..." She lowered her gravelly voice one octave. "...Do not have a chance without your men. We offer a fair fight in exchange for our king's freedom."

Okay. She could be lying. Perhaps not. Anyone with a brain could see they were three inexperienced, young women—yes, filled with passion and purpose and a love of shoes and all things shopping, in the case of Helena and Emma—but they didn't know the first thing about fighting wars. Especially ones that might end in a big hairy apocalypse prophesied to be just eight months away.

Sure, they had powerful, slightly insane, dysfunctional deities and battalions of beefy vampires and human soldiers on their side. However, that was like giving a tank to a kindergartner. Sort of funny in a Sunday comics *Beetle Bailey* kinda way, but not in real life.

"Don't agree to it," Helena pleaded from the flank. "We'll find another way to free them."

"She's right, Pen," Emma whimpered, clearly in pain.

Penelope took another step. They were right; they'd have to find some other way to get the prisoners back. Chaam was too dang dangerous. "And if we refuse?"

The Maaskab woman laughed into the air above, her teeth solid black and the inside of her mouth bright red.

Yum. Nothing like gargling with blood to really freshen your breath.

"Then," Granny said, "we shall kill both men—yes, even your precious Votan; we have the means—and the end of days will begin. It is what Chaam would have wanted."

Granny had conveniently left out the part about killing her and her friends before she departed this room. Why else would the evil Maaskab woman have come in person when an evil note would have done the evil job? Or how about an evil text?

No. Emma's grandmother would kill them if the offer was rejected. She knew it in her gut.

Penelope didn't blink. *No fear. No fear.* The powerful light tingled on the tips of her fingers. She was ready.

"Then you leave us no choice. We agree." Penelope held out her hand. "Shake on it."

The Maaskab woman glanced down at Pen's hand. Pen lunged, grabbed the woman's soot-covered forearm, and opened the floodgates of heat. Evil Granny dropped to her knees, screaming like a witch drowning in a hot, bubbling cauldron.

"No! No!" Emma screamed. "Don't kill her! Don't, Pen!"

Crackers! Penelope released the woman who fell face-forward onto the cold Saltillo tile. Steam rose from her naked back and dreadlock-covered skull.

"Grandma? Oh, God, no. Please don't be dead." Emma dropped to her knees beside the eau-de-charred roadkill. "She's still breathing."

The room suddenly filled with Penelope's private guards. They looked like they'd been chewed up and spit out by a large Maaskab blender—tattered, dirty clothes and bloody faces.

That explained what had taken so long; they must've been outside fighting more Maaskab.

The men pointed their rifles at Emma's unconscious grandmother. Zac, God of Who the Hell Knew and Penelope's right hand since she'd been appointed the interim leader of the gods—yes, yes, another long story—blazed into the room, barking orders. "Someone get the Maaskab chained up."

Zac, dressed in his usual black leather pants and tee combo that matched his raven-black hair, turned to Penelope and gazed down at her with his nearly translucent, aquamarine eyes. "Are you all right?"

Penelope nodded. It was the first time in days she'd felt glad to see him. He'd been suffocating her ever since Kinich—

"Oh, gods!" They'd completely forgotten about Kinich! Her eyes flashed up at the clock.

Tick.

Sundown.

A gut-wrenching howl exploded from the other room. Everyone stiffened.

"He's alive!" Pen turned to rush off but felt a hard pull on her arm.

"No. You've had enough danger for one day. I will go." Zac wasn't asking.

Penelope jerked her arm away. "He won't hurt me. I'll be fine. Just stay here and help Emma with her grandmother." She snatched up the two bags of blood from the floor where Helena had dropped them.

"Penelope, I will not tell you again." Zac's eyes filled with anger. Though he was her right hand, he was still a deity and not used to being disobeyed.

"Enough." Penelope held up her finger. "I don't answer to you."

Zac's jealous eyes narrowed for a brief moment before he stiffly dipped his head and then quietly watched her disappear through the doorway.

She rushed down the hallway and paused outside the

bedroom with her palms flat against the hand-carved double doors. The screams had not stopped.

Thank the gods that Kinich, the ex–God of the Sun, was alive. Now they would have a chance to put their lives back together, to undo what never should have been— such as putting her in charge of his brothers and sisters— and she would finally get the chance to tell him how much she loved him, how grateful she was that he'd sacrificed everything to save them, about their baby.

This was their second chance.

She only needed to get him through these first days as a vampire. *And orchestrate a rescue mission for the God of Death and War and the General of the Vampire Army. And deal with the return of Emma's evil granny. And figure out how to stop an impending apocalypse set to occur in eight—yes, eight!—months. And deal with a few hundred women with amnesia they'd rescued from the Maaskab. And manage a herd of insane egocentric, accident-prone deities, with ADHD. And carry a baby. And don't forget squeezing in some time at the gym. Your thighs are getting flabby!*

"See? This Kinich vampire thing should be easy," she assured herself.

She pushed open the door to find Kinich shirtless, writhing on the bed. His muscular legs and arms strained against the silver chains attached to the deity-reinforced frame. He was a large, beautiful man, almost seven feet in height, with shoulders that spanned a distance equal to two widths of her body.

"Kinich!" She rushed to his side. "Are you okay?" She attempted to brush his gold-streaked locks from his face, but he flailed and twisted in agony.

"It burns!" he wailed. "The metal burns."

"I know, honey. I know. But Helena says you need to drink before we can let you go. Full tummy. Happy vamp—"

"Aaahh! Remove them. They burn. Please," he begged. *Oh, saints.*

He would never hurt her. Would he? Of course not.

"Try to hold still." She went to the dresser, pulled open the top drawer, and grabbed the keys.

She rushed to his ankle and undid one leg, then the other.

Kinich stopped moving. He lay there, eyes closed, breathing.

Without hesitation she undid his right arm and then ran to the other side to release the final cuff.

"Are you okay? Kinich?"

Without opening his eyes, he said, "I can smell and hear everything."

Helena had said that blocking out the noise was one of the hardest things a new vampire had to learn. That and curbing their hunger for innocent humans who, she was told, tasted the yummiest. Helena also mentioned to always make sure he was well fed. Full tummy, happy vampire. Just like a normal guy except for the blood obviously.

Penelope deposited herself on the bed next to Kinich with a bag of blood in her hands. "You'll get used to it. I promise. In the meantime, let's get you fed. I have so much to—"

Kinich threw her down, and she landed on her back with a hard thump and the air whooshed from her lungs.

Straddling her, Kinich pinned her wrists to the floor.

His turquoise eyes shifted to hungry black, and fangs protruded from his mouth. "You smell delicious. Like sweet sunshine."

Such a beautiful face, she thought, mesmerized by Kinich's eyes. Once upon a time his skin had glowed golden almost, a vision of elegant masculinity with full lips and sharp cheekbones. But now, now he was refined with an exotic, dangerous male beauty too exquisite for words.

Ex-deity turned mortal, turned vampire. *Hypnotic. He is...hypnotic.*

He lowered his head toward her neck, and her will suddenly snapped back into place. "No! Kinich, no!" She squirmed under his grasp. Without her hands free, she couldn't defend herself. "I'm pregnant."

He stilled and peered into her eyes.

Pain. So much pain. That was all she saw.

"A baby?" he asked.

She nodded cautiously.

Then something cold and deadly flickered in his eyes. His head plunged for her neck, and she braced for the pain of having her neck ripped out.

"Penelope!" Zac sacked Kinich, knocking him to the floor. "Go!" he commanded.

Penelope rolled onto her hands and knees and crawled from the room as it was overrun with several more of Kinich's brethren: the perpetually drunk Acan, the Goddess of the Hunt they called Camaxtli, and the Mistress of Bees they called—oh, who the hell could remember her weird Mayan name?

"Penelope! Penelope!" she heard Kinich scream. "I want to drink her! I must drink her!"

Penelope curled into a ball on the floor in the hallway, unable to stop herself from crying. *This isn't how it's supposed to be. This isn't how it's supposed to be.*

Helena appeared at her side. "Oh, Pen. I'm so sorry. I promise he'll be okay after a few days. He just needs to eat." She helped Penelope sit up. "Let's move you somewhere safe."

Penelope wiped away the streaks of tears from her cheeks and took her friend's hand to stand.

The grunts and screams continued in the other room.

"I can't believe he attacked me, even after I told him." Tears continued to trickle from Penelope's eyes. Why hadn't he stopped? Didn't he love her?

"In his defense, you really do smell yummy. Kind of like Tang."

"Not funny," Penelope responded.

"Sorry." Helena braced Penelope with an arm around her waist and guided her to a bedroom in the other wing of the house.

Helena deposited Penelope on the large bed and turned toward the bathroom. "I'll get you a warm washcloth."

Ironically, Penelope's mind dove straight for a safe haven—that meant away from Kinich and toward her job, which generally provided many meaty distractions, such as impending doom and/or anything having to do with Cimil, the ex–Goddess of the Underworld.

"Wait." Penelope looked up at Helena, who'd become her steady rock of reason these last few weeks. "What happens next?"

Helena paused for a moment. "Like I told you, Kinich needs time to adjust."

Penelope shook her head. "No. I mean, you heard

Emma's grandmother; without Niccolo and Guy, we can't defeat the Maaskab. We have to free them."

"Well—"

"I know what you're going to say," Pen interrupted. "We can't release Chaam, but—"

"Actually," Helena broke in. "I've been meaning to tell you something."

"What?"

"We've been looking for another way to free them, and I think we found it."

"Found what?" Penelope asked.

"A tablet."

Glossary

(In No Particular Order Because Cimil Said So)

Yum Cimil: Goddess of the Underworld, also known as Ah-Puch by the Mayans, Mictlantecuhtli (try saying that one ten times) by the Aztecs, Grim Reaper by the Europeans, Hades by the Greeks...you get the picture! Despite what people say, Cimil is actually a female, adores a good bargain (especially garage sales) and the color pink, and has the ability to see all possible outcomes of the future. She's also batshit crazy.

Cenote: Limestone sinkholes connected to a subterranean water system. They are found in Central America and southern Mexico and were once believed by the Mayans to be sacred portals to the afterlife. Such smart humans! They were right. Except cenotes are actually portals to the realm of the gods.

(If you have never seen a cenote, do a quick search on the Internet for "cenote photos," and you'll see how freaking cool they are!)

The Pact: An agreement between the gods and good vampires that dictates the dos and don'ts. There are many parts to it, but the most important rules are vampires are not allowed to snack on good people (called Forbiddens), must keep their existence a secret, and are responsible for keeping any rogue vampires in check.

Obscuros: Evil vampires who do not live by the Pact and like to dine on innocent humans since they really do taste the best.

K'ak: The history books remember him as K'ak Tiliw Chan Yopaat, ruler of Copan in the 700 ADs. Really, King K'ak (don't you just love that name? Tee-hee-hee...) is one of Cimil's favorite brothers. We're not really sure what he does.

Kinich: Also known by many other names depending on the culture, Kinich is the Sun God. He likes to go by Nick these days, but don't let the modern name fool you. He's not so hot about the gods mingling with humans. Although...he's getting a little curious what the fuss is all about. Can sleeping with a woman really be all that?

Votan: God of Death and War. Also known as Odin, Wotan, Wodan, the God of Drums (he has no idea how the hell he got that title; he hates the drums) and Lord of Multiplication (okay, he is pretty darn good at math so that one makes sense). These days, Votan goes by Guy Santiago (it's a long story—read Book #1), but despite his deadly tendencies, he's all heart. He's now engaged to Emma Keane.

Chaam: God of Male Virility. He's responsible for discovering black jade, figuring out how to procreate with humans, and kicking off the chain of events that will eventually lead to the Great War. Get your Funyuns and beer! This is gonna be good.

Black Jade: Found only in a particular mine located in southern Mexico, this jade has very special supernatural properties, including the ability to absorb supernatural energy—in particular, god energy. When worn by a human, it is possible for them to have physical contact with a god. If injected, it can make a person addicted to doing bad things. If the jade is fueled up with dark energy, then released, it can be used as a weapon. Chaam personally likes using it to polish his teeth.

Payal: Though the gods can take humans to their realm and make them immortal, Payals are the true genetic offspring of the gods but are born mortal, just like their human mothers. Only firstborn children inherit the gods' genes and manifest their traits. If the firstborn happens to be female, she is called a Payal. If male, well...then you get something kind of yucky!

Maaskab: Originally a cult of bloodthirsty Mayan priests who believed in the dark arts. It is rumored they are responsible for bringing down their entire civilization with their obsession for human sacrifices (mainly young female virgins). Once Chaam started making half-human children, he decided all firstborn males would make excellent Maaskab due to their proclivity for evil.

Uchben: An ancient society of scholars and warriors who serve as the gods' eyes and ears in the human world. They also do the books and manage their earthly assets.

Book of the Oracle of Delphi: This living, ancient text tells the future. But as events unfold, the pages rewrite themselves. Currently, the good vampires are in possession of this text.

The Gods: Though every culture around the world has their own names and beliefs related to beings of worship, there are actually only fourteen. And since they are able to access the human world only through the portals in the Yucatán region, the Mayans were big fans.

The gods often refer to each other as brother and sister, but truth is, they are just another species of the Creator.

Demilords: (Spoiler alert for Book #2—yes, this book!) This group of immortal badasses are vampires who've been infused with the light of the gods. They are extremely difficult to kill and hate their jobs (killing Obscuros) almost as much as they hate the gods who control them.

THE DISH

Where Authors Give You the Inside Scoop

♥ ♥ ♥ ♥ ♥ ♥ ♥ ♥ ♥ ♥ ♥ ♥ ♥ ♥ ♥

From the desk of Jennifer Haymore

Dear Reader,

When Mrs. Emma Curtis, the heroine of THE ROGUE'S PROPOSAL, came to see me, I'd just finished writing *The Duchess Hunt*, the story of the Duke of Trent and his new wife, Sarah, who'd crossed the deep chasm from maid to duchess, and I was feeling very satisfied in their happily ever after.

Mrs. Curtis, however, had no interest in romance.

"I need you to write my story," she told me. "It's urgent."

I encouraged her to sit down and tell me more.

"I'm on a mission of vengeance," she began. "You see, I need to find my husband's murderer—"

I lifted my hand right away to stop her. "Mrs. Curtis, I don't think this is going to work out. You see, I don't write thrillers or mysteries. I am a romance writer."

"I know, but I think you can help me. I really do."

"How's that?"

"You've met the Duke of Trent, haven't you? And his brother, Lord Lukas?" She leaned forward, dark eyes serious and intent. "You see, I'm searching for the same man they are."

My brows rose. "Really? You're looking for Roger Morton?"

"Yes! Roger Morton is the man who murdered my husband. Please—Lord Lukas is here in Bristol. If you could only arrange an introduction...I know his lordship could help me to find him."

She was right—I did know Lord Lukas. In fact...

I looked over the dark-haired woman sitting in front of me. Mrs. Curtis was a young, beautiful widow. She seemed intelligent and focused.

My mind started working furiously.

Mrs. Curtis and Lord Luke? Could it work?

Maybe...

Luke would require a *lot* of effort. He was a rake of the first order, brash, undisciplined, prone to all manner of excess. But something told me that maybe, just maybe, Mrs. Curtis would be a good influence on him... If I could join them on the mission to find Roger Morton, it just might work out.

(I am a *romance* writer, after all.)

"Are you *sure* you want to meet Lord Lukas?" I asked her. "Have you heard the rumors about him?"

Her lips firmed. "I have heard he is a rake." Her eyes met mine, steady and serious. "I can manage rakes."

There was a steel behind her voice. A steel I approved of.

Yes. This could work.

My lips curved into a smile. "All right, Mrs. Curtis. I might be able to manage an introduction..."

And that was how I arranged the first meeting between Emma Curtis and Lord Lukas Hawkins, the second brother of the House of Trent. Their relationship proved to be a rocky one—I wasn't joking when I said Luke was a rake, and in fact, "rake" might be too mild a term. But Emma proved to be a worthy adversary for him, and they ended up traveling a dangerous and emotional but ultimately sweetly satisfying path in THE ROGUE'S PROPOSAL.

Come visit me at my website, www.jenniferhaymore .com, where you can share your thoughts about my books, sign up for some fun freebies and contests, and read more about THE ROGUE'S PROPOSAL and the House of Trent Series. I'd also love to see you on Twitter (@ jenniferhaymore) or on Facebook (www.facebook.com/ jenniferhaymore-author).

Sincerely,

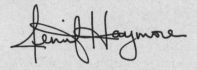

♥ ♥ ♥ ♥ ♥ ♥ ♥ ♥ ♥ ♥ ♥ ♥ ♥ ♥ ♥

From the desk of Hope Ramsay

Dear Reader,

My mother was a prodigious knitter. If she was watching TV or traveling in the car or just relaxing, she would always have a pair of knitting needles in her hand. So, of course, she needed a steady supply of yarn.

We lived in a medium-sized town on Long Island. It had a downtown area not too far from the train station, and tucked in between an interior design place and a quick lunch stand was a yarn shop.

I vividly remember that wonderful place. Floor-to-ceiling shelves occupied the wall space. The cubbies were filled with yarn of amazing hues and cardboard boxes of incredibly beautiful buttons. The place had a few cozy chairs and a table strewn with knitting magazines.

Mom visited that yarn store a lot. She would take her knitting with her sometimes, especially if she was having trouble with a pattern. There was a woman there—I don't remember her name—but I do remember the half-moon glasses that rode her neck on a chain. She was a yarn whiz, and Mom consulted her often. Women gathered there to knit and talk. And little girls tagged along and learned how to knit on big, plastic needles.

I went back in my mind to that old yarn store when I created the Knit & Stitch, and I have to say that writing about it was almost like spending a little time with Mom, even though she's no longer with us. There is something truly wonderful about a circle of women sharing stories while making garments out of luxurious yarn.

I remember some of the yarn Mom bought at that yarn store, too, especially the brown and baby blue tweed alpaca that became a cable knit cardigan. I wore that sweater all through high school until the elbows became threadbare. Wearing it was like being wrapped up in Mom's arms.

There is nothing like the love a knitter puts into a garment. And writing about women who knit proved to be equally joyful for me. I hope you enjoy spending some time with the girls at the Knit & Stitch. They are a great bunch of warm-hearted knitters.

Hope Ramsay

♥   ♥   ♥

From the desk of Erin Kern

Dear Reader,

So here we are. Back in Trouble, Wyoming, catching up with those crazy McDermotts. In case you didn't know, these men have a way of sending the ladies of Trouble all into a tizzy by just existing. At the same time there was a collective breaking of hearts when the two older McDermotts, Noah and Chase, surreptitiously removed themselves from the dating scene by getting married.

But what about the other McDermott brother, you ask? Brody is special in many ways, but no less harrowing on those predictable female hormones. And, even though Brody has sworn off dating for good, that doesn't mean he doesn't have it coming. The love bug, I mean. And he gets bitten, big time. Sorry, ladies. But this dark-haired heart-breaker with the piercing gray eyes is about to fall hard.

Happy Reading!

Erin Kern

♥ ♥ ♥ ♥ ♥ ♥ ♥ ♥ ♥ ♥ ♥ ♥ ♥ ♥ ♥ ♥

From the desk of Mimi Jean Pamfiloff

Dear Reader,

"If you love her, set her free. If she comes back, she's yours. If she doesn't...Christ! Stubborn woman! Hunt her down, and bring her the hell back; she's still yours according to vampire law."

> Niccolo DiConti, General of the
> Vampire Queen's Army

I always like to believe that the universe has an all-knowing, all-seeing heart filled with the wisdom to grant us not what we want, but that which we need most. Does that mean the universe will simply pop that special something into a box and leave it on your doorstep? Hell no. And if you're Niccolo DiConti, the universe might be planning a very, very long, excruciating obstacle course before handing out any prizes. That is, if he and his over-bloated, vampire ego survive.

Meet Helena Strauss, the obstacle course. According to the infamous prophet and Goddess of the Underworld, Cimil, Niccolo need only to seduce this mortal into being his willing, eternal bride and Niccolo's every wish will be granted. Thank the gods he's the most legendary warrior known to vampire, with equally legendary looks. Seducing a female is hardly a challenge worthy of such greatness.

Famous last words. Because Helena Strauss has no interest in giving up long, sunny days at the beach or exchanging her happy life to be with this dark, arrogant, deadly male.

Mimi

♥ ♥ ♥ ♥ ♥ ♥ ♥ ♥ ♥ ♥ ♥ ♥ ♥ ♥ ♥

From the desk of Jessica Lemmon

Dear Reader,

Imagine you're heartbroken. Crying. Literally *into* your drink at a noisy nightclub your best friend has dragged you to. Just as you are lamenting your very bad decision to come out tonight, someone approaches. A tall, handsome someone with a tumble of dark hair, expressive amber eyes, and perfectly contoured lips. Oh, *and* he's rich. Not just plain old rich, but rich of the *filthy, stinking* variety. This is exactly the situation Crickitt Day, the heroine of TEMPTING THE BILLIONAIRE, finds herself in one not-so-fine evening. Oh, to be so lucky!

I may have given the characters of TEMPTING THE BILLIONAIRE a fairy-tale/fantasy set-up, but I still wanted them rooted and realistic. Particularly my hero. It's why you'll find Shane August a bit of a departure from your typical literary billionaire. Shane visits clients personally, does his own dishes, makes his own coffee. And—get ready for it—bakes his own cookies.

Hero tip: Want to win over a woman? Bake her cookies.

The recipe for these mysterious and amazing bits of heavenly goodness can be traced back to a cookbook by Erin McKenna, creator of the NYC-based bakery Babycakes. What makes the recipes so special, you ask? They use *coconut oil* instead of vegetable oil or butter. The result is an amazingly moist, melt-in-your-mouth, can't-stop-at-just-one chocolate chip cookie you will happily burn your tongue on when the tray comes out of the oven. Bonus: Coconut oil is rumored to help speed up your metabolism. I'm not saying these cookies are healthy...but I'm not *not* saying it, either.

Attempting this recipe required a step outside my comfort zone. I tracked down unique ingredients. I diligently measured. I spent time and energy getting it right. That's when I knew just the hobby for the down-to-earth billionaire who can't keep himself from showing others how much he cares. And if a hero is going to bake you cookies, what better place to be served *said cookies* than by a picturesque waterfall? None, I say. (Well, okay, I can think of another location or two, but admit it, a waterfall is a pretty dang good choice.)

As you can imagine, Crickitt is beyond impressed. And when a rogue smear of chocolate lands on her lips, Shane is every bit the gentleman by—*ahem*—helping her remove the incriminating splotch. Alas, that's a story for another day. (Or, for chapter nineteen...)

I hope you enjoy losing yourself in the very real fantasy world of Shane and Crickitt. It was a world I happily immersed myself in while writing; a world I *still* imagine myself in whenever a certain rich, nutty, warm, homemade chocolate chip cookie is melting on my tongue.

Happy Reading!
www.jessicalemmon.com

Jessica Lemmon